The Janissary Tree

Jason Goodwin fell under the spell of Istanbul while studying Byzantine history at Cambridge University. Fifteen years ago, following the success of *The Gunpowder Gardens: Travels in China and India in search of Tea*, he made a six-month pilgrimage across Eastern Europe to reach the city for the first time, a journey recounted in *On Foot to the Golden Horn*, which won the John Llewellyn Rhys/*Mail on Sunday* Prize 1993.

Intrigued by the enduring influence of the Ottoman Turks on Eastern Europe, Jason went on to research and write *Lords of the Horizons: A History of the Ottoman Empire*. Jan Morris called it 'a high-octane work of art', and the *New York Times* praised its 'dazzling beauty . . . The rare coming together of historical scholarship and curiosity about distant places with luminous writing'.

He is married to Kate, his companion on the walk to Istanbul; they live in rural Sussex with their four children.

Praise for *The Janissary Tree*

'*The Janissary Tree* is a tremendous first novel, born of a deep engagement with the culture of which Goodwin writes. It is beautifully written, perfectly judged, humane, witty and captivating.'
Michael Bywater, *Daily Telegraph*

'Beguiling . . . In Yashim the eunuch, Goodwin creates a detective who deserves many further outings as a subtle sleuth in the seraglio.' Boyd Tonkin, *Independent*

'Terrific . . . Brings 19th century Istanbul to life, almost as if [Goodwin] is walking the reader through it, and his descriptions of the city are a continual pleasure. Combine that with a protagonist whose own predicament gives him special insight into the complexities of power and sexuality, and it is a racing certainty that Goodwin's Ottoman detective will be a winner.' Joan Smith, *Sunday Times*

'Goodwin brings all the scholarship and aplomb of his prizewinning non-fiction to his first novel, which steams with the stink of the tanneries and dazzles with the whirl of the dervishes.' *Independent on Sunday*

'Fast-moving and labyrinthine . . . Brilliantly conjures up the exoticism of Istanbul.' Michael Arditti, *Daily Mail*

'A clever, accomplished book.' *Literary Review*

The Janissary Tree

JASON GOODWIN

The Janissary Tree

faber and faber

First published in 2006
by Faber and Faber Limited
3 Queen Square London WC1N 3AU
This paperback edition first published in 2007

Typeset by Faber and Faber Limited
Printed and bound in England by Bookmarque Ltd, Croydon, Surrey

A CIP record for this book
is available from the British Library

ISBN 978-0-571-22923-9

2 4 6 8 10 9 7 5 3 1

For Kate

For those who have Awareness,
a hint is quite enough.
For the multitudes of heedless
mere knowledge is useless

Haji Bektash Veli

Yashim flicked at a speck of dust on his cuff.

'One other thing, Marquise,' he murmured.

She gazed at him levelly.

'The papers.'

The Marquise de Merteuil gave a little laugh.

'Flûte! Monsieur Yashim, depravity is not a word we recognise in the Académie.' Her fan played; from behind it she almost hissed: 'It is a condition of mind.'

Yashim was already beginning to sense that this dream was falling apart.

The Marquise had fished out a paper from her décolletage and was tapping it on the table like a little hammer. He took a closer look. It *was* a little hammer.

Tap tap tap.

He opened his eyes and stared around. The Chateau de Merteuil dissolved in the candle light. Shadows leered from under the book-lined shelves, and from the corners of the room – a room and a half, you might say, where Yashim lived alone in a tenement in Istanbul. The leatherbound edition of *Les Liaisons Dangereuses* had slipped onto his lap.

Tap tap tap.

'Evet, evet,' he grumbled. 'I'm coming.' He slipped a cloak around his shoulders and his feet into a pair of yellow slippers, and shuffled to the door. 'Who is it?'

'Page boy.'

Hardly a boy, Yashim considered, as he let the spindly old man into the darkened room. The single candle guttered in the sudden draught. It threw their shadows around the walls, boxing with one another before the page's shadow stabbed Yashim's with a flickering dagger.

Yashim took the paper scroll and glanced at the seal, feeling the floor still moving beneath his feet, the lurching candlelight taking his mind back to a swaying lamp in a tiny cabin far out at sea, and the anxious hours spent scanning a dark horizon, peering through the drizzle for lights and the sight of land.

He broke the seal and tried to concentrate on the ornate script.

He sighed and laid the paper aside. There was a lamp. Blue flames trickled slowly round the charred cloth as he lit it with the candle. Yashim replaced the glass and trimmed the wick until the fitful light turned yellow and firm. Gradually the lamplight filled the room.

He'd been lucky to find a ship at all. The Black Sea was treacherous, especially in the winter, and the captain was a barrel-chested Greek with one white eye and the air of a pirate, but even at the worst moments of the voyage, when the wind screamed in the rigging, waves pounded on the foredeck and Yashim had tossed and vomited in his narrow bunk, he had told himself that anything was better than seeing out the winter in that shattered palace in the Crimea, surrounded by the ghosts of fearless riders, eaten away by the cold and the gloom.

He picked up the scroll the page had given him, and smoothed it out.

Greetings, etcetera. At the bottom he read the signature of the seraskier, city commander of the New Guard, the imperial Ottoman army. *Félicitations*, etcetera. He scanned upwards. From practice he could fillet a letter like this in seconds. There it was, wedged into the politesse: an immediate summons.

'Well?'

The old man stood to attention. 'I have orders to return with you to barracks immediately.'

He glanced uncertainly at Yashim's cloak. Yashim smiled, picked up a length of cloth, and wound it around his head. 'I'm dressed,' he said. 'Let us go.'

Yashim knew that it hardly mattered what he wore. He was a tall, well-built man in his late thirties, with a thick mop of black curls; a few white hairs, no beard, but a curly black moustache. He had the high cheekbones of the Turks, and the slanting grey eyes of a people who had lived on the great Eurasian steppe for thousands of years. In European trousers, perhaps, he would be noticeable; but in a brown cloak – no. Nobody noticed him very much. That was his special talent, if it was a talent at all. More likely, as the Marquise had been saying, it was a condition of mind. A condition of the body.

Yashim had many things – innate charm, a gift for languages, and the ability to open those grey eyes suddenly wide. Both men and women had found themselves strangely hypnotised by his voice, before they had even noticed who was speaking. But he lacked balls.

Not in the vulgar sense: Yashim was reasonably brave.

But he was that creature rare even in nineteenth-century Istanbul.

Yashim was a eunuch.

2

In the Abode of Felicity, in the deepest, most forbidden district of Topkapi Palace, the sultan lay back on his pillows and picked fretfully at the satin coverlet, trying to imagine what could amuse him in the coming hours. A song, he thought, let it be a song. One of those sweet, rollicking Circassian melodies: the sadder the song, the brighter the melody.

He had wondered if he could just pretend to be asleep. Why not? Ruler of the Black Sea and the White, ruler of Rumelia and Mingrelia, lord of Anatolia and Ionia, Romania and Macedonia, Protector of the Holy Cities, steely rider through the realms of bliss, Sultan and Padishah, he had to sleep sometimes, did he not? Especially if he was ever to reclaim his sovereignty over Greece.

But he knew what would happen if he tried to pretend. He'd done it before, dashing all the hopes and ambitions of the lovely gözde, the girl selected to share his bed that night. It would mean listening to her sighs, followed by timid little scratches against his thighs or his chest, and finally tears; the whole harem would throw him reproachful glances for a month.

Soon she'd be here. He'd better have a plan. Riding the rooster was probably safest: he was quite fat, frankly, and he didn't want anyone hurt. If only he could be lying in bed with Fatima instead, who was almost as cuddly as himself, having his feet rubbed!

His feet! On a reflex he pulled his knees up slightly under the coverlet. Ancestral tradition was all very well, but Sultan Mahmut II had no intention of letting any fragrant Circassian girl lift the covers and start crawling up towards him from the foot of his bed.

He heard a slight commotion in the corridor outside. A sense of duty brought him up on one elbow, arranging his features into a smile of welcome. He could hear whispers. Last-minute nerves, perhaps? The swooning slave suddenly resistant? Well, it wasn't likely. She'd got this far: almost to the moment she'd been trained towards, the event she had given her life to attend. A jealous squabble was more likely: *those are my pearls!*

The door opened. But it wasn't a bangled slave-girl with swaying hip and full breasts who entered. It was an old man with rouged cheeks and a big waist who bowed and loped into the room on bare feet. Catching sight of his master, he sank to his knees and began to crawl until he reached the edge of the bed, where he prostrated himself on the ground. He lay there, mute and quivering, like a big jelly.

'Well?' Sultan Mahmut frowned.

Out of the enormous body there came at length a voice, piping and high.

'Your Magnifishensh, my lord, my mashter,' the slave finally began to lisp. The sultan shifted uncomfortably.

'It has pleased God to catht a mantle of death over the body of one daughter of felithity whothe dreams were about to be fulfilled by Your Magnificenth, my master.'

The sultan frowned.

'She died?' His tone was incredulous. Also he was taken aback: was he so very fearsome?

'Thire, I do not know what to thay. But God made another the inthtwument of her detheathe.'

The eunuch paused, groping for the proper form of words. It was awfully hard.

'My master,' he said at last. 'She has been stwangled.'

The sultan flopped back onto the pillows. There, he said to himself, he was right. Not nerves at all. Just jealousy.

Everything was normal.

'Send for Yashim,' the sultan said wearily. 'I want to sleep.'

3

Asleep or awake, the sultan was the Commander of the Faithful, and chief of the Ottoman armed forces; but it was many years since he had unfurled the standard of the prophet and put himself at the head of his soldiery, securing his throne by a single act of nerve. His navy was commanded by the Kapudan Pasha, and his troops controlled by the seraskier.

The seraskier did not rise for Yashim, but merely motioned him with dabbling fingers to a corner of the divan. Yashim slipped off his shoes and sat down cross-legged, his cloak settling around him like a lily pad. He inclined his head and murmured the polite greeting.

Clean-shaven, in the new fashion, with tired brown eyes set in a face the colour of old linen, the seraskier lay awkwardly on one hip, in uniform, as though he had received a wound. His steel-grey hair was cut close to his skull, and the red fez perched on the back of his head emphasized the weight of his jaws. Yashim thought he would be passable in a turban, but Frankish practice had instead dictated a buttoned tunic, with blue trousers piped in red and a shoal of braid and epaulettes: modern uniform for modern war. In the same spirit he had also been issued with a solid walnut table and eight stiff-looking uphol-stered chairs, which stood in the middle of the room and were lit by candelabra suspended from the coffered ceiling.

He sat up and crossed his trousered legs so that the seams bulged. 'Perhaps you would rather we moved to a table,' he sug-gested irritably.

'As you wish.'

But the seraskier evidently preferred the indignity of sitting on the divan in his trousers to the unpleasant exposure of the cen-tral table. Like Yashim himself, he found sitting on a chair with his back to the room faintly disquieting. So instead he drew a long sigh, folding and unfolding his stubby fingers.

'I was told you were in the Crimea.'

Yashim blinked. 'I found a ship. There was nothing to detain me.'

The seraskier cocked an eyebrow. 'You failed there, then?'

Yashim leaned forwards. 'We failed there many years ago,

6

Effendi. There is little that can be done.' He held the seraskier's gaze. 'That little, I did. I worked fast. Then I came back.'

There was nothing else to be said. The Tartar Khans of the Crimea no longer ruled the southern steppe, like little brothers to the Ottoman state. Yashim had been shaken to see Russian Cossacks riding through Crimean villages, bearing guns. Disarmed, defeated, the Tartars drank, sitting about the doors of their huts and staring listlessly at the Cossacks while their women worked in the fields. The Khan himself fretted in exile, tormented by a dream of lost gold. He had sent others to recover it, before he heard about Yashim – Yashim the guardian, the lala. In spite of Yashim's efforts, the khan's gold remained a dream. Perhaps there was none.

The seraskier grunted. 'The Tartars were good fighters,' he said. 'In their day. But horsemen without discipline have no place on the modern battlefield. Today we need disciplined infantry, with muskets and bayonets. Artillery. You saw Russians?'

'I saw Russians, Effendi. Cossacks.'

'That's the kind we're up against. The reason we need men like the men of the New Guard.'

The seraskier stood up. He was a bear of a man, well over six feet tall. He stood with his back to Yashim, staring at a row of books, while Yashim glanced involuntarily at the curtain through which he had entered. The groom who had ushered him in was nowhere to be seen. By all the laws of hospitality the seraskier should have offered the preliminary pipe and coffee; Yashim wondered if the rudeness was deliberate. A great man like the seraskier had attendants to bring him refreshment, as well as a pipe-bearer to select his tobacco, keep the equipment in good clean working order, accompany his master on outings with the pipe in a cloth and the tobacco pouch in his shirt, and ensure the proper lighting and draw of the pipe. Rich men who vied with one another to present their guests with the finest leaf and the most elegant pipes – amber for the mouthpiece, Persian cherry for the stem – would no more think of functioning without a pipe-bearer than an English milord could dispense with the services of a valet. But the room was empty.

'Less than two weeks from today, the Sultan is to review the troops. Marches, drill, gunnery displays. The sultan will not be the only one watching. It will be –' the seraskier stopped, and his head snapped up. Yashim wondered what he had been about to say. That the review would be the most important moment of his career, perhaps. 'We are a young troop, as you know. The New Guard has only been in existence for ten years. Like a young colt, we startle easily. We have not had, ah, all the care and training we might have wished for.'

'Nor always quite the success that was promised.'

Yashim saw the seraskier stiffen. In their newfangled European jackets and trousers, the New Guard had been put through their paces by a succession of foreign instructors, ferenghi from Europe who taught them drilling, marching, presenting arms. What could you say? In spite of it all the Egyptians – the *Egyptians*! – had dealt them humiliating reverses in Palestine and Syria, and the Russians were closer to Istanbul than at any time in living memory. Perhaps their victories were to have been expected, for they were formidable opponents with up-to-date equipment and modern armies; yet there remained, too, the debacle in Greece. No more than peasants in pantaloons, led by quarrelsome windbags, even the Greeks had proved to be more than a match for the New Guard.

All this left the New Guard with a single sanguinary triumph. It was a victory achieved not on the battlefield but right here, on the streets of Istanbul; not against foreign enemies but against their own military predecessors, the dangerously overweening Janissary Corps. Once the Ottoman Empire's crack troops, the

8

Janissaries had degenerated – or evolved, if you liked – into an armed mafia, terrorising sultans, swaggering through the streets of Istanbul, rioting, fire-raising, thieving and extorting with impunity. Outgunned and outdrilled by the armies of the west, stubbornly they had clung to the traditions of their forefathers, contemptuous of innovation, despising the common soldiers of the enemy and rejecting every lesson the battlefield could teach, for fear of their grip loosening. For decades they had held the empire to ransom.

The New Guard had finally settled the account. Ten years ago that was, on the night of 16 June 1826: the Auspicious Event, as people were careful to refer to it. Right here, in Istanbul, New Guard gunners had pounded the Janissaries to pieces in their barracks, bringing four centuries of terror and triumph to a well-deserved end.

'The review will be a success,' the seraskier growled. 'People will see the backbone of this empire, unbreakable, unshakeable.' He swung round, sawing the air with the edge of his hand. 'Accurate fire. Precise drill. Obedience. Our enemies, as well as our friends, will draw their own conclusions. Do you understand?'

Yashim shrugged slightly. The seraskier tilted his chin and snorted through his nose.

'But we have a problem,' he said. Yashim continued to gaze at him: it was a long time since he had been woken in the dead of night and summoned to the palace. Or to the barracks. He glanced out of the window: it was still dark, the sky cold and overcast. *Everything begins in darkness.* Well, it was his job to shed light.

'And what, exactly, does your problem consist of?'

'Yashim Effendi. They call you the lala, do they not? Yashim Lala, the guardian.'

Yashim inclined his head. Lala was an honorific, a title of

9

respect given to certain trusted eunuchs who attended on rich and powerful families, chaperoning their women, watching over their children, supervising the household. An ordinary lala was something between a butler and a housekeeper, a nanny and the head of security: a guardian. Yashim felt the title suited him.

'But as far as I understand it,' the seraskier said slowly, 'you are without attachment. Yes, you have links to the palace. Also to the streets. So tonight I invite you into our family, the family of the New Guard. For ten days, at most.'

'The family, you mean, of which you are the head?'

'In a manner of speaking. But do not think I am setting myself up as the father of this family. I would like you to think of me, rather, as a kind of, of –' the seraskier looked uneasy: the word did not seem to come easily to him. Distaste for eunuchs, Yashim knew, was as inbound amongst Ottoman men as their suspicion of tables and chairs. 'Think of me – as an older brother. I protect you. You confide in me.' He paused, wiped his forehead. 'Do you, ah, have any family yourself?'

Yashim was used to this: disgust, tempered with curiosity. He made a motion with his hand, ambiguous: let the man wonder, it was none of his business.

'The New Guard must earn the confidence of the people, and of the sultan, too,' the seraskier continued. 'That is the purpose of the Review. But something has happened which might wreck the process.'

It was Yashim's turn to be curious, and he felt it like a ripple up the back of his neck.

'This morning,' the seraskier began, 'I was informed that four of our officers had failed to report for morning drill.' He stopped, frowned. 'You must understand that the New Guard are not like any other army the empire has seen. Discipline. Hard work, fair pay and obedience to a superior officer. We turn up for drill. I know what you are thinking, but these officers were particularly fine young gentlemen. I would say that they were the flower of our corps, as well as being our best gunnery officers. They spoke French,' he added, as if that concluded it. Perhaps it did.

'So they had attended the engineering university?'

'They passed out with top marks. They were the best.'

'Were?'

'Please, a moment.' The seraskier raised a hand to his forehead. 'At first, in spite of everything, I thought like you. I supposed they had had some adventure and would reappear later, very shamefaced and sorry. I, of course, was ready to tear them into strips: the whole corps look up to those young men, do you see? They set, as the French say, the tone.'

'You speak French?'

'Oh, only a very little. Enough.'

Most of the foreign instructors in the New Guard, Yashim knew, were Frenchmen, or others – Italians, Poles – who had been swept into the enormous armies the Emperor Napoleon had raised to carry out his dreams of universal conquest. Fifteen, ten years ago, with the Napoleonic Wars finally at an end, some of the more indigent remnants of the Grande Armée had found their way to Istanbul, to take the sultan's sequin. But learning French was a business for the young, and the seraskier was pushing fifty.

'Go on.'

'Four good men vanished from their barracks last night. When they did not appear this morning, I asked one of the banjee, the cleaners, and found out that they had not slept in their dormitory.'

'And they're still missing?'

'No. Not exactly.'

'What do you mean, not exactly?'

'One of them was found tonight. About four hours ago.'

'That's good.'

'He was found dead in an iron pot.'

'An iron pot?'

'Yes, yes. A cauldron.'

Yashim blinked.

'Do I understand,' he said slowly, 'that the soldier was being cooked?'

The seraskier's eyes nearly bulged out of his head. 'Cooked?' He echoed weakly. It was a refinement he had not considered.

'I think,' said the seraskier, 'you should just come and take a look.'

◄◄ 4 ►►

Two hours later, Yashim had seen just about all that he wanted to see for one morning. For any number of mornings.

Summoning a lantern bearer, the seraskier walked him eastwards through the empty streets, following the city's spine towards the imperial stables. Outside the Beyazit Mosque torches flickered in the dark; they passed the Burnt Column close to the entrance to the Grand Bazaar, now shuttered and still, holding its breath as it guarded its treasures through the night. Further on, near the Sehzade Mosque above the Roman aqueduct, they ran across the night watch, who let them go when he saw who it was. Eventually they reached the stables. The stables, like the Guard itself, were new. They had been erected close below the ridge, on the southern side, on an area of ground which had been vacant since the suppression of the Janissaries ten years before, when their vast and rambling barracks had succumbed to bombardment and conflagration.

They found the cauldron, just as the seraskier had described.

It stood in a corner of one of the new stables, surrounded by bedding straw and lit by large, globular oil lamps suspended on heavy chains from the tie beam way overhead. The horses, the seraskier explained, had been removed.

'It was the horses' disturbance that brought the matter to light,' he added. 'They do not like the smell of dead men.'

Yashim had not realised when the seraskier described it that the cauldron was so very big. It had three short legs and two metal loops on either side for handles; even so Yashim could barely see over the top. The seraskier brought him a mounting stool, and Yashim climbed it to look inside.

The dead soldier was still in his uniform. He was coiled in a foetal position at the bottom of the pot, just covering the base: his arms, which were tied at the wrist, were drawn up over his head making it impossible to see his face. Yashim stepped down and brushed his hands automatically, though the rim of the pot was perfectly clean.

'Do you know who he is?'

The seraskier nodded. 'Osman Berek. I took his pocket book. You see . . .'

He hesitated.

'Well?'

'I am sorry to say, the body has no face.'

Yashim felt a chill of disgust.

'No face?'

'I . . . I climbed in. I turned him just a little. I thought I would recognise him, but – that's all. His face has been hacked off. From below the chin to above the eyebrows. It was done, I think, at a single blow.'

Yashim wondered what force was needed to sever a man's face from his body at a blow. He turned around. 'The cauldron is always here? It seems an odd place for it.'

'No, no, the cauldron came with the body.'

13

Yashim stared.

'Please, effendi. Too many surprises. Unless you have more?'

The seraskier considered. 'No. The cauldron simply appeared overnight.'

'And nobody heard or saw anything?'

'The grooms heard nothing. They were asleep in the lofts.'

'The doors are barred?'

'Not usually. In the event of a fire . . .'

'Quite.' According to an old saying, Istanbul suffered three evils – plague, fire, and Greek interpreters. There were so many old wooden buildings in the city, too closely packed: it only took a careless spark to reduce whole sections of the city to ashes. The unlamented Janissaries had been the city's firemen, too: it was typical of their degeneration that they had combined their fire-duty with the more profitable occupation of fire-raising, demanding bribes to put out fires they themselves had started. Yashim vaguely remembered that the Janissaries had manned an important fire-tower on the edge of their old barracks here, which ironically collapsed in the conflagration of 1826. Subsequently the sultan had ordered the construction of an extraordinary new fire-tower at Beyazit, a 260-foot-high pillar of stone, topped with an overhanging gallery for the fire-watchers. Many people thought that the Beyazit Tower was the ugliest building in Istanbul; it was certainly the tallest, standing as it did on the Third Hill of the city. It was noticeable, all the same, that there were fewer fire-alarms these days.

'And who found the body, then?'

'I did. No, this is not a surprise. I was called because of the cauldron, and because the grooms were unhappy about the state of the horses. I was the first one to look inside. I am a military man, I've seen dead men before. And . . .' He hesitated. 'I had already begun to suspect what I might see.'

Yashim said nothing.

'I gave nothing away. I ordered the horses out and had the doors barred. That's all.'

Yashim pinged the cauldron with his fingernail. It gave a tinny sound. He pinged again.

The seraskier and he looked at each other.

'It's very light,' Yashim remarked. They were silent for a moment. 'What do you think?'

'I think,' said the seraskier, 'that we do not have much time. Today is Thursday.'

'The review?'

'Ten days. To find out what is happening to my men.'

It had been a difficult morning. Yashim went to the baths, was soaped and pummelled, and lay for a long time in the hot room, before returning home in his freshly laundered clothes. Finally, having explored the matter in his mind in every way he could think of in an effort to draw a lead, he turned to what he always considered the next best thing.

How do you find three men in a decaying, medieval, mist-benighted city of two million people?

You don't even try.

You cook.

Getting up he moved slowly over to the other side of the room, which lay in darkness. He struck a Lucifer and lit the lamp, trimming the wick until the light burned steadily and bright. It fell on a neat arrangement of stove, high table and a row of very sharp-looking knives, suspended in mid-air by a splice of wood.

There was a basket in the corner and from it Yashim selected several small, firm onions. He peeled and sliced them on the block, first one way and then the other, while he set a pot on the stove and slipped enough olive oil into it to brown the onions. When they were turning, he tossed in a couple of handfuls of rice which he drew from an earthenware crock.

Long ago he'd discovered what it was to cook. It was at about the same time that he'd grown disgusted with his own efforts to achieve a cruder sensual gratification, and resigned himself to more stylised pleasures. It was not that, until then, he had always considered cooking as a woman's work: for cooks in the empire could be of either sex. But he had thought of it, perhaps, as a task for the poor.

The rice had gone clear, so he threw in a handful of currants and another of pine nuts, a lump of sugar and a big pinch of salt. He took down a jar from the shelf and helped himself to a spoonful of oily tomato paste which he mixed into a tea glass of water. He drained the glass into the rice, with a hiss and a plume of steam. He added a pinch of dried mint and ground some pepper into the pot and stirred the rice, then clamped on a lid and moved the pot to the back of the stove.

He had bought the mussels cleaned, the big three-inch mussels from Therapia, up the Bosphorus. He opened them one by one with a twist of a flat blade and dropped them into a basin of water. The rice was half-cooked. He chopped dill, very fine, and stirred it into the mixture, then tipped it out onto a dish to cool. He drained the mussels and stuffed them, using a spoon, closing the shells before he laid them head to toe in layers in a pan. He weighted them down with a plate, added some hot water from the kettle, put on a lid and slid the pan over the coals.

He took a chicken, jointed it, crushed walnuts on the flat of the cleaver and prepared Acen Yahnisi, with pomegranite juice.

When everything was done he picked up a swan-necked ewer and very carefully washed first his hands, then his mouth, his face, his neck and, lastly, his private parts.

He took out his mat and prayed. When he had finished he rolled up the mat once more and put it away in a niche.

Soon, he knew, he would have a visitor.

 6

Stanislaw Palewski was about fifty-five years old, with a circle of tight grey curls around his balding pate and a pair of watery blue eyes whose expression of beseeching sadness was belied by the strength of his chin, the size of his Roman nose and the set determination of his mouth, which at this moment was compressed into a narrow slit by the rain and wind backing off the Marmara shore.

He walked, as he did every Thursday night, along the road which ran from the New Mosque up the Golden Horn, a conspicuous figure in a top hat and frock coat. The coat, like the hat, had seen better days; once black, it had been transmuted by wear and the damp airs of Istanbul into something more nearly approaching sea-green; the velvet nap of the topper had worn smooth in many places, particularly around the crown and on the rim. Approaching a pair of ladies swathed in their chadors, accompanied by their escort, he stepped politely into the road and automatically touched the brim of his hat in salute. The ladies did not directly acknowledge his salutation, but they bobbed about a little and Palewski heard a muffled whisper, and a giggle. He smiled to himself, and stepped back onto the pavement to resume his walk.

As he did so, something chinked in his bag, and he stopped to check. Nothing explicitly forbade the diplomatically accredited representative of a foreign power from walking through the city carrying two bottles of 52 per cent proof bison grass vodka, but

Palewski wasn't eager to put the case to the test. For one thing, he was not absolutely sure that there hadn't ever been, in the whole tumultuous history of the city, an edict which made carrying liquor a flogging offence. For another, his diplomatic immunity was at best a fragile kind of favour. He had no gunboats at his disposal to ride up the Bosphorus and bombard the sultan into a more amenable frame of mind if things went wrong, as Admiral Duckworth had done for the English in 1807. He had no means of exerting government pressure as the Russians had done in 1712, when their ambassador was clapped up in the old prison of the Seven Towers. Forty years ago, the rulers of Russia, Prussia and Austria sent their armies into Poland to wipe the country from the map. Palewski, in truth, had no government at all.

The Polish Imperial Ambassador to the Sublime Porte rearranged the damp cloth which protected his bottles, drew the strings of his bag tight again, and walked on through a dwindling series of streets and alleyways until he came to a very small porte cochère in one of the back alleys of the old town down by the Golden Horn. The door was small because it was sunken: only the upper three-fifths showed above the level of the muddy ground. A scattering of small boys tore past him, no doubt rubbing yet another layer of shine into the back of his old coat. A snapping bell, clapped between the fingers, announced the approach of a man in a tiny donkey cart, weaving his way with miraculous precision through the narrow interstices of the close medieval streets. Hurriedly, Palewski knocked on the door. It was opened by an old woman in a blue wimple who silently stood back to let him enter. Palewski, stooping, stepped in just as the cart swept by with a pattering of tiny hooves and a shout from the man at the reins.

Outside, the light, such as it was, was fading; inside, it had never, apparently, risen. Palewski wondered briefly whether sunlight had penetrated to this spot at all in the past fifteen hundred years: the sunken doorcase, he had long suspected, was early Byzantine work, and he had no reason to imagine that the dark wooden handrail, to which he was now clinging as he swung blindly but unfalteringly upstairs, was anything but Byzantine itself, like the stone of the house, and the window embrasures, and the very probably Roman vaulting overhead.

At the head of the stairs he paused to catch his breath and analyse the peculiar mixture of fragrances seeping through the lighted crack at the foot of the door in front of him.

Yashim the eunuch and Ambassador Palewski were unlikely friends, but they were firm ones. 'We are two halves, who together become whole, you and I,' Palewski had once declared, after soaking up more vodka than would have been good for him were it not for the fact, which he sternly upheld, that only the bitter herb it contained could keep him sane and alive. 'I am an ambassador without a country and you – a man without testicles.' Yashim had considered this remark, before pointing out that Palewski might, at a pinch, get his country back; but the Polish ambassador had waved him away with a loud outbreak of sobs. 'About as likely as you growing balls, I'm afraid. Never. Never. The bastards!' Soon after that he had fallen asleep, and Yashim had employed a porter to carry him home on his back.

The impoverished diplomat sniffed the air and adopted a look of cunning sweetness which was entirely for his own benefit. The first of the smells was onion; also chicken, that he could tell. He recognised the dark aroma of cinnamon, but there was something else he found it hard to identify, pungent and fruity. He sniffed again, screwing his eyes shut.

Without further hesitation or ceremony he wrenched open the door and bounded into the room: 'Yashim! Yashim! You raise our souls from the gates of hell! Acem Yahnisi, if I'm not mistaken – so like the Persian fesinjan. Chicken, walnuts – and the juice of the pomegranate!' he declared.

Yashim, who had not heard him come up, turned in astonishment. Palewski saw his face fall.

'Come, come, young man, I ate this dish before you were weaned. Tonight let us give it in all sincerity a new and appropriate name: The ambassador was out of humour, and now is delighted! How's that?'

He presented the bottles to his host. 'Still cold, you feel! Marvellous! One day I shall take a light and go down into that cellar and find out where the icy water comes from. It may be a Roman cistern. I shouldn't be surprised. What a find!'

He rubbed his hands together while Yashim, smiling, handed him a glass of vodka. They stood for a moment looking at one another, then tossed back their heads simultaneously, and drank. Palewski dived on the mussels.

It was going to be a long evening. It *was* a long evening. By the hour of the dawn prayer, Yashim was aware he had just nine days left.

❖ 7 ❖

The Street of the Tinsmiths ran slightly above and to the west of the Mosque of Rustem Pasha, itself half-buried in the alleys and back-doubles which surround the southern entrances of the Grand Bazaar. Like most of the artisans' quarters, it consisted of a narrow funnel of open workshops, each no bigger than a very big wardrobe, where the smiths worked with forge, bellows and hammers over the standard articles of their trade: tin pots, little kettles, weakly hinged or plainly lidded boxes of every size and shape, from the tiny round tins used for storing kohl and tiger balm to banded trunks for sailors and the linen trade. They made knives and forks; they made badges and insignia; spectacle frames and ferrules for walking sticks. Every one of them worked at a specialism, rarely if ever straying from, say, the remorseless production of amulets designed to contain a paper inscribed with the ninety-nine names of God to, for example, the perpetual manufacture of pin boxes. These were guild rules, laid down hundreds of years before by the market judges and the sultan himself, and they were broken only under very special circumstances.

Would the manufacture of an enormous cauldron, Yashim wondered, constitute a special circumstance?

The tin market was not a place for the crowds who infested some of the other industrious highways of Istanbul: the food markets, the spice bazaars, the makers of shoes. Even the Street of the Goldsmiths was more busy. So Yashim walked along easily in the middle of the street, and attracted few glances. Once the smiths had satisfied themselves that he was a stranger, they thought no more about him: they hardly cared to notice if he was rich, poor, fat or thin, for no man alive was likely to bring them any greater profit than the modest profit they enjoyed by the terms of their guild membership. No one was going to stop by and offer to buy – at a wild price – any of their humdrum manufactures. The regulations of the guild were fixed: there was a quality, and a price, neither more nor less.

Yashim knew all this. For the moment he merely watched. Most of the smiths worked in the opening of their shops, closest to the light and air and away from the smoky furnaces which blazed in the background. From here, tapping incessantly with their hammers, they slowly pushed out a succession of little products. He glanced up: the usual arrangement of latticed windows overhead advertised the dwelling places of the men, their wives and their children. The apprentices, Yashim thought, would sleep in the shops.

He took a turn into a courtyard and looked back. Up an alley thick with rubbish, the upper storeys were approached by rickety staircases leading, in every case, to a mean doorway hung with a faded strip of carpet, or a blanket cut into ribbons against the flies. Which left, he imagined, the flat roofs where the women could go in the day to get some air, unobserved. And at night, who used those roofs? Enough people, he supposed: you could never be sure. With a shrug he dismissed a faint idea and returned his inspection to the courtyard.

The sound of hammers beating against the tin was fainter here: it broke upon the courtyard like the musical note of frogs tinkling in a nearby lake. Few smiths were working in the alcoves of the courtyard itself: it served, instead, as a caravanserai where tin merchants brought the raw materials of the trade and sold it, at need, to the smiths outside. Here were piled thick sheets of tin in apparently random shapes; and their owners sat among them on low stools in quiet contrast to the arrhythmic tintinnabulation of the street beyond, sipping tea and telling their beads. Now and again one of them would make a sale; the tinsmith cut the sheet, the tin merchant weighed it out, and the smith carried it away.

Yashim wandered out for a last look. The bigger objects – lanterns, in the main, and trunks, were being assembled on the ground outside the shops. But Yashim was satisfied that nowhere, either inside or out, was there a place where a cauldron with a base big enough to fit a man could be discreetly built.

Someone, he thought, would have seen.

And that person, he thought, would have been legitimately puzzled. Why, in the name of all things holy, should anyone want to make a cauldron out of tin?

Of such a size, too! The biggest cauldron anyone had seen since – when?

Yashim froze. All around him the tinsmiths beat out their

meaningless bird-like paean to industry and craftsmanship, but he no longer heard. He knew, in a flash, when that moment had been.

Ten years before. The night of 15 June 1826.

8

Yashim felt conspicuous as soon as the thought flashed upon him. It was as if the knowledge had made him glow.

In a nearby café, the proprietor brought him a coffee while Yashim looked with unseeing eyes down the street. The noise of the tinsmiths insistently hammering had melded with a memory of that terrifying sound, ten years ago, of the Janissaries battering on their upturned cauldrons. It was an age-old signal that nobody in the palace, or in the streets, or in their homes in the city, could misunderstand. It was the mother of all dins, and it hadn't meant that the Janissaries wanted more food.

It meant that they wanted blood.

Up through the centuries that driving and sinisterly insistent sound of the Janissaries beating on their cauldrons had been the prelude to death in the streets, men torn apart, the sacrifice of princes. Had it always been so? Yashim knew well what the Janissaries had achieved. Each man was selected from a levy of the empire's toughest, likeliest, most wide-awake Christian boys. Brought to Istanbul, renouncing the faith of the Balkan peasants who had borne them, swearing allegiance as slaves to the sultan mounted at their head, they became a corps. A terrifying fighting machine that the Ottoman sultans had unleashed against their enemies in Europe.

If the Ottoman empire inspired fear throughout the known world, it was the Janissaries who carried the fear to the throats of the unbelievers. The conquest of Sofia and Belgrade. Istanbul itself, wrested from the Greeks in 1453. The Arab peninsula and with it, the Holy Cities. Mohacs, 1526, when the flower of Hungarian knighthood was cut down in the saddle and Suleiman the Magnificent led his men to Buda, and on, fleetingly, to the gates of Vienna. Rhodes and Cyprus, Egypt and the Sahara. Why, the Janissaries had even landed in France in 1566, and spent a year in Toulon.

Until – who could say why? – the victories dried up. The terms of engagement changed. The Janissaries sought permission to marry. They petitioned for the right to take up trades when there was no fighting, to feed their families. They enrolled their sons into the corps, and the corps grew reluctant to fight. They were still dangerous: loaded with privilege, they lorded it over the common people of the city. Designed to die fighting at the lonely borders of an ever-expanding empire, they enjoyed all the licence and immunity that the people and the sultan could bestow on men who would soon be martyrs. But they no longer sought to martyr themselves. The men who had been sent to terrify Europe made a simple discovery: it was easier – and far less dangerous – to terrorise at home.

The palace made efforts to reason with them. Efforts to discipline them. In 1618 Sultan Osman tried to overturn them: they had him killed, as Yashim knew, by the compression of his testicles, a mode of execution which left no traces on the body. Special man; special death. It was considered fitting for a member of the imperial family. Later still, in 1635, Murad IV rounded up 30,000 Janissaries and marched them to their deaths in Persia. But the corps survived.

And slowly, painfully, the Ottomans had come to realise that they could no longer properly defend themselves. Unreliable as they were, the Janissaries still insisted on being the supreme military power: they had become unassailable. The common people were afraid of them. In trade, they exploited their privileges to become dangerous rivals. Their behaviour was threatening and insolent as they swaggered through the city streets fully armed and wielding sticks, uttering loutish blasphemies. Outside the Topkapi Palace, between Aya Sofia and the Blue Mosque, lay the open space called the Atmeidan, the ancient Hippodrome of the Byzantines. In it grew a huge plane tree to which the Janissaries had always rallied at the first sign of any trouble, for the blotched and peeling trunk of the Janissary Tree stood at the centre of their world; as the palace lay at the centre of Ottoman government, and Aya Sofia at the heart of religious faith. Beneath its branches the Janissaries divulged their grievances and secrets, and plotted mutinies. From the swaying limbs of the tree, too, they would hang the bodies of men who had displeased them: ministers, viziers, court officials, sacrificed to their blood-lust by a terrified succession of weak and vacillating sultans.

Meanwhile, lands that had been conquered by the sultan's armies in the name of Islam were being lost to the infidels: Hungary was the first to go. In Egypt, Ali Pasha the Albanian built on the experience of the Napoleonic invasion to train the fellahin as soldiers, western-style. And when Greece disappeared, from the very heartland of an empire where every other man was Greek by speech, it was the final blow. The Egyptians had held the fort, for a while: they were to be commended. They had drill, and discipline; they had tactics and modern guns. The sultan read the message and began to train his own, Egyptian-style force: the seraskier's New Guard.

That was ten years ago. The sultan issued orders that the Janissaries should adopt the western style of the New Guard, knowing that they would be provoked and affronted. And the Janissaries had rebelled on cue. Caring only for their own privileges, they turned on the palace and the fledgling New Guards. But they had grown stupid, as well as lazy. They were loathed by the people. The sultan had made ready. When the Janissaries overturned their cauldrons on the night of Thursday, 15 June, it took a day to accomplish by modern means what no one had managed to achieve in three hundred years. By the night of the sixteenth, efficient modern gunnery had reduced their mutinous barracks to a smouldering ruin. Thousands were already dead: the rest, fleeing for their lives, died in the city streets, in the forests outside the walls, in the holes and lairs they crept into to survive.

It was a trauma, Yashim reflected, from which the empire still waited to recover. Certain people might never recover at all.

≪ 9 ≫

A man with grime up to his elbows and a leather apron was working on a lantern in the street outside his shop. With a pair of tongs he crimped the tin sheets, fixing them together with a speed and dexterity Yashim was content simply to admire, until the man looked up questioningly.

'I've got something slightly unusual I'd like a price for,' Yashim explained. 'You seem to make large objects.'

The man grunted in agreement. 'What is it you want, effendi?'

'A cauldron. A very big cauldron – as tall as me, on legs. Can you do it?'

The man straightened up and pulled his hand over the back of neck, wincing.

'Funny time of year for a big cauldron,' he remarked.

Yashim's eyes widened.

'You can do it? You've done it before?'

The smith's answer took him by surprise.

'Do it every year or so. Big tin cauldrons for the soup-sellers' guild. They use them for the city procession.'

Of course! Why hadn't he thought of that? Every year, when the guildsmen process through the streets to the Aya Sofia, each guild drags a juggernaut loaded with the implements of their craft. The guild of barbers have a huge pair of scissors and offer free haircuts to the crowd. The fishmongers make their float like a ship, and stand casting nets and hauling on the ropes. The bakers set up an oven and toss hot rolls to the people. And the soup-sellers: huge black cauldrons of fresh soup, which they ladle out into clay pannikins and distribute to the crowd as they go along. Carnival.

'But a tin cauldron wouldn't take the heat or the weight,' Yashim objected.

The smith laughed.

'They're not real! The whole float would collapse if they were real. You don't think, effendi, the barber cuts people's hair with that giant pair of scissors? They put a smaller pot of soup inside the tin cauldron, and just make believe. It's for a laugh.'

Yashim felt like a dimwitted child.

'Have you made one of those cauldrons recently? Out of season, even?'

'We make the cauldrons when the guild orders them. The rest of the year, well,' he spat on his hands and picked up the tongs, 'it's just lanterns and such. The cauldrons get a bit battered and they split, so we make more at the right time. If you're looking for one, I'd talk to the soup-men's guild if I were you.' He looked at Yashim and creases of amusement showed around his eyes. 'You're not the mullah Nasreddin, are you?'

'No, I am not the mullah,' Yashim laughed.

'Sounds like some kind of prank anyway. If you'll excuse me . . .'

The girl lay on the bed in her vestal finery, her eyes closed. Her hair was elaborately braided, fastened with a malachite clasp. Perhaps it was the kohl, but her eyes seemed very dark, while the skin of her beautiful face seemed almost to glitter in the slatted sunlight that filtered through the shutters of the room. Heavy tassels of gold thread hung from the gauze scarf she wore around her breasts, and her long legs were encased in pantaloons of a satin muslin so fine it was as though she were naked. A small golden slipper dangled from the toe of her left foot.

The tongue that protruded slightly between her rouged lips suggested that she needed more than a kiss to waken her now.

Yashim bent over and examined the girl's neck. Two black bruises on either side of her throat. The pressure had been severe, and she'd been killed from in front: she would have seen the killer's face before she died.

He glanced down at the girl's body and felt a pang of pity. So flawless: death had made her more like a jewel, lustrous and cold, her beauty beyond all power of touch. And, he thought sadly, I will die like her: a virgin. More mangled, in my case. He blocked the thoughts, quickly: years ago they had maddened and tormented him, but he had learned to control them. They were his thoughts, his desires, and so he could sheath them like a sword. He was alive. That was good.

His eyes travelled over her skin. The pallor of death had left it like cold white butter. He almost missed the tiny suggestion that she was not, after all, absolutely without a flaw. Around the middle finger of her right hand he spotted the very slight trace of a narrow band where the skin had been squeezed. She had worn a ring; she was not wearing it now.

He raised his head. Something in the atmosphere of the room

had changed – a slight shift in pressure, perhaps, a shift in the balance of the living to the dead. He turned quickly and scanned the room: hangings, columns, plenty of places for someone else to hide. Someone who had already killed?

Out of the shadows a woman glided forward, her head slightly cocked to one side, her hands outstretched.

'Yashim, *chérie! Tu te souviens de ta vieille amie?*'

It was the Validé Sultan, the queen mother herself: and she spoke, he noticed without surprise, in the voice of the Marquise de Merteuil. It was she who had given him the book. In his dreams, the marquise spoke French with what Yashim was not to know was a Creole twang.

She took his hands and pecked him on the cheek, three times. Then she glanced down at the lovely form laid out in death for his inspection.

'*C'est triste*,' she said simply. Her eyes came up to meet his. 'Poor you.'

He knew exactly what she meant.

'*Alors*, you know who did it?'

'Absolutely. A Bulgarian fisherman.'

The Validé Sultan put a pretty hand to her mouth.

'I was about fifteen.'

She waved him away, smiling.

'Yashim, *sois sérieux*. The little girl's dead and – don't shout now – also my jewels have gone. The Napoleon jewels. We are all having a very bad time in the *appartements*.'

Yashim gazed at her. In the half-light she looked almost young; in any light she was still beautiful. He wondered if the dead girl would have looked so good at her age – or would have survived so long. Aimée – the sultan's mother. It was the role that every woman in the harem fought for: to sleep with the sultan, bear a son and, in due course, engineer his elevation to the throne of Osman. Each step required a greater concentration of miracles. The woman in front of him had possessed a singular advantage, though: she was a Frenchwoman. One miracle under her belt from the start.

'You're not telling me that I never showed you the Napoleon jewels?' she was saying. 'Well, my God, you are the lucky man. I bore everyone with these jewels. I admire them, my guest admires them – and I'm quite sure they all think them as ugly as I do. But they came from the Emperor Napoleon to me. *Personellement!*'

She darted him a roguish look.

'You think – sentimental value? Rubbish. They are, however, part of my *batterie de guerre*. Beauty is cheap within these walls. Distinction, though, comes at a price. Look at *her*. Not all the mountains of Circassia could produce a creature so lovely again – but my son would have forgotten her name in a week. Tanya? Alesha? What does it matter?'

'It mattered to somebody,' Yashim reminded her. 'Somebody killed her.'

'Because she was beautiful? Pah, everyone is beautiful here.'

'No. Perhaps because she was about to lie with the sultan.'

She eyed him suddenly: at times like this he knew exactly why she was validé, and no one else. He held her gaze.

'Perhaps.' She gave a pretty little shrug. 'I want to tell you about my jewels. Ugly, very useful – and worth a fortune.'

He wondered if she needed money: but she had read his thoughts. 'One never knows,' she said, tapping him on the arm. 'Things are never quite as one expects.'

He bowed slightly to acknowledge the truth of her remark. In his life, it was true. In hers? Without question: and with an unexpectedness that was fantastic.

Fifty years before a young woman had boarded a French packet en route from the West Indies to Marseilles. Raised on the Caribbean island of Martinique, she was being sent to Paris to complete her education, and find a suitable husband.

She never arrived. In the eastern Atlantic her ship was taken by a North African *xebec*, and the beautiful young woman became the prisoner of Algerian corsairs. The corsairs presented her to the Dey of Algiers, who marvelled at her exotic beauty and her white, white skin. The dey knew she was far too valuable to be retained. So he sent her on, to Istanbul.

But that was only half the story: the half that was merely unusual. Over the centuries other Christian captives had made their way into a sultan's bed. Not many; some. But the whim of destiny is powerful and inscrutable. On Martinique, young Aimée had been almost inseparable from another French Creole girl called Rose Tascher de la Pagerie. A year after Aimée set out on her fateful voyage to France, young Rose had followed. Same route: a luckier ship. Reaching Paris, she had weathered revolution, imprisonment, hunger and the desires of ambitious men to become the lover, the wife, and finally the Empress of Napoleon Bonaparte, Emperor of France. Aimée, the friend of Rose's youth, had vanished to the world as the Validé Sultan. Rose was Empress Josephine.

One never knows.

She reached up and gave him a chaste kiss. At the door she turned.

'Find my jewels, Yashim. Find them soon – or I swear I'll never lend you another novel as long as I live!'

11

In the rain, in the night, even a city of two million souls can be quiet and deserted. It was the dead hour between the evening and the night prayers. A rat, its wet fur glistening, scrambled out of an overflowing drain and began to scuttle along the foot of a building, looking for shelter. The rising water pursued it almost imperceptibly.

Slowly the puddle rose, from one cobble to the next, probing the joints for a means of escape. When it found one, it began to trickle through, blindly but unerringly seeking its path downhill. From time to time it stopped, pooled, and started over, insistently seeking its own way to the Bosphorus, lining the banks of its own clear trail with mud, twigs, hairs, crumbs. It spread across a lateral street but pooled again on the other side where a flight of stone steps ran down to the Mosque of the Victory, just newly completed on the shore.

The rain, continuing to fall, continued to back up against the drain. At the hour of the morning star the janitor of the mosque sent two workmen to trace the torrent that was threatening to seep into the cement floors and spoil the carpets. They hitched their woollen cloaks over their heads with their elbows against the rain, and started up the steps.

About two hundred yards uphill they found a section of road which had turned into a pond, and cautiously probed the muddy water with their rods.

Eventually they located the drain, and started work trying to unblock it: first with the rods and later, standing up to their chins in the freezing, filthy water, with their hands and feet. The obstruction was a soft package of some sort, so tightly bound with cords that neither man, slipping foot-first into the icy murk for a few seconds at a time, could get a proper purchase on it. At last, shortly before daybreak, they managed to guide a rod between the package and the wall of the drain, and lever it away far enough to let the water escape with a gurgle.

The workman who leaned in up to his chest and gripped the obstruction finally saw what looked at first like a gigantic turkey, trussed for roasting.

What he saw next made him a very sick workman indeed.

Yashim rolled out of bed, slipped on a djellabah and slippers, took his purse from a hook and went down into the street. Three turns brought him to Kara Davut Sokaği, where he drank two cups of thick, sweet coffee and ate a borek, layers of honeyed pastry fried in oil. Often in the night, at the time when people tend to lie awake and follow their plans out until they drift away into a happy sleep, Yashim thought of moving from his rooms in the tenement to somewhere bigger and lighter, with proper views. He'd designed a small library for himself, with a comfortable, well-lit alcove for reading, and a splendid kitchen, too, with a room off the side for a servant to sleep in – someone to riddle up the fire in the morning and fetch him his coffee. Sometimes it was the library which looked out over the blue Bosphorus, sometimes it was the kitchen. The water threw soothing patterns of light onto the ceiling. An open window caught a glimmer of the summer breeze.

And in the morning, coming down to the Kara Davut, he always decided to stay where he was. He'd leave his books to glower in the half-light, and his kitchen would fill the room with the scent of cardamom and mint and throw steam onto the windows. He'd labour up and down flights of steep stairs and crack his head, from time to time, on the lintel of the sunken doorway. Because the Kara Davut was his kind of street. Ever since he'd found this café, where the proprietor always remembered how he liked his coffee – no spice, a hint of sugar – he'd been happy in the Kara Davut. The people all knew him, but they weren't prying, or gossipy. Not that he gave them anything to gossip about: Yashim led a quiet, blameless life. He went to mosque with them on Fridays. He paid his bills. In return he asked for nothing more than to be left in peace over his morning coffees, to watch the street show, to be waved over by the fishmonger with news of an important haul or to visit the Libyan baker for his excellent sprouted grain bread.

Was that quite true? Did he, really, want to be left in peace by these people – by any people? The seraskier's note, the sultan's summons, the fishmonger winking and the coffee done right for him each day: weren't these exactly the links he craved? Yashim's air of invisibility sometimes struck even him as a protective pose, a version of the stagey mannerisms of those little gelded boys who grew to become the eunuch guardians of a family, and slip-slopped after their charges, frowning and moue-ing and letting their hands flutter towards their hearts. Perhaps detachment was a mannerism he had adopted because the agony was too biting and too strong to bear without it. A very fragile kind of make-believe.

Yashim looked along the street. An imam in a tall white cap lifted his black robe a few inches to avoid soiling it in a puddle and stepped quietly past the café, not turning his head. A small boy with a letter trotted by, stopping at a neighbouring café to ask the way. From the opposite direction a shepherd kept his little flock in order with a hazel wand, continually talking to them, as oblivious to the street as if they were following an empty pathway among the hills of Thrace. Two veiled women were heading for the baths; behind them a black slave carried a bundle of clothes. A porter, bent double beneath his basket, was followed by a train of mules, with logs for firewood, and little Greek children darted in and out between their clattering hooves. Here came a cavass, a thickly-padded policeman with a red fez and pistols thrust into his belt, and two Armenian merchants, one swinging his beads, the other counting them with slender fingers while he spoke.

Once he had hated them all, for having things he could never have – not just the children who would never run and play catch with his; but also knowledge of women who'd speak the truth to their lovers in the quiet, and turn over the small business of the day with them; and the company of men who joked, jostled and held their common secret like ripe melons.

Yashim sipped his coffee, and ground his teeth. Even now, he found himself from time to time with a thwarted urge to leap up, waving his arms: to lacerate himself on barbs of scandal by rutting and roaring among these veiled women and their quiet, all-too-well satisfied men. But the hatred, at least, had passed. It had ebbed away slowly, like a receding flood, leaving only its shining imprint in his mind, the dangerous outline of bitterness and rage. These days he walked warily where the flood had been, trying to recognise old landmarks, to piece together the elements of an honourable life out of the jumble of everyday objects he encountered. If he could not be one of the people – if he could not suffer their hurts, and their joys, and their fears the way they did – then he told himself that he could hold to clarity all the faster; he could watch and intervene. For the people were too busy loving, and backsliding and cheating, and boasting and calculating to see, like him, the comedy complete. They trod on rakes which sprang up to hit them in the eye. They sat on stools which somebody whisked away at the last moment. And sometimes they carried vipers hidden in the folds of their cloaks.

Yashim squeezed his eyes shut tight, to focus on the order of the day. He had to visit the seraskier. Standing by that cauldron in the wee hours of yesterday morning, there were any number of questions he'd been too surprised to ask. What had the soldiers been doing on the night they disappeared? What did their relatives think of the affair? Who were their friends? Who were their enemies?

Then there was the cauldrón to reckon with: the oddest and most sinister part of the whole affair. He needed to visit the Soup Sellers to see what they had to say.

As for the girl in the palace, and the validé's jewels – that was, you might say, a more private affair. In every family home lay a region that was harem, forbidden to outsiders. In the Topkapi palace, this region was almost an acre in size, a warren of corridors and courtyards, of winding stairs and balconies so cunningly contrived that it was sealed from the world's gaze as effectively as if it had been built in the great Sahara, instead of in the middle of one of the greatest cities in the world.

With the rarest exceptions, no man but the sultan himself, or men of his family, could enter the harem.

Yashim was one of the exceptions. He could go where no ordinary man could go, on pain of death.

It did not do to make too much of the harem itself. It wasn't the harem which made eunuchs, though many of them worked there, and the black eunuchs, led by the Kislar Agha, effectively controlled it. Unlike Yashim, unlike many of the white eunuchs, unlike the castrati of the Vatican, the black eunuchs of the palace were utterly clean-cropped: shaved to the quick in a single sweep of the sickle blade, wielded by a slaver in the desert. Each of them now carried a small and exquisite silver tube, tucked into a fold of their turban, for performing the most modest of bodily functions.

Yet men had been gelded for service in the time of Darius and Alexander, too. Ever since the idea of dynasties arose, there had been eunuchs who commanded fleets, who generalled armies, who subtly set out the policies of states. Sometimes Yashim dimly saw himself enrolled into a strange fraternity, the shadow-world of the guardians: men who since time immemorial had held themselves apart, the better to watch and serve. It included the eunuchs of the ancient world, and of the Chinese emperor in Beijing, and the whole Catholic hierarchy in Europe, too, which had supplied the celibate priests who served the kings of Christendom. Didn't the Pope in Rome himself serve man and

36

God? The service of barren men, like their desires, began and ended with their death; but in life they watched over the churning anthills of humankind, inured from its preoccupation with lust, longevity and descent. Prey, at worst, to a fondness for trinkets and trivia, to a fascination with their own decline, a tendency to hysteria and petty jealousies. Yashim knew them well.

As for the harem, none of the women there could come or go at will, of course. So Yashim's current business in there was, in that sense, a more private affair. Even time, Yashim reflected, ran differently on the inside: the harem could wait. Outside, as the Seraskier had warned, he had just nine ordinary days.

Brushing the crumbs of the borek from his lips, Yashim decided that he would visit first the Guild, and then pay his call on the Seraskier. Afterwards, depending on what he learned, he would go and question various people in the harem.

13

Mustafa the Albanian sniffed suspiciously at the bowl of tripe. There were, he knew, certain parties in the city who had embraced heretical doctrines. Daily, he was certain, they were extending their dangerous influence over the weaker, more impressionable members of society: young men, people from out of town, even students at the medreses who surely should know better, found it all to easy to succumb to the subtle blandishments of these rogues. Some of them, he was well aware, simply abused the authorities' trust. Others – and who could say they were not encouraged by that baleful example? – recognised no authority at all. Well, he thought grimly, he was there to root them out.

He sniffed again. The colour of the soup was good: no obvious sign of innovation there. Mustafa was of the school that followed the saying of the Prophet, peace be on him: in change there is innovation, innovation leads to blasphemy, blasphemy leads to hell fire. The notion that a good tripe soup needed the addition of a pinch of pounded coriander was the kind of innovation which, if left unchecked, would gradually undermine the whole guild and destroy its ability to serve the city as it should. It made no difference whether the heretics charged extra for the spice, or not: the confusion would have entered men's minds. Where there was a weakness to be exploited, there would greed find its encouragement.

Mustafa sniffed again. Lifting the horn spoon that hung around his neck as a symbol of his office, he dipped it into the bowl and turned the contents over. Tripe. Onions. Regularly shaped, faintly caramelised. He dug down to the bottom of the bowl and examined the spoon carefully in the light for any specks or impurities. Satisfied, he lifted the spoon to his lips and sucked noisily. Tripe soup. He smacked his lips, his immediate fears allayed. Whatever secrets this young apprentice held in the recesses of his heart he could definitely make the proper article on demand.

Two anxious pairs of eyes followed the spoon to the guild master's lips. They saw the soup go in. They heard the soup flow about Mustafa's palate. They watched anxiously as he held his hand close to his ear. And then they watched, delighted, as he nodded curtly. An apprenticeship redeemed. A new master soupier born.

'It is good. Keep an eye on the onions: never use them too large. The size of your fist is good, or smaller.' He brought up his own massive paw and curled the fingers. 'Too big!' He shook the fist and laughed. The apprentice tittered.

They discussed arrangements for the apprentice's formal

induction into the guild, his prospects, the extent of his savings and the likelihood of his finding an opening within the next few years. Mustafa knew that this was the most dangerous moment. Newly fledged soupiers always wanted to start right away, whatever the circumstances. It took patience and humility to carry on working for an old master while you waited for a shop to come free.

Patience, yes. Impatience led to coriander and hell fire. Mustafa tugged at his moustache and squinted at the young man. Did he have patience? As for himself, he thought, patience was his second skin. How could he have lived his life, and not acquired patience in positively redemptive quantities?

14

It was a singular request, for what use could a man have for a play cauldron at this time of the year? Mustafa the Albanian seemed to hear a dangerous word whispered in his ear. Was it not an innovation, to let a stranger examine the store-rooms of the guild of soup-makers? It certainly seemed an insidious precedent.

Yashim blinked, smiled and opened his eyes wide. He thought he could guess exactly what was going through the old soup master's mind.

'I'm known at the palace: the gate-keepers there could vouch for me, if that's a help.'

The guild master's frown remained firmly in place. His massive hands lay quietly folded over his paunch. Perhaps, Yashim thought, the palace card was the wrong one to try: every institution in the city had its pride. He decided on another throw.

'We live in strange times. I'm not so young that I can't

remember when things were . . . better ordered, in general, than they are today. Every day, right here in Istanbul, I see things I'd never have dreamed of seeing in my young days. Foreigners on horseback. Dogs literally starving to death on the streets. Beggars in from the countryside. Buildings removed to make way for strange mosques. Frankish uniforms.' He shook his head. The soup master gave a little grunt.

'The other day I had to return a pair of slippers that had cost me forty piastres: the stitching was coming away. And I'd only had them a month!' That was quite true: Yashim had bought the slippers from a guildsman. For forty piastres they were meant to last a year. 'Sometimes, I'm sorry to say, I think that even our food doesn't taste quite the way it used to.'

Yashim noticed the soup master's fingers clench and wondered if he'd gone a bit far. The soup master put a hand up to his moustache and rubbed it between his finger and thumb.

'I'm a eunuch,' Yashim said.

'Aha,' the soup master said complacently. Well, he thought, that bit about the palace was probably true.

'Tell me,' he rumbled. 'Do you like coriander seed? In soup?'

It was Yashim's turn to frown.

'What a peculiar idea,' he said.

Mustafa the Albanian got to his feet with surprising agility.

'Come,' he said simply.

Yashim followed the big man onto the balcony around the courtyard. Below the balustrade, under the arcade, men were busy frying tripe. Apprentices staggered to and fro with buckets they'd filled from the well in the centre of the court. A cat slunk through the shadows, weaving between the legs of enormous chopping blocks. Yashim thought: even the cat has its position here.

They descended a flight of stairs and came out into the arcade. A man wielding a shiny cleaver looked up as they appeared, his eyes streaming with tears. His cleaver fell and rose automatically on a peeled onion: the onion stayed whole until the man swept it aside with a stroke of the blade, and selected another from the basket hanging at the side of the block. Mechanically he began to chop and peel it. Not once did he so much as glance down at his fingers.

Now that, Yashim thought with admiration, is a real skill. The onion man sniffed and nodded a greeting.

The master entered a corridor and began fumbling at his belt for keys. At length he felt what he was looking for and drew it out on a chain. He stopped in front of a thick oak door, banded with iron, and placed the key into the lock.

'That's a very old key,' Yashim remarked.

'It's a very old door,' the master replied sensibly. Yashim almost added: 'And none the worse for that,' but decided against it. The lock was stiff; the master winced and the key slid sideways in the slot, depressing the necessary pins. The door opened lightly.

They were in a large, low-ceilinged room, lit by an iron grating so high up in the opposite wall that a portion of the ceiling had been sloped upwards to meet it. A few dusty rays of the winter sun fell on a curious collection of objects, ranged in shelves along the side walls. There were wooden boxes, a stack of scrolls, and a line of metal cones of varying sizes whose points seemed to rise and fall like the outline of a decorative frieze. And there, at the back of the hall, stood three enormous cauldrons.

'All our old weights,' said the master. He was looking lovingly at the metal cones. Yashim repressed his impatience.

'Old weights?'

'Every new master sees to it that the guild weights and measures are renewed and re-confirmed on his appointment. The old ones then are stored here.'

'What for?'

'What for?' The master sounded surprised. 'For comparison. How else can any of us be sure that the proper standards are being kept? I can place my weights in the balance and see that they accord to a hair's breadth with the weights we used at the time of the Conquest.'

'That's almost four centuries ago.'

'Exactly, yes. If the measures are the same, the ingredients must also be the same. Our soups, you understand, are not merely in conformability with the standards. They are – I do not say the standard itself, but a part of it. An unbroken line which comes down to us from the days of the Conquest. Like the line of the house of Osman itself,' he added, piously.

Yashim allowed for a suitably impressed pause.

'The cauldrons,' he suggested.

'Yes, yes, that is what I'm thinking about. There seems to be one missing.'

❧ 15 ❧

The seraskier sat on the edge of the divan, staring down at his shiny leather riding boots.

'Something will have to be announced,' he said finally. 'Too many people know what's happened as it is.'

The workmen had been too scared to touch the obstruction in the drain once they knew what it was. Leaving it still concealed across the mouth of the drain, they had fled downhill to inform the caretaker of what they had found. The caretaker informed the imam, who was at that moment setting out to climb the minaret to call the morning prayer. In a hurry, not quite knowing what to do, the imam sent the caretaker to track down the morning watch: the old man could hear the sound of the prayer breaking out all over the city as he scurried through the streets.

There is no God but God, and Mohammed is His Prophet.

By dawn light, a group of men could be seen milling about the drain. One of them had been sick. Another, hardier, braver or more desperate than the rest for the night watch's proffered sequins, had manipulated the grotesquely misshapen corpse out of the drain and onto the cobbles, where it was finally bundled onto a sheet, wrapped and hoisted onto a donkey cart that went slipping and swaying down the slope to the Nusretiye, the Mosque of the Victory.

The workman who had made the discovery had already gone home, to sleep off his horrors or sluice them away in the vivid warmth of the baths. His mate, better shielded from the shock, remained to enjoy his moment with the crowd. Already his story, somewhat improved from its first rendition, was being retailed with appropriate embellishments among latecomers to the scene, and within the hour several versions of events were circling through the city. By lunchtime these stories were so finely rounded that two of them were able to actually pass each other without the slightest friction, leaving some people to believe that it had been a day of oddities in which an Egyptian sphinx had been dug up out of the foreshore while in Tophane a nest of cannibals had been surprised at their gory breakfast.

The seraskier had intercepted the rumours considerably earlier. He heard that a man, very possibly one of his missing recruits, had been found in bizarre circumstances close to the Mosque of the Victory. He sent to the mosque for more information, and learned that the body had been put into an outhouse normally used by some of the workers on the site. He dispatched a note to Yashim, who was at that moment eating his borek in

43

the café on Kara Davut Sokaği, suggesting they meet at the mosque, and rode over to see.

Thoroughly shaken and repelled by the condition and appearance of the naked corpse, he had returned to his apartments to find Yashim – in a state of ignorance and unconcern – examining the spines of the military manuals and regulation books that filled the bookshelves opposite the divan.

The seraskier became very angry.

≪ 16 ≫

The master of the soup-makers' guild had been angry with Yashim, too. The fact that the stranger knew more about the missing cauldron than he did seemed to him in some degree sinister.

'Is this some kind of a joke?' he demanded furiously, when his eyes had – rather superfluously, Yashim thought – devoured the store-room in a fruitless search for the enormous missing cauldron. After all, you could hardly conceal a cauldron the size of an ox behind a few scrolls and hand-weights. At the same time Yashim felt sorry for the master: such a thing, he was almost certain to say, had never happened before in all the history of the guild. Now it had happened on his watch: a theft.

'I can't believe it. I have the key.' He held the key up and stared at it, as if it might suddenly break down and confess to illicit behaviour. Then he shook it angrily. 'This is highly irregular. Twenty-four years!' He glared at Yashim. 'I've been here twenty-four years.'

Yashim shrugged amiably.

'Do you keep the key with you all the time?'

'In the name of God, I sleep with my keys!' the master snapped.

44

'You might update the lock.'

The master cocked his head and leaned slowly towards Yashim.

'You say you come from the palace,' he growled. 'What is this? You are some inspector?'

Yashim nodded slowly. This is a man, he thought, who feels easy with power. He glanced again at the master's hands. The massive fingers were loosely curled.

'You could say that.' More briskly he added: 'When did you last come in here?'

The soup master drew breath through his nose, and as he exhaled Yashim wondered what he was considering: the answer to the question? Or whether to answer the question?

'I don't know,' he said finally. 'About a month ago. Maybe more. Nothing was missing.'

'No. Who guards the place at night?'

In Istanbul it was always people who mattered. Who you knew. The balance of favours.

The soup master's breath was rapid.

'How is the guild house guarded after hours?'

'We employ guards. I myself sleep overhead.'

'How many guards?'

'Oh, two, maybe three.'

Yashim's face remained expressionless.

'They have keys?'

'I told you, I sleep with the keys. They have the key to the main gate, of course – I give it to them at night and collect it back first thing in the morning.'

'May I see it?'

The master fished up the loop and ran his fingers through a bunch of keys. Finding the right one, he showed it to Yashim, who raised his eyebrows. It was another of the old-fashioned sort, something like a big comb of wood, with pegs of varying length for teeth.

'You say two or three guards. Do you mean two? Or do you mean three? Which?'

'Well, I –' the master broke off. 'It depends.'

'On what? The weather? Their mood? What I see here is a place that runs by the book, yes? No deviation from routine, no innovation, no coriander in the soup. Right?'

The master lifted his chin.

'But when we come to the regulation of the night watch, you don't know how many guards are employed. Two *or* three? Maybe it's five. Maybe none.'

The master of the soup-makers' guild lowered his head for a second. He seemed to be thinking.

'It's like this,' he said slowly. 'There are always enough guards. Sometimes it's two, sometimes three, just as I said. They aren't always the same men, night after night, but I know the bunch. I trust them, always have. We go back a long way.'

Yashim noticed something imploring in the man's tone. He caught his eye.

'They're Albanians, aren't they?'

The master blinked. He looked steadily at Yashim. 'Yes. What of it?'

Yashim made no answer. He reached out and took the master's hand in his, and with the other he gripped the man's sleeve and rolled it back. The master jerked away with an oath.

But Yashim had already seen what he had expected. A small, blue tattoo. He had not been quick enough to recognise the actual symbol, but there was only one reason why a man would carry a tattoo on his forearm.

'We can talk,' he suggested.

The master compressed his lips and closed his eyes.

'All right,' he said.

17

While he waited for the seraskier's anger to blow itself out, Yashim questioned him about the discovery of the second corpse, asking for details about the position of the drain and the condition of the body. The effort of describing the way the corpse was trussed seemed to rob the seraskier of his temper, but he kneaded the back of a chair with his fingers, making it creak. Yashim wondered if he would sit down.

'I had thought,' the seraskier concluded bitterly, 'that we might have got somewhere by now. Have we got anywhere?'

Yashim pulled at his nose.

'Effendi. I still do not understand how the men went missing. Did they go out together?'

'Yes, so I understand.'

'Where?'

The seraskier sighed. 'That's just it. Nobody seems to know. They came off duty at five. They went back to their dormitory and spent some time there – I know, because they overlapped with the men coming on for night duty.'

'Doing what?'

'Nothing much, apparently. Loafing on their bunks. Books, a game of cards, something like that. The last man out saw two of them playing cards.'

'For money?'

'I . . . I don't know. Probably not. I hope not. These were good young men.'

'The man who saw them playing, was he the last man to see them at all?'

'Yes.'

'So nobody checks on people as they leave the barracks?'

'Well, no. The sentries are there to check people as they come

47

in. Why should they check people going out?'

To help a man like me in a situation like this, Yashim thought. That was one reason; he could think of others. A question of order and discipline.

'Do the men generally go out, for whatever reason, in uniform?'

'Five or ten years ago, it was uncommon. Now we encourage the men to wear uniform at all times. It is better for the people of Istanbul to become acquainted with the new ways, and better for the men. It improves their morale.'

'And useful for you, too, to check on how they behave.'

The seraskier cracked a rare, dry smile.

'That too.'

'Would they visit a brothel? Did they have girls? I'm sorry, effendi, but I have to ask.'

'These men were officers! What are you saying? The men, yes, the ordinary men see women in the streets. I know about that. But these were officers. Of good family.'

Yashim shrugged.

'And there are good brothels, too, by all accounts. It doesn't seem very likely that these four went and sat out the whole evening in a well-lit café, in their uniforms. That's no way to go missing, is it? Instead, somewhere along the line, sometime in the course of their evening, their paths had to cross the path of their abductor. Their murderer. Somewhere – what? Murky, out of the light. In a boat, maybe. On a dark path. Or in some place shady – a brothel, a gambling saloon.'

'Yes, I see.'

'May I have your permission to interview the officers who shared their dormitory?'

The seraskier blew the wind between his teeth and stared down at the floor. Yashim had been here before. People wanted solutions, but they always hoped they could reach them without creating a fuss. The seraskier wanted to make a public announcement but was not, it seemed, quite ready to risk offending or alarming anyone. The forces of the padishah, he would aver, are working ceaselessly and with complete confidence to bring the perpetrators of this evil deed to light – and he wouldn't mean a word he said.

'Effendi, either we must try to find out what happened, or there is no point in my proceeding with this case.'

'Very well. I will write you a chit.'

'A chit. Will that be enough, do you think? To talk, perhaps. In the murky place: will a chit hold out?'

The seraskier looked straight into Yashim's grey eyes.

'I'll support you,' he said wearily.

18

Yashim arrived early at the little restaurant beneath Galata Point and chose a quiet alcove which overlooked the channel of the Bosphorus. The Bosphorus had made Istanbul what it was: the junction of Europe and Asia, the pathway from the Black Sea into the Mediterranean, the great entrepot of world trade from ancient times to the present day. From where he sat he could watch the waterway he loved so much, the narrow sheet of gunmetal which reflected back the shape of the city it had built.

The water was as ever thick with shipping. A mountain of white sail rose above the deck of an Ottoman frigate which was tacking up the straits. A shoal of fishing smacks, broad-beamed and single- masted, held out under an easterly wind for the Sea of Marmara. A customs boat swept past on its long red oars like a scurrying water-beetle. There were ferries, and skiffs, and over-laden barges; lateen-rigged cutters from the Black Sea coast, house-boats moored by the crowded entrance to the Golden

49

Horn. Across the jostling waterway, Yashim could just make out Üsküdar on the opposite shore, the beginning of Asia.

The Greeks had called Üsküdar Chalcedon, the city of the blind. In founding the city, the colonists had ignored the perfect natural setting across the water, where centuries later Constantine was to turn the small town of Byzantium into a great imperial city which bore his name. For a thousand years Constantinople was the capital of the Roman empire in the east, until that empire had shrunk to a sliver of land around the city. Ever since the Conquest in 1453, the city had been the capital of the Turkish Ottoman empire. It was still officially called Constantinople, though most ordinary Turks referred to it as Istanbul. It remained the biggest city in the world.

Fifteen hundred years of grandeur. Fifteen hundred years of power. Fifteen centuries of corruption, coups and compromises. A city of mosques, churches, synagogues; of markets and emporia; of tradesmen, soldiers, beggars. The city to beat all cities, overcrowded and greedy.

Perhaps, Yashim sometimes reflected, the Chalcedonians hadn't been so blind, after all.

He had half-expected the Albanian to stay away, but when he looked up there he was, massive and grim, hitching his cloak. Yashim gestured to the divan and he sat down.

'Ali Pasha of Janina,' said the soup master. 'The name means something to you?'

Ali Pasha was the warlord who by guile and cruelty had built up a semi-independent state in the mountains of Albania and northern Greece. It was fourteen years since Yashim had seen his head displayed on a pillar at the gates of the seraglio.

'The Lion,' Mustafa rumbled. 'We called him that. I soldiered in his army – it was my country. But Ali Pasha was foxy, too. He gave us peace. I wanted war. In 1806 I went to the Danube. That is where I joined the corps.'

'The Janissaries?'

The soup master nodded.

'As a cook. I was already a cook, even then. To fight – it's not so much for a man. For an Albanian, it's nothing. Ask a Greek. But cooking?' He grunted with satisfaction.

Yashim clasped his hands and blew into them.

'I am a man of tradition,' the soup master continued. 'For me, the Janissaries were the tradition. This empire – they built it, didn't they? And it is hard for an outsider to understand. The Janissary regiment was like a family.'

Yashim pulled a sceptical face. 'Every regiment says that.'

The soup master shot him a scornful look. 'They say that because they are afraid, and must fight together. That is nothing. There were men in the corps I loved because they could handle a falcon, or make poetry, better than anyone in the world before or since. Believe me. There was a brave fighter who trembled like a leaf before each battle, but fought for ten. We looked after each other, and we loved each other – yes, they loved me because I could make them food anywhere, the same way we loved the cobbler who would see us shod even when he had nothing but bark and pine needles to work with. We were more than family. We had a world, within a world. We had our own food, our own justice, our own manner of religion. Yes, yes, our own manner. There are various ways to serve God and Mohammed. To join a mosque is one way, the way of the majority. But we Janissaries were mostly Karagozi.'

'You're saying that to be a Janissary was to follow a form of Sufism.'

'Of course. That and all the other rituals of being a Janissary. The traditions.'

The traditions. In 1806 the sultan, Selim, had begun to train up a parallel army to the Janissaries. In that respect it had been a forerunner of Mahmut's New Guard. But Selim, unlike

Mahmut, had had little time to organise: the result was that when the Janissaries rebelled against their sultan, they crushed him, and destroyed his reformed army. The rebel Janissaries had been led by Bayraktar Mustafa Pasha, commander on the Danube.

'So you were there,' Yashim suggested, 'when Selim was forced off the throne, in favour of his brother Mustafa.'

'Sultan Mustafa!' The Albanian ground out the title with scorn, and spat. 'Girded with Osman's sword, maybe, but mad like a dog. After two years the people were thinking how to get Selim back. Bayraktar had changed his mind as well, like all the rest of us. We were in Istanbul, at the old barracks, and for a night we prayed for guidance, talking with the Karagozi dervishes.'

'They told you what to do?'

'We stormed the Topkapi Palace next day. Bayraktar ran through the gates, crying for Selim.'

'At which point,' Yashim recalled, 'Mustafa ordered Selim to be strangled. Along with his little cousin – just in case.'

The soup master bowed his head.

'So it was. Sultan Mustafa wanted to be the last of the House of Osman. Had he been the last, I think he would have survived. Whatever else we might have been, we Janissaries were loyal to the House. But God willed otherwise. Even though Selim was killed, the little cousin escaped alive.'

Thanks to his quick-thinking mother, Yashim reflected. At the crucial moment, with Mustafa's men scouring the palace with their bowstrings, the crafty Frenchwoman he now knew as the Validé Sultan had hidden her boy beneath a pile of dirty laundry. Mahmut became sultan by the grace of a heap of old linen.

'You were there?'

'I was in the palace when they brought the boy to Bayraktar Pasha. I saw the look on Sultan Mustafa's face: if he had seemed

52

mad before, then –' The soup master shrugged. 'The chief Mufti had no choice but to issue a fetwa deposing him. And Mahmut became sultan.

'For myself, I was tired of this kind of soldiering. Rebellion, fighting in the palace, the murder of Selim.' He gestured with his arm: 'Back and forth, here, there. I'd had enough.'

The soup master took a deep breath, and blew the air through his cheeks.

'I left the corps at the first opportunity. I was a good cook, I had friends in Istanbul. In five years I was working for myself.'

'Did you give up your pay-book, too?' Plenty of men had been on the payroll, drawing a Janissary's wage and enjoying all the privileges of the corps without the slightest intention of turning up for war. It was a well-known scam.

Mustafa hesitated. 'Not immediately,' he admitted. 'But within a few years I no longer needed help, and I gave it in.'

Yashim doubted it, but said nothing.

'You can check the records. I ceased to be a Janissary in May 1815. It took courage. You wouldn't understand.'

Yashim did his best. 'They didn't want to let you go? Or you wanted the money?'

The Albanian shot him a look of contempt.

'Listen. I go where I want. Today is an exception. I didn't need the money, I was doing well.' Yashim blinked, believing him. 'I found it hard to break with them.'

Yashim leaned forwards.

'How did you do it?'

The guild master spread his huge hands and looked at them.

'I learned to trust myself. I saw with my own eyes what had happened to the Janissaries. What they had allowed to happen to the real tradition, the one that mattered. They no longer served the empire.'

He looked up.

'You think that's obvious? I was only waiting – many, like me, only waiting – for the tradition of service to come back to us. In the end, I decided I could wait no longer. I saw that we were doomed to repeat our mistakes. You think the Janissaries were lazy, cowardly, arrogant. The mutinies. The interference.'

The soup master stroked his beard and narrowed his eyes at Yashim, who sat transfixed.

'I tell you, the men we hung upon the Janissary Tree were all too easily taken. When we got angry, then someone fed us names, and we shouted: Kill him! Kill so-and-so! They threw them to us. We thought it would go better after that.

'You put coriander in the soup. Well, some people like it, some don't, some don't even notice. Forget the people who don't like it. You add some beans. Some carrots. The same thing. Some like it, some don't. But more people don't care much either way. By the end, you can take out the tripe. Call it soup. Nobody will know any better. Only a few.'

He tugged at his moustache.

'The Janissaries were like that. Like a recipe that has been quietly and completely altered. In the city I made tripe and onion soup from tripe and onion. But in the barracks, so to speak, they wanted me to believe in a kind of tripe and onion soup made of beans and bacon. In the end, I had to leave.'

Yashim could admire the older man's guts. So much in this city was founded on pretence: it took a certain kind of temper for a man to step aside. But then, the Albanian hadn't stepped away entirely. Not if what Yashim suspected about the guards at the guild were true.

'Your old friends,' he suggested.

'No, no, they had no hold over me, not what you might think. They didn't blame me, either. But they remembered me. Our lives went separate ways. But they remembered.'

He picked up a pastry with a clumsy sweep of his arm and

stuffed it into his mouth. Yashim watched him deliberately chew it down. His eyes were sparkling.

'The fifteenth of June was the worst night of my life. I heard the cauldrons – we all did, didn't we? Eighteen years the sultan had waited. Eighteen years for a boy to become a man, and all that time with one resolve, to destroy the force which had destroyed Selim.'

Perhaps, Yashim thought. But Mahmut's motives were more complex than mere vengeance for his uncle's death. He wanted to rid himself of the men who had almost casually brought him to the throne, as well: to expunge a debt, as well as avenge a death. The Janissaries had crudely expected gratitude, and took carte blanche. Yashim could remember the cartoon that was stuck up on the palace gate one night, showing the sultan as a dog led by a Janissary. 'You see how we use our dogs,' the notice ran. 'While they are useful and let themselves be led, we treat them well; but when they stop being of service, we kick them out into the streets.'

'The people of the city were scared. Boom boom! Boom boom! It was a frightening sound, wasn't it? Night falling, and not a sound in the streets as we listened, all of us. I went up onto my roof, treading like a cat. Oh, yes, there was a tradition all right. They said the voice of the Janissaries was the voice of the people. The men believed it. The cauldrons were beating for the empire, as they'd beaten for centuries. Only the sound of the cauldrons drumming, and the barking of the pye-dogs in the streets.

'Look, I stood on the roof and I heard the sound and I wept for those fools. I wept for a sound. I knew I would never hear it again, not if I lived for a thousand years.'

He wiped his hands over his face.

'Later, after the killing and the demolition, some of them came to me asking for a quiet job. One of them had been living for days in a foxhole when they torched the Belgrade woods to flush them out. They had to avoid their families and relatives, for their sakes. They were lost. They were hunted. But we had broken bread together. I gave them money and told them to slip away, get out of Istanbul. Nobody would be interested in them any more, not after a few weeks, a few months.

'And slowly some of them started coming back. Looking for quiet jobs, out of sight – stokers, watchmen, tanners. I knew a few. There must have been thousands, I suppose, unknown to me.'

'Thousands?'

'I knew a handful, so I gave them the work. Night duties. Discreet.' He closed his eyes and shook his head slowly. 'I can't understand it. Ten years, and all good, quiet men. Grateful for the work.'

'So what would they want a cauldron for, do you suppose?'

The soup master opened his eyes and fixed them on Yashim.

'That's what I don't understand. It was only a pretend cauldron, anyway. You can't do it with a cauldron made of black tin. It would only be make-believe.'

Yashim thought of the dead officer, coiled in the cauldron's base.

'It was always pretending, wasn't it?' Yashim asked. 'That's what you said. Tripe soup made of beans and bacon.'

The soup master looked at him in surprise, and folded his hands.

❦ 19 ❧

'You must get Yashim back!' The Validé Sultan crooked her finger and wagged it at her son. 'We may all be murdered in our beds.'

Sultan Mahmut II, Lord of the Horizons, Master of the Black

Sea and the White, put up his hands and rolled his eyes. It was scarcely conceivable, he thought, that three hundred able-bodied women – and in this sum he included his mother, for sure – could be actually murdered, one by one, in the very sanctum of imperial power.

All the same he allowed himself to play with the idea. He would keep the delightful Fatima safely by his side at all times and by the end, through a simple process of elimination, they would know who the killer was. Then he and Fatima would spring out among the throttled beauties and despatch her. He would announce that he was too shaken by the experience to take on any more wives; it would be unfair on them, he was far too old. He would marry Fatima, and she would rub his feet.

'Validé,' he said politely. 'You know as well as I do that these things happen. There is probably a very good explanation.'

He wanted to point out that it would almost certainly be a very trivial explanation, but he sensed that his mother would feel slighted by the insinuation. This was her realm, shared with the Kislar Agha, the chief black eunuch, and everything which happened in it had to be serious.

'Mahmut,' the validé said sharply. 'I can think of a very good explanation. The murderess wants you.'

'Me?' The sultan frowned.

'Not in bed, you silly fool. She wants to kill you.'

'Aha. It was dark, and she mistook some ambergrised houri for her sultan and throttled her before she realised her mistake.'

'Of course not.'

'So what was that girl, then? Strangling practice?'

The Validé Sultan cocked her head.

'Maybe,' she admitted. 'I suppose it might take practice. I don't suppose many of the girls have done a lot of strangling before they come.' She patted the cushion beside her, and Mahmut sat down.

'I was more worried that she might simply be hurrying the moment,' the validé continued. 'She has her place in the order. Sooner or later she will be alone with you. She wants it sooner. Then she can kill you.'

'So she knocks off the nice girl and moves up one on the list? I see.'

'You make it sound ridiculous, but I have been here a lot longer than you. I know just how ridiculous things can turn out to be extremely serious. Trust me. Trust a mother's intuition.'

'I trust you, of course. But what I don't see is why the murderess is in such a rush. And by killing the girl she's slowed the thing down, anyway. After this, I shan't have to see any of them for days. My nerves, mother.'

'It makes the thing more sure. That unfortunate girl might have infatuated you. You might have kept after her for weeks on end. She might have, I don't know, rubbed your feet the way you like.'

She gave him an arch look. Mahmut grinned ruefully: the validé knew everyone's secrets.

'And there's the Edict, isn't there? The great announcement. If you die, there will be no Edict. Don't tell me someone doesn't want to murder you over that!'

'To get me out of the way in time, you mean?'

'Exactly. I think you should send for Yashim right away.'

'I have. He's working on it.'

'Nonsense. He's not working on it at all. I haven't seen him here all day.'

20

Yashim had, in fact, found time to visit the harem that day; but
he had gone in quietly, alerting no one, simply to see where the
body had been found, and where the girl had lived.

Her room, which she had shared with three other girls, had
iron bedsteads and several rows of pegs on which the girls hung
their clothes and the bags which held the scented soaps they
were fond of, a few shawls and slippers, some well-laundered
strips of linen, and such bangles and jewels as they possessed. As
cariyeler, harem maids, her room mates had not yet been
advanced to the rank of gözde: but they were hoping.

Two girls had spread an old sheet across their bed, and were
busy depilating themselves with a sticky green ointment they
took from a plain brass bowl that stood on a small octagonal
bedside table. One of them, a redhead with green eyes and pale
skin, was carefully anointing herself with a spatula when Yashim
came to the door and bowed. She chucked her chin in a casual
greeting.

'The gözde's bed?' Yashim enquired.

The girl on her knees gestured with the spatula.

The other girl, spreadeagled, raised her head and squinted
down her body.

'They ought to take her stuff out, poor thing,' she said. 'It's
not very nice for us.'

'I'm sorry,' Yashim said. 'I just want to see what there is.' He
ran his hands over her clothes, then pulled two bags off the pegs
and emptied their contents onto the bed. 'You must have been
friends.'

The girl who was kneeling got off the bed and came across for
a better look. She had her elbow out, to keep the ointment on
her armpit in the air, and with one hand she tugged her black

hair back into a pony tail. Her skin was olive, and her lips were dark like old wine, the same colour as the nipples of her breasts, rising in firm curves.

Yashim glanced back, and then stirred the belongings strewn across the empty bed.

'She was my size,' the girl said, reaching forwards to pick up a bundle of transparent gauze. 'We all knew that.'

The girl on the bed giggled.

'She was!' The girl shook the thing in her hand and then gathered it to her chest, working her free arm so that it lay across one breast, the transluscent silk ribbons dangling against her tummy. There was something so innocent and so obscene about the gesture, that Yashim blushed.

The girl on the bed saved him from speaking.

'Put it back, Nilu. It's too creepy. Have you, lala, come to take her things away?'

Nilu let the bustier flutter back onto the bed, and turned to her friend.

Yashim carefully surveyed the gözde's belongings.

'What was she like?' He asked.

The girl called Nilu climbed back onto her friend's bed; Yashim heard the mattress creak. There was a silence.

'She was . . . all right.'

'Was she a friend?'

'She was nice. She had friends.'

'Enemies?' Yashim turned around. The two girls were sitting side by side, staring at him.

'Ow!' The girl suddenly put a hand between her legs. 'It's stinging!'

She jumped off the bed, her pale breasts swinging, one hand clamped between her slender legs.

'Come on, Nilu. I've got to wash.'

Nilu reached for a towel on a peg.

'She had friends,' she said. She scampered to the doorway. 'Lots of friends,' she added, over her shoulder.

21

'Well, hello precious.'

The speaker was a raw-boned girl of about forty in a glossy black wig, a sequinned bustier with padded breasts, a long diaphanous skirt and a pair of large beaded slippers. She was also wearing half a pound of make-up. It made her look older, Yashim realised with a slight pang.

But it was what – eighteen years? They were both of them older than when he first came to the city in the retinue of the great Phanariot merchant-prince, George Mavrocordato. Mavrocordato had been quick to see where Yashim's talent lay, setting him to work at the ledgers for the sake of his cultivated hand, sending him down to the port to pick up useful information, asking him to con over the manifests, and identify new articles of trade. Yashim had learned a great deal, and with his gift for languages – a gift greater, if possible, even than his employer's, who spoke Ottoman Turkish, Greek ecclesiastical and demotic, Romanian, Armenian and French, but Russian badly, and Georgian not at all – he had made himself indispensable to the Mavrocordato clan. He'd discovered a talent for being invisible, a knack of holding himself quiet and saying little, so that people tended to overlook his presence.

But while he was grateful for the long hours which kept his mind sharp, still the old torment, all the worse for being fresh, had flourished in the heavy atmosphere of trade and politics, a secret agony among secrets: to be a eunuch was, for Yashim at that time, the grammar of a language he could not understand.

And so he had felt himself isolated in the most cosmopolitan society in Europe.

He had met Preen at a party which Mavrocordato threw for a pasha he wanted to impress, hiring dancers for the evening. Yashim had been sent to pay them off afterwards, and he had found himself talking to Preen.

Of all the traditions that bound Istanbul together, the long history of the köçek dancers was probably the least celebrated, and possibly the oldest. Some said that they were descended – in a spiritual sense – from Alexander's dancing boys. The foundation of Constantinople would have occurred almost a thousand years after the köçek tradition had migrated from its homelands in northern India and Afghanistan to the frontiers of the Roman empire. The köçek were creatures of the city, and the rise of a city on the banks of the Bosphorus would have sucked them in like dust to a raging fire. What was certain was that the Greeks had entertained these dancers, selecting them from the ranks of boys who had been castrated before puberty and subjecting them to rigorous training in the stylised arts and mysteries of the köçek dance. They danced for both men and women; under the Ottomans, it was usually for men. They performed in troupes of five or six, accompanied by a musician who plucked at a zither while they whirled and stamped and curved their wrists. Each troupe was responsible for engaging new 'girls' and training them. Many of them, of course, slept with their clients; but they were adamantly not prostitutes, whom they regarded as utterly wanton – and unskilled. 'Any girl can open her legs,' Preen had once reminded him. 'The köçek are dancers.'

But it was undoubtedly true that the köçek were not too picky about their friends. They stood on the very lowest rung of Ottoman society, above beggars, but with the jugglers, actors, conjurers and others who made up the despised – and well-patronised – class of professional entertainers. They had their snobberies – who doesn't? – but they lived in the world and knew the way it turned.

Yashim had been amused by Preen and her 'girlfriends', at first. He liked the open way they spoke, their roguishness and candour, and in Preen he came to admire the chirpy cynicism which concealed a heart plunged in romantic dreams. Compared to the heavy secrecy and dark glances of the Phanariot aristocracy, Preen's world was rough but full of laughter and surprises. And when the Peloponnesian rebellion cast ominous shadows over the Greeks in Istanbul, Preen had reacted to his proposals without thought of her own danger or of the prejudice flaring in the streets. For two days, she had sheltered Mavrocordato's mother and his sisters, while Yashim arranged the ruse that would carry them to the island of Aegina, and safety.

Sometimes he wondered what she saw in him.

'Come on in.' She twirled from the door and returned to her face in the mirror. 'Can't stop, sweetie. The other girls'll be here in a moment.'

'A wedding?' Yashim knew the form. Many times since that year of drama he'd helped Preen prepare for the weddings, circumcision celebrations and birthdays for which people required the presence of the köçek dancers. In return, perhaps without quite knowing it, Preen had prepared him for his days: those new, flat days when agonies of lust and anger gnawed at him from the inside, and all the better days that were to come.

'Boys' night,' she said, without looking round. 'You're lucky to find me.'

'Business is good?'

'Never better. There. How do I look?'

'Eye-catching.'

She turned her head this way and that, following her reflection the mirror.

'Not old?'

'Certainly not,' said Yashim quickly. Preen put her fingers to her cheek and gently pushed the skin up. She let it drop, and Yashim saw her look at him in the mirror. Then she smiled brightly and turned to face him.

'Fixing a party?'

Yashim grinned and shook his head. 'Looking for information.'

She raised a finger and wagged it at him.

'Darling, you know I never betray a confidence. A girl has her secrets. What kind of information?'

'I need a quick line on the gossip.'

'Gossip? Why on earth would you come to me?'

They both laughed.

'Men in uniform,' Yashim suggested.

Preen wrinkled her nose and made a moue.

'The New Guards, from the Eskeshir Barracks.'

'I'm sorry, Yashim, but the thought revolts me. Those tight trousers! And so little colour. To me they always look like a bunch of autumn crickets hopping to a funeral.'

Yashim smiled. 'Actually, I want to know where they *do* hop. Not the men so much as the officers. Boys from very good families, I'm told. I wouldn't bother you about the ordinary soldiers, Preen, you wouldn't know about that. But the officers . . .'

He left it hanging. Preen raised her eyebrows and touched her hand to the back of her hair.

'I can hear the girls now. No promises, but I'll see what I can do.'

22

The room was tiny, more like a cell, sparsely furnished with a pine footstool, a sagging rope bed and a row of wooden hooks, from which hung several large bags, bulking black in the yellow light. The room had no windows and smelt fetid and damp, a queasy amalgam of scent, and sweat, and the oil that smoked blackly from the lamp.

The person whose room it was moved swiftly towards the bags and fumbled at the neck of the smallest, groping around inside until their fingers closed on another, smaller bag which they proceeded to pull out, plucking at the drawstrings. The contents fell onto the mattress with a soft, metallic chink.

A pair of glittering black eyes stared with hatred at the jewels which glittered back. There was a golden chain bearing a dark lapis. There was a silver brooch, a perfect oval, set with diamonds the size of new peas. There was a bracelet – a smaller version of the gold chain, its clasp hidden beneath a ruby anchored to a silver roundel – and a pair of earrings. There was no doubting where the jewels had originated. On every face, painstakingly inlaid into the lapis, between the diamonds, over the ruby, that loathsome and idolatrous symbol, Z or N, zigzagging back and forth, crooked as the man.

That was the way it had all begun, for sure. It wasn't easy to follow the exact steps – those Franks were cunning as foxes – but Napoleon had been the author of it all. What was it that the French kept pressing on the world? Liberty, equality, and something else. A flag with three stripes. There was something else. No matter, it was all lies.

That flag had fluttered over Egypt. Men like scissors had gone about scratching, scraping, digging things up, writing it all down in little books. Other scissor men, led by a half-blind infidel, had burned their ships within the shadow of the Pyramids, and Napoleon himself had run away, sailed off in the night. Then those infidels had marched and starved, thirsted for water and died like flies in the deserts of Palestine.

But that was only the beginning. You would have thought, wouldn't you, that everyone would see the folly of the foreigners? But no: the Egyptians tried to be more like them. They'd seen how the French had gone about, behaving like the masters in the dominion of the sultan. They put it down to the trousers, to the special guns the French had left behind, to the way the French soldiers had marched and wheeled, fighting like a single body in the desert, even while they were dropping like flies.

New ways. New stuff which came out of little books. People always scribbling and scribbling, sticking their noses into books until their eyes went red with the effort. Pretending to understand the French gibberish.

Napoleon. He'd killed the French king, hadn't he? Invaded the Domain of Peace. Thrown sand in the eyes of his own men and all the world. Why else could no one see what was going on? And these jewels – were we to sell ourselves for baubles?

Valuable as they are.

It was a pity that the girl had seen. That killing had been an unexpected duty, and dangerous. Perhaps an over-reaction. She might have seen nothing, understood nothing. Other things on her mind. A secret smile of triumph and expectation on her pretty face. Nothing like the bewilderment with which she fought for breath, seeing whose hands lay around her neck. The hands which had taken the jewels.

Ah, well, there were the others. In here it paid to act swiftly, without remorse.

A ball of spit landed on the lapis and began to trail slowly down the upright of the letter N.

23

Preen felt the ouzo scorch the back of her throat and then plummet like something alive into the pit of her empty stomach. She set the glass back on the low table, and selected another.

'To the sisters!'

A round of little glasses swayed in the air, chinked, and were tossed back by five raven-haired, slightly raddled-looking girls. One of them hiccupped, then yawned and stretched like a cat.

'Time's up,' she said. 'Beauty sleep.'

The others cackled. It had been a good evening. The men, silent while the köçek danced, had showed their appreciation in time-honoured fashion by slipping coins beneath the seams of their costume as they danced close. You couldn't always tell, but the house had looked clean and the gentlemen sober. Some reunion, she never found out exactly what.

She liked her gentlemen sober, but after a performance she didn't mind getting a little drunk herself. They'd asked the carriage to drop them off at the top of the street which led down to the waterfront, and teetered away into the dark until they reached the door of a tavern they knew. It was Greek, of course, and full of sailors. That in itself was no bad thing, Preen thought with a ghost of a smile, for as it happened there were two of them throwing surreptitious glances at them now and then, two young, rather handsome boys she didn't know. Only fishermen from the islands, but still . . .

Two other girls decided to leave, but Preen thought she'd prefer to stay. Just her and Mina, together. Another drink, maybe.

She was having her second when the sailors made their move. They were from Lemnos, as she'd guessed, and they had shifted a big catch at the morning market, a little tight themselves on their last night in town and with money to spend. After a few minutes, Preen noticed the man's sunburnt hand moving towards her leg. Go on! she smiled.

But out of the corner of her eye she saw a small, slightly hunchbacked man with a pockmarked face enter the tavern. Yorg was one of the port pimps, one of the weaselly crowd who accosted newly arrived seamen and offered them cheap lodgings, a visit to their sister or, if it seemed safe, a free drink at their place. Yorg's place, of course, was a brothel where haggard girls from the countryside turned trick after trick, night after night, until they were either let loose on the streets or bumped off and dumped into the Bosphorus. They were part of the human detritus that floated around the docks and the men who sailed from them; their life expectancy was short.

Preen shuddered. Very gently she brushed away the hand which had just settled on her thigh, put a finger to the sailor's lips and slipped past him, with a flash of an elegant waist. He'd hold, she thought. Right now, she had a little job to do.

A girl doesn't like to break her promises.

24

There's a section of Istanbul, right up under the city walls at the head of the Golden Horn, which has never been fully built up. Perhaps the ground is too steep for building on, perhaps in the days of the Byzantines it was forbidden to build so close to the palace of the Caesars; so it had lingered on into the beginning of the nineteenth century as a sort of ragged wilderness, planted with rocks and scrubby trees.

If you knew where to look you could find men living there, and sometimes women, too; but it was unwise to poke about too diligently. Some of the denizens of this patch were more often abroad by night than by day, and at any hour an air of resigned criminality hung about the tired trees and the little caves and crannies where some of the city's rubbish had been carefully drawn up to form a dismal kind of shelter. Benders, shacks and bustees artfully constructed by a shadowy people who had somehow slipped through the net of charity – or the hangman's noose.

Now and again the city authorities would order a sweep-out of the hillside, but invariably most of its inhabitants would appear to have crept away, unseen. The sweeps turned up a lot of rubbish which was burned at the foot of the ravine, sometimes a corpse, a starving feral dog or someone too far removed from the world to do more than stare, with unseeing eyes, at this emanation of men from a city they had long since lost and forgotten. The noisy men, armed with long sticks, would finally depart; the hill-dwellers would silently sift back, and the creation of shelters would begin again.

Someone was now fumbling their way very slowly down the ravine, moving noiselessly and carefully from rock to rock. There was a little moon, but a heavy rolling bank of cloud blotted it out entirely for minutes at a stretch; and in one of those dark interludes the figure stopped, waiting, listening. 'All quiet?'

The answer came in a whisper.

'All quiet.'

Two men groped past one another in the dark. The newcomer dropped feet-first into a shallow cave, squatted on his haunches and leaned his back against the wall.

Minutes later the cloud parted. The moonlight showed the man all he needed to see. A little opium box, propped against the wall. A dark pile of what he knew to be the uniforms. And at the back of the cave two men, trussed and gagged. The head of one was tilted back, as if he were asleep. But the eyes of the other man were flaring like the eyes of a terrified animal.

The newcomer glanced instinctively at the little box, grateful at least that the choice was made.

25

Yashim threw back his head as the moonlight came streaming through a break in the cloud. It seemed to him, as he stood with two hands touching its bark, that the tree was taller than he remembered: the black and twisted limbs corkscrewed upwards overhead, a nest of branches so thick and so high that even the moonlight struggled to break through between them.

The Janissaries had chosen this tree as their own. Some happy instinct had led them to adopt a living thing, in a part of the city that was stiff with monuments to human grandeur. Compared to this massive plane tree, Topkapi seemed cold and dead. To his left, Yashim could make out the black silhouette of the palace erected long ago by a vizier who thought himself to be all-powerful, before he was strangled with the silken bow-string. To the north lay Aya Sofia, the Great Church of the Byzantines, now a mosque. Behind him stood the Blue Mosque, built by a sultan who beggared his empire to have it done. And here was this tree, quietly growing on the ancient Hippodrome, generous with its shade in the heat of the day.

Nobody had tried to blame it for what it had come to represent: the jeering power of the Janissary corps. That, Yashim reflected, was never the Turkish way. The same instinct that prompted the Janissaries to adopt the tree made the people reluctant to do away with it now that the very name of the Janissaries was consigned to oblivion. People liked trees, and they disliked change: the Hippodrome itself was proof of that. A few steps away stood an obelisk with incised hieroglyphs, which a Byzantine emperor had brought from Egypt. Further on, there was a massive column erected by some Roman emperor long ago. There was also the celebrated Serpent Column, a bronze statue of three green twining serpents that once stood at the Greek Temple of Apollo at Delphi. The serpents' heads were missing now, it was true: but Yashim knew that the Turks could hardly be blamed for that.

He smiled to himself, remembering the night in the Polish residency when Palewski, drunk and whispering, had revealed to him the astounding truth. Together they had peered by candlelight into the depths of a vast and elderly armoire, where two of the three heads, which had been a wonder of the ancient world, lay on a pile of dusty linen, practically untouched since they were snapped off the column by some revelling youths in the Polish ambassador's suite a century ago. 'Too dreadful,' Palewski had murmured, shuddering at the sight of the brazen heads. 'But too late, now. What's broken is better not mended.'

So the Janissary tree remained. Yashim leaned his forehead against the peeling bark, and wondered if it were true that a tree's roots were as long and deep as its branches were high and wide. Even when a tree was felled, its roots continued to live, sucking up moisture from the ground, forcing new growth from the stump.

It was only ten years since the Janissaries had been suppressed. Many had been killed, not least those who barricaded themselves in the old barracks when the artillery was brought up and reduced the building to a smoking shell. But others had escaped – if the Albanian soup master were to be believed, more than Yashim would have guessed.

And that was only counting the regiments stationed in Istanbul. Every city of the empire had had its own Janissary contingent: Edirne, Sofia, Varna in the west; Üsküdar, Trabzon, Antalya. There were Janissaries established in Jerusalem, in

Aleppo and Medina: Janissary regiments, Janissary bands, Karagozi imams, the works. From time to time, their power in provincial cities had allowed them to form military juntas, who controlled the revenues and dictated to the local governor. How many of those still existed?

How many men had formed the corps?

How effectively had they been put down?

Ten years on, how many Janissaries had survived?

Yashim knew just where to ask the questions. Whether he would be vouchsafed any answers, he was not so sure.

He looked up at the branches of the great plane tree for a last time, and patted its massive trunk. As he did so his hand met something that was thinner and less substantial than the peeling bark.

Out of curiosity he tugged at the paper. In the last of the moonlight he read:

Unknowing
And knowing nothing of unknowing,
They spread.
Flee.

Unknowing
And knowing nothing of unknowing,
They seek.
Teach them.

Yashim glanced uneasily around. As the cloud blotted out the moon, the Hippodrome seemed to be deserted.

Yet he had an uncomfortable feeling that the verses he had read were intended for him. That he was being watched.

26

The gigantic records of the Ottoman administration were housed in a large pavilion that formed part of the division between the second and third, or more inward, court of the palace at Topkapi. It was entered from the second court, through a low doorway protected by a deep porch guarded by black eunuchs day and night. An archivist was always in attendance, for it had long ago been observed that although most of the sultans avoided much strenuous work after hours, their viziers could demand papers at any time. Even now, as Yashim approached, two torches blazed at the entrance to the Archive Chambers. The light revealed four muffled shapes crouching in the doorway, the eunuch guard.

The night was cold and the men, drawing their heavy burnouses closely round their heads, were either fast asleep or wishing to be so. Yashim stepped lightly over them, and the door yielded soundlessly to his fingertips. He closed it behind him without a sound. He was standing in a small vestibule, with an intricately modelled ceiling and a beautiful swirl of Kufic letters incised around the walls. Candles burned in glimmering niches. He tried the door ahead, and to his surprise he found it opened.

In the dark it looked even bigger than the book-barn he remembered: the stacks which took up space in the centre of the room were invisible in the gloom. Down one side of the room ran a low bench, or reading table, with a line of cushions; and far away, almost lost in the echoing darkness, was a very small point of light that seemed to draw the darkness closer in upon it. As he watched, the light snapped off, then leaped out again.

'An intruder,' a voice announced, pleasantly. 'How nice.'

The librarian was coming down the room. It was the exaggerated sway of his walk, Yashim realised, that had blocked the candlelight for a moment.

'I hope I'm not disturbing you.'

The librarian stepped up to a lamp by the door and gently trimmed the wick until the light was bright enough for them to look at one another. Yashim bowed, and introduced himself.

'Charmed. My name's Ibou,' the other said simply, with a slight bob of his head. He had a light and almost girlish voice. 'From Sudan.'

'Of course,' said Yashim. The most sought-after eunuchs at the palace came from the Sudan and the Upper Nile, lithe, hairless boys whose femininity belied their enormous strength and even more colossal powers of survival. Hundreds of boys, he knew, were taken every year from the Upper Nile and marched across the deserts to the sea. Only a few actually arrived. Somewhere in the desert, the operation was performed; the boy was plunged into the hot sand to keep him clean, and kept from drinking for three days. If, at the end of those three days, he was not mad, and could pass water, his chances were very good. He would be the lucky one.

The price, in Cairo, was correspondingly high.

'Perhaps you can help me, Ibou.' Somehow Yashim doubted it: most probably the delicious young man was in the library as a favour to some infatuated older eunuch. He scarcely looked old enough to know what a Janissary was, let alone to have mastered the system in the archives.

Ibou had put on a serious, solemn expression, his lips pursed. He really was very pretty.

'What I'm looking for,' Yashim explained, 'is a muster roll for all the Janissary regiments in the empire prior to the Auspicious Event.' The Auspicious Event – the safe, stock phrase had tripped out by force of habit. He'd have to be more explicit. 'The Auspicious Event –', he began. Ibou cut him off.

'Shh!' He raised one hand to his lips, and fanned the air with the other. His eyes rolled from side to side, pantomiming caution. Yashim grinned. At least he knew something about the Auspicious Event.

'Do you want names? Or only numbers?'

Yashim was surprised.

'Numbers.'

'You'll want the digest, then. Don't go away.'

He turned and teetered away into the darkness. At length, Yashim saw the distant candle begin to move, swaying a little until it disappeared. Behind the stacks, he supposed.

Yashim did not know the archive well, just well enough to understand that its organisation was comprehensive and inspired. If a vizier at the divan, or council meeting, needed a document or reference, be it ever so remote in time, or obscure by nature, the archivists would be able to locate it in a matter of minutes. Four or five centuries of Ottoman history were preserved in here: orders, letters, census returns, tax liabilities, proclamations from the throne and petitions running the other way, details of employment, promotion – and demotion, biographies of the more exalted officials, details of expenses, campaign maps, governor's reports – all going back to the fourteenth century, when the Ottomans first expanded out of Anatolia across the Dardanelles, into Europe.

He heard footsteps returning. The candle and its willowy bearer appeared out of the darkness. Apart from the candle, Ibou's hands were empty.

'No luck?' Yashim could not keep a trace of condescension out of his voice.

'Mmm–mmm,' the young man hummed. 'Let's just take a look.'

He turned up a series of wall lights above the reading bench, and knelt on a cushion. Above the bench itself ran a shelf containing nothing but tall, chunky ledgers with green spines, one of which the boy pulled down with a thud and opened on the bench. The thick pages crackled as he turned them over, humming quietly to himself. Eventually he ran his finger down a column on the page and stopped.

'Got it now?'

'We'll get there eventually,' Ibou said. He closed the ledger with a heavy whump! and lifted it lightly back into place. Then he sauntered over to a set of drawers built into the wall near the door, and pulled one out. From it, he selected a card.

'Oh.' He looked at Yashim: it was a look of sadness. 'Out,' he said. 'Not you. You're nice. I mean the records you wanted.'

'Out? To whom?'

'Tsk, tsk. That's not for me to say.'

Ibou waved the little card in front of his face as if he were opening and shutting a fan, with a flick of the wrist.

'No. No, of course not.' Yashim frowned. 'I was hoping though –'

'Yes?'

'I wondered if you could possibly tell me what revenue the beyerlik of Varna derived from . . . from mining rights in the 1670s.'

Ibou put his lips together and blew. He looked, thought Yashim, as if he were about to give the figures from memory.

'Any particular year? Or just the whole decade?'

'1677.'

'One moment please.'

He popped the card face down on the open drawer, picked up the candle, and in a moment had vanished behind the stacks. Yashim stepped forward, picked up the card and read:

Janissary rolls; 7-3-8-114; digest: fig., 1825.
By command.

He put back the card, puzzled.

A minute later, as he and Ibou pored over a thick roll of yellowing parchment which smelt powerfully of sheepskin and on which, to his infinite lack of interest, various sums and comments were recorded relative to the Varna beyerlik for the year 1677, he popped the question.

'What does 'By command' mean, Ibou? The sultan?'

Ibou frowned.

'Have you been peeping?'

Yashim grinned. 'It's just a phrase I've heard, somewhere.'

'I see.' Ibou's eyes narrowed for a moment. 'Don't touch the scroll, please. Well, it could mean the sultan. But it probably doesn't. It certainly won't mean, for instance, the Halberdiers of the Tresses, or the gardeners, or any of the cooks. Obviously we'd put them in, by their rank and place.'

'Then who?'

Ibou gestured slyly to the parchment roll. 'Are you interested in this, or is it just an excuse to come and chat?'

'It's just an excuse. Who?'

The archivist carefully rolled the parchment up. He tied it again with a length of purple ribbon and picked it up.

'Just let me set everything in order.'

Yashim chuckled to himself as he watched the boy prowling, loose-limbed and insufferably fluid, over to the drawers. He tucked the card back into its place, ran the drawer shut with his long fingers, and disappeared into the stacks with the candle. God help the older men! He'd never known such *coquetterie*. But he was also impressed. Ibou looked and sounded like a bit of African fluff but he certainly knew his way around. And not just among the dusty records, either, as he could see.

He came back very quickly.

'By command,' Yashim prompted.

'The imperial household. The sultan, his family, his chief officers.'

'The imperial women?'

'Of course. All the sultan's family. Not their slaves, mind you.'

'By command.' Yashim mused. 'Ibou, who do you think
wanted the book?'

'I don't know.' He frowned. 'Could it be –'

He shrugged, gave up.

'Who? Who are you thinking of?'

The archivist flipped his hand dismissively.

'No one. Nothing. I didn't know what I was going to say.'

Yashim decided to let it pass.

'I wonder, though, where I could find out what I want to
know?'

Ibou cocked his head and gazed at one of the lamps on the
wall.

'Ask one of the foreign embassies. I shouldn't be surprised.'

Yashim began to smile at the sally. *But why not?* he wondered.
It was exactly the sort of information they would be likely to
have.

He looked curiously at Ibou. But Ibou had raised the back of
his hand to his chin and was gazing, innocently, at the lamp.

27

'Damn!' Preen hadn't thought of money.

Yorg the Pimp thought of nothing else.

'What, köçek dancer, are we just sitting round together having
a drink? Swapping tales? No. You come across and ask me for
some information. Something you want, perhaps I have. A
trade.'

He gave her a crooked smile and tapped his head. 'My shop.'

To Preen, it looked as though Yorg's information was stored elsewhere: in his hump. Poisonous stuff, and he was full of it.

'What do you want?' she asked.

Yorg's eyes clicked past her like a lizard's.

'You've got friends, I see.'

'Some boys. You haven't answered my question.'

His eyes swivelled back to her.

'Oh, I think so,' he said softly. 'You've got something I can use, right, köçek? A drunken sailor for Yorg.'

She glanced back over her shoulder. Her Greek sailor sat with a frown on his face, tilting his glass back and forth. Mina and the other boy had their heads together, until he said something that made Mina give a whoop of laughter and rock back, one hand fluttering at her chest.

'Really!'

She looked back at Yorg. His eyes were cold as stone. His fingers curled around a glass: they were almost flat, with huge, misshapen knuckles.

'You'd be doing him a favour, köçek,' he spat.

He watched her, sensing a little victory.

'That guy deserves a real woman, don't you think?' Köçek dancers! Ancient traditions, years of training, blah blah. What gave those sad bastards the right to look down on him? 'Yes, a woman. And maybe, why not, a young one.'

Preen stiffened.

'You're mean, Yorg. I think you'll regret this one day. You take the sailor.'

She went back to her table. Mina looked up, but the smile on her lips vanished when she saw the crookbacked pimp in tow. The sailor looked from Preen to Yorg in surprise.

'I've got to go,' Preen bent forward to whisper in his ear. A little louder, she said: 'This is Yorg. He looks like the devil's toenail but tonight – he wants to buy you a drink. Isn't that right, Yorg?'

Yorg gave her a sick look and then turned and put out his hand.

'Hello Dmitri,' he croaked.

 28

Dear Sis,

. . . awfully jolly. Ask a great deal after you.

I am trying to write all my Impressions, just as you wanted me to, but there are so many I hardly know where to begin. Imagine you were trying to write a letter describing everything you ever saw in grandmama's china cabinets, you know the thing – Cups all piled up helter skelter, & little saucers, & Shepherdesses & Coffee pots & coloured sugar Pots, with domed lids: that's what the whole place seems like to me. Not to mention a blue riband of water, on which the whole thing seems to rest – not the cabinet, I mean – Constantinople.

Fizerly says the Turks don't give a thought for yesterday or tomorrow – all Fatalists – he once went into the great church built by Justinian – Aya Sofia (in Greek, pls) – all disguised as a Mohammedan (Fizerly, I mean, not Justinian – whizz!) and says it's just awful, with nothing but some dinner gongs hanging in the corners to show what Mustafa has done there in the last 400 years. He's a good fellow, Fizerly, and you should get to meet his Sister for he says, and I believe him, we shall be fast Friends.

On the same line, though, I have passed my first Great Test in Diplomacy. Fizerly'd hardly finished telling me the Turks live for the moment when one of them shambled up to the

embassy door – they all wear cloaks, you see, and look like
wizards – Turks not doors I mean – and declared himself to
be an historian! Fizerly spoke some turkish to him and the
chap replied in perfect French. Fizerly and I exchanged
glances – I thought I would die of laughter – but the turk v
serious and wanted to investigate Janissary regiments &c.
The Amb says Istanbul is much duller without the
Janissaries, Fizerly tells me. Not too dull for

> *Yr loving bro.,*
> *&c*

'Who are you working for?'

Compston spoke French badly. Yashim wished he would go away and leave him to get on with the assessment. The Englishman seemed puzzled.

Yashim said: 'Let us say I work for myself.'

'Oh. A freelance?'

Yashim rolled the unfamiliar word around his tongue. A free lance? He supposed he did: at least it was unencumbered by the plums that other men had gobbling at their groins.

'You are very perceptive,' he said, inclining his head.

The young man flushed. He felt certain that he was being laughed at, but could not quite understand the exchange. Perhaps he'd better just shut up for a while. More diplomatic. He folded his arms and sat stiffly on the upholstered seat, watching the Turk scribbling down lists. After a minute he said: 'Jolly bad business about the Janissaries, was it?'

Yashim looked up in surprise.

'For the Janissaries, yes,' he observed drily.

The boy nodded vigorously, as if Yashim had just made a profound remark.

'Whew! Yes! Rotten for them.'

He shook his head and raised his eyebrows.

'Not much fun, being burned alive,' Yashim murmured. *Pas trop amusant.*

The boy goggled dutifully. 'Not my idea of amusement, certainly!' He lowered his head and gave a big laugh. Yashim carried on writing.

'I say,' the boy chirped up. 'What do chaps do for amusement here, in Istanbul?'

He was leaning forward now, his hands dangling between his knees, with a screwed up look on his face.

Yashim narrowed his eyes. When he spoke it was almost a whisper.

'Well, some men use a dead sheep.'

The boy startled. 'A sheep?'

'They cut it and remove its – what do you say – its bladder.'

The boy's face was frozen into an expression of horror.

'One of them, it's usually the strongest, puts his lips to the urethra –'

'Oh quite. I . . . I see. Please, it's not what I meant.'

Yashim put on a puzzled expression.

'But don't you play football in your country, too?'

The boy stared at him, then sagged.

'I'm sorry, yes, of course. I . . . I . . .' he was quite red in the face. 'I think I'll just go and get a glass of water. Please excuse me.'

Yashim gave a short smile, and went back to the books.

He had found what he needed. They were, he imagined, only estimates; but if the figures were even roughly correct they made for sobering reading.

How many Janissaries had died in the events of June 1826? A thousand, possibly, at the barracks. Several hundred more accounted for in the hunt which followed – say five hundred. There had been hangings and executions, but surprisingly few, mostly of known ringleaders.

The rest had been allowed to melt away. Three of them, maybe a few more, had found jobs at the soup-makers' guild, as Yashim knew.

Which still left, if these figures were a guide, a lot of men unaccounted for. Living quiet, unobtrusive lives somewhere. Bringing up families. Working for a living. Well, that would be a shock to the system.

Yashim sat back on the chair and stared at his totals. A lot of rueful and regretful men.

About fifty thousand of them, in fact.

29

The imam winced. Could he plead another engagement? He knew that the eunuch prayed in his mosque, but they had never spoken until today. He'd approached him after the noon prayer and asked for a word. And the imam had inclined his head, quite graciously, before he realised who was asking.

As the eunuch fell into stride behind him, the imam reflected that he had no right to withhold his sympathy, or his advice. He didn't want to lie. Anyway, it was too late. Yet he viewed their discussion with foreboding.

How could a man be a good Muslim, if so many of those avenues by which a Muslim approached his God were, so to say, already blocked? The imam considered himself a teacher, certainly. But so much of his teaching was bound up with considerations of family: the blessing of children, the regulation that was appropriate to married life. He advised fathers about their sons, and sons about their fathers. He taught men – and women – how to conduct themselves in marriage. Straying husbands. Jealous wives. They came to him as a judge, with questions. It was his job to consider the questions, and answer yes, or no; usually it was through questions that they reached an understanding of their position. He guided them to the right questions: along the way they had to examine their own conduct, in the light of the Prophet's teaching.

What could he discuss with a creature who had no family?

They reached his room. A divan, a low table, a pitcher on a brass tray. A few cushions. The room was sparsely furnished, but it was still sumptuous. Running from the floor to shoulder height, the walls were decorated with a fabulous treasury of Iznik tile-work, centuries old, from the best period of the Iznik kilns. The blue, geometric designs seemed to have been applied only yesterday: they shone brilliant and pure, catching the sunlight which streamed through the windows overhead. In the corner, a black stove threw out a welcome warmth.

The imam gestured to the divan, while he stood with his back to the stove.

The eunuch smiled, a little nervously, and settled himself on the divan, kicking off his sandals before tucking his feet up beneath his burnous. Inwardly the imam groaned. This, he thought, was going to be difficult. He ran a fingertip across one eyebrow.

'Speak.'

His voice rumbled: Yashim was impressed. He was used to meeting people with something to hide, their speech marred by doubt and hesitancy, and here was a man who could give him answers stamped with authority. To be an imam was to live without uncertainty. For him, there would always be an answer. The truth was palpable. Yashim envied him his security.

'I want to know about the Karagozi,' he said.

The imam stopped polishing his eyebrow as it raised itself away from his fingertip.

'I beg your pardon?'

Yashim wondered if he had said the wrong thing. He said it again.

'They are a forbidden sect,' said the imam.

Not only the wrong thing, thought Yashim. The wrong man. Completely the wrong man. He began to get up, thanking the imam for his clarification.

'Stay, please. You want to know about them?' The imam had put up a hand. A discussion about doctrine now, that was another case entirely. The imam felt a great weight roll from his shoulders. They needn't talk about lust or sodomy or whatever it was that eunuchs wished to talk about when they visited their imam. Whether it was possible for a man without bollocks to enjoy the houris of paradise.

Yashim resumed his seat.

'The Karagozi were prominent in the Janissary Corps,' the imam remarked. 'Perhaps you know this?'

'Yes, of course. I know that they were unorthodox, too. I want to know how.'

'Sheikh Karagoz was a mystic. This was long ago, before the Conquest, when the Ottomans were still a nomadic people. They had a few mosques, here and there in the towns and cities they had conquered from the Christians. But the fighters were gazi, holy warriors, and they were not used to living in cities. They hungered after truth, but it was difficult for teachers and imams to stay amongst them. Many of these Turkish gazi listened to their old babas, their spiritual fathers, who were wise men. I say wise: they were not all enlightened.'

'They were pagan?'

'Pagan, animist, yes. Some, however, were touched by the words of the Prophet, peace be on him. But they incorporated into their doctrines a great deal of the old traditions, many esoteric teachings, even errors they had gathered up among the unbelievers. You must remember that those were tumultuous times. The little Ottoman state was growing, and many Turks were attracted to it. Every day, they encountered new lands, new peoples, unfamiliar faiths. It was hard for them to understand the truth.'

'And the Janissaries?'

'Sheikh Karagoz forged the link. Imagine: the early Janissaries were young men, uncertain in their faith, for they had been plucked from the ranks of unbelievers and had to forget many errors. Sheikh Karagoz made it easier for them. You know the story, of course. He was with the sultan Murad, who first created the Janissary corps from among the prisoners he took in his Balkan wars. When the Sheikh blessed them, with his hand outstretched in a long white sleeve, that sleeve became the mark of the Janissary, the headgear that they wore like an egret in their turbans.'

'So Sheikh Karagoz was a baba?'

'In a sense, yes. He lived somewhat later than the last babas of Turkish tradition, but the principles were the same. His teachings were Islamic, but they dwelt on mystery and sacred union.'

'Sacred union?'

The imam pursed his lips.

'I mean union of faiths, union with God. We say, for example, that there is only one path to truth, and that is written in the Koran. Sheikh Karagoz believed that there were other ways.'

'Like the dervish. Ecstatic states. Liberation of the soul from the prison of the body.'

'Exactly, but the means were different. You might say, more primitive.'

'How so?'

'A true adept considered himself to be above all earthly bonds and rules. So rule-breaking was a way of showing their allegiance to the brotherhood. They would drink alcohol and eat pork, for instance. Women were admitted under the same conditions as men. Much of the clear guidance of the Koran was simply brushed aside, as unimportant, or even irrelevant. Such transgressions helped to create a bond between them.'

'I see. Perhaps that made it easier for the Christian-born to approach Islam?'

'In the short term, I agree. They gave up fewer of their base pleasures. You know what soldiers can be like.'

Yashim nodded. Wine, women and song: the litany of the camp fire in every age.

'If they ignored the guidance of the Koran,' he said slowly, 'what guidance did they receive?'

'A very good question.' The imam put his fingertips together. 'In one sense, none at all. The true Karagozi believed in no one but himself: he believed that his was the soul that persisted in every state – creation, birth, death and beyond. The rules were irrelevant. But the ridiculous thing is, he had rules of his own, too. Magic numbers. Secrets. Superstitions. A Karagozi will not set his spoon on the table, or stand on a threshold, that sort of thing.

'Obeying the petty regulations of the order allowed him to break the laws of God. It is scarcely to be wondered at that all sorts of bad types were attracted to the Karagozi order. Let's not exaggerate. The original impulse, if confused, was pure. The Karagozi followers thought of themselves as Muslims. That is, they attended prayers in the mosque, like everyone else. The Karagozi element was another layer in their spiritual allegiance, a secret layer. They were organised in lodges, what we call tekkes. Places of gathering and prayer. There were many of them, in Istanbul and elsewhere.'

'Were all the Karagozi Janissaries?'

'No. All the Janissaries were Karagozi, broadly speaking. Which is not the same thing. Perhaps, my friend, we have been too quick to speak of them and their doctrines in the past tense. The blow to the Janissaries? A setback. Maybe, in the end, a creative one. You know, faith may sharpen itself in adversity. I would imagine that we have not heard the last of the Karagozi. Perhaps not under that name, but the currents of spirituality they tap are deep.'

'But proscribed, as you said. Forbidden.'

'Ah, well, here in Istanbul, yes. But they have made a long journey. Once they listened to a baba from the steppe. Since then they have passed through the heartlands of Islam, the Domain of Peace, and now they stand on its borders. As sentinel, perhaps.'

The imam smiled.

'Don't look so surprised. The doctrine of the Karagozi won many frontiers for Islam. Perhaps it will do so again.'

'Which borders? Where do you mean?'

'They are strong where you'd expect them to be. In Albania. Where the Janissaries were always strong.'

Yashim nodded.

'There's a poem. You seem to know a lot, so perhaps you know this, too.'

He recited the verses he had found nailed to the Janissary Tree.

> Unknowing
> And knowing nothing of unknowing,
> They spread.

> *Flee.*

> Unknowing
> And knowing nothing of unknowing,
> They seek.

> *Teach them.*

The imam frowned. 'It is, I recall, an Karagozi verse. Yes, I know it. Highly esoteric, don't you agree? Typically secretive. It goes on to suggest some form of mystical union with the divine, as far as I remember.'

'What do you mean, it goes on?'

'The poem you've quoted is incomplete.' The imam looked surprised. 'I'm afraid I can't recite it exactly.'

'But you could, perhaps, find out?'

'By the grace of God,' said the imam placidly. 'If you're interested, I can try.'

'I would be grateful,' Yashim said, rising.

They bowed to one another. Just as Yashim turned to go, the imam turned his face to the window.

'Sufic mysteries,' he said quietly. 'Beautiful in their way, but ethereal. I don't think they would mean much to the ordinary people. Or perhaps, I don't know, too much. There's a lot of passion, and even faith, in this kind of poetry, but in the end it doesn't suit the believers. It's too free, too dangerous.'

I don't know about free, Yashim reflected.

But dangerous, yes.

Certainly dangerous.

Even murderous.

30

He saw her swinging down the street, tall and graceful and challenging the men to stare. A few yards from him she slowed and began to look around.

He put up a hand and waved her across.

She dragged back a stool and sat down abruptly. A group of old men playing backgammon at the next table rubbernecked with obvious stupefaction; but Preen didn't notice, or care.

'Coffee,' she said.

Yashim ordered two, avoiding the tray boy's curious stare. Not for the first time in his life he wanted to stand up and explain. She's not, in fact, a woman, so everything is as it should be. She's a man, dressed as a woman. But he admired her courage in coming to the café. He nodded grimly at the old men.

With scarcely a trace of make-up, the flush in Preen's cheeks was real: she looked, Yashim thought, better for it.

'We can't talk here,' he said. 'I'll cut along home, and you can join –'

'We'll talk here,' she replied through gritted teeth. The boy served the coffees, and began to flick a duster over an adjoining table. Yashim caught his eye and jerked his head. The boy sloped off, disappointed.

'I've got reasons for discretion, Preen.'

She drew breath through her nose. Her chest heaved.

'Such as?'

He looked at her. 'You're looking good today,' he said.

'Cut it out.'

She sounded tough, but she kept her eyes on the table and moved her head slowly from side to side. A trace of pleasure.

'It's better if we're not seen together at the moment. It's my job to blend in, to slip by unobserved. As for you, well, I'm not sure what we're into here.'

'I'm a big girl,' said Preen. Her lip quivered. Yashim grinned. Preen covered her mouth with a hand and shot him a look. Then she giggled.

'Oh, I know I'm naughty, sweetie. I just couldn't help it. I had to do something a bit wild, see someone I like. Shock them, too. To feel alive.' She let a shiver of pleasure run through her body. 'I've been talking to Istanbul's most disgusting man.'

Yashim raised his eyebrows.

'I'm amazed you can be so sure.'

90

'A hunchbacked pimp, from the docks? I'm sure. He says someone saw your friends the other night.'

Yashim leaned forwards.

'Where?'

'Somewhere reasonably salubrious. Is salubrious the word I want, Yashim?'

'Possibly. Your – informant – he wasn't there himself?'

'Not that he told me. Don't you want to know where?'

'Of course I want to know.'

'It's some sort of gardens,' Preen explained. 'Along the Bosphorus.'

'Ah.' Perhaps salubrious *was* the word Preen wanted: all things are relative, after all.

'There's a kiosk there, apparently, perfectly clean. There are even little lanterns in the trees.' Preen sounded almost wistful. 'You can sit there and talk, and watch the boats in the straits, and have a coffee or a pipe.'

Or an assignation, Yashim thought. The Yeyleyi Gardens were once a favourite of the court: the sultan would take his women to picnic there, among the trees. That must have been almost a century ago. The sultans had stopped coming when the place became popular; in time it grew faintly notorious. Not entirely respectable, the Yeyleyi Gardens had been the sort of place where lovers used to arrange to meet by accident, communicating in the tender and semi-secret language of flowers. These days the encounters were more spontaneous, but even better arranged, and the language possibly mercenary. He could quite imagine it being visited – a little hopefully – by what the seraskier called boys of good family.

'So – what? They arrived, had a pipe and a coffee, and left together?'

'So I'm told.'

'By boat?'

'I don't know. He didn't say anything about a boat. No, wait, I think they left in a cab.'

'All four of them together?'

'All five.'

Yashim looked up sharply. Preen tittered.

'Four came, but five left.'

'Yes, I see. And do you, Preen, know anything about this Number Five?'

'Oh, yes. He was a Russian.'

'A Russian? You're sure?'

Yashim thought about this. Stambouliots had a tendency to mark down everyone vaguely foreign, and fair, as a Russian these days. It was a function of the late war; and of all the wars the Porte had fought with the czar's men over the last hundred years; increasingly ending with the defeat of the sultan's army, and further tough demands.

'I think it must have been true,' Preen said. 'He was in a uniform.'

'What?!'

Preen laughed. 'White, with gold braid. Very smart. *Ve-ry* big guy. And a sort of medal on his chest, like a star, with rays.'

'Preen, this is gold dust. How did you get it?'

She thought of the young Greek sailor.

'I made a few sacrifices,' she smiled. Then she thought of Yorg and her smile faded.

❦ 31 ❧

Istanbul was not a city which kept late hours. After ten, for the most part, when the sun had long since sunk beneath the Princes' islands in the Sea of Marmara, the streets were quiet and deserted. Dogs sometimes snarled and snapped in the alleyways, or took to howling down on the shore, but those sounds, like the muezzin's call to prayer at first light, were the night noises of Istanbul, and no one thought more about them.

Nowhere in the city was quieter than the Grand Bazaar, a labyrinth of covered streets which twisted and writhed like eels all the way down the hill from Beyazit to the shores of the Golden Horn. By day, the hum of the bazaar belonged to what was, even then, perhaps the most fantastic caravanserai in the world, an emporium of gold and spices, of rugs and linens, soaps and books and medicines and earthenware bowls. But it wasn't just the place where the produce of the world was traded; within that square mile of alleyways and cubicles, some of the most delicate and useful products of the empire were manufactured daily. It was a concentration of the empire's wealth and industry; it was served by its own cafés, restaurants, imams and hamams; and the strictest rules were laid down for its security.

The heights which commanded the bazaar – the so-called Third Hill of Istanbul – on which the Beyazit Mosque stood, had been chosen by the Conqueror, Sultan Mehmed, for his imperial palace; but the building was still incomplete when he began work on another palace, Topkapi on Seraglio Point, destined to be far greater and more magnificent than the first. The old palace, or Eski Serai, later served as a sort of annexe to Topkapi. It was a school where palace slaves were trained; a company of Janissaries were stationed in its walls; but its only royal inhabitants were women of previous sultans, despatched from Topkapi on the death of their lord and master to gloomy retirement in Eski Serai.

That dismal practice had lapsed many years before. Eventually, the Eski Serai sank into disrepair, and finally into ruin; its remains were cleared and from the rubble rose the fire-tower which still brooded watchfully over the Grand Bazaar.

The bag, which arrived in the night, was tied by its drawstrings to a heavy iron grille which protected the Grand Bazaar from prying eyes and enterprising thieves. By dawn more than a dozen people had commented on it, and within the hour, in front of a very squeezed-up crowd, it was finally brought to the ground.

No one was eager to be the one who opened it. Nobody thought it contained treasure. Everyone thought that whatever it contained, it would be horrible; and everyone wanted to know what it was.

In the end, it was decided to carry the bag, unopened, to the mosque, and ask the kadi for an opinion.

32

Several hours later the bag was opened for the second time that morning.

'It is a terrible thing,' the kadi said again, wringing his hands. He was an old man, and the shock had been great. 'Nothing like this . . . ever . . .' His hands fluttered in the air. 'It has nothing to do with us. Peaceful people . . . good neighbours . . .'

The seraskier nodded, but he was not listening. He was watching Yashim drag at the cords. Yashim stood up, and tipped the bag over onto the floor.

The kadi gripped a doorway for support. The seraskier skipped to one side. Yashim himself stood breathing heavily, staring at the pile of white bones and wooden spoons. Wedged in the pile, unmistakably dark, was a human head.

Yashim hung his head and said nothing. The violence is terrible, he thought. And what have I done to stop it? Cooked a meal. Gone looking for a toy cauldron.

Cooked a meal.

The seraskier put out a booted foot and stirred the heap with his toe. The head settled in its grisly nest. Its skin looked drawn and yellow, and its eyes glittered faintly beneath half-lowered lids. Neither of them noticed the kadi leave the room.

'No blood,' said the seraskier.

Yashim squatted down beside the bones and spoons.

'But one of yours?'

'Yes. I think so.'

'You think so?'

'No, I'm sure. The moustache.' He gestured faintly to the severed head.

But Yashim was more interested in the bones. He was laying them out, bone by bone, paying particular attention to the shin, the femur, the ribs.

'It's very odd,' he murmured.

The seraskier looked down. 'What's odd?'

'There's not a mark on them. Clean and whole.'

He picked up the pelvis and began turning it this way and that between his hands. The seraskier pulled a face. He'd dealt with corpses often enough – but fondling bones. Euch.

'It was a man, anyway,' Yashim remarked.

'Of course it was a fucking man. He was one of my soldiers.'

'It was just a thought,' Yashim replied pacifically, setting the pelvis in position. From overhead it looked almost obscenely large, thrusting out from the skeletal remains spread on the marble floor. 'Maybe they'd used another body. I wouldn't know.'

'Another body? What for?'

Yashim stood up and wiped his hands with the hem of his cloak. He stared at the seraskier, seeing nothing.

'I can't imagine,' he said.

The seraskier gestured to the door, and heaved a sigh.

'Like it or not,' he said, 'we're going to have to tell the people something.'

Yashim blinked.

'How about the truth?' He suggested.

The seraskier looked at him levelly.

'Something like that,' he said abruptly. 'Why not?'

Fine cities whose contented citizens support an intelligent administration do exist, containing not a single dilapidated public building, a solitary weed-strewn building lot, or even a crumbling palazzo; but a great city must have them all, for decay, too, is a sign of life. In the right ear, dereliction whispers of opportunity. In another ear, of delinquency and corruption. Istanbul in the 1830s was no exception.

The ragged bell-pull that now lay, inert, in Yashim's hand as he stood at the top of the steps by the front door of a building in Pera, Istanbul's so-called 'European' quarter across the Golden Horn, inspired a similar reflection. He sensed that in some way the broken bell claimed kinship with much that was already ragged and mouldering in the ancient metropolis, from cracked basilicas to sagging wooden houses, from the office of the Patriarch to waterlogged pilings in the port.

At the last, mortal wrench of the cord, a bell had pealed somewhere inside the old mansion. For the first time in weeks, and the last time in years, a bell announced to the Polish ambassador that he had a visitor.

Palewski manoeuvred himself off the divan with an oath and a tinkle of broken glass.

At the head of the stairs he gripped the balustrade and began to descend, quite slowly, towards the front door. He stared for a moment or two at the bolts, then stretched, flexed the muscles in his back, ran a hand across his hair and around his collar, and wrenched it open. He blinked involuntarily in the sudden rush of winter light.

Yashim shoved the remains of the bell pull into his hands and stepped inside. Palewski closed the door, grumbling.

'Why don't you just come in through the windows at the back?'

'I didn't want to surprise you.'

Palewski turned his back and began to mount the stairs.

'Nothing surprises me,' he said.

Yashim glimpsed a dark corridor, which led to the back of the Residency, and a sheet covering some furniture stacked in the hall. He followed Palewski up the stairs.

Palewski opened a door.

'Ah,' he said.

Yashim followed his friend into a small, low-ceilinged room, lit by two long windows. Against the opposite wall stood an elaborate chimney piece, decorated with sheaves of carved shields and the bows and arrows of a more chivalric age; in the grate a fire glowed dully. Palewski threw on another log and kicked the fire; a few sparks shot up. The flames began to spread.

Palewski threw himself into a massive armchair and motioned to Yashim to do the same.

'Let's have some tea,' he said.

Yashim had been in this room many times before; even so, he looked about with pleasure. A mottled mirror in a gold frame hung between the louvred windows; beneath it stood Palewski's little writing desk and the only hard chair in the room. The two armchairs, drawn up to the fire, were leaking their stuffing, but they were comfortable. Over the fireplace hung a portrait in oils of Jan Sobieski, the Polish king who lifted the Turkish siege of Vienna in 1683; two other oils, one of a man in a full wig on a prancing horse, and another family scene, hung on the wall by the door, over a mahogany side-table. Palewski's violin was perched on it. The further wall, and the alcoves by the fire-place, were ranged with books.

Palewski reached forwards and yanked once or twice on a tapestry bell pull. A neat, Greek serving girl came to the door and Palewski ordered tea. The girl brought a tray, and set it down on the charpoy in front of the fire. Palewski rubbed his hands together.

'English tea,' he said. 'Keemun with a trace of bergamot. Milk or lemon?'

The tea, the fire and the rich tones of the German clock on the mantelpiece soothed the Polish ambassador into a better mood. Yashim, too, felt himself relax. For a long while neither man said anything.

'The other day you quoted something to me – an army marches on its stomach. Who said that? Napoleon?'

Palewski nodded, and pulled a face. 'Typical Napoleon. In the end his armies marched on their frozen feet.'

Not for the first time, Yashim promised himself to probe Palewski's attitude to Napoleon. It seemed a combination of admiration and bitterness. But instead he asked: 'Does anything about the way the Janissaries named their ranks strike you as significant?'

'Significant? They took titles from the kitchen. The colonel was called the soup cook, wasn't he? And there were other ranks I remember – scullion, baker, pancake maker. Sergeant-majors carried a long wooden ladle as a badge of office. As for the men, to lose a regimental tureen in battle – one of the big cauldrons they used for making pilaff – was the ultimate disgrace. They had the provisioning sorted out. Why the Janissaries?'

Yashim told him. He told him about the cauldron, about the man trussed ready to roast, the pile of bones and wooden spoons. Palewski let him speak without interruption.

'Forgive me, Yashim, but weren't you in Istanbul ten years ago? They call it suppression, don't they? Laughter can be suppressed. Emotion. But we're talking about flesh and blood. This was history. This was tradition. Suppressed? What happened to the Janissaries wasn't even a massacre.'

To Yashim's surprise, Palewski was scrambling to his feet.

'I was there, Yashim. I never told you this, because no one – not even you – would have wanted to know. It's not the Ottoman way.' He hesitated, with a rueful smile. '*Have* I told you this before?'

Yashim shook his head. Palewski raised his chin.

'June the sixteenth, 1826. Sunny day. I was over in Stamboul on some errand or another, I forget,' he began. 'And boom – the city explodes. Kettles drumming on the Etmeidan. Students in the medreses, humming like ripe cheese. Get back, I think. Down to the Golden Horn, grab a caique, tea on the lawn and wait for news.'

'Tea?' Yashim interjected.

'It's a figure of speech. Rather like the lawn. But never mind: I never made it here. Golden Horn. Silence. There were the caiques, drawn up on the Pera side. I waved and capered on the landing stage, but not a miserable soul stepped forward to ferry me across. I tell you, Yashim, it made the hairs prickle on the back of my neck. I felt as if I'd been quarantined.

'I had a rough idea of what was brewing. I thought of some of the pashas I knew – but then, I thought, they'd have trouble enough without me tagging along. To be honest, I wasn't sure it was wise to be barricaded into some grandee's mansion at the moment of crisis, which we all knew was coming. Guess where I went instead.'

Yashim creased his brow. I know just where, old friend, but I won't spoil it. 'A Greek tavern? A mosque? I don't know.'

'The sultan. I found him in the seraglio, at the Circumcision

99

Kiosk – he'd just arrived from Besiktas up the Bosphorus. Various commanders with him. The Grand Mufti, too.' Palewski gave Yashim a long, hard look. 'Don't talk to me about suppression. I was there. "Victory or death!" the pashas shouted. Mahmut took the Holy Standard of the Prophet in his two hands. "Either we win today," he said, "or Istanbul will be a ruin for cats to prowl through." I'll say this for the House of Osman: it may have taken them two hundred and fifty years to make the decision, but when they made it, they meant it.

'Students came pouring into the great court at Topkapi. They were given arms, and they carried the Holy Standard to the Sultan Ahmet Mosque – all that end of the city was ours, around the Hippodrome, Aya Sofia and the palace. The rebels were at the end of the street closer to their barracks, around the Beyazit Mosque and down by the old clothes bazaar. Old Byzantine street, and Janissary stronghold, too. That's where the sultan's troops attacked first. Grapeshot. Like Napoleon at the Tuileries. A whiff of grapeshot.

'Just two cannons – but under a fellow they called Ibrahim. Infernal Ibrahim. The Janissaries ran back to the barracks and started to barricade the doors with stones – not a thought for their companions left out in the streets. Even when the artillery had surrounded them, they refused to talk about surrender. Just crowded together inside the Great Gate, apparently. The first cannonade which blew it open killed dozens of them, there and then.

'We saw the flames, Yash. They burned the Janissaries out – some of them, anyway. It was like dismantling a straw-rick, killing the rats as they scamper out. The prisoners were sent to the Sultan Ahmet Mosque, but those who were strangled on the spot were dumped under the Janissary Tree – there were half a dozen corpses there by nightfall. The next day, the Hippodrome was a heap of bodies.

'It's always made me feel sick, that tree. Thinking of the men hanged in the branches, like fruit. And the Janissary corpses piled around its trunk. It must have blood in it, Yash. Blood in its roots.

'But that's what I saw, and I'm saying this. I've known pogroms and massacres. I've seen worse, to be frank, than what the Janissaries got in the end. Women and children – I've seen that. The Janissaries were men, and they deserved it in a way, poor fools, for what they'd done, and what men before them had done and been doing, time out of mind. They knew the racket they'd joined. It was killing the empire slowly, and they must have known that one day there'd be a reckoning.

'Perhaps they didn't expect it, coming quite like that, so utter and complete. It wasn't "party's over and leave your sabres on the counter as you file out", was it? It was annihilation, Yash. Ten thousand dead? Burning them out of the Belgrade Forest. Winkling them out of the provincial cities. Tartar horsemen, flying across the empire to spread the news. The Auspicious Event, that's the phrase, isn't it? The Janissaries don't even get a mention on their own death certificate. They're gone, and beyond trace, too.

'You know, a few weeks afterwards, I saw the sultan with an executioner, in a cemetery among the cypress trees. Their ancient dead. The loyal and the brave, as well as the venal and corrupt. The executioner beheaded every gravestone with a heavy sword.'

Yashim raised a finger.

'There's one left. Over in Uskudar, with the sleeve carved into the stone.'

Palewski waved him away.

'There's always one left. And maybe dozens. It doesn't mean anything. The Ottoman empire endures. It endures because everything has changed. And everything has changed because the Janissaries are gone. They were the bedrock of the empire, don't you see? They were all that stood in the way of – what? The sultan riding on a European saddle. The army drilling like Napoleonic soldiers. Christians opening liquor shops in Pera, men in fezzes instead of turbans, all that. And more: the Janissaries were thieving, overweening, narrow-minded bastards, but they were poets, and artisans of skill, too, some of them. And all of them had culture of a kind. Something that was bigger than them, bigger than their greed and faults.

'Do I regret them? No. But I mourn them, Yashim. Alone in this city I mourn them, because they were the soul of this empire, for good and ill. With them, the Ottomans were unique. Proud, strange and – in a way – free. The Janissaries reminded them of who they were, and what they wished to be. Without them? Very normal now, I'm afraid. Too normal: even the memory of the Janissaries is blotted out. And the empire can't jig along with this normality, I think, for very long. It's too thin, too brittle, without memory. Being able to remember – that's what makes a people. It's the case for us Poles, too,' he added, suddenly morose.

He swept into an armchair and was silent, brooding with a hand across his eyes. Yashim took a sip of his tea, found it cool and drained the cup.

'I'm sorry,' he said. 'I shouldn't have bothered you.'

Palewski slowly raised his head.

'Bother me, Yashim. Bother as much as you want. I'm only the ambassador, what do I know about anything?'

Yashim felt himself humbled. He had a boyish urge to get up and go away. 'I wondered about the bones,' he said, 'because they were so clean. How many days have they had – six? How do you strip the bones of a man clean in such a short time?'

'Well,' Palewski murmured, feeling rather queasy. 'You boil him.'

'Mmm. And whole, too – in a huge pot. There isn't a mark of a knife on the bones.'

Palewski poured more tea. He noticed that his hand was trembling.

'Think of the smell,' Yashim was saying. 'Someone would be sure to have noticed.'

'Yashim, my friend,' Palewski protested. 'Are there any aspects of this mystery which don't involve cookery? I feel we may have to suspend our Thursday evenings until this is all over. I'm not sure I'm up to it.'

Yashim seemed not to have heard.

'The way the bodies appear, it's almost as if they're signalling their reach – first at the new stables above Aksaray, then way over the Golden Horn in Galata, near the Mosque of the Victory. Finally, today, we get one at the very gates of the Bazaar. Corpses materialising out of thin air – and another to come,' he added. 'Unless we get there first.'

'You could only do that if – what? – there were some sort of pattern. Something about each of those locations which suits the murderer, however far apart they are. Delivering corpses all around the city, and even to Galata, has to be more difficult than just letting them bob up in the Bosphorus.'

Yashim looked up and nodded. 'But for some reason the killers think the added difficulty is worthwhile.'

'A pattern, Yashim. You need to get hold of a decent map and plot the points.'

'A decent map,' Yashim repeated flatly. It was many years since anyone had attempted to make a good map of Istanbul.

Palewski knew that as well as he did.

'All right, what else do you have?'

'One Sufic verse. May or may not be relevant. One uniformed Russian,' Yashim replied.

'Ah. A Russian. Now that I can help you with.'

Yashim told him what Preen had discovered about the decorated fifth man.

'Order of Vasilyi, I shouldn't wonder. Only awarded for battlefield experience, but it's not immensely high grade. You
wouldn't wear it if you could get something grander.'

'Which means?'

'Which means that your boy is probably a good soldier, but
not a grandee. Fourth rank aristocracy, or lower. Could be a
career soldier.'

'In Istanbul?'

'Attached to the embassy. There's no other explanation. I'll
find him for you right now.'

Palewski unwound himself from his armchair and dug about
in a low shelf. He dragged several copies of *Le Moniteur*, the
Ottoman court gazette, back to his seat and began flicking
through the pages.

'It'll be in here – who's come, who's left, who's presented their
credentials at court. Look, new boy at the British embassy,
American chargé d'affaires upscaled to consular rank, Persian
emissary plenipotentiary received, blah blah. Next one. New
Russian trade agent, wrong line of country, departure of French
consul – ah, wish I'd gone to that party – etcetera, no. Next.
Here you are. N. P. Potemkin, junior attaché to the assistant
attaché of military affairs presents his credentials to the viziers of
the court. Pretty lowly. Not full accreditation. I mean, he never
got to see the sultan.'

Yashim smiled. Palewski's own reception by the sultan had
been the high point of his otherwise stillborn diplomatic career.
As well as making a story which Palewski told in the driest way
possible.

By a quirk of history, the Polish ambassador was maintained
in Istanbul at the sultan's expense. It was a throwback to the
days when the Ottomans were too grand to submit to the ordinary laws of European diplomacy, and would not allow any king
or emperor to claim to be the sultan's equal. An ambassador,

they reasoned, was a kind of plaintiff at the fount of world justice rather than a grandee vested with diplomatic immunity, and as such they had always insisted on paying his bills. Other nations had successfully challenged this conception of what an embassy was about; the Poles, latterly, could not afford to. Since 1830 their country had ceased to exist when the last parcel, around Cracow, was gobbled up by Austria.

The stipend the Polish ambassador received didn't seem to cover the cost of maintaining the embassy itself, Yashim had observed, but it at least allowed Palewski to live in reasonable comfort. 'We talk of Christian justice,' Palewski would explain, 'but the only justice that Poland has ever received is at the hands of its old Muslim enemy. You Ottomans! You understand justice better than anyone in the world!' Palewski would be careful not to complain that the stipend he received had not changed for the last two hundred years. And Yashim would never say what both of them knew: that the Ottomans only continued to recognise the Poles to irritate the Russians.

'So it seems,' Yashim mused, 'that junior attaché Potemkin springs into a coach with four of the brightest New Guard cadets – and they're never seen alive again.'

Palewski's eyebrows shot up.

'Meet a Russian – disappear – it's a common phenomenon. It happens all the time in Poland.'

'But why would they meet a Russian official in the first place? We're practically at war with Russia. If not today, then yesterday and probably tomorrow.'

Palewski put up his hands in a gesture of ignorance.

'How can we know? They were selling secrets? They all met at the Gardens, by chance, and decided to make a night of it?'

'No one meets anyone at the Gardens by chance,' Yashim reminded him. 'As for selling secrets, I get the impression that it's us who need their secrets, not the other way round. What could the cadets be selling – old French trigonometry tables? Details of cannon they probably copied off Russian designs in the first place? The name of their hatter?'

Palewski scowled and thrust out his lips.

'I think that's enough tea,' he said thoughtfully. 'The penetration of arcane mysteries requires something stronger.'

But Yashim knew the consequences of following Palewski's well-meaning advice. So he made his excuses, and left.

34

Yashim walked quickly away to the Pera quay on the Golden Horn, and crossed by caique to the Istanbul side. His friend was right: it looked as though another body, the fourth, was going to wind up on his plate tomorrow night. And that was just the beginning of his difficulties.

A jogging donkey-cart blocked his progress as he walked back to his lodgings. The driver looked round and raised the handle of his whip in acknowledgement, but the alleys were too narrow to let him by, and Yashim was forced to drag his feet, smouldering with impatience. At last the cart turned into his own alley, and at that moment Yashim saw a man loitering, about halfway down. His outfit of scarlet and white indicated that he served as a page of the interior service of the palace. He was looking up the other way, and Yashim slipped back into the alley he'd come from.

He leaned against the wall and considered his position. The seraskier had given him ten days: ten days before the great Review that would show the sultan at the head of an efficient, modern army that could match anything the empire's enemies could put into the field against it. Four days had already gone, and time seemed to be running out: there was the question of the upcoming murder, Palewski's well-founded observation that he needed to get his hands on a good map, and the problem of the Russian attaché, Potemkin. But there was the strangling at the palace, too, and the validé's lightly couched threat that he had better find her jewels if he ever wanted another French novel. Well, he did want another: but Yashim wasn't naive. Novels were the least of it. Favour. Protection. A powerful friend. He might need that any day.

He wasn't ungrateful, either. The palace had discovered – and then allowed him to exercise – his particular talents, the same way that for hundreds of years the palace had selected and trained its functionaries to exploit their natural gifts.

Apart from the sultan himself, and the palace eunuchs, he was the only man who could take up an invitation to enter the women's quarters. The only man in the whole empire who could come and go at will. And when the palace turned to him for help it was his duty to oblige.

But that put him in a difficult position. He was engaged by the seraskier: the seraskier had called him in first.

A killing in the harem was bad. But what he was dealing with outside looked worse.

For the fourth cadet, time was running out.

But why?

Why now?

He took a deep breath, pulled back his shoulders, and walked around the corner into his street.

35

The Dresser of the Girls looked beseechingly at Yashim, then at the Kislar Agha, the chief black eunuch, who was spreading his considerable bulk across a chaise longue. Neither the Dresser or Yashim had been invited to sit.

Yashim privately cursed his impetuosity. He'd been taken into the palace just when the Validé Sultan took her evening nap, and the Kislar Agha had swiftly taken control. The Kislar Agha never slept. When Yashim had told him what he had to say, he had sent immediately for the dresser.

That was how the system worked, Yashim knew. Everyone had their own ideas about the imperial harem, but essentially it was like a machine. The sultan, pumping a new recruit in the cohort of imperial concubines, was simply a major piston of an engine designed to guarantee the continuous production of Ottoman sultans. All the rest – the eunuchs, the women – were cogs.

Christians viewed the sultan's harem quite differently. Reading his way through some of the validé's favourite French novels, it had slowly dawned on Yashim that westerners, as a rule, had an intensely romantic and imaginative picture of the harem. For them it was a honeyed fleshpot, in which the most beautiful women in the world engaged spontaneously at the whim of a single man in salacious acts of love and passion, a narcotic bacchanal. As though the women had only breasts and thighs, and neither brains nor histories. Let them dream, Yashim thought. The place was a machine, but the women had their lives, their will and their ambition. As for the hints of lasciviousness, the machine simply let them off as steam.

The dresser was a case in point. He was something like a squeezed lemon, a sour and fussy creature, black, skinny, forty-five, meticulous about detail, with all the spontaneous effervescence of a dripping tap. The dresser's tasks ranged from preparing the gözde, or chosen girl, for a sultan's bed to buying their underwear. His staff included hairdressers, tailors, jewellers and a perfumier, whose own job involved, among other things, crushing and grinding scents, blending perfumes to suit the sultan's taste, preparing soaps, oils and aphrodisiacs, and overseeing the making of the imperial incense. If anything went wrong, the dresser was the one to take the blame: but he always had lesser functionaries he, in turn, could kick.

'A ring, dresser,' the Kislar Agha was saying. 'According to our friend here, the girl wore a ring. I do not know if she was wearing it when the unfortunate circumstance occurred. Perhaps you will tell us.'

The slight annular depression on the dead girl's middle finger which Yashim had noticed before the Validé Sultan had interrupted his inspection of the body had interested him at the time. For all her finery and precious jewels, it had been the missing ring which recalled, however fractionally, her existence as a living person, with thoughts and feelings of her own. Perfectly engineered for the task she was never destined to perform – flawless, beautiful, perfectly accoutred, bathed and perfumed – had she nonetheless prepared to approach the sultan's bed with the tiniest trace of an imperfection, a cold, white indentation on the middle finger of her right hand: the faint imprint of a choice?

Was the ring removed at the time of her death, or even later?

The dresser glanced at Yashim, who watched him without expression, arms folded patiently across his chest. The dresser gazed upwards, drumming his fingers nervously against his closed lips. Yashim had the impression that he already had the answer they wanted. He was trying to control his panic and work out the probable consequences of what he was about to say.

'Indeed. A ring. Just the one. She did wear the ring.'

The Kislar Agha tugged at his earlobe. He turned a bloodshot eye on Yashim, who said: 'And the Page of the Chamber found the body. Can we talk to him?'

The Page of the Chamber, whose task was to lead the gözde to the sultan, was produced: he knew nothing about a ring. The Kislar Agha, who had been next on the scene, gave Yashim his answer only by a slight lowering of his eyelids.

'She was laid out in the bridal chamber, just as you saw her.'

'By –?'

'Among others, the dresser.'

The dresser could not remember if the ring had been missing then.

'But you might have noticed if it had been gone?' Yashim suggested.

The dresser hesitated.

'Yes, yes, I suppose that would have struck me. After all, I arranged her hands. Put like that, effendi, it's obvious that she was wearing the ring when she – ah – she –'

'She died. Can you describe it?'

The dresser swallowed.

'A silver ring. Not of account. I've seen it quite often. Different girls wear it, pass it around. There are a lot of small pieces like that, not very special, that belong to the women in general, as it were. They wear them for a bit, tire of them, give them away. Frankly, I consider those sort of trinkets as beneath my notice – unless they are ugly, or spoil a composition, of course.'

'And you let her wear this ring to attend the sultan?'

'I thought it more prudent that she should keep the ring, than have an unsightly mark on her finger. I didn't mention it.'

The dresser turned and twisted involuntarily from side to side.

'I did right, chief, didn't I? It was only a ring. It was clean, silver.'

The Kislar Agha fixed him with a stare. Then with a shrug and a wave of his hand, he dismissed him from the room. The dresser backed out, bowing nervously.

The Kislar Agha picked up a peach and bit into it. The juice ran down his chin.

'Do you think he took it?'

Yashim shook his head.

'A bit of silver, why would he bother? But somebody took it. I wonder why?'

'Somebody took it,' the Kislar Agha repeated slowly. 'So it must still be here.'

'Yes, I suppose so.'

The black man leaned back and examined his hands.

'It will be found,' he said.

His excellency Prince Nikolai Derentsov, Order of Czar Peter, First Class, hereditary Chamberlain to the Czars of all the Russias, and Russian ambassador to the Sublime Porte, watched his knuckles whiten against the edge of his desk.

He was, as he would have been the first to admit, an extraordinarily handsome man. Now in his late fifties, well over six foot, his broad shoulders exaggerated by a high-collared, cutaway coat, his neck in a starched cravat, lace at his sleeves, he looked both elegant and formidable. He wore his steel-grey hair short, and his side-whiskers long. He had a fine head, cold blue eyes, and a rather small mouth.

The Derentsov family had found that life was expensive. Despite vast estates, despite access to the highest positions in the land, a century of balls, gowns, gambling and politics in St Petersburg had led Prince Nikolai Derentsov to the uncomfortable discovery that his debts and expenses greatly exceeded his income. His ability to attract a very beautiful young wife had been the talk of the late season – although beautiful young women are as common in Russia as anywhere else.

What animated the talk – what spurred the envy and congratulation – was that through his marriage the prince had also secured the benefit of her considerable fortune. Not that the people Derentsov moved among always put it that way. Behind his back they sniffed that the girl – for all her beauty – was Trade. Her father had made millions in fur.

'It appears that you have been careless,' Derentsov was saying. 'At my embassy I cannot afford to maintain people who make mistakes. Do you understand me?'

'I am so sorry, Your Excellency.'

The young man bent his head. Nikolai Potemkin certainly looked sorry. He *was* sorry, too: not for what he had done, which was not his fault, but because the chief was angry and unfair and sounded as if he were going to sack him on the spot. He had been here only two months, slipping from a dead-end desk job in the Russian army to the diplomatic on the back of an elderly relative's interest at court – a distant relative, the slenderest interest. The chance would not come again.

He was, like his chief, over six foot tall; but he was not handsome. His face, scarred from a sabre cut received in the Turkish war, had never healed well: a livid weal ran from the corner of his left eye to his upper lip. He was very fair, and his almost lashless eyes were watery and pale. In that struggle with a Turkish cavalier he had grappled the sabre with his bare left hand, and three of his fingers were now curled into a useless hook. Young Potemkin had come to understand that it was the diplomatic or . . . nothing. Five thousand acres on the borders of Siberia. A third-rate estate, shackled with debt, a thousand miles from anywhere at all.

Prince Derentsov drummed on the desk with his finger tips.

'The damage is done. In a few minutes we will talk to an emissary of the Sublime Porte. Let's get it clear. You met the men once. You spoke in French. You gave them a lift and dropped them – where?'

'Somewhere near their barracks, I'm not sure. I've only been out in the city a few times.'

'Hmph.' The prince grunted. 'Nothing else, understand? Very well.'

He rang a bell, and asked the orderly to bring in the Ottoman gentleman.

37

The Russians noted Yashim's appearance.

An insignificant fellow, the ambassador thought. No rank.

Junior Attaché Potemkin felt a surge of relief, struck by the thought that if the Turks themselves gave this interview such low priority, his chief could hardly rank his error as a sacking offence.

They watched Yashim bow. The ambassador did not offer him a seat.

'I'm grateful for your help today,' Yashim said. The prince sneered and looked away. Yashim caught the expression and smiled.

'We understand that Count Potemkin spent some time with four officers of the Imperial New Guard last week. You are Count Potemkin.'

Potemkin bowed.

'If I may ask, were you friends? You have not been long in Istanbul.'

'No. I still hardly know my way around.' Potemkin bit his lip: that was supposed to come later. 'We weren't friends. Just friendly.'

'Of course. Then you had met before?'

'Not at all. We met at the gardens, by pure chance. I suppose we were all slightly curious. We spoke, in French. I'm afraid my

French is not good,' Potemkin added.

Yashim saw no reason to flatter him.

'And you discussed – what?'

'To tell the truth, I hardly remember. I think I told them about this.' Potemkin raised his palsied hand to his face. 'War wounds.'

'Yes, I see. You are a man of experience in battle.'

'Yes.'

'What were you doing in the gardens?'

'Looking round. Taking a walk.'

'A walk? What for?'

'I thought maybe I could get some exercise. Somewhere quiet, where I would not attract so much attention.'

Yashim thought the mangled Russian could probably cause quite a stir in a city street.

The ambassador yawned, and prepared to stand.

'Is that all? I am sure we all have our duties to perform.'

Yashim bowed. 'I merely wanted to ask the attaché, how did he leave the gardens?'

The ambassador sighed, stood up, and waved a hand.

Potemkin said: 'We left together. I dropped them off, somewhere near the barracks, I think. I don't know the city well.'

'No, I understand. You took a cab?'

Potemkin hesitated and glanced at his chief.

'Yes.'

'How did you share the fare?'

'I'm sorry?'

'You dropped them off. I assume you came on here, to the embassy.'

'That's right.'

'So how was the cabman paid? Did you share the fare?'

'Oh, I see what you mean.' Potemkin ran his fingers through his hair. 'No, no, it was my treat. I paid. I was coming back anyway, as you say.'

'Can you remember how much? It might be very important.'

'I don't think so,' the ambassador intervened, in a voice of deep scorn. 'As I just said, we are all busy. So, if you will allow us –'

Yashim had turned to face the ambassador. He cocked his head slightly to one side and put up a hand.

'I am sorry,' he said, very deliberately. 'But I must insist. Count Potemkin, you see, was the last man to see the guards alive.'

The ambassador's eyebrows flickered for an instant. Potemkin's eyes widened.

'Good Lord!' he said. He did not look at Yashim.

'Yes, it is very sad. So you see, anything we can do to trace the men's last movements could be helpful. Such as finding the cab driver.'

It was a punt, Yashim thought. Not quite impossible.

'I am quite sure that Count Potemkin will not remember how much the cab cost,' the prince said smoothly. 'We do not encourage our officials to carry much money. Cabs are paid off by porters, at the entrance.'

'But of course,' Yashim said. 'I am afraid I have been stupid. The porters, naturally, would keep a record of their disbursements.'

The prince stiffened, realising his mistake. 'I will have Count Potemkin look into it. If we learn anything, of course we will inform you.'

Yashim bowed. 'I do hope the Count has no travel plans. It may be necessary to speak with him again.'

'I am sure there will be no need,' said the prince, gritting his teeth.

Yashim went out, closing the door.

The prince sat down heavily at his desk.

'Well!' he said.

Potemkin said nothing. The interview, he felt, had gone rather well.

He would not, after all, be going home.

Once outside the prince's office Yashim stood for a moment in the vestibule, frowning. A liveried footman stood to attention by the open mahogany doors. Lost in thought, Yashim walked slowly round the room until he found himself standing in front of a framed map which he pretended to examine, seeing nothing.

Nobody, he reflected, had asked him any questions. Was that odd? The work of an embassy was to pick up information; but they had shown no interest in his enquiry. They might have heard that the men were dead, true. But he said that Potemkin was the last man to see the men alive, and nobody asked him how he knew. It was as if the subject failed to interest them, and that was interesting.

Even more interesting, though, was the lie about the cab.

The lie – and the fact that the prince had known about it.

The fact that the prince himself had attempted to cover up.

'*Excusez-moi, monsieur.*'

Yashim turned. For once, he was almost nonplussed.

He hadn't noticed her come in.

Yet standing beside him now was the most beautiful woman he had ever seen.

∼≪ 39 ≫∼

'Madame,' he murmured. She was tall, almost as tall as him, and he guessed that this was the princess, the ambassador's wife, although he might have expected someone older. The princess looked barely twenty. Her hair was drawn up to reveal her slender neck and shoulders, though a few black ringlets danced exotically against her fair skin. He noticed the tips of her ears, the soft curve of her chin, the almost Turkish slant of her cheekbones. Her large black eyes sparkled.

She was looking at him with an air of amusement.

Yashim could hardly understand how the footman could stand there unmoved, when the most ravishing creature, dark-eyed, black-haired, her face seemingly sculpted from the virgin snow, glided in front of him unchaperoned. Was he blind?

'I am Eugenia, monsieur. *La femme de l'Ambassadeur le Prince.*'

The ambassador's wife. The ambassador's woman. Her voice was singularly low. Her lips barely moved when she spoke.

'Yashim,' he murmured. He noticed that she had extended her hand, the fingers pointing to the ground. As if in a dream he took it and pressed it to his lips. The skin was warm.

'You should be more adventurous, Monsieur Yashim,' she said, dimpling her cheek.

Yashim's eyes widened. He felt the blood rush to his face. 'I . . . I am sorry –'

'I meant, of course, looking at old maps of your city.' She looked at him again, with curiosity. 'You do speak French, or am I dreaming? Wonderful.

'The map? Interesting, of course – it's one of the first detailed maps of Istanbul ever made, shortly after the Conquest. Well, a hundred years or so. 1599, Flensburg, Melchior Lorich. All the same, I suggest we look at some of the paintings. Then, perhaps, you can form an idea of what *we* are like.'

Yashim was scarcely listening to what she was saying. The sensation he was experiencing was unlike any he had ever known before, and he recognised that it was not merely the effect of her beauty which produced it. Ordinary men might be staggered, he supposed, but for Yashim? Ridiculous! Beautiful women paraded by him every time he entered the sultan's harem.

He saw them, sometimes, all but naked: how often they teased him, with their perfumed breasts and full thighs! How they pleaded with him, these perfect creatures, for a stray touch of what was forbidden and unknown! Yet they always seemed to him, in some fundamental sense, to be clothed, veiled, forbidden.

Here was a woman almost fully dressed – though he gazed at her lips, at the hollow in her throat, at her bare slender shoulders. It was she who seemed the more naked.

Never, in a public room, had a woman spoken to him like this. Allowed him to touch her skin with his lips.

She laid a hand on his arm and led him along the paintings which hung on the wall.

'Tell me, monsieur, does this shock you at all?'

The hand shocked him.

They were standing in front of a family portrait of the Czar Alexander, his wife and children. It was an informal composition, in the French style: the czar seated beneath a tree in the sun, the czarina, like a ripe apple, leaning against him, and several small, fair boys in silk breeches and girls in white frocks grouped around them.

Yashim tried to examine the picture but yes, she was right.

'It does shock me, a little.'

'Aha!'

'Not the woman' – Yashim, you liar! – 'but the intimacy. It . . . it's so public. It makes a show of something that should be private, between the man and the woman.'

'So you do not believe in the representation of the human form? Or you would set other limits?'

Even her voice, he thought, was scandalous. Her curiosity was more like a slow caress, as if he were being explored, limb by limb.

'I'm not sure how to answer. When I read a novel I find, there, a representation of form. Also the same intimacy – and other states of emotion, too. In the novel they delight me. They seem shocking to me in some of these paintings. You will accuse me of being inconsistent.'

'I'll accuse you of nothing, monsieur. When you read – perhaps you possess the characters yourself? What passes between you and them remains private. But the paintings are very public, as you say.'

She looked at him shyly from the corner of her eye.

'You Turks, I think, understand a great deal about private matters.'

Yashim gazed wildly at the painting on the wall.

'Harem – it is forbidden, is it not?'

'But not to you, madame,' Yashim replied.

Eugenia stifled a little gasp of surprise. 'Oh? As a woman, you mean?'

'Of course. And by virtue of your rank, I have no doubt you could visit the sultan's own apartments, if you wished.' He saw the eagerness on her face, and half-regretted his remark.

'By invitation, surely?' Her voice was coaxing now.

'But I am sure that an invitation could be arranged,' Yashim answered thickly, wondering at his own behaviour. What was he doing?

'I had never thought of it,' she said quietly. 'By you?'

Yashim was about to reply when the door to the ambassador's office swung open and the prince appeared, followed by Potemkin.

'What the devil –' The oath froze on the ambassador's lips.

Eugenia gave him a small, cold smile.

'Monsieur Yashim and I were having a most interesting conversation. About art,' she added. 'Am I right?'

Yashim bowed slightly. 'Certainly, princess.'

The prince looked heavily from Yashim to his wife.

'The gentleman was on his way out,' he snapped. 'I am sure he is very busy. As are we all. Good day, monsieur.'

Yashim put a hand to his chest and inclined his head. Once again he kissed Eugenia's slender hand. She said: 'Forgive me for detaining you. I do hope we can continue our conversation another time.'

Her tone was impeccably ambassadorial. Cool. Disinterested.

But Yashim's fingers were hot where she had squeezed them lightly with her own.

At the baths he wanted heat, and more heat. When his head seemed banded with flaming hoops he let the masseur pummel him like dough and then plunged himself into the icy water of the frigidarium.

Later on his way home he fell upon the vegetable market in a sort of frenzy: his old friend George, the Greek vendor who arranged his wares like weapons in an armoury, or jewels on a tray, actually stepped out from behind his stall to lay a heavy hand on Yashim's arm.

'Slow. Slow,' he said in his bass profundo. 'You puts in this basket like a Greek robbers, this, that, everything. Say to George, what you wants to cook.'

He prised the basket from Yashim's hands and stood there massive and barrel-chested in his dirty tunic, hands on his hips, blocking Yashim's way.

Yashim lowered his head.

'Give me the basket, you Greek bastard,' he said.

George didn't move.

'The basket.'

'Hey.' George's voice was very soft. 'Hey.' Louder. He picked up some baby cabbages. 'You wants?'

Yashim shook his head.

'I understand,' George said. He turned his back on Yashim and began to unload all the vegetables from his basket. Over his shoulder he said: 'Go, buy some fish. I will give you a sauce. You kebabs the fish, some Spanish onion, peppers. You puts on the sauce. You puts him in the fire. You eats. Go.'

Yashim went. When he had the fish, he came back and George was crushing walnuts open with his hands and peeling cloves of garlic, which he put together in a twist of paper.

'Now you, effendi, go home and cook. The pepper. The onion. No, I don't take money from crazy mans. Tomorrow you comes, you pays me double.'

When Yashim got home he laid the fish and vegetables on the block and sliced them with a thin knife. The onions were sharp and stung his eyes. He riddled up the stove and chucked in another handful of charcoal. When he had threaded the pieces onto skewers he smashed the walnuts and the garlic with the flat of a big knife and chopped, drawing together the ever-dwindling heap with the flat of his hand until the hash was so sticky he had to use the blade to scrape it off his skin. He anointed the fish with the sauce and let it lie while he washed his hands in the bowl his housekeeper set out for him every morning and afternoon.

He laid the skewers over the dull embers and drizzled them with a string of oil. When the oil hissed on the fire he waved the smoke with a cloth and turned the skewers, mechanically.

Shortly before the fish was ready to flake from the stick he sliced a loaf of white bread and laid it on a plate with a small bowl of oil, some sesame seeds and a few olives. He stuffed a tiny enamelled teapot with sprigs of mint, a piece of white sugar and a pinch of Chinese tea leaves rolled like gunshot, poured in water from the ewer and crunched it down into the charcoal until its base bit into the glow.

Finally he ate, sitting in the alcove, wiping the peppers and the fish from the skewer with a round of bread.

Only then did he pick up the small folded note that had been waiting for him when he got home.

It was from the imam, who sent his greetings. He had done a little research, as well. In a firm hand he had written out the final verses of Yashim's Sufi poem.

Unknowing
And knowing nothing of unknowing,
They sleep.

Wake them.

Knowing,
And knowing unknowing,
The silent few become one with the Core.

Approach.

Yashim sat up and crossed his legs. Then he propped the window ajar, rolled himself a cigarette the way an Albanian horse-merchant had shown him how, with a little twist at one end and a half-inch of cardboard at the other, and drank a glass of scalding sweet mint tea while he read the verses through again.

He lay down on his side. Fifteen minutes later his hand snaked out and groped for the old fur that lay rumpled somewhere by his legs. He hauled it over his body.

In three minutes – for he was already half-dreaming – Yashim the eunuch was fast asleep.

The Polish Residency was favoured by the dark. As dusk gathered, even its railings seemed to shed their rust, while the ragged curtain of overgrown myrtles which sheltered the carriage-sweep from the eyes of the street jostled together more closely, bulking black and solid as the darkness deepened. Then empty rooms, long since uninhabited, where the plaster sifted in eddying scales from the ornate ceilings and settled on wooden floors that had grown dull and dusty through disuse, gave out false hints of life within, as if they were merely shuttered for the night. And as night fell, the elegant mansion reassumed an appearance of weight and prosperity it hadn't known for sixty years.

The light which flickered unevenly from a pair of windows on the *piano nobile* seemed to brighten as the evening wore on. These windows, which were never shuttered – which could not, in fact, be shuttered at all, owing to the collapse of various panels and the slow rusting of the hinges in the winter damp – revealed a scene of wild disorder.

The room where only a few hours before Yashim had left the Polish ambassador dithering over whether to open the bison grass or simply a rustic spirit supplied to him, very cheap, by Crimean sailors on the sly, looked as if it had been visited by a frenzied bibliophile. A violin lay bridge down on a tea tray. A dozen books, apparently flung open at random, were scattered across the floor; another twenty or more were wedged haphazardly between the arms of a vast armchair. Tallow dripped from a bracket onto the surface of a well-worn escritoire, on which was piled a collection of folio volumes and tiny glasses. It seemed as if someone had been searching for something.

Stanislaw Palewski lay on the floor behind one of the armchairs. His head was thrown back, his mouth open, his sightless eyes turned upwards towards the ceiling.

Now and then he emitted a faint snore.

The seraskier picked up a handful of sand and sprinkled it across the paper. Then he tilted the sheet and let the sand run back into the pot.

He read through the document one more time and rang a bell.

He had thought of having the notice printed for circulation, but on reflection he decided to have it simply transcribed, by hand, and delivered to the mosques. The imams could interpret it in their own fashion.

From the Commander of His Imperial Highness's New Guard in Istanbul, greetings and a warning.

Ten years ago it pleased the Throne to secure the peace and prosperity of the Empire through a series of Auspicious Acts, intended to extirpate a lying heresy and put an end to an abuse which His Imperial Highness was no longer prepared to tolerate. As by his wars, so by his acts, the sultan achieved a complete victory.

Those who, by dealing death, would wish to return the city to its former state, take heed. The forces of the Padishah do not sleep, nor do they tremble. Here in Istanbul, a soldier meets death with scornful pride, secure in the knowledge that he sacrifices what is unreal for what is holy, and serves the greater power of the Throne.

In all your strength you will be crushed. In all your cunning you will be outfoxed. In all your pride, humbled and brought forwards to face the supreme penalty.

Once again you will flee and be brought from your holes by the will of the Sultan and his people.

You have been warned.

The seraskier felt that he had made an effort to clarify the situation. Rumour was an insidious force. It had this in common with the passion for war: it could be, and needed to be, controlled.

Drill the men. Straighten the rumour. Keep the initiative and leave the enemy guessing. The eunuch suspected some kind of Janissary plot, but the seraskier had prudently decided to keep his terms vague. The implication was there, of course, between the lines.

A textbook approach.

The seraskier stood up and walked to the darkened window. From here he could look down on the city it was his duty to defend. He sighed. In daylight he knew it as an impossible jumble of roofs and minarets and domes, concealing a myriad crooked streets and twining alleyways. Now specks of lamplight blended in the dark, softly glowing here and there, like marshlight shimmering over a murderous swamp.

He curled his fingers around the hem of his jacket and gave it a smart tug.

43

Yashim's first waking thought was that he'd left a pan on the coals. He shot from the divan and stood unsteadily in the kitchen, rocking on his heels. He looked around in bewilderment. Everything was as it should be: the stove banked low, its hotplate barely warm; a stack of dirty pans and crockery; the blocks and knives. But he smelled burning.

From outside there rose a confused medley of cries and crashes. He glanced at the open window. The sky was lit with a glow like the early dawn, and as he watched an entire roofscape was suddenly picked out in silhouette by a huge roar of flame which shot upwards into the sky, and subsided in a trail of sparks. It was, he judged, barely a hundred yards away: one, maybe two streets off. He could hear the crack of burning timber, and smell the ashes in the air.

An hour, he thought. I give it an hour.

He looked round at his little apartment. The books ranged on the shelves. The Anatolian carpets on the floor.

'Ah, by the jewels!'

The blaze had broken out in an alleyway which opened out into the Kara Davut Sokaği. The mouth of the alley was blocked by a throng of eager sightseers, anxious householders, many of them bare-headed, and women in every stage of dishabille, though every one of them contrived to cover her nose and lips with a scrap of cloth. One woman, he noticed, had yanked up her pyjama jacket, exposing a delicious ripple of flesh around her belly while concealing her face. They were all staring at the fire, as if frozen.

Yashim looked around. In the Kara Davut, people were emerging from their houses. A man Yashim recognised as the baker was urging them to go back and fetch their buckets. He stood on a step beside the fountain at the head of the street, gesticulating. Yashim suddenly understood.

'Get these women out of here,' he shouted, prodding the men next to him. 'We need a line!'

He jostled the men: the spell that had fallen over them was broken. Some of them woke up to the sight of their women, half-dressed.

'Take them over to the café,' Yashim suggested. He intercepted a young man running forward with a bucket.

'Give me that – get another!' He swung the bucket to a man standing nearby.

'Form a chain – take this and pass it on!'

The man seized the bucket and swung it forwards, into a pair of waiting hands. Another boy ran up to Yashim with a loaded bucket. The back of the line needed attention, Yashim realised. 'You, stay here. Pass that bucket and be ready to take another.'

He darted back, seizing bystanders and hustling them into positions a few feet apart. More buckets were being produced; as fast as they came the baker swung them through the fountain and passed them down. Yashim ran along the chain, checking for gaps, and then on to the head of the line to make sure that empty buckets were being returned. For the first time he found himself in the alley.

The flames were gusting along the narrow street: as Yashim looked, a window burst in a shower of sparks and a long tongue of flame shot out and licked into the eaves of the neighbouring house. The flame retreated; but in a moment it had burst out again, tunnelled to its neighbour by the wind that was already being drawn like a bellow's blast into the narrow opening of the alley. Yashim, standing several paces back, could feel the wind ruffling his hair even as he felt the heat on the side of his face. He felt powerless. Suddenly he remembered what had to be done.

'A break! A break!' He darted into the nearest doorway and found a whole family working the well in the backyard. 'We must make a break – not here, across the street.' Nobody paid him the slightest attention: they were all busy fetching water, sloshing it onto the facade of their house which was already beginning to scorch and blister in the heat. 'An axe! Give me an axe!'

The man of the house nodded to a woodpile in the corner of the yard. With a jerk Yashim flipped the broad-headed splitting axe out of the log where it had been buried and dashed out into the street.

'A break!' he yelled, brandishing the axe. Several bystanders stared at him. He turned on them. 'Get your tools, people. We've got to take down this house.'

Without waiting for their reaction he whirled his body round with a shout and embedded the axe in the plaster infill. A piece the size of a hand fell away. He struck again: laths splintered and gave way. In a few minutes he had cleared a space large enough to wield an axe against the upright timbers. By now a few others had joined him: two men he sent through the house to check that there was no one still inside, and then to set to on the other side. He paused to catch his breath, leaning on the axe. The four men at work were stripped to the waist, the approaching firelight reflected in vivid glints in the sweat on their skin.

'Janissary work,' said one, through gritted teeth, as he chopped with the flat of his axe in short, savage blows against a tenon pin. The wooden pin was growing mashed at the end; the man made a few swift passes and cut it again, and with a heave on the flat of his axe sent it loose out the other side. Yashim gripped the pin and jerked it out.

The building gave a lurch. Several panels of plaster from the upper storey crashed down at their feet and exploded into a powder that was immediately whipped away by the rush of hot wind flaring down the street. Yashim glanced back. Two houses along, the fire was beginning to take hold. Sparks were flying past: one of the men he'd sent to the back of the house stuck his head out through a pair of uprights leaning at a drunken angle to the ground and hurriedly withdrew it. Everyone laughed.

'They'll be out in a moment. And none too soon,' a man said. They scented victory: their mood had changed.

Sure enough, the two men appeared suddenly on the other side of the frame and darted out through the collapsed doorway.

'To think we used to get the Janissaries from the Beyazidiye Pound to do this for us!'

They were enjoying themselves now. A slithering crash from overhead told them that the joists had sprung: the planking of the upper floor leaned at an angle that was already putting pressure on the roof supports, forcing them up.

'It's going wide!' Yashim bellowed. It was true: the whole frame of the house was sagging towards them, spinning around. 'Watch out!' Yashim backed, darted forward down the street away from the fire. The others followed. At twenty yards they stopped to watch the whole frame of the house take a sudden lurch into the street like a drunk wheeling from the wall. The roof tiles seemed to hang suspended in the air until, with a crash that could be heard over the crackling of the fire and the shouts from the upper end of the street, the edifice fell with a sudden *whump!* and a scouring plume of dust and fragments picked up by the wind billowed towards them like an angry djinn.

Yashim hit the ground, cradling his head in his arms: it was like a desert sandstorm flying overhead. Someone nearby screamed. He pressed his face into the dirt, even as the storm of debris began to ebb. A few pieces of broken tile skittered along the ground and harmlessly struck his arms.

Cautiously he peered up over the crook of his elbow. Further along the street the fire still raged: it had caught up with them now, and the shutters of the last house standing blew open with a force that sent them rocking wildly on their hinges. But the flames that shot from the casements darted out in vain. Where there had been wood and eaves, there was only a black gap and a few stray timbers dangling from a skinny beam.

Someone stooped and helped him to his feet. He recognised the man with the axe: they shook hands and then, because the excitement had been intense and the labour was won, they embraced, three times, shoulder to shoulder.

'You did us a favour, my friend,' the other man said. He looked like a ghost, his face blanched by the dust. 'Murad Eslek, me.'

Yashim grinned.

'Yashim Togalu.' Not Yashim the eunuch. 'At the sign of the Stag, Kara Davut.' And then, because it was true, he added: 'The debt is all mine.'

The note of cultivation in his voice caught the man by surprise. 'I'm sorry, effendi. In the dark . . . all this dust . . . I did not –'

'Forget it, friend. We are all one in the sight of God.'

Murad Eslek grinned, and gave Yashim the thumbs up.

⋘ 44 ⋙

Yashim stirred his coffee mechanically, trying to identify what still bothered him about the night's events.

Not the fire itself. Fires were always breaking out in Istanbul – though it had been a close-run thing. What if he had left the window shut – would the smell of smoke have reached him in time? He might have gone on sleeping, oblivious to the jagged screen of flame dancing its way towards his street: roused when it was already too late, perhaps, the stairwell filled with rolling clouds of black smoke, the windows shattering in the heat . . .

He thought of the crowd he'd seen that morning, the women and children standing dazed in the street. Dragged from their sleep. By God's mercy they, too, had woken up in time.

A phrase of the Karagozi poem leaped into his mind. *Wake them.*

The spoon stopped moving in the cup.

There was something else. Something a man had said.

Janissary work. *To think we used to get the Janissaries from the Beyazidiye Pound to do this for us.*

A Janissary fire-brigade had been stationed close to the Beyazit Mosque, the first and perhaps, in its way, the greatest of the mighty mosques of the sultans: for even Sinan Pasha, the master architect whose sublime Suleymaniyye surpassed Aya Sofia, acknowledged that the Beyazit Mosque had shown the way. But it wasn't the mosque which mattered: it was its position. For the Beyazit Mosque straddled the spine of the hill above the Grand Bazaar, one of the highest points in Stamboul.

A unique vantage point. So unique, in fact, that it was selected as the site of the tallest and perhaps the ugliest building in the empire: the Fire Tower which bore its name. The bag of bones had been discovered only yards away.

And there had been another Janissary watch, across the city, operated from the Galata Tower. The Galata Fire Tower. High over the drain which held the nauseating corpse of the second cadet.

And at the Janissaries' old centre of operations, the old barracks now razed and replaced with the imperial stables, there'd been a tower which Yashim could still vaguely recall.

Palewski had suggested that there could be a pattern to explain the distribution of the bodies – so if each body had been placed in the vicinity of an old fire-station, a Janissary fire-watch, a tower . . . Yashim probed the idea for a moment.

Fire had always been the Janissaries' special responsibility. It had become their weapon, too. People were roused from their beds by the firemen's tocsin. *Wake them.*

Where, then, had the other fire-station been? There were to be four corpses. There had to be four fire-stations. Four towers.

Perhaps, Yashim thought fiercely, he might still be in time.

The Kislar Agha had the voice of a child, the body of a retired wrestler and weighed eighteen stone. No one could have guessed his age, and even he was not completely sure when he had crawled from his mother's womb beneath the African sky. A few pounds of unwanted life. Another mouth to feed. His face was covered in dark wrinkles, but his hands were smooth and dark like the hands of a young woman.

It was a young woman he was dealing with now.

In one of those smooth hands he held a silver ring. In the other, the girl's jaw.

The Kislar Agha dragged the girl's head sideways.

'Look at this,' he hissed.

She closed her eyes. He squeezed his hand tighter.

'Why – did – you – take – the – ring?'

Anuk squeezed her eyelids shut, feeling the stabbing tears of pain. His fingers had caved in on the soft part of her mouth and she opened it suddenly very wide. His fingers slipped between her teeth.

She bit down hard. Very hard.

The Kislar Agha had not screamed for many years. It was a sound he had not heard himself since he was a little boy in a Sudanese village: the noise of a piglet squealing. Still squealing, he brought his left hand up between her legs, sagging slightly for a better grip. *Don't mark the goods.*

His thumb searched for the gate. His fingers stretched and encountered a tight bunch of muscle. His hand clamped shut, with iron force.

The girl gave a gasp and the Kislar Agha pulled himself free. He put his sore fingers under his armpit, but he did not let go.

He wriggled his fingers and the girl jerked her head back. The

Kislar Agha pressed harder. The girl felt herself being pressured to roll aside, and she obeyed the pressure.

The eunuch saw the girl flip over and fling out her arms to meet the ground. He gave a sudden pull with the pincer of his hand.

Panting now, he dropped to his knees and began to fumble at the folds of his cloak.

He'd forgotten all about the silver ring.

He remembered only the need for punishment, and the itch for pleasure.

≪ 46 ≫

Preen had found it hard to believe what the imam seemed to be saying. A revival of the Janissaries? New Guard cadets found murdered in despicable ways?

She picked up a pair of tweezers and began to pluck her eyebrows.

She wondered, looking into the mirror, if the imam's message had anything to do with the information she had brought her friend Yashim.

Murder.

Her heart skipped a beat.

Today she would take the line ever so slightly higher: she could always heighten the curve with kohl. She began to hum.

Nothing she'd heard in the mosque had anything to do with Yashim, or her, or that disgusting pimp.

She worked briskly with a practised hand along the arch of her brow, watching herself in the mirror.

But Yorg could be involved in anything. With anyone.

She'd only peddled a little ordinary gossip. It was nothing.

Though Yashim had been pleased. Gold dust, he called it.

But Yashim wouldn't tell. She moved her hand and began on the other eyebrow.

Yorg would tell. Yorg would tell *anything*, if he was paid enough.

Or frightened enough.

Preen sucked in her breath. The idea of Yorg being afraid was, well, scary.

She lowered her tweezers and snapped up a piece of kohl between their jaws. Carefully she started to thicken the line.

What would Yorg do, she wondered, if he heard about the murdered soldiers? Not at mosque. The Yorgs of this world heard nothing at mosque. They wouldn't even go.

But if he heard, and started putting two and two together?

The kohl wavered. The face in the mirror was very white.

He'd squeal, for sure.

◆ 47 ◆

Fire-officer Orhan Yasmit cupped his hands around his mouth and blew into them. It had been a filthy morning, not just because it was damp and cold but because the mist made it almost impossible for him to work properly. Who could spot a fire in this miasma? He could scarcely see across the Golden Horn.

He stamped a few times to warm up, then crossed the tower to the southern side and peered gloomily down towards the Bosphorus. On good days, the Galata Tower presented him with one of the finest views the city could afford, almost three hundred feet up above the Golden Horn, across to Stamboul with its minarets and domes, south to the Bosphorus and Üsküdar on the farther side – sometimes he could actually see the mountains of Gule, purple in the distance.

It was a solid tower of massive dressed stone, built by the Genoese almost five hundred years before, when the Greek emperor ruled in Byzantium and Galata was its Italian suburb. Since then it had survived wars and earthquakes – even fires. The face of the city had no doubt changed, as minarets replaced the spires, as more and more people settled in the burgeoning port, building their wooden houses cheek by jowl, fragile wooden houses crammed like dry tinder into the declivities of the seven hills. And they'd been kicking over their braziers, letting their candles tilt, sending out careless sparks for centuries, too. Hardly ten years ran by without some section of the city burning to the ground. That any of it still stood at all was a testament to the wisdom of the Genoese master-builders who erected the Galata Tower.

The trick with any fire was to catch it early, contain it quickly. And to use it wisely, in the Janissary days – to control and shape it to the Janissaries' best advantage. Orhan Yasmit was too young to have known those days personally, but he had heard the stories. Oh, the Janissaries put out fires – in the end.

Orhan Yasmit leaned on the parapet, wondering how much longer it would be before he was relieved. He looked down. He had no trouble with vertigo. He liked to watch the people bustling back and forth so far below him: with the sun on his back there were times when he came close to feeling like a flying bird, skimming the rooftops and the marketplaces. From above, in their turbans, the people looked like birds' eggs, rolling about beneath his feet: the foreigners with their small heads looked weird. More like insects.

Hearing footsteps, he eased himself off the parapet and turned around. He expected to see the duty fireman, but the man who stepped out onto the platform was a civilian, a stranger in a plain brown cloak. Orhan frowned.

'I'm sorry,' he said sharply. 'I don't know how you got in, but civilians aren't allowed up here.'

The stranger smiled vaguely, and looked around.

'Two pairs of eyes are better than one,' he remarked. 'I won't detain you.'

Orhan could make nothing of this.

'You might say that we're both working for the same service. I'm here for the seraskier.'

Orhan instinctively stood a little straighter.

'Well,' he said grudgingly, 'it's no use your being here anyhow. No one could see a thing on a day like this.'

Yashim blinked at the fog.

'No, no, I suppose not.' He went to the parapet and leaned out. 'Amazing. Do you often look down?'

'Not much.'

Yashim cocked his head.

'I expect you hear stuff, though. I've noticed that myself. The way sounds can carry much further than you expect. Especially upwards.'

'True.' Orhan wondered what all this was leading up to.

'Were you on duty the day they found that body?'

'I was on the night before. Didn't hear or see anything, though.' He frowned. 'What do you want up here, anyhow?'

Yashim nodded, as if he understood. 'This tower must have been here a long time.'

'Five hundred years, they say.' The fireman slapped a hand on the parapet. 'The Stamboul Tower, Beyazit, that's mostly new.'

'Mostly new?'

'There's always been a fire-watch over there, see, but the tower used to be shorter. Good look-out over the bazaar and such, but to the east you've got the mosque, haven't you, and that used to block the view that way. Didn't matter so much, not with the Janissary Tower beyond to cover the ground.'

'Ah. I thought there'd been another fire-tower there – above Aksaray?'

Orhan nodded. 'Proper job, by all accounts. Gone now, along with the tekke underneath and all the rest.'

'Tekke? What tekke do you mean?'

'Tekke, prayer-room, whatever. Like here, downstairs. For that Janissary Karagoz mumbo-jumbo. Oldest Karagozi tekkes in the city, apparently. That tower's gone now, like I said. Got burned down during the – well, a few years back, you know what I mean? So what they did was, they raised the tower at Beyazit. To get the lift, see, over the mosque? Must have doubled its height, I reckon – and all in stone, now, like this one. The old ones were wood, and kept burning down. So there you are, we've got the two towers as good as the old three. Better, really, being all stone.'

'I'm sure. Go on. Tell me about the fourth tower.'

Orhan gave the stranger a look.

'There isn't a fourth. Galata, Stamboul, that's it.'

'There must be another. Yedikule, maybe?'

'Yedikule?' The fireman grinned. 'Tell me who'd be sorry if Yedikule caught fire.'

Yashim frowned: the fireman had a point. Yedikule was the sink of the city, down in the south-east where the walls of Byzantium joined the sea. Apart from the dirt, and the feral dogs which prowled its mean, dark streets, the tanneries were there; also a grim edifice, old even when the Ottomans took Istanbul, known as the Castle of the Seven Towers, variously used as a mint, a menagerie and a prison, particularly the latter. Many people had died within its walls; still more had wanted to.

'But you can watch Yedikule from the new tower at Beyazit, effendi. Stamboul and Galata, like I told you. Cover the city.'

Yashim winced. The second verse of the poem swam into his head.

Unknowing
And knowing nothing of unknowing,
They seek.
Teach them.

He was obviously a slow learner.

'Look,' Orhan said affably. 'You can ask old Palmuk, if you like.'

A whiskered face appeared in the hatch. Palmuk was not really old, only perhaps twice Orhan's age, with thick white moustaches and a noticeable paunch. He came out of the hatch wheezing.

'Those bloomin' stairs,' he muttered. Yashim noticed that he was carrying a paper twist of sugared buns. 'No babies, then?' He winked at Yashim.

'Now, Palmuk, I don't think the gentleman wants all that. He is from the seraskier.'

Palmuk took the warning with an exaggerated roll of his eyes.

'Oho, old Frog's Legs, eh? Well, effendi, you tell him not to worry about us. We get cold, we get wet, but we do our duty, ain't that right, Orhan?'

'You might not think it, effendi,' Orhan said, 'but Palmuk's got the best pair of eyes in Galata. You'd think he could smell a fire before it's even started.'

Palmuk's face twitched. 'Steady, there, boy.' He turned to Yashim. 'You wondering about them babies I mentioned? It's fireman's talk, that is. Baby – that's a fire. A boy's a fire on the Stamboul side. We hang out the baskets that way' – he gestured to four huge wicker baskets leaning against the inside of the parapet – 'and that puts the lads in the right direction, see? A girl, that's Galata-side.'

Yashim shook his head. However long you lived, however well you thought you knew this city, there was always something else to learn. Sometimes he thought that Istanbul was just a mass of codes, as baffling and intricate as its impenetrable alleys: a silent clamour of inherited signs, private languages, veiled gestures. He thought of the soup master and his coriander. So many little rules. So many unknown habits. The soup master had been a Janissary once. He looked at Palmuk again, wondering if he, too, wore a tattoo on his forearm.

'You've been a fireman a long time, then?'

Palmuk stared at him, expressionless.

'Twelve, thirteen years. What's it about?'

Orhan said: 'Gentleman wants to know about another tower. Not the old barracks place. A fourth tower. I told him there wasn't one.'

Palmuk dug into his paper twist and took out a bun, looked at it, and took a bite.

'You did right, Orhan. You can cut along now, old Palmuk's in command.'

Orhan yawned and stretched. 'I could use a kip,' he said. 'Fire in?'

'Warm and bright, mate.'

With a happy sigh, and a small bow to Yashim, Orhan lowered himself down the hatch and went off to enjoy the brazier in the fireman's cuddy down below.

Palmuk took a turn round the walls, looking out and finishing his bun.

Yashim hadn't moved.

Palmuk leaned over the parapet and looked down.

'Funny,' he said. 'As you get older, you lose your head for heights. They ought to pay me more, don't you think?'

He looked back at Yashim, his head cocked.

'Know what I mean?'

Yashim eyed the fireman coldly.

'A fourth tower?'

Palmuk bent over a basket and wedged his cone of buns between the wickerwork. Then he stood looking out towards Stamboul. He appeared not to have heard.

Suppressing a sigh, Yashim fished for his purse beneath the folds of his cloak. Selecting three coins, he chinked them together in the palms of his hand. Palmuk turned.

'Why, effendi, I call that handsome. A welcome contribution to the Fund.'

The money disappeared into a pocket of his tunic.

'It's information you want, mate. Effendi. A hint to the wise, am I right? You've been handsome with me, so I'll be handsome with you, as the saying goes. All right: there isn't a fourth tower. Never was, as far as I know.'

There was a silence. The fireman ran a hand over his moustaches.

Their eyes locked.

'Is that it?'

The fireman shrugged. 'It's what you asked for, ain't it?'

'Right.'

Neither man moved for a few moments. Then Palmuk turned his back on Yashim and stood by the parapet, looking south to the Bosphorus, lost in the fog.

'Mind the stairs as you go down, effendi,' he said, not looking round. 'They're slippery when it's wet.'

48

'It's mine,' said the girl.

It was the only thing she'd said so far.

Yashim bit his lip. He'd been trying to talk to her for half an hour.

Lightly, at first. Where was she from? Yes, he knew the place. Not the exact place but . . . he drew her a picture in words. Mountains. Mist. Dawn creeping down the valley. Was that like it?

A blank.

'It's my ring.'

Heavy: we don't think it belongs to you. Serious suspicion, serious charge. Unless you tell us what you know it'll be the worse for you, girl.

'It's mine.'

Cajolery: come on, Asul. You have a life half the women in Circassia would die for. Whims granted. Luxuries. A safe and honourable and *enviable* position. A lovely girl like you. The sultan's bed and then – who knows?

She pushed out her lips and turned her head, threading a curl with her fingers.

Yanked the curl savagely, pressed her lips together.

'My ring,' she blurted.

'I see. She gave it to you?' Yashim asked gently.

'Don't believe a word,' the Kislar Agha interrupted. 'They all lie like hyenas.'

Yashim raised his shoulders and swallowed his irritation. 'Asul may answer as she pleases, but I hope it will be the truth.'

The kislar snorted. The girl flashed him a contemptuous look.

'She never gave it to me.'

'Um. But did you have some agreement, some understanding about the ring?'

The girl gave him a strange look.

'I don't know what you're talking about. What does it matter anyway? She's dead, isn't she? Fucking fish food. What does it matter if I took the ring?'

Yashim frowned. Did he have to explain the idea of theft? There was something particularly repugnant about stealing from a corpse. A sacrilege. If she didn't at least feel that, where could he begin?

'It may matter very much indeed. Was she dead or alive when you took the ring?'

But the gorgeous little face had clammed up again.

Yashim knew these mountaineers, raised among the far-off peaks of the Caucasus. Hard as their stony houses, as their frozen tracks in winter. Living on air, forever feuding with their neighbours. God had made them beautiful, especially their women: but he made them hard.

Wearily he put the question again. Alive? Or dead?

She made no response.

Perhaps she was right, after all. What did it matter? Yashim looked again at the ring in the palm of his hand. The dresser was right. It was no better than market tat, a plain band of silver, with a worn motif on the annulus which seemed to show two snakes swallowing each other's tails.

He glanced at the girl. She was wearing bangles, a torque: all gold. Not unusual here, in the harem, where gold and jewels from across the empire went to satisfy the cravings of the women for – what had the validé called it – distinction? Yet he knew how objects like these could take on a resonance no outsider could ever detect or guess at: how they could become the focus of spite or jealousy in spite of their intrinsic worthlessness, the cause of livid arguments, rages, tears, fights.

The sultan's women had been raised on the hardscrabble. What was death out there? Babies died. Women died giving birth to babies who died, and men got shot in the back for an unlucky word – or lived to be a hundred. Death was nothing: honour counted. In the mountain world they came from people took offence at the lightest word, and allowed feuds to develop into bloodshed over generations, long after their original causes were forgotten.

Was it possible, Yashim asked himself, for a feud like that to have been carried into the palace? The distance which separated the Caucasus from Istanbul was too great. More than geographical.

The snakes, what did they mean? Round and round they ran, forever swallowing their tails: a symbol of eternity, was it, derived from some impious mumbo-jumbo peddled by shamans in the mountains?

Yashim sighed. He had the feeling that he was stirring up problems where they didn't exist, making trouble where it wasn't needed. Wasting his own time. All he had achieved was to sharpen the animosity he detected flying between Asul and the Kislar Agha.

'That's it,' he said. He bowed to the black eunuch and, taking him by the arm, drew him aside. 'Five more minutes, kislar. Give me that. Alone.'

Looking into his bloodshot eyes, Yashim found it hard to know what he was thinking.

The kislar grunted.

'You are wasting your time,' he said. His eyes slid round to fasten on the girl.

'The lala will talk to you in private.' She glanced up, expressionless. 'You know what we expect.'

And he left the room.

Asul watched the door close, and very slowly turned her eyes to look at Yashim. He had the feeling that she had never looked at him until now. Perhaps never really registered his presence in the room.

'Here,' he said softly. 'Catch.'

The girl's eyes followed the ring through the air. At the last moment, with a movement snake-like in its speed, she put out a hand. She clenched the ring in her fist, balled against her chest.

'I've seen you before,' she said in a small voice.

Yashim blinked slowly, but said nothing.

Asul glanced down, and uncurled her fingers. 'He will take it from me again,' she said.

'But I will ask him not to,' Yashim said.

The girl almost smiled. A weary flicker of expression crossed her face. 'You.'

Yashim pressed his palms to his face. 'When you are hurt,' he began slowly, 'when you have lost something – or someone – it makes you sad, doesn't it? Sometimes change is good, and sometimes it makes us only want to cry. When you are young, it is hard to believe in pain or loss. But sadness is what makes us alive. The dead don't grieve.

'Even here, there is plenty of sadness. Even in the Abode of Felicity. The Happy Place.'

He paused. Asul had not moved, except to rub the ring slowly between her fingers.

'You don't have to say anything, Asul. Not now. Not to me. The sadness is yours, and only yours. But I want to give you something else, besides that ring.'

Asul raised her chin.

'Advice.' Yashim inclined his head, wondering how much he might say. How much she might understand. 'Nothing can be changed, Asul. The loss is never repaired, the pain is never fully over. That is our fate, as men or women.

'Bitterness is not a better kind of grief, Asul. Grief has its place, but bitterness invades a wound like rot. Slowly, bit by bit, it shuts you down. And in the end, even though you are alive, you are really dead. I've seen it happen.'

Asul pressed her lips together. She glanced downwards, blinking. 'Will I keep the ring?' Her voice was small, unsteady.

Yashim gazed at her, silent for a moment. A few minutes longer, and she would tell him what she knew. And with that single act of self-betrayal, perhaps, the bitterness would return.

He found the handle of the door.

'I will speak to the validé myself,' he said.

He needed to speak to her anyway, he thought. To fulfil a promise. To procure an invitation.

The seraskier clawed his way to the edge of the divan with his heels and clambered to his feet.

'You should have told me.' His voice was clipped, correct. 'I did not ask you to speak to foreigners. Unbelievers.'

Yashim, sitting on the divan, put his chin upon his knees.

'Do you know why I brought you in? Do you think it was because I wanted discretion?' He glared at Yashim. 'Because you're supposed to be fast. My men are dying. I want to know who is killing them, and I don't have a lot of time. It is one week exactly before the Review. Days have gone by, and you've told me nothing. You were quick enough in the Crimea. I want to see that right here. In Istanbul.'

The veins on his temples were pulsing.

'Poems. Taxi rides. They tell me nothing.'

Yashim got to his feet and bowed. When he reached the doorway, the seraskier said: 'Those meetings were fixed up by me.'

Yashim's cloak swirled. 'Meetings?'

The seraskier stood against the window with his hands behind his back.

'Meeting the Russians. I've made it my business to see that my boys get an education. Present arms and salute your superior officer! Fine. Learn how to load a breech gun or to drill like a Frenchman? That's the half of it. Someday we are going to be fighting the Russians. Or the French. Or the English.

'How do they think? How willingly do the men fight? Who are their heroes? You can learn a lot if you understand another man's heroes.'

The seraskier cracked his knuckles.

'I could pretend that none of that matters. There was a time when we met our enemies on the field, and crushed them underfoot. We were very good. But times have changed. We are not as fast as we were, and the enemy has become faster.

'We can't afford to ignore them – Russians, Frenchmen. Yes, even those Egyptians can teach us something, but not if we suck on narghiles here, in Istanbul, trying to imagine what they are like. It's for us to go out and learn how they think.'

Yashim scratched his ear. 'And you think your officers can learn all this by having coffee with the Russian military attaché?'

The seraskier thought: he is not a military man. Not a man at all.

He spoke with exaggerated precision. 'You asked me the other day if I spoke French. In fact I do not. Nowadays we have a book, a dictionary, which gives all the words in Turkish and French so that our men can read some of the French textbooks. This book never existed when I was young. Apart from the officers we engage to teach our men, I have never met a Frenchman. Or an Englishman or a Russian. And never, of course, any of their ladies. Of course not. I would not know how to –'

He broke off, gripping the air with outstretched hands.

'How to act. How to speak with them. You know? Thirty years ago the idea would not have occurred to me. Now I think about it all the time.'

146

'I understand.' Yashim felt a wave of pity for the seraskier, in his western kit, his efficient boots, his buttoned tunic. These were symbols he endured, not knowing exactly why, like one of those simpletons in the bazaar who feel that no medicine is good unless it causes them some pain. Magic boots, magic buttons. Ferenghi magic.

'Things are moving fast. Even here.' The seraskier rubbed a hand across his chin, watching Yashim. 'The sultan recognises that our military review presents him with an opportunity. Next Monday, all the city will be watching. People will see the banner of the Prophet at the head of the troop. The jingle of cavalry, brightwork sparkling, beautiful mounts. There'll be the deep lines of soldiery, marching in step. Whatever they think of us now, they'll be moved. They will be impressed, I'm sure of that. Better still, it's going to make them proud.'

The seraskier raised his chin with the population, and his nostrils flared as if pride were something he already smelled in the air.

'To coincide with the display, the sultan will issue an Edict. An Edict that will move us all along in the direction he wants us to take. It is up to us to support him. To try and learn the good things that the infidels can teach us now. Even, as you say, by having coffee with the Russians.'

But Yashim had stopped listening. 'An Edict?'

The seraskier lowered his voice.

'You may as well know. Changes will be made in many areas. Equality of the people under a single law. Administration. Ministers instead of pashas, that sort of thing. It will follow the way the army has been reformed on western lines, and it will not be enough. Naturally.'

Yashim felt flattered. What did he really know about anything? In six days, an imperial Edict. An order for change. With an effort he pushed the thoughts that crowded in aside.

'Why the Russians? Why not send our boys to have tea with

the English? Or drink wine with the French ambassador?'

The seraskier rubbed a hand across the back of his enormous neck. 'The Russians . . . were more interested.'

'And that didn't strike you as being suspicious?'

'I'm not naive. I took a risk. The boys from the Guard were . . . what shall I say? Sheltered. I thought it safer for them to make some mistakes now, in Istanbul, than to be ignorant later, on the battlefield.'

Yet they might have survived a battle, Yashim thought.

In Istanbul they didn't have a chance.

The man who kills in the dark is not afraid of darkness.

He waits for it. It is reliable, it always comes.

Darkness is his friend.

His feet were bare, to make no sound. He knew he would make no sound.

Years ago, he was one of the Quiet Men. One of the elite. Now he watched the daylight ebb from the grating that lay overhead. In four hours' time he would lift the grating as easily and silently as a feather, and begin his work. But now he would wait.

He remembered the day of selection. The colonel had sat with a rose on his lap and a blindfold over his eyes at the centre of the barracks hall and dared the men to approach him, one by one. To lift the rose – and return to their place. The reward: a commission in the sappers.

The stone floor of the hall was strewn with dried chickpeas. Nobody had the dexterity and the patience that he had. His self-control. One or two others reached the rose: but their eagerness betrayed them.

They taught him how to move in the dark, making no sound. It was easy.

They taught him how to live underground. They buried him alive, breathing through a cane.

They explained to him how shadows worked, what the eye could see, the difference between movement and movement.

They ordered him to be a shadow. Live like a rat. Work like a miner. Kill like a snake.

Patience. Obedience. Time, they said, is an illusion: the hours pass like seconds, seconds can seem like lifetimes.

Inch forward under the enemies' lines. Burrow into his defences like a rat. Listen for the enemy sappers, the counter-mines, the creaking of the props. Absorb the dark like a second skin. Kill in silence.

And if he was captured – it happened, that far forward of the lines – say nothing. Give nothing.

They didn't talk much anyway. That suited him, too, he'd never been a talker. The sappers were the Quiet Men.

He hadn't needed friends when he had the corps. He belonged. He shared faith. And the faith carried him through, didn't it? Through the cramped tunnel. Beyond the cramped muscle. Over fear and panic into the timeless and immobile centre of all things.

Then came the Betrayal. The shelling of the barracks. Dust, falling masonry, splinters of stone. A wall that hung in the air before it fell. He remembered that moment: an entire wall, thirty feet high, blown from its foundations and sailing, hanging in the air.

He remembered how it flexed and buckled like the flanks of galloping horse. As if the air itself was thick as water. It was a moment that seemed like an eternity.

It gave him ample time, then, to seek the hollow and roll up into it.

Like a man entombed. But not dead. Breathing through an aperture in the rubble. Working the rubble gradually from head to toe like a worm coming up for the dew.

The grating overhead was now invisible. The sapper could see it, though, by moving his head just a fraction of an inch. By using the light that no one else could see.

He raised his chin. This was the time.

Patience was all that mattered.

Obedience was all that mattered.

People would die. People had to die.

Only death could sanctify the empire's rebirth.

Only sacrifice could cleanse and protect the holy shrines.

The four pillars of the Karagozi.

The assassin felt in his pouch. He touched the ground with the palm of his hand.

And then, like a cat, he began to move.

Yashim leaned forward and fixed his eyes on page thirty-four of *Les Liaisons Dangereuses*. But it was no use. The book had been open on the same page for half an hour.

Whose law would it be? Would it be like the Frankish laws, which allowed the Greeks to have a country but denied the same convenience to the Poles? And would it work as well in the highlands of Bulgaria as in the deserts of Tripolitana?

The necessary leap? Perhaps. A single law for everybody, regardless of their faith, their speech, their parentage. Why not? He doubted that such a thing was sacrilegious, but then . . . plenty of others would think it was.

As he resolved these questions in his mind, Yashim wondered who else, precisely, knew about the Edict. The sultan and his viziers, of course. High-ranking dignitaries like the seraskier himself, no doubt. The religious leaders – the Mufti, the Rabbi, the Patriarch? Probably. But the rank and file – priests and imams, say? No. And not the common people of the city. For them it was to be a surprise. As it had been for him.

He snapped the book shut, and closed his eyes, leaning back on the divan.

In the past few hours he had thought this through a dozen times. There was going to be trouble, he could be sure of that.

But there was something else, wasn't there?

Something he knew was there, like a face in the crowd. Something he'd missed.

53

The man sat suddenly upright.

The assassin thought: *he smells me*. It made things more interesting. He'd been trained to infiltrate like an odour, not as a man. Now the odour clung to him.

The man sniffed.

Click.

Very slowly the man got to his feet. A knife in his hand.

Now where had that come from?

The assassin smiled. He felt for his pouch. His fingers closed on something hard.

The man with the knife stood crouching, craning his neck.

'Who's that? What do you want?'

The assassin didn't move.

A breeze caught the tattered curtain at the window and it

flapped. The man with the knife wheeled round, then back again. He peered into the dark.

He craned his neck. Very slowly he turned his head.

He was trying to hear.

The assassin waited. Watching.

The man's head moved through the midway point of its turn.

The assassin flicked his wrist and the cord snaked out. He plucked it back with a fierce grunt and the man with the knife was jerked off balance, scrabbling with both hands at his neck.

The assassin gave the cord another savage tug.

The man started sawing at the air, searching to cut the cord. The assassin stepped out of the shadows and pushed him down. He caught the knife-wrist and wedged his thumb between the tendons: the knife clattered to the floor as the hand spasmed open.

The assassin was astride him now. He put a hand to his belt and slid out a wooden spoon.

The man on the floor was choking.

The assassin slackened the cord for an instant. His victim gave a shuddering gasp, but it was a false respite. The assassin slipped the wooden spoon beneath the cord and began to twist it round.

⋘ 54 ⋙

A fat man, eager for sleep, felt himself rolled off the bed and hit the ground. He opened his eyes and saw a pair of women's feet.

'All right, petal? Here's your kit. Shove it on, love, I'm done. Go on.'

The fat man scrambled blearily into his robes. Get out, he thought. Five on the table, he'd be gone before she knew.

The woman watched him scurry through the door.

She was done for the night. Done with outside business, anyhow. No one would come now.

Upstairs would know the final customer had left. She was left with one more trick to turn, the worst.

Carrying her lamp she climbed the stairs. At the top she paused, hearing nothing.

Very slowly she pushed the door ajar. The room smelt terrible.

Silently she put in her head. She stretched out her hand, carrying the little lamp, and the shadows started to flicker round the room.

Months ago, the woman had lost her faith in God. She had begged, she had prayed, she had pleaded with Him night after night, and every dawn had brought the same answer. So she cursed him. Nothing changed. In the end, she had forgotten Him.

But what she saw now was like a revelation.

'Thank God,' she said.

⚜ 55 ⚜

Yashim went down to the water stairs at first light, still clutching the note which the kadi had written shortly after the morning prayer. By the time he was settled in the bottom of the boat, the note was limp with the exhalations of Istanbul's morning damp, between fog and drizzle, but he didn't need to read it again.

While the rower dragged busily at his heavy sculls and sent the caique skimming towards Seraglio Point, Yashim drew up his knees on the horsehair cushion and automatically let his weight settle on his left arm, to trim the fragile boat. A wooden spoon, the kadi had written: having seen the bag of bones and wooden spoons tipped out over his floor only yesterday, the coincidence had inspired him to inform Yashim.

Twenty minutes later, the rower turned the caique and backed it neatly against the Yedikule stairs in a flurry of backstrokes and shouts.

As soon as Yashim saw the little man sprawled face down in the mud with a wooden spoon bound tightly to the back of his neck he knew that this was not the fourth cadet. The corpse's hands were by his ears, his knees slightly bent, and there was a curve in his back which made him look, Yashim thought, as if he were simply peering down into a hole in the mud.

Yashim rolled the corpse over and looked at its face.

The staring eyeballs. The protruding tongue.

He shook his head. The night watchman, who had been squatting close to the body for several hours, spat on the ground.

'Do you know him?'

The night watchman shrugged.

'Fings 'appen, innit?' He glanced over at the corpse, and brightened. 'Yer, good lad an' all. Did some blokes a favour. Women, y'know, and all that.'

He scratched his head.

'Mind you, fackin' tough.' His simple mind slipped into the reverse key. 'Bit too 'eavy, if you ask me. They didn't like 'im, not the women.'

Yashim sighed.

'These women. Are you saying he ran a brothel?'

'Yeah. Funny lookin' geezer, too.'

Yashim walked away, squelching in mud up to his ankles. Up on the quay he saw the entrance to a courtyard and picked his way across a scattering of rubbish to a pump. He cranked the handle. A thin trickle of brown water dribbled from the spout.

People were stirring in the apartments around the courtyard. A shutter banged and a woman leaned out of an upstairs window.

'Hey, what you doin'?'

'I'm washing my feet,' Yashim muttered.

'I'm chuckin' this bucket, so watch out.'

Yashim beat a hasty retreat, the mud still clinging to his feet. What a foul district this was!

He walked around the corner, hoping to find a cab or a sedan chair. Every doorway seemed to have its ragged beggar or snoring drunk: some of them stared blearily at Yashim as he walked past. The bars were supposed to close at midnight, but Yashim knew that they tended to stay open for as long as anyone had money to spend, finally pushing them into the street when their purses were empty and their guts were full. He couldn't understand the attraction. Preen had once argued with him, saying that she enjoyed the bars, their mixture of happy and sad.

'Except for drunks, you can never tell who you'll meet, or why they're there. Everybody has a story. I like stories,' she had said.

Too many of those stories ended like this, Yashim felt, soaking up your own vomit in a cold doorway. Or head-down in the mud, dead, like that crookbacked brothel keeper he'd just seen, maintaining the tone of the neighbourhood.

Hadn't Preen mentioned speaking to a hunchback?

A sleazy port-rat who made her feel dirty.

Who told her about the cadets meeting the Russian up at the Yeyleyi Gardens.

Her informant.

And down in the mud, freshly dead, a crookbacked pimp.

Not the victim, by any stretch of the imagination, of a crime of passion. The blow that fell too hard. The carving knife that simply came to hand.

No. It had been a professional killing. Someone who killed with a length of cord – and a wooden spoon.

Yashim broke into a run.

56

Every city has districts which teeter on the fringes of respectability, which have nothing to do with their proximity to the moneyed and desirable centre. However roomy the houses, however convenient they seem, they are always tainted in some indefinable way by the incessant passage of other people: people who take their lodgings by the week, or even by the night; people who come and go, and may or not come back again, and whose purposes are too fleeting and too diffuse to be properly understood. Nobody asks. Nothing is assumed. Services are paid for in advance, and trust is at a premium. Prices are always a bit higher than elsewhere, but the clientele are happy to save themselves a walk, or know no better, being strangers.

Preen, however, was something of a fixture, and paid rent accordingly. Her landlord had nothing to complain of: he barely knew of her existence, being sent out to a café where all day he played backgammon with other old fellows and was only asked back if his wife needed to vet a new applicant or frighten a recalcitrant lodger. Guarding her modesty, Preen's landlady conducted most of her business by shrieking from behind a latticed screen at the foot of the stairs. There was a small window people could use to pay her: they held the money by the hole and she would snatch it up. If she needed to take a look she could press her eye against the lattice-work. Her own room behind was fairly dark.

At the moment she was watching a small black man struggling with a yoke, from which hung two swaying china pots. Paying no attention to the eyes he knew were watching him behind the screen, the man carried his burden past the door and ran bow-legged into the court outside. The landlady followed his movements with envy and irritation.

It wasn't that the landlady wanted to haul slops to the drain every morning. It was that the little black man she had engaged to perform the task knew everything that was going on before she did.

The slop-carrier returned with his empty pots and set them down in a row beside the others to dry. He faced the lattice.

'Three gents in number five. Eight not slept in, but it smell werry bad.'

The landlady sucked in her lips and pushed them out again. Number five was let for the week, to a single gentleman. She'd have it out with him when they tried to sneak out later on. As for number eight, it wasn't the first time she'd stayed out overnight. A bad smell was the reason she discouraged her tenants from bringing food into the premises.

If she had time, she thought, she'd go and get rid of whatever was festering in Preen's room.

A man came in at the door. She recognised him as a friend of number eight.

She rapped on the lattice with her knuckles.

'You can save yourself the stairs,' she croaked, in what she hoped was a kindly tone. Number eight was her best tenant. 'Gone out.'

Yashim squinted at the lattice.

'Gone out this morning, you mean?'

It was an unlikely idea. The slop-carrier picked up a mop and began to poke it around the corridor, grinning.

'Whatever,' the landlady replied. 'She's not there now. I can let her know you called, effendi.'

'Yes, thank you. And give her this message, will you?' He tore a leaf from a little notebook he carried, scribbled a few words and folded it. The flap in the lattice dropped down and a withered hand shot out to take the paper.

'It's important she gets this as soon as possible,' Yashim added. 'You don't know where she's gone?'

'I'll see she gets it,' the landlady said firmly.

Yashim hesitated. Was there anything else he could do? He thought of going up to leave a message in her room, but it was too late for that. The crone at the lattice had the message, and the black servant had already wetted the corridor floor ahead.

He bid the lattice good-day, and went out into the street.

57

It was already dark when Preen got back to her boarding house. Not that she had done very much that day: the action had taken place last night, at a stag-night where alcohol had been served and Preen had agreed to take a drink herself, after the dancing. It broke one of her cardinal rules, but even cardinal rules are made to be broken, she'd thought, as one drink became two and the groom-to-be asked her agitated questions about the wedding night.

So she'd ended up staying over, sleeping late, and waking up with a hangover. The other guests had left long since, taking the groom with them: she had a faint recollection of hearing stifled laughter and groans in the early morning, before she rolled over and went back to sleep. A very fat Armenian woman, sniffing with disapproval, had made her some coffee, and she had spent the rest of the day at the baths with a towel over her head.

She'd stopped for a pastry on the way home, but the hangover had taken away her appetite and she only nibbled at the corner before she asked the vendor to wrap it. It was in her bag now, but really she only wanted to go upstairs and sleep. She pushed the door, and her landlady rapped immediately on the lattice.

'Message for you,' she screeched. The flap dropped, and Preen saw her hand shoot out clutching a folded note.

'Thanks,' she said. 'May I have a light?'

'Urgent, he called it. It was that gentleman of yours who came by the other day. Nicely spoken. Here you are.'

She means Yashim, Preen thought as she took the candlestick. As usual, the candle was only a stub: the landlady was careful with things like that. She wondered if she should turn around and try to find Yashim right away: she certainly wasn't going to be able to read the note, but she didn't want the landlady to know that.

Perhaps, if she hadn't been standing at the foot of the stairs with the candle, she would have gone to look for Yashim. Or if the landlady hadn't added, in what passed for a confidential undertone, that she'd be grateful if everyone would remember not to take food upstairs – the smell in her room had disturbed the help.

Preen climbed the stairs slowly. At this time of year there was a perpetual draught in the old house and the stubby candle needed shielding. On the second floor she turned left down a low corridor past two doors, both shut and silent within, to reach the tiny, crooked flight of stairs that led to her own door. Gradually she mounted, following the sharp twist she never liked because it somehow put her at odds with the rest of the house, shutting her in. She glanced up and saw the door. In the narrow stairwell the shadows flickered like a troop of wild monkeys.

She stopped and sniffed. There was a smell, just as the landlady had said. For the first time she wondered what it might be. Perhaps a rat had died under the floorboards. She shuddered, and put out her finger.

And that was something else she didn't like about those stairs, about that door: having to reach into the dark hole to finger the latch on the inside.

It was like sticking her finger into a dark mouth.

❧ 58 ❧

Yashim had returned to the Imperial Archives after leaving his message with Preen's landlady. In daylight, with a weak winter sun filtering through the high windows, the place looked more ordinary, the atmosphere flatter. There was another reason for the change, too. Several archivists were in attendance, but Ibou the Sudanese boy was not among them. The Library Angel, Yashim thought.

The head archivist was a mournful fellow with drooping moustaches, not a eunuch but a superannuated graduate of the palace school.

'The divan is in session,' he explained gloomily. 'Come back this afternoon.'

But Yashim did not want to come back that afternoon. 'This is urgent,' he said.

The archivist stared at him with sad eyes. He looked infinitely put-upon, but Yashim suspected he was merely lazy.

'Help me now. You can break off if any orders come from the viziers' council.'

The archivist nodded slowly, blowing out his cheeks.

'Put your request in writing. We'll see what we can do.'

Yashim leaned his elbows on the reading desk and chewed at a pencil. Eventually he wrote:

'Istanbul fire-towers. Location details.' And then as an after-thought he added: 'Summaries of renovation/maintenance costs 1650–1750,' as being more likely to turn up what he wanted to know.

The archivist acknowledged the paper slip with a brief grunt but made no effort to read it. It lay on his desk for over twenty minutes while he thumbed through a quarto volume of figures and Yashim paced to and fro by the entrance. Eventually he picked it up, glanced at it, and rang a bell.

His subordinates moved in imitation of their master's ponderous ennui, shaking their heads and glancing up at Yashim now and then as if they suspected he had come merely to try their patience. At long last one of them disappeared into the stacks. He was gone about an hour.

'Nothing specific on location. There are two volumes of accounts, which refer to the fire-service in general. They straddle your stated time-frame. Do you want to see them?'

Yashim mastered an urge to pull the man's nose.

'Yes, please,' he said evenly.

The archivist shuffled off. He came back with two surprisingly small books, smaller than Yashim's own hand and bound in blue cloth. The older book, which roughly speaking covered a period from the beginning of the seventeenth century to 1670, was quite badly worn, and the signatures which bound the pages together were so badly rotted that pages slipped from position in clumps, threatening to slide out of the covers altogether.

The archivist frowned.

'I'm not sure we can allow you to examine this one,' he began.

Yashim exploded.

'I haven't waited all morning to be told I'm incapable of keeping a few pages of a book in order. I'm going to look at the book here, on the bench. Not fan it about, or shake it, or chuck it in the air.'

Yet the books proved to be a disappointment. After half an hour Yashim had only turned up three references, two dealing with the Stamboul Tower, which had burnt down twice, and the other referring only in the vaguest way to the fire-towers, without numbering or naming them. Entries had been made in the books by many hands, which made the business of deciphering some of the older entries in particular both exacting and frustrating.

It was while he was trying to make out an entry written in particularly antiquated script that Yashim suddenly thought of his message to Preen. He had written it clearly enough, and if she followed his advice she would be probably be safely tucked up in some corner of the café in Belol Oglu, waiting for him and challenging the men to stare. That thought made him smile, but the smile died suddenly.

He had written Preen a warning, making his instructions clear. Stifling the poetics of the written word, exaggerating the loops of his script, he'd written a few lines that anyone could read, even a child.

Even, but only.

Only a literate child.

❧ 59 ❧

Preen poked her finger into the little black hole in the door and crooked it, feeling upwards for the slim wooden latch.

She felt it resting against the edge of her nail, and clicked it up. As the door swung open a sudden draught, laden with the unpleasantly sweet smell of rotten meat, snuffed out the candle in her hand. She gave a small cry of dismay and stepped backwards in the dark.

The swinging door struck against the side wall. At the same moment Preen felt something brush across her face, with a whirr like an insect against her skin. She jerked her head back, stumbled, and lost her footing on the top step of the darkened stairs. She fell with a crash, ricocheting off the back wall and plunging sideways down the narrow stairs.

Preen landed in a bruised tangle, her face pressed against the corridor floor. Her right arm throbbed. For a few seconds she did not move, hearing only the sound of blood pulsing in her head and the gasp of her own breath. In the darkness it sounded shockingly loud.

But then came a muffled crack behind her on the stairs, close to her feet, like the sound of someone testing their weight on a wooden step.

The sound of someone joining her in the dark.

Somebody was coming down the stairs, from her own room.

With a convulsive jerk, she pulled up her legs and somersaulted out into the corridor. As her weight fell upon her arm a jolt of pain seared upwards through her shoulder into her neck and she opened her mouth to scream.

But then the sound died on her lips.

 60

Yashim, mounting the stairs two at a time, heard the crash of Preen falling backwards, and at the top of the stairs he grabbed the wall and swung himself round the corner into the corridor. The darkness disoriented him. He heard another movement in the passage and shouted:

'Preen!'

Without hesitation he took two steps into the dark. Only two – but they saved his life. He had got no further when he was suddenly smashed backwards with a force that seconds earlier would have catapulted him down the stairs. He felt a savage blow to his face and the breath knocked out of his lungs as he was hurled back against the wall.

Two things flashed through his mind as he retched for air. One, that he was already too late. Another, that the killer who had struck him and who was at this very moment flinging himself down the darkened stairs, flight by flight, was not going to get away easily.

He put out a hand and gripped the banisters. The movement seemed to let air back into his chest; another brought him to his feet. For a moment he stood, heaving, and then with an oath he plunged down the stairs.

He reached the corridor on the ground floor and tore out of the entrance into the street, where he swivelled and glanced about. A black man he recognised from the morning lay sprawled in the dust, still holding two chamber pots aloft in either fist. He jerked his head and swung a pot over his shoulder. Yashim began to run.

There were still many people about, and while it was hard to see how many, or where they were until he was almost upon them, because it was very dark, something in the way people shrank back at his approach told Yashim that he was on the right track. A man runs through a crowd, he thought, and the crowd instinctively expects another, on his trail: quarry and hunter, the pursued and the pursuer, old as man himself, older than Istanbul. A picture of two snakes swallowing each other's tails swam in his mind. He ran.

He reached the corner of the street and plunged left, guided by a sharp rage and an instinctive urge to climb, to take to the higher ground. Figures shrank away at his approach. At a corner lit by the torches of a coffee-house he caught sight of people turning their heads back to focus on him and he thought: *I'm closing*. But the streets were narrowing again. At a junction of three alleyways he almost paused, and almost lost his way: but then a faint something in the air, a sickly-sweet trace he had smelled before but couldn't identify, gave him the lead he sought and, ignoring a well-lit empty alley and another he thought he recognised as a cul-de-sac, he plunged down the darkest and the meanest of them all. Whether he was trailing by instinct, or magic, or by signs he could not even pause to decipher – a faint incline, a preference for the dark over the light, an unreasoned and unexamined knowledge of the difference between a street and a dead-end which he had imbibed, as it were, from years of living in Istanbul – he did not know: had he stopped to think he would have stopped altogether, for the breath was flying to his lungs like an angry lizard: he could feel its scales upraised, its scrabbling claws.

He swerved to the wall and flung out his hand to meet it and stood for a few seconds, breathing heavily. Ahead, lights flickered and glittered red in the darkness, a string of little street shrines lit by candles glowing behind the coloured glass. He guessed where he was. And at that moment he realised, too, where he was going.

And he ran on with such a fierce, formless and glowing conviction that at the next alley he swerved suddenly to the right and almost knocked a man to the ground.

It was a glancing blow, shoulder to shoulder, but it made the man wheel; and as he wheeled, Yashim turned his head and caught sight of his face. It contained, he saw, a whole range of expressions – anger, confusion, and a spark of sudden recognition.

'The fire!' The man cried out, almost with a laugh.

Yashim waved an arm and sped on, but the man was at his back. 'Effendi!'

Yashim recognised the voice. And at that very moment the alley made a sudden shallow curve and a light was burning at its far end: and right in his line of sight he caught a glimpse of what he already knew had been in his mouth all along, like the tail of a snake: a fleeting glimpse of a man who disappeared.

A voice came from behind: 'I saw him! Let's go!'

Yashim glanced sideways as the other man, fresh to the chase, loped up at his shoulder.

'Murad Eslek!' He panted. Yashim remembered the street on

fire, the man black with soot who grinned and shook his hand.

Reaching an alley which offered a choice to run right or left, Yashim hesitated. He seemed to have lost his sense of direction: Eslek's sudden appearance confused him. He was aware that he had been running for a long time. He sensed he was very close – but he felt his own anger and confusion, pounding heavy-footed down an ordinary alleyway in Istanbul. What he had taken for inspiration had suddenly resolved itself into commonplace: it had become no more than coincidence.

'The tanneries!' Yashim gasped. The scent had both eluded and directed him for what seemed like hours. He had smelled it the moment Preen's killer made explosive contact with him at the head of the stairs. It had drawn him along the streets, sucked him instinctively into alleyways, urged him left and right and now, within sight of his prey, it enveloped him.

Doggedly, feeling the weight on his feet for the first time, Yashim trotted left at a junction of mean alleys. Even in the darkness he could see that the walls around him were not continuous. Here and there a dim glow told him that he was passing a dwelling of some sort, but for the most part he moved in darkness where the lane bled out into scrub, and goats and sheep were tethered and corralled into flimsy yards. He heard them shift, with a low tinkle of bells; once he stumbled into a gate where the lane curved. His companion had long since dropped away: his quarry was nowhere to be seen. Nowhere to be sensed.

The reek of the tanneries had blotted him out.

≪ 61 ≫

The first thing Yashim noticed, after the stench he was forced to suck down into his heaving chest, was the light.

It rose in eerie columns from the vats into which, across an area of several acres, the animal skins were lowered for boiling and dyeing. Against a forest of flickering torches, each vat threw out a spume of coloured vapour, red, yellow and indigo blending and slowly dissolving into the darkness of the night air. The air stank of fat, and burned hair, and worst of all the overreaching odour of dog shit used to tan the leather. A vision of hell.

A hell into which Yashim's quarry had disappeared.

Yashim dropped to one knee and took a careful look around.

He'd heard about the tanning yard, and smelt it, too, but this was the first time he had seen it with his own eyes. A high wall enclosed a space about the size of a football field, and crammed together, almost touching at the rim, the vats lay embedded in a raised floor of clay and cement, which glinted greasily in the torchlight, and allowed the tanners to walk between them and stir their bubbling contents with a long pole. Moulded of clay, lined with tiles, each vat was about six feet across. Here and there crude derricks had been set up for hauling the heavy bundles of wet skins in and out of the dyes, and at the junction of each four vats, in a space that resembled a four-pointed star, circular iron grilles had been fixed, Yashim imagined, to feed air to the flues that ran underneath. Several of these grilles were visible from where he stood.

Of the assassin there was no sign, but Yashim knew that he was there, somewhere, hidden behind the lip of one of the vats, perhaps, or standing motionless against the shadowed walls. Yashim knew almost nothing about the killer, except that he could operate in the dark: it was in the dark that he had launched himself against him, in darkness he had killed Preen, in the night he had stolen in to garrotte the hunchback. The dark, Yashim thought, is this man's friend.

He scanned the tannery again. It was surrounded by high walls: only at the farther end of the tannery across the dancing glow of colour could he see other darkened doorways. He did not think the killer had found time to reach them.

Yashim shifted focus to look at the vats closest to him. The colours in the steam were less vivid, perhaps because of the way the light caught them; it was only further out, as the pillars of steam overlapped, that they showed a rainbow iridescence. Some of the nearer vats appeared to be empty.

Yashim edged closer on bended legs, holding up the skirt of his cloak. He stepped out onto the clay. It was surprisingly slippery, beaded with droplets of steam and fat, and he moved cautiously, planting his feet with elaborate care. He could feel the heat from the vats but, yes, there were empty vats among them. They were drained, he now saw, by means of a wooden bung attached to a chain which ran up the inside of each vat and was secured by a metal loop at the rim. He had a vision of the killer dropping down into one of them: like the soldier lying dead in the cauldron at the stables, long ago.

He reached into his cloak and unsheathed the little dagger at his belt. For a moment its blade glinted fiercely in the weird light, and then dulled as the vapour which filled the air condensed on the cold metal. He held it out, the handle beneath his thumb and nestling into his curled fingers, using it like a pointer.

He put one foot on top of the grating, feeling a rush of hot air up his leg; he tried it with his weight and felt the grating rock, with an almost imperceptible metallic sound. He pushed again, a little harder. Again the same slight yielding to pressure, but this time the metal grille gave a distinct knock against the frame.

Yashim stepped back and crouched down to inspect the grating. It was about twenty inches in diameter, set with rounded iron bars about two inches apart. He raised his head, considering. There had been so little time to hide. Crouched in one of the empty vats, the killer would be caught like a bear in a pit: it would be only a matter of time before Yashim found him, and then . . .

He put out his hand and pushed the far side of the grating, watching it rock very slightly away from him. It was not properly bedded at one side, and by rocking it to and fro he worked out the pivotal point. Yashim ran his fingers along the edge and gave a grunt as his fingers closed on a small twist of cloth no bigger than a fingernail that protruded from the joint.

He stood up and stepped back, carefully, to take a flaming torch from a bracket in the wall. Once more he scanned the tannery, but nothing moved. By the grating he knelt down and thrust the torch against the grille.

Tunnels. These grilles had to be more than air-vents: they must also act as access-points to a network of tunnels for the tanners to feed the fires that boiled the water in the vats. The killer could have dropped down here into the tunnels: in his haste, though, a corner of his sleeve must have caught in the join as he replaced the grille overhead.

It has already been said that Yashim was reasonably brave: but that was only when he stopped to think.

Without a moment's reflection, he heaved up the grille and swung his legs into the pipe. The next moment he was crouched at its base, about five feet below, peering in astonishment at what was revealed in the flickering light of his torch.

62

The assassin hung for a moment on all fours, to catch his breath. Strong: yes, he was very strong. But the running was for a younger man, perhaps; a man in training. He had not trained that way for ten years.

Move, he told himself. Crawl away from under the grating. For the first time in forty-eight hours he felt tired. Jinxed.

The mission had failed. He had waited for hours in that room, focusing on the door. Once or twice he had tried the latch, to see how long it took for the door to swing open. Darkness had come: his element.

He had heard her coming. He saw the light approach, watched with satisfaction as a finger snaked in to flick the latch. His hand coiled around the weight at the end of the twine.

And then, in the darkness, it had all gone wrong. The dancer stepped back, not forwards. The weight sliced through the empty air, and then the crashing. It would have been possible to go on – but someone had come.

If there's any risk of being discovered, abort.

The assassin began to move again, silently, creeping away from the grating down the sluice. Forget the failure, he thought. Hide. Go to earth.

The movement consoled him. His breathing softened. Rest now. No one would follow him down here, and later he could rectify his mistake. Sleep now.

Sleep among the altars.

Each altar topped by a glowing brazier.

The air was fetid and warm.

The air was full of sleep.

The assassin squirmed through a low arch and found a clear space on the warm brick. He also found a day-old loaf of bread on the ledge of a brazier and stuffed a piece of it into his mouth. He took the stopper from an earthenware bottle and drank a long draught of warm water.

At last he stretched out on the warm bricks, clasping his hands behind his head.

And then, looking up at the curving belly of the vats, the assassin screamed.

63

Yashim saw he had been wrong about the spaces that lay below the vats. From what he could make out, a succession of air-wells all dropped to a huge and very low chamber, raised on shallow brick vaults. Between the vaults, at regular intervals, wide braziers were set on stacks of bricks to heat the tiled cauldrons overhead: in the dim and smoky light the cauldrons were suspended like the teats of a monstrous she-devil.

His eyes ran from the wooden bungs which hung like nipples to the brickwork that composed the floor on which he now crouched. In a way he had been right. He had expected a maze of tunnels, but what he found was the impress of a maze, as if the floor of the tannery had been scored by a huge wheel: as if the tunnels he had imagined had been abandoned when they were only a few inches high. They were thick with coloured grease.

He shuffled forwards, the torch in one hand, the knife in the other. He felt the grease pile up beneath his toes: looking down, he saw it gathered in a slick ridge at his feet. Looking ahead, he saw that the grease was actually moving sluggishly towards him. Someone had already sloshed it aside, in a faint but unmistakable track, and it was quietly oozing back, revealing its direction as it rolled.

Struck by an idea, he inched back to the air-vent and stood up. He put the torch on the ground above his head and gripped the edge of the grating, hauling himself back into the not-so-fresh air.

For the next five minutes, Yashim crept this way and that around the vats. He went to the far end of the tannery and removed the grating, thrusting his torch down the pipe. He watched the oozing grease for a few moments.

He went towards the centre of the tannery and fiddled with a rope attached to one of the derricks used for raising and lowering bundles of skins into the vats.

When he was ready, he put a hand on one of the chains that stretched out of the vats and yanked on it.

Then he dived for another, and another, pulling with all his might.

And somewhere in the distance, as if from underground, he heard a scream.

64

The assassin saw the first bung disappear.

Ten years before, he had watched a wall collapse on top of him, and counted that moment an eternity.

Now, for an eternity, he made no sound.

For an eternity he scrambled for an explanation.

And he rolled aside only when the bung was replaced by a black tube of scalding fat and water which exploded onto the brick.

It ricocheted onto his back, the hot fat clinging like needles.

And he screamed.

Spouts of heavy boiling dye erupted all around him. The culvert he lay in was suddenly filled with swirling liquid. In terror he ploughed his hands into the scalding torrent and fought his way to an opening. He reached up, placed his scalded hands on the grating, and heaved.

And as he dragged himself up out of the vent he scarcely noticed the coiled rope that cinched very tight against his burning ankles.

65

Yashim lunged on the counterweight and had the satisfaction of seeing the assassin swept from his feet. But as the slipknot ran up against the pulley, the arm of the derrick swung heavily towards him and the rope went slack. Yashim lunged further backwards to regain his hold but at that moment the rope bearing the assassin's weight kicked between his hands, almost knocking him off his feet: the rope sped through his palms and he found himself suddenly scrabbling against the sweaty slope. He kicked with both feet: his left leg slithered off the edge and his foot touched boiling water. He jerked it back with a gasp, and went down on his side.

Flailing to regain a foothold on the slimy surface, Yashim saw the rope slowly oozing through his fingers, slick with grease. He made a lunge with his left hand and caught the rope, tight as a bar, a few inches higher up, hauling hand over hand until he was able to get into a crouch. For a moment he felt his sandals skating on the greasy floor, so he leaned back to balance the weight. Everything had happened so fast that when he finally looked up he could make no sense of what he saw.

A few yards ahead of him, something like a giant crab was working its pincers in a jet of pinkish steam.

Bound at the ankles, upside down, the assassin's legs were opening and closing at the knee. His tunic had fallen over his head, but his arms were flailing upwards from the cloud of cloth, struggling to take a grip of his own legs. The hem of the tunic floated in a bath of dye. He was suspended directly over a boiling vat, where the derrick had carried him the moment it felt the weight of his body against its arm.

Yashim dragged at the rope and hauled himself upright, but the moment he slacked his hold on the rope the assassin dropped. Yashim hauled back, wrapping a length of rope around his waist and leaning back over the vat behind him.

I can't let go, he thought.

The flailing man's legs opened again. What was he doing? Yashim cast a glance over his shoulder: he was hanging out over a roiling tub of evil-smelling liquid. He could see the skins rolling over and over. He needed to keep his weight balanced there, keep his feet set against the rim of the vat, move them along the greasy ledge, and gradually bring the rope up hard against the derrick.

Then he saw what the man was trying to do: with a knife in his hands he was lunging upwards, scissoring his legs to close the distance, lunging at the knot with the blade.

He didn't know where he was.

If the rope severed, the assassin would dive into the dye.

Yashim, meanwhile, was also hanging out over a vat of poisonous, boiling liquid. Only the assassin's weight was keeping his feet on the rim of the vat.

And at any moment the rope would whip through the block and Yashim would plunge backwards into the boiling broth.

They were balanced.

The rope gave a thud, and sagged a quarter of an inch.

Yashim tightened his grip. He glanced across the pillars of purple and yellow and saw that the dark doorways at the far end of the tanneries were growing wider.

A knot of men detached themselves from the darkness of the door and began loping across the glistening surface of the tanneries towards him.

And from the direction they came from, and the way they moved, Yashim did not think that they looked very friendly.

 66

The rope gave another jerk and Yashim scrabbled to keep his balance on the edge of the vat. His right foot lost its hold and for a moment he swung out over the scum. To regain his footing he had to pay out more rope until he was almost horizontal. He could feel the heat on the back of his neck, and the weight of the liquid seeping into his cloak.

It was not so much a decision as an instinct which made him haul savagely on the rope to regain his footing. The response of his human counterweight brought him momentarily upright: the assassin dropped and as the bundle hit the boiling water his legs convulsively scissored for the last time as the rope finally parted. Yashim floundered, his arms sawing the air while the assassin continued his descent into the vat. Regaining his balance, Yashim was in time to see one hand fling itself out of the pot before it sank into the churning water.

He had no time to consider what had happened. Avoiding the slippery surface between the vats, the men from the doorway were now fanning out into two lines around the edge close to the walls, to cries of 'Block him!' and 'Close the entrance!' Yashim began to scramble back in a zigzagging diagonal line towards the gate at the corner by which he had come in. But he had to move cautiously, while the others, further from the edge of the vats and with the wall to help them, were already closing in.

Several tanners were already at the gate when Yashim came past the grating he had first descended. He reached down and scooped up the grille in his left hand, like a shield; in the other he fingered the short-bladed knife. But he knew already that the gesture was futile. The men at the gate were hunched over their own knees, bow-legged, waiting for a fight. And the others, sensing their chance, had left the wall to approach him across the vats.

He whirled round. A man at his back lunged, and Yashim whipped him across the face with the knife. Another man closed and Yashim plunged the grille against him like an iron glove, knocking him back. Turning, he saw that the gate was infested with men: there was no escape in that direction.

He sensed a movement and turned, a little too late. He had only time to see a face blackened with rage before he felt a stunning blow over his right eye and he fell to the ground. He stuck out the knife blindly and waited for the man either to run upon it or dodge in and grapple with him, but when nothing happened he rolled round to raise the grating as a shield.

Just in time to see the black-faced man wheeled to the right by a tug on his arm. The man who was tugging ducked, rose like a fish and nutted the black-faced assailant expertly on the tip of his nose. The assailant dropped and the man who had delivered the blow turned to Yashim and grinned.

'Let's get you the fuck out,' he said.

 67

It was said that the battle – they only called it a brawl – continued long after Murad Eslek had helped Yashim punch, kick and slash his way out of the tanneries and into the silent darkness beyond.

As they groped their way down the alleys, small lights glowed behind shutters overhead. Now and then a door banged. Away in the distance a dog began to bark. Their footsteps echoed softly on the cobbles, thrown back by buildings asleep, and at peace. A cold wind carried the smell of damp plaster, and the lingering scent of the evening's spices.

'Phew! You stink, my friend,' said Murad Eslek, grinning.

Yashim shook his head.

'If it hadn't been for you,' he said, 'there'd have been nothing left to smell. I owe you my life.'

'Forget it, effendi. It was a good scrap, and all.'

'But tell me, how –' Yashim winced. Now that the excitement was over his scalded foot was beginning to smart.

'Easy enough,' Eslek replied. 'I sees you running like a demon – maybe you got robbed, or something. But when you started in for the tanneries it didn't look so good – I mean, they're rough, them guys. That's when I started to think you were going to need some heavy artillery. So I whipped back and raised the boys. I went round a couple of caffs. Put the word out. Ding dong up the tannery? *No* problem. Why, when we came and saw what trouble you were in the lads moved in like donkeys on a carrot. Lovely job.'

Yashim smiled. They were back in the city by now. The streets were empty and it was too late, he thought, to get a bath. Eslek seemed to guess his thoughts.

'Me, I'm in transport. We work nights, effendi. Cover the markets – veg, mainly, and small livestock. I was going in there when we ran into each other again. There's a hammam we use, open all night, which you as a gentleman might not know about. It's small, yes, but I reckon it's clean. Leastways save you going back and stinking up your own gaff. No disrespect,' he added hurriedly, 'but them tanneries don't half get into your skin. It's the fat.'

'No, no, you're perfectly right. I'd be grateful, really. But you've done so much for me this evening, I don't want to take you out of your way.'

Eslek shook his head.

'Almost there,' he said.

At the door of the hammam they parted, with a handshake. Yashim had murmured – and Eslek had protested.

'Drop it, effendi. You came out all right for us on the night of the fire. I've got a wife and kiddies up the street what know as you did a grand job for them. I was going to swing round and see you – sign of the Stag, you said, right? – and thank you proper. My advice is, don't go messing with them tanners any more. They're dirty, effendi, and it ain't just the fat.'

Yashim was grateful for the baths. Eslek was right: they were clean. The proprietor, a sallow old Armenian with a weary and intelligent face, even agreed to send a boy to fetch clean clothes from Yashim's landlady while Yashim sluiced away the coloured grease that had sunk between his toes and the miasma of shit that clung to his skin. All the time he fought not to remember what he knew.

Yashim unwound his turban and scooped water over his hair. *Preen was dead.* He concentrated on his surroundings. When the attendant offered him a bar of soap it smelled, he noticed, of Murad Eslek. He touched his left cheek: tomorrow he'd have a black eye. He continued to use the scoop, rhythmically ladling the hot water over his head, massaging the soap into his scalp, behind his ears, over his aching neck. His ribs were bruised where the assassin had plunged against him on Preen's corridor. *And Preen was dead.* Yashim jerked his head up, to watch the attendant bringing him a basin of cold water for his scalded foot. There was nothing he could do about his knee. It looked red, and felt sore. It would heal.

He forced himself to remember the chase through the alleys. Palewski had told him once how Napoleon had entered Italy, winning battle after battle with the Austrians, until he had felt that the earth itself was flying under his feet. He had felt the same, pursuing the man who had killed the hunchback, through the inclined alleys of Istanbul. Pursuing the man who killed Preen.

He had not been able to save the assassin, that was true. Otherwise he could have made him talk. To have learned – what? Details, names, locations.

Even now, he could not decide whether the killer had been aware of what was happening when he had struggled to cut the rope that bound him to the derrick. Yashim had been hoping to inch him back, away from the boiling vat. Had the killer known where he was? Was it suicide? Yashim was pious enough to hope it was not.

Yet he could not rid himself of the idea that the killer, like himself, understood that they were both at an end of the same rope: bound for minutes in perfect mutual understanding. He wanted us both to go together, Yashim suspected.

All he had really learned, instead, was how the third cadet to die had been boiled so that all his bones were clean. And that, he reasoned, was something he could have guessed. After all, the soup master had already told him how the Janissaries had come back to Istanbul, taking jobs that were out of the way. Watchmen. Stokers. *Tanners*. He remembered the scarred and blackened face of the man who knocked him down.

Was it for this that Preen had died?

Yashim squeezed his hair.

Preen was dead.

And why was the assassin so determined to die?

What was there, apart from the threat of justice, that made a man decide to die rather than talk?

Yashim could think of only two things.

One was fear.

The other was faith: the martyr's death.

He pulled back suddenly, gasping for breath, his eyes stinging.

Preen had died alone, for nothing, in the dark.

Wise and wayward, loving and forever doomed, she died because of him.

He had asked her to help.

It wasn't that. Yashim whined, teeth bared, his eyes screwed up tight, knocking his head against the tiled wall.

He had never properly taught her to read.

68

The morning dawned bright. On the street, Stambouliots congratulated one another on the re-appearance of good weather, and expressed the hope that the gloom which had settled over the city in the last week might finally be lifted. Optimists declared that the spate of murders seemed to have come to an end, proving that the message from the imams had worked. Pessimists predicted more fog ahead. Only the fatalists, who in Istanbul number hundreds of thousands, merely shrugged their shoulders and said that, like fire and earthquake, God's will would be done.

Yashim made his way down early to the café on Kara Davut. The proprietor noticed that he was limping, and without a word offered him a cushioned divan off the pavement where he could still enjoy watching the doings on the street. When he had brought the coffees, Yashim asked: 'Is there anyone who could take a message for me, and fetch an answer? I'd ask your son, but it's pretty far.'

He gave the address. The café proprietor frowned and turned down his mouth.

'It is time,' he said gruffly. 'Mehmed can go. Eh, hey! Mehmed!'

A little boy of about eight or nine bounced out of the back of the shop at his father's shout. He bowed solemnly and stood looking at Yashim with his big brown eyes, rubbing one foot against his other leg.

Yashim gave him a purse, and carefully explained where to go. He told him about the old lady behind the lattice. 'You should knock. When she answers, present my compliments. Give her the money, and tell her these are . . . expenses – for the lady Preen, in room eight. Whatever she says, don't be frightened. Remember what you are told.'

The boy nodded and darted through the door, where a small crowd had gathered to watch a dervish perform his dance on the street. Yashim saw the boy dive unhesitatingly between the folds of their cloaks, and so away, down the street. A funeral errand, he thought; the father would not be pleased.

'A good boy,' he said, guiltily. 'You should be proud.'

The father gave a noncommittal wag of his head and started polishing glasses with a cloth.

Yashim took a sip of coffee and turned to watch the perform-ance in the street.

The dervish danced in the space defined by a ring of bystanders, who every now and then had to stand aside to let someone in or out of the café, giving Yashim a glimpse of the performer. He wore a white tunic, white puttees, and a white cap, and he flexed his hands and legs in time to some inner melody, his eyes closed. But the dancer was not entranced: from what Yashim could see, it looked like one of the simpler dances of the seeker after truth, a stylised rendition of Ignorance search-ing for the Way.

He put up a hand to rub his eyes and gave an involuntary yelp. He'd forgotten the bruising.

A fire-station. Another tower. His exploration of the files in the Imperial Archives had been inconclusive, to say the least. The references to fire-towers had been too scanty to work on: they did not signify anything either way. All you could say was that fire-towers existed; Galata, Beyazit. Everyone knew that. Perhaps he'd been reading in the wrong book.

If only he could get hold of that helpful young Sudanese. Ibou. He'd gone looking for evidence of a fourth tower. He hadn't found any.

Perhaps there wasn't one.

What if the fourth location wasn't a tower at all?

But if there wasn't a tower, what was he looking for?

The second verse of the Karagozi poem came to his mind.

> Unknowing
> And knowing nothing of unknowing,
> They seek.

Well, here he was. Unknowing, searching. And the refrain?

Teach them.

All well and good, he thought, but teach them what? Enlightenment? Of course, it would be that. But it meant nothing to him. As the poem said, he didn't even know what he didn't know. He could go round in circles like this for ever.

So who were these other people, the people who were supposed to teach? Teachers, simply. Imams, for example, dinning the Koran into their restless little charges with the cane. Ferenghi gunnery instructors, perhaps, trying to explain the rules of mathematics to a fresh-faced batch of recruits. And at the medreses, the schools attached to city mosques, clever boys learned the rudiments of logic, rhetoric and Arabic.

Outside on the pavement the dervish had finished his dance. He pulled a cap from his belt and passed through the café, soliciting alms. To everyone who gave him something, he put out a hand and murmured a blessing. Out of the corner of his eye, Yashim saw the proprietor watching with folded arms. He had no doubt that had the man been a simple beggar he would have shooed him away, maybe with a coin, but a dervish – no, the babas had to be given respect because they showed people the way. The path to a higher truth.

The dervish were teachers of higher truths.

The Karagozi, also, were teachers of their Way.

Yashim hunched his shoulders, trying to concentrate.

He'd had that verse in his head, recently. *Unknowing they seek. Teach them.* And he had said – or perhaps it was just a thought – that he must be a slow learner.

Where was it? He had an impression that he had, after all, learned something then. He had thought of that verse, and heard something useful. But the time and place eluded him.

He shut his eyes. In his mind he groped for an answer.

A slow learner. Where had he thought that before?

His mind was blank.

He had guessed that there were four towers. Old Palmuk, the fire-watcher, had denied it.

Then he remembered. It wasn't the old man; it was the other one, Orhan. It was Orhan who had told him about the towers as they stood on the parapet of the Galata Tower, in the fog. He'd described the tower that was lost, and how they raised the Beyazit Tower to compensate. The old tower had burnt, he'd said: along with the tekke. A tekke, like the one downstairs.

So both towers had been furnished with a Karagozi tekke. He couldn't yet be sure about the fire-tower at Beyazit, but a tekke was certainly where the truth was taught, as the Karagozi perceived it. *Unknowing they seek. Teach them.* And the tekkes in the fire-towers were, coincidentally, the earliest tekkes in the city.

'I've had the whole thing back to front,' Yashim announced. He stood up abruptly and saw a dervish blinking, smiling, putting out his cap for alms. The dervish's cap swam under his nose.

Yashim walked out.

The dervish stretched out both his arms in blessing. In his cap he had seen a whole silver sequin.

69

'*Charmante! Tout à fait charmante!* If I were younger, my dear, I would be positively jealous.'

Eugenia blushed slightly, and curtseyed. There was no doubt in her own mind that the validé, who was reclining against cushions scattered around a window seat, must have been ravishing herself. With the soft light at her back she had the easy poise of a beautiful woman. And the cheekbones to go with it.

'I am so glad we were able to persuade you to come,' the validé continued, without a hint of irony. She raised her lorgnette and peered at Eugenia's dress. 'The girls will think you quite *à la mode*,' she pronounced. 'I want you to sit here by me, before they come to devour you. We can talk a little.'

Eugenia smiled and took a seat at the edge of the divan.

'It was so kind of you to invite me,' she said.

'Men don't think it, but there is so much we women can arrange, *n'est ce pas?* Even from here. *Tu ne me crois pas?*'

'Of course I believe you, validé.'

'And you Russians are very much in the ascendant these days. Count Orloff, your husband's predecessor, was a good friend to the empire during the Egyptian crisis. He had a very plain wife, I understand. But no doubt they were very happy together.'

Eugenia's eyes narrowed a fraction. 'She was a Voronsky,' she replied.

'Believe it or not,' the validé said, 'I have never been impressed by the claims of old family. Neither I nor my dear childhood friend Rose were precisely Almanac de Gotha. We were clever, and that counts for much more. She became Empress. Her husband Napoleon, of course, came from nowhere at all. The Ottomans, I'm delighted to say, have no snobberies of that kind.'

Eugenia blinked lazily, and smiled.

'Surely,' she said carelessly, 'there's one old family in the empire whose claims have to be respected?'

The validé put out a hand and rested it on Eugenia's arm. 'Perfectly right, my dear. But my son was brought up to defend those claims, rather than rely on them. It doesn't matter if you're the fifth or the twenty-fifth or – in Mahmut's case – the twenty-eighth sultan of the Ottoman empire, and in direct descent from Osman Bey himself, if you can't prove that the empire needs you. Mahmut has exceeded my expectations.

'I'd like you to meet him. He would be delighted by you, of course.' The validé saw the surprise in Eugenia's expression, and laughed softly. 'Oh, don't be alarmed. My son is no Suleyman.'

Eugenia found herself laughing. Suleyman the Magnificent, the great Renaissance sultan, had fallen head over heels for a Russian courtesan, Roxelana. He wound up marrying her – the last time any sultan had married at all.

The validé gave her arm a squeeze. 'And *entre nous*, he prefers them rather more upholstered. You'll see.'

She raised her hand. As if by magic, two girls entered and bowed. One of them held a tray containing coffee in tiny china cups. The other, a narghile.

'Do you smoke?'

Eugenia gave the validé a startled look. The validé shrugged.

'One forgets. It is a harem vice, I'm afraid. One of several. Parisian fashions are another.'

She gestured to the girls, who set down the tray and the pipe. One of them knelt prettily at Eugenia's feet and presented her with a coffee cup.

'The inspection has begun,' said the validé drily. Eugenia took the cup and murmured a thank you. The girl made no effort to move, but touched her hand to her forehead and addressed a few words to the validé.

'As I expected,' the validé said. 'The girls have been wondering whether you would like to join them in the bath.'

70

As Yashim climbed the spiral staircase he was still elated by the news.

The boy had found him on the pavement outside the café. He stood very stiffly to attention and blurted out the message he had memorised on the run back from Preen's landlady.

'The lady says your friend is not going to die and I should not ask about such things. She says she has hurt her arm and needs a lot of rest. She says . . . she says . . .' – he screwed up his face. 'I cannot remember the other thing, but it was like the first bit. I think.'

Yashim had made him repeat the message. He stood stock still for several moments, then he laughed. 'You've done very well – and brought me the best news. Thank you.'

The boy took the coin with grave ceremony and ran back into the café to show it to his mother. Yashim turned up the street and limped away in the direction of the Golden Horn, humming.

His mood didn't change when he put his head through the hatch and saw old Palmuk, the fire-watcher, leaning on the parapet with his back turned towards him. On the contrary. With a smile he moved quietly onto the roof. He stood behind Palmuk and made a sudden grab for his waistband. Before the fire-watcher could react he had hoisted him over the parapet.

'Aaargh! Aaaargh! Don't do that! Orhan! Aaaargh! Let go! You bastard. Oh. Oh. Me heart. Orhan?'

'It isn't Orhan,' said Yashim levelly. 'It's the man you lied to yesterday. The tower? Remember? I think you said, too, that you don't like heights. But what am I to believe?'

'I don't like 'em, effendi, I don't. And I swear I never lied.'

Old Palmuk's legs were thrashing about but his arms were too far over the parapet to reach back. Yashim gave him a little shove.

'No, please!' He was almost screaming now, the words coming in rigid little bursts. 'What I said – I wanted the money. I'll give it back.'

'A tekke,' Yashim shouted. 'There's a fourth tekke, isn't there?'

But the man had gone limp. Yashim's eyes narrowed. He wondered if it was a ruse. He'd pull him back and then – wham! Old Palmuk would be at his throat.

'Over you go, then,' he said loudly.

Either old Palmuk was in a faint or he was a very steely customer.

Yashim thought of the assassin, plunging himself into the boiling dye. He pulled old Palmuk back onto the roof.

The man's face was the colour of putty. His eyes moved wildly to left and right, and he seemed to be having trouble breathing. He emitted a series of dry clicks.

Yashim laid him on his back and tore at the neck of his shirt. He massaged his chest, pumping with his forearms. A little colour returned to old Palmuk's cheeks, and the rapid movement of his eyes slowed. At last he drew a long, shuddering wheeze and closed his eyes.

Yashim said nothing. Waited.

The old man's eyes half-opened, and slid towards him.

'You didn't ought to have done that,' he mumbled. 'You took advantage, didn't ya? Eh? Effendi?'

Yashim, squatting, rocked back on his heels and breathed hard through his nose.

'You lied to me,' he said coldly.

A sly grin spread over old Palmuk's face, and he hiccupped mirthlessly.

'It's what you wanted, innit?' He spoke very quietly. 'Old Palmuk, serve the customer. Hey, Palmuk, tell us a story.' He closed his eyes again. 'You didn't ought to have done that.'

Yashim bit his lip. Last night he'd as good as murdered a man. And today –

'I'm sorry,' he said.

Palmuk put a hand to his chest and clawed at his shirt, crumpling the torn edges together.

'It was a new shirt, effendi.'

Yashim sighed.

'I'll get you another. I'll get you two. But first, tell me this. Did the Karagozi have a tekke at the Beyazit Fire Tower? Like the one here?'

Old Palmuk stared. 'Tekke? The Beyazit Tower?' He began to wheeze. It took Yashim a moment to realise that he was laughing.

'What's the joke?'

'A tekke at Beyazit, you said?' Old Pamuk rubbed his nose with the palm of his hand, sniggering. 'There was a tekke there, all right. The whole tower was built on it.'

Yashim froze. 'The Eski Serai?'

'It's what I heard. Way back when, them Janissaries used to guard the old palace. It fell apart, didn't it? But the Karagozi didn't abandon the tekke. They found a way to keep it – protected, like. They got the whole fire-tower built atop of it, see?'

Yashim saw. 'Another tekke, then. That's what I need. The fourth.'

The fire-watcher cracked a smile. 'There were dozens, effendi. Hundreds.'

'Yes. But for the fire-watchers? Was there . . . a special one?'

Old Palmuk wrestled himself upright. He swayed over his lap, shaking his head.

'I wish I knew, effendi. I wish I knew what you were on about.

I don't know who you think I am, but you've got the wrong man. I . . . I don't know what you mean.'

He turned to look at Yashim, and his grey eyes were round.

'I used to be a gofer. On the docks.' He was nodding now, staring at Yashim as if for the first time. 'Get this, effendi. I weren't there.'

Yashim thought: it's true.

I give the fellow money. I buy him shirts. And he really doesn't know a thing.

⋘ 71 ⋙

Yashim found the Polish ambassador in a silken dressing gown, embroidered with lions and horses in tarnished gold thread, which Yashim supposed was Chinese. He was drinking tea and staring quietly at a boiled egg, but when Yashim came in he put up a hand to shield his eyes, turning his head this way and that like an anxious tortoise. The sunshine picked out motes of dust climbing slowly towards the long windows.

'Do you know what time it is?' Palewski said thickly. 'Have tea.'

'Are you ill?'

'Ill. No. But suffering. Why couldn't it be raining?'

Unable to think of an answer, Yashim curled up in an armchair and let Palewski pour him a cup with a shaking hand.

'Meze,' Yashim said. He glanced up. 'Meze. Little snacks before the main dish.'

'Must we talk about food?'

'Meze are a way of calling people's attention to the excellence of the feast to come. A lot of effort goes into their preparation. Or, I should say, their selection. Sometimes the best meze are the simplest things. Fresh cucumbers from Karaman, sardines from

Ortakoy, battered at most, and grilled . . . Everything at its peak, in its season: timing, you could say, is everything.

'Now take these murders. You were right – they're more than isolated acts of violence. There is a pattern, and more. Taken together, you see, they aren't an end in themselves. The meal doesn't end with the meze, does it? The meze announce the feast.

'And these killings, like meze, depend on timing,' he continued. 'I've been wondering over the last three days, why now? The murders, I mean, the cadets. Almost by chance, I discover that the sultan is set to issue an Edict in a few days. A great slew of reforms.'

'Ah yes, the Edict,' Palewski nodded and put his fingertips together.

'You know about it?' Yashim's argument collapsed in astonishment.

'In a roundabout way. An explanation was given to, ah, selected members of the diplomatic community in Istanbul a few weeks ago.' He saw that Yashim was about to speak, and raised a hand. 'When I say selected, I mean that I for one was not included. It isn't hard to see why, if I'm right about the Edict and what it means. One of its purposes – its primary purpose, for all I know – is to make the Porte eligible for foreign loans. Poland, obviously, is in no position to influence the bond market. So they left me out. It was essentially a Big Power arrangement. I heard about it from the Swedes, who got it from the Americans, I believe.'

'You mean the Americans were invited?'

'Odd as it seems. But then, you know what Americans are? They're the world experts at borrowing money in Europe. The Porte wants them on side. Perhaps they can co-ordinate their efforts. And, to be frank, I don't think the Porte has ever quite managed to work out whose side the Americans are on. Your pashas are still digesting the Declaration of Independence sixty years after the event.'

Palewski reached for the teapot. 'The idea of a republic has always fascinated them, in a schoolboy sort of way. The House of Osman must be the longest-lived royal line in Europe. Some more tea?'

Yashim put out his cup and saucer. 'I've been stupid,' he said. 'I've been wondering who knew about the Edict. Foreign powers never occurred to me.'

'But foreign powers,' said Palewski, with patient cynicism, 'are the whole point: Foreign Powers, foreign loans.'

'Yes. Yes, of course.'

They drank their tea in silence for a moment, marked only by the ticking of the German clock.

'Your Janissaries,' Palewski said, after a while. 'Do you still believe that they exist?'

Yashim nodded. 'Like it or not, I'm sure. You saw them blotted out, you told me. Very well. Poland, as the world supposes, vanished fifty years ago. You can't even find it on a map. But that's not what you tell me. You say it endures. Poland exists in language, in memory, in faith. It lives on, as an idea. I'm talking about the same thing.

'About the fire-towers, I was only partly right. I made a link between the three fire-towers I knew about – the two still standing, as well as the one which was burned and demolished in 1826 – and the cadets, whose bodies all turned up nearby. I needed to find a fourth fire-tower, didn't I? But I can't. There never was a fourth tower. But I knew the pattern was right. The fire-towers had the hand of the Janissaries on them, just like these murders. It had to be right.'

'Perhaps. But without a fourth tower it makes no sense.'

'That's what I felt, too. Unless there was something else about the fire towers that I couldn't see – something that could link all three of them to another place which isn't a fire-tower at all.'

Palewski thrust out his lower lip and sighed. 'I hate to say it,

Yash, but you're skating on very thin ice. Let's forget my reservations for a moment. You suspect the Janissaries of murdering these cadets, because of the wooden spoons and all the rest of it.' He wrinkled his nose. 'The pattern of the fire-towers comes to you because the Janissaries once manned them, as the city's firemen. Abandon the fire-towers, and what happens to your Janissary theory? Tell me that. You can't have it both ways.'

Yashim smiled. 'But I think I can. I found what I needed to know a couple of days ago, but it wasn't until today that I saw how it all fits together. The Galata Tower housed a Karagozi tekke, a place sacred to the Janissaries. The lost watch tower at the Janissary barracks had one, too.'

'But the Beyazit Tower,' Palewski objected, 'is modern. And that's exactly what I mean. By the time it was built the Janissaries – and the Karagozi, too – were already history. Really, Yash, this Janissary obsession is only getting in your way.'

'I don't think so. I just discovered that the Beyazit Tower was built smack on top of an old Karagozi tekke at the Eski Serai. So that makes three. What I'm looking for now is another Karagozi tekke – and I don't even know where to start.'

Palewski groped on the table beside him and produced a set of leather boards. Inside was a single foolscap sheet of paper, folded in two, but loose. He opened the sheet and there, to Yashim's surprise, was a meticulously executed bird's eye view of Istanbul, in ink. Where the sky should have been, the air was thick with names, notes and numbers.

'You were asking for a map. Last night, I remembered Ingiliz Mustafa,' he said.

'English Mustafa?'

'He was actually a Scotsman. Campbell. He came to Istanbul about sixty years ago, to start up a school of mathematics for the artillerymen. Became a Muslim, too.'

'He's still alive?'

Palewski snorted.

'No, no. I'm afraid even the practice of Islam couldn't do that for him. One of his pet obsessions was the holiness of Istanbul – how the city was steeped in faith. I daresay he became a very good Muslim, but you can't easily overcome a Scottish training in the sciences. This map shows all the mosques, saintly tombs, dervish tekkes and such that he could locate in the city. He had it printed here, too.'

He dipped into the pocket of his dressing gown for a pair of reading glasses.

'Look, every holy place in the city has a number. The key is up here. Fourteen: Cammi Sultan Mehmed. Mehmed's mosque. Twenty-five: Turbe Hasan. The tomb of Hasan. Thirty, look, Tekke Karagoz. And another one. Here, too.'

Yashim shook his head in disbelief.

'Only a foreigner would do something like this,' he said. 'I mean it's so . . . so . . .' He was going to say pointless, but thought better of it. 'So unusual.'

Palewski grunted. 'He wanted to show how his adopted faith was embedded in the very fabric of the city. Plenty of Karagozi tekke to choose from too.'

Yashim peered at the map for a while.

'Too many,' he murmured. 'Which is the right one? Which is the fourth?'

Palewski leaned back with his fingers over his eyes, thinking. 'Didn't you tell me that the three fire-stations were also the oldest tekkes in the city? Isn't that what the fire-watchers said?'

Yashim's mind began to race. Palewski continued: 'Perhaps I'm just saying this because I'm a Pole, and all Poles are at bottom antiquarians. This dressing gown, for instance. You know why I wear it?'

'Because it's cosy,' said Yashim absently.

'Yes and no. It's Sarmatian. Years ago, you see, we Poles

193

believed that we were connected to a half-mythical tribe of warriors who came from Sarmatia, somewhere in central Asia. I suppose we didn't know properly where we came from, and went looking for pedigree, if you like. There was a rage for it, and the supposed Sarmatian style – you know, silk and feathers and crimson leather. I found this hanging in a wardrobe when I came here. It's a relic from another age. That's what I like best about it. Every morning I envelop myself in history. In the fancied glory of the past. Also it's jolly comfortable, as you say.

'Well, what makes me sit up is the thought that these tekkes are old, really old. Maybe the first ever established in the city. That's your pedigree, if you like. That's where your chaps might want to begin. Maybe the fourth tekke is also one of the original lodges in the city. The first, or the fourth, whatever. So you need to look for a tekke that's as old as the other three you know about.'

Yashim nodded. The four original tekkes. It fitted: it was what traditionalists would want.

'Which might explain something else that's been bothering me,' he said aloud. 'Not the timing – that's the Edict – but the number. Why four? If you're right, if someone is going back to the beginning, trying to start over, then four's the obvious number. Four is the number of strength, like the legs of a table. It's a reflection of earthly order. Four corners of the earth. Four winds. Four elements. Four is bedrock.'

'And it's going back, to the very origins of the whole Ottoman enterprise! Holy War – and Istanbul as the very navel of the world.'

Yashim could hear the soup master explaining that the Janissaries had built the empire: that they, under the guidance of the Karagozi babas, had won this city for the faith.

'Whenever things have gone wrong, people have stepped forward to explain that we've simply deviated from the true old ways, that we should go back and try to be what we were when the whole of Europe lay trembling at our feet.'

'Well,' said Palewski drily, 'not the whole of Europe.'

'Poland excepted, the valiant foe.' A look of doubt crossed Yashim's face.

'But how do we work out which was the original, fourth tekke? Your map here doesn't give dates, even if anyone knew them.'

Palewski bit his nails.

'If we had an older map,' he said slowly. 'A really good one, to cross reference with this one. Most of these tekkes, after all, would-n't exist. You might get somewhere by a process of elimination.'

He rubbed his palms together.

'It would have to be a very good map,' he mused. Then he shook his head. 'To be honest, I'm not sure there's anything early enough for you. I certainly don't have such a thing.'

Yashim set his jaw, and stared into the fire.

'Does the name Lorich mean anything to you?' He asked qui-etly. 'Flensburg. Fifteen something.'

Palewski's eyes widened.

'How on earth, Yash? It's the most astonishing panorama of the city ever made. Or so I've heard. I've never seen it, to be hon-est. There must have been several copies but you won't find one here in Istanbul, that's for sure.'

'An astonishing panorama,' Yashim echoed. 'But you're wrong, my friend. I think I know just where to find it.'

Half an hour later Yashim was standing in the portico of the Russian embassy, toying with the irritating reflection that knowing was not altogether the same thing as finding. He was only half a mile from Palewski's ambassadorial Residency, and scarcely twenty yards from the map which he had seen hanging in the gallery in the vestibule upstairs. But for all his ability to reach the map, it might have been in Siberia.

The ambassador, it appeared, was not at home. Yashim wondered if he kept Palewski's hours: perhaps he was even now in bed with his luscious wife. The idea upset him, and he asked to see the First Secretary instead. But the First Secretary could not be contacted, either. It occurred to Yashim to ask to see the ambassador's wife: but common sense, as well as inherited notions of propriety, ruled that out. Even Christian women didn't come to the door for every man who knocked.

'Is there anyone I can speak to? It's very urgent.'

The moment he heard the deliberate, military tread Yashim knew who could be found to speak to him. The crippled hand. The ugly scar.

'Good afternoon,' Potemkin said. 'Won't you come in?'

As he followed the young diplomat into the great hall his eyes flickered automatically to the stairs.

'The staff do not usually admit people without an appointment. I am sorry if you have been waiting a long time. The ambassador and his staff have a heavy workload today. His excellency is expected at the palace tonight. I am afraid it is impossible that they should be interrupted.'

He sounded nervous, on edge, Yashim thought. He said: 'You may be able to help me. The other day I saw an interesting map outside the ambassador's office, which I'd like to look at again. I wonder . . .?'

Potemkin looked puzzled. 'A map?'

'Yes. By Melchior Lorich. It is hanging in the vestibule upstairs.'

'I am sure His Excellency would be delighted to show it to

you,' Potemkin said, more smoothly. 'If you would care to put your request in writing, I will personally see that it receives his attention.'

'Now?'

Potemkin managed a half-smile. 'I'm afraid that's impossible. Requests of this nature take, what, a month or so to organise. Perhaps we can cut it down, though. Shall we say three weeks?'

'I know the map is just there, up the stairs. I'll disturb no one.'

Potemkin continued to smile, and said nothing.

'Fifteen minutes,' Yashim said desperately.

'You forget, monsieur, that this is a working embassy. It is neither a museum, nor a public gallery. But I am sure that His Excellency the Prince would be delighted to consider your request – in good time. In the meantime, unless you have anything else . . .?'

'I don't suppose you have had a chance to look at the porter's accounts yet,' Yashim observed sardonically.

'No,' the attaché agreed softly. 'Not a chance. Allow me to show you out, monsieur.'

❦ 73 ❧

The ambassador's wife, at that very moment, was being helped to undress by five eager handmaidens, who took each garment as it was relinquished and examined it with varying degrees of excitement and admiration.

The validé's suggestion that she should bathe with the women of the sultan's harem, coming on top of her offer of a puff on the narghile, had temporarily robbed Eugenia of the power of speech. She was not easily nonplussed, but it had occurred to her immediately that the sultan might take it into his head to enjoy a bathe himself. Alternatively, that he might choose to enjoy the spectacle from a concealed lattice. Finally she wondered if the validé was simply teasing her.

'It's quite all right,' the validé said. 'The sultan never uses the women's bath. The girls would be delighted, but if you'd rather not . . .'

That's two of my three concerns answered, at least, Eugenia thought. 'I'd be charmed,' she answered.

Minutes later she was laughing as the girls examined her stays, pulling funny faces. One girl puffed up her cheeks and blew. Another, to general merriment, mimed turning a little lock with a key. With a shrug of her firm, creamy shoulders, she demonstrated to Eugenia that Ottoman women enjoyed certain freedoms denied their European cousins. But when Eugenia stepped out of her petticoat, they stood back with what looked like sincere admiration for the effect – until they caught sight of her pubic hair. At this, with equal sincerity, they simply goggled in surprise. Then they helped her unlace, and escorted her into the bath.

Later, Eugenia was to reflect on the difference between a Turkish bath, and a Russian one. On her father's estates outside Moscow she had often leaped from the steamy log cabin to gasp with pleasure in the snow, while the bathing attendants scrupulously beat her skin to a glow with a whippy bundle of birch twigs. In the harem bath the pleasure was attained without the pain, such as it was: the pleasure seemed infinite and curiously detailed. She was soaped, and rubbed, and massaged, and it seemed that no part of her body escaped the attentions of the girls, or of the stalwart woman who flexed her limbs, cracked her neck, and even bent her fingers and toes. It was only through a massive effort of will, which she afterwards half-regretted, that she conveyed her opinion of the hot wax and a razor which the bath attendant automatically produced. By the time she had bathed, and she was lounging naked on a sofa in the room beyond, surrounded by other women smoking, sipping coffee, and assessing their prize – and all her clothes – Eugenia had no idea how much time had passed. The chirruping of the women was very restful, and their birdlike cadences mingled with the smell of applewood and tobacco to take her back, when she closed her eyes, to a childhood in autumn, by a river far away, and not so long ago.

She was woken by a cool hand on her shoulder. Automatically she pushed herself upright and found the Kislar Agha staring down at her impassively. Then he nodded several times, and showed his little teeth, making a gesture that she was to rise.

She got up slowly, smiling to her new friends. They smiled back, but fleetingly, and helped her to dress. She climbed into her petticoat first, then wrapped her corset around her front. One of the girls laced it at the back; she would have preferred it tighter, but somehow the atmosphere of levity that would have let her ask the girl to pull harder was missing now. She glanced to where the chief black eunuch was standing by the door, his gaze flickering around the room. When she was dressed she tilted her chin and looked him lazily in the eye. He gave a barely perceptible bow, and opened the door.

When she regained the validé's suite, she found the old lady on her divan, chatting with a plump middle-aged man who sat straddling a western chair, rocking it back and forth.

The sultan turned and rose with a slight effort.

'Princesse!' He bowed, took her hand and pressed it to his lips. Eugenia sank in a low curtsey.

'Bravo!' The validé clapped her hands. 'You escaped, I see, dressed just as beautifully as before. The girls,' she explained, 'might easily have stolen her clothes.'

'Her clothes?' The sultan looked confused. 'But we send to Paris every year, validé.'

Eugenia laughed pleasantly.

'I think, Your Majesty, it's not the clothes themselves we women find interesting. It's the way they're worn. And everyone,' she added, unable to think of a suitable epithet for the sultan's women, 'has been delightful.'

By everyone she did not include the Kislar Agha. The Kislar Agha gave her the creeps.

≪ 74 ≫

'Back again?'

'Stanislaw Palewski,' Yashim announced, 'we have exactly four hours. You are going to a party.'

Palewski smiled and shook his head.

'I know what you're thinking: the ambassadors' concert at the palace. All very tempting, but I don't do them any more. These days, I –' He spread his fingers. 'To be frank, Yash, it's a question of dress.' He lowered his voice. 'A question, you might say, of moth.'

Yashim held up an imperious hand. 'We aren't talking about those horrible beetling jackets you people all wear. You have the most splendid clothes, and four hours in hand. I have already sent for the tailor. Tonight, you are set to appear at the palace as the living embodiment of Polish history.'

'Eh?'

'You're going as a Sar – what's it?'

'Sarmatian?'

'Exactly.'

The Polish ambassador folded his arms stubbornly.

'Of all the fool ideas. Who do you think you are? My fairy godmother?'

Yashim blinked, and Palewski gave a dry chuckle.

'Never mind, it's an old story.' He frowned. 'What are you doing?'

For Yashim had raised his arms and flicked out his hands, taking a backward step, as if Palewski were the djinn he had just conjured up out of the thin air.

Palewski narrowed his eyes suspiciously. 'I'm sorry, Yash. I'd do anything for you, you know that. But only within reason. As the ambassador of Poland to the Sublime Porte I have a higher responsibility. Mine is a fallen nation, I know that. But stubborn, sir, very stubborn.' He wagged a finger. 'Call it pride, or vanity if you like – but I tell you this. Not for your sake – not even for the sake of the Black Madonna of Czestechowa herself – will I mingle with my peers in a mouldy old dressing gown.'

75

'His Excellency is not at home,' the butler rumbled.

He stood with the door ajar, peering at the Turk who had rung the bell.

'I would prefer to wait,' Yashim said. 'My time is of no consequence.'

The butler weighed up this remark. On the one hand, it implied a compliment to his master who was, of course, a busy man. On the other, nobody in Istanbul ever said quite what they meant. He studied Yashim. His clothes were certainly clean, if simple. He'd like to rub that cloak in his fingers, to make sure it was really cashmere, but yes . . . he might be a man of consequence, after all.

'If you will step in,' the butler intoned, 'you may find a chair in the hall.'

Yashim did, and sat down on it. The butler closed the door behind them with an audible click. Yashim sat facing the door he had just come through, and two enormous sash windows that descended almost to the floor. The staircase to his left swirled up at his back to the vestibule overhead. The butler walked majestically across to a bewigged footman, in breeches, who stood solemnly at the foot of the stairs, and murmured a few words in Russian. The footman stared out straight before him, and made no response.

'I trust you will not have too long to wait,' the butler said, as he passed Yashim and disappeared through a door to his right.

Yashim sat with his hands folded in his lap.

The footman stood with his hands by his sides.

Neither of them moved for twenty minutes.

At the end of that time, Yashim suddenly started. He raised his head. Something had attracted his attention at the window. He leaned slightly to one side and peered, but whatever it was that caught his eye seemed to have gone. He kept a watch on the window nonetheless.

About thirty seconds later he was almost on his feet, staring. The footman's eyes slid over him, and then to the window, but the window was black and revealed nothing to him.

But Yashim's attention was called to something almost out of sight. Curious, he leaned further over to the right, to follow it better. From where he stood, the footman realised that he couldn't see what the foreigner was looking at.

He wondered what it could be.

Yashim gave a little smile, whistled through his nose, and continued to watch, craning his head.

The footman rubbed his fingers against his palms.

The foreigner, he noticed, had jerked his head slightly, to keep up with the event occurring outside. It seemed to be moving away, out of his line of sight, because the fellow was leaning forward now.

Very slowly, Yashim leaned back in his chair. He looked puzzled. In fact, he simply could not imagine the significance of what he appeared to have seen.

Something within the grounds, the footman knew.

When there should be nothing. No one.

The footman wondered what it could have been. It had to be a light. A light in the dark, in the grounds. Going round the side of the embassy.

What would the butler have done? The footman glanced at the Turk, who was still sitting exactly where he had sat half an hour before. Wearing a slight frown.

Having seen something he hadn't expected. That nobody else had observed.

The footman took a measured step forwards, hesitated, then continued to the front door and opened it.

He glanced to the left. The spaces between the columns of the portico were dark as pitch. He took a step out, and another, craning for a better view.

He sensed a darkness at his back and half turned. The Turk filled the doorway.

The Turk held out his hands, palms up, and shrugged. Then he gestured to himself and to the gatehouse.

'I'm going,' he said in Turkish.

The footman understood the gesture. His anxiety increased.

The Turk descended the steps.

The footman waited until he had cleared the portico, and then ran very quickly down the steps himself, and headed left, into the dark.

Privately he relished the little cold wind which hit him on the face but could not in a thousand years ruffle his artificial hair. Still he saw nothing. He darted to the corner of the building and looked down the side of the east wing.

It was as far as he dared to go.

76

Yashim sprinted back up the steps, crossed the empty hall and took the stairs three at a time. At the top he slowed and put his hand on the doorknob of the vestibule.

What if there was another footman, as before, standing sentinel in there?

He squeezed the handle and stepped inside.

The room was almost dark. Two candles burned in their sconces at the far side of the room, really too far away to be of any use to him. He turned to the right, gliding along the gallery. The oils were hard to make out, but as he passed one of them he paused. He stepped aside, to let the meagre light reveal it, and even though it was mostly shadow, the composition of figures closely grouped at its centre was unmistakeably that of the czar and his amorous czarina, with their little children.

He went back up the gallery.

Two shoulder-length portraits. A full-sized rendition of a man on a horse. A scene he could not decipher, including a river and a mass of men and horses surging towards it. Another portrait.

And he was back at the door. He could hear the footman banging the door downstairs.

He looked around in astonishment.

The vestibule still housed, as he remembered, a positive Parliament of Russian nobles, a Hermitage of royal heads. As for landscapes, well, many versts of the Russian steppe had been crammed in there, too, where Cossack hussars stooped in village streets to kiss their sweethearts farewell.

There wasn't a map of Istanbul to be seen.

Where the map had been, he was looking at a portrait of a gouty czar.

He took a step closer. The czar looked surprised: perhaps he didn't like to be ignored. Even in the feeble candlelight Yashim could still make out the faint outline of the frame, bleached against the painted woodwork.

They had got rid of the map.

Yashim hardly had time to register this appalling thought when he heard footsteps mounting the stairs.

Without a second's hesitation Yashim lunged for the door at the far end of the room. The handle turned easily, and in a moment he was through.

The Russian ambassador put a monocle to his eye and then let it fall without a sound as his eye expanded in surprise.

'This I do not believe!' he muttered, to no one in particular. A Second Secretary, standing close by, stooped as if to gather up the remark and put it to his ear; however he heard nothing. He raised his head and followed his master's gaze.

Standing by the entrance with a glass of champagne in one hand and a pair of kid gloves in the other was Stanislaw Palewski, the Polish ambassador. But he was like no Polish ambassador that the Russian had ever seen.

Palewski was dressed in a calf-length, padded riding coat of raw red silk, fantastically embroidered in gold thread, with magnificent ermine trim at the neck and cuffs. His long waistcoat was of yellow velvet: unencumbered by anything so vulgar as buttons it was held at the waist by a splendid sash of red and white silk. Below the sash he wore a pair of baggy trousers of blue velvet, stuffed into flop-topped boots so highly polished that they reflected the chequerboarding of the palace floor.

The boots, Yashim's tailor had said defiantly, were beyond his help.

But now, thanks to a some judicious polishing of the ambassador's feet, it was impossible to detect that the boots were holey at all.

'It's an old trick I read about somewhere,' Palewski had earlier remarked, calmly blacking his toes with a brush. 'French officers did it in the late war, whenever Napoleon ordered an honour guard.'

78

Yashim pulled the door closed behind him, releasing the handle gently so as to make no sound.

He was just in time: even as he put his ear to the door he could hear the other door being flung open. Someone marched into the room, and then stopped.

In five seconds they'll be through this door, too, Yashim thought. He looked round, hoping to find a hiding place.

And realised immediately that the Russian ambassador's gorgeous young wife, wearing a shimmering sable cape, was sitting at a mirror, gazing at him open-mouthed.

And apart from the fur, she was naked.

79

Prince Derentsov flung a look at the Austrian ambassador, a man with no visible neck, a vast moustache and a belly like a Bukovina wineskin. He had been standing with his back to the doors, so that Derentsov had the satisfaction of watching his reaction to Palewski as, noticing some change in the expression of the little man he was speaking to, he turned and caught sight of the Polish ambassador.

His heavy jaw dropped. His eyes bulged from his head. He went from sallow to a sort of imperial purple.

Silly fool, Prince Derentsov thought. Certainly the Pole's coming here tonight, dressed like that, was a deliberate insult to the Powers that had silenced his bickering little nation forty years before. But that Austrian sausage-merchant's reaction would give the Pole some satisfaction.

The Austrian was trying to catch his eye, dabbing a plump paw in the air like a wounded seal. Derentsov turned on his heel and began to speak to his Second Secretary.

The British ambassador, without disturbing his conversation, allowed his eyes to flicker now and then from his Austrian counterpart to Prince Derentsov. He tugged at his lip to restrain a smile.

The American ambassador said: 'I'll be danged!' He wanted to walk right up and shake Palewski by the hand, but he was new, not only to Istanbul but to the ways of diplomatic protocol. I'll talk to that fellow before the evening's out, he thought.

The French ambassador edged around slightly so that when Palewski moved into the room he quite naturally gravitated into the Frenchman's little group.

And the imperial bandmaster, Giacomo Donizetti, being Italian and highly romantic, held a whispered discussion with the first violin. His programme of light German occasional music drew to a discreet end and, after a moment of rustling scores, the band launched into the latest Chopin polonaise. Some of the cleverer people in the ballroom broke into applause. Prince Derentsov, naturally, continued his conversation.

Sultan Mahmut chose this moment to enter the room. He heard the applause and, feeling his confidence revive – for he hated these international affairs – moved to speak to the French ambassador.

Later on he tried to explain it to his mother.

'I thought he looked damn fine. So did Concordet, I suppose. I wish we could have regiment like that, all sash and colour. Palewski looked like one of us.'

'That much I understand,' the Validé Sultan broke in crisply. 'What I can't understand is why you had to have him locked up.'

The sultan twisted his fingers.

'Don't be ridiculous, validé. Nobody was locked up. I merely had him escorted to a side-room. I . . . I interviewed him later. Same with the Russian, Derentsov, and it was all his fault, suggesting the duel. Practically under my nose!'

The validé saw his point. It was on her advice, several years ago, that the sultan had issued a formal decree, backed by the ulema, forbidding the practice of duels within the empire. It was aimed principally at those stubborn Circassian mountaineers whose distant feuds occasionally brought heartache and anxiety into the sultan's harem, and irritated the Validé Sultan; but it applied also to the touchy foreigners of Galata.

'The British ambassador brought Palewski within earshot of the Russian,' the sultan explained. 'So it was his fault, too. I wasn't there, but Stratford Canning apparently made some effort to catch Derentsov's attention and the Russian swerved so abruptly that he elbowed Palewski's glass and ended up with champagne all down his shirt. You know what they're like. Well, you can imagine, anyway. Derentsov claimed he had been insulted. The Pole pulled out a handkerchief and started to swab Derentsov's chest – hee hee hee!'

'Mahmut!'

'Well, it was funny, validé. The Russians have never once

acknowledged Palewski's existence. They always pretend they haven't seen him. But here was Derentsov calling for pistols at dawn, and the Polish ambassador dabbing at him with a napkin!'

The validé, too, gave herself up to the humour of the situation.

'But what did the Pole say?'

Mahmut rocked about, his eyes closed.

'He said – hee hee hee – he said – ah ha ha – "Well in that case I accept the challenge and you can use your own handkerchief!" Hee hee hee!'

The Validé Sultan, who had not laughed for several years, felt carried along by her son's laughter. It was many years since she had been to a party, but she knew how funny men could look together.

Sultan Mahmut simmered down first, with an occasional snort of hilarity interrupting his story.

'After that, I had to separate them. The Pole came away very politely. I talked to him, and let him go. Derentsov was snarling by the time I got to him – jabbered about infringement of his diplomatic rights and all that. I let him rant and then I said my piece about duels and the law, just as I'd told the Polish ambassador. I said that the mark of a civilised nation was its respect for the individual, and the individual's respect for law, and that of course I understood that other nations had different principles, but that within the empire which I control duelling is forbidden. This, I said, is why we have laws – and laws, I added, that will be strengthened and clarified in a matter of days. In the meantime, I asked only for his apology.'

'And?'

'If his release had been dependent on his apology, validé, the Russian ambassador might still be waiting in that room. I took some mumbled words – curses, I'm sure – as a sign of contrition, and told him so. Then I suggested he go home, and walked out.'

'Flûte, *mon brave*! You are very clever!'
The validé took her son by the ears, and gave him a kiss.

 80

Before Yashim could recover himself, Eugenia had pointed with an imperious finger.

'You could try under the bed,' she said.

Yashim needed no second bidding. He fairly dived for the bed, and wriggled beneath it. He saw Eugenia approach the door in her bare feet; she plucked something from the bed as she passed. A silk peignoir swished through the air and swirled around her ankles.

There was a knock on the door. Yashim strained to hear, but all he could make out was Eugenia's 'nyet – nyet' and a few murmured words. The door closed, and the feet stood again by the edge of the bed. Then the peignoir slid to the floor in a soft cloud, and the feet disappeared.

Eugenia was sitting in bed, right on top of him. She was waiting for her Turk to emerge. She wore a little smile, and nothing else.

Feeling ridiculous, Yashim scrambled to his feet and bowed.

'Forgive me, Excellency,' he said. 'I lost my way. I had no idea –'

Eugenia pouted. '*No* idea, Monsieur Ottomane? You disappoint me. Come.'

She ran her hand down between her breasts. By the jewels, Yashim thought, she is lovely: lovelier than the girls in the sultan's harem. Such white skin! And her hair – black as shining ebony.

She drew one knee up and the silk sheet rode up, exposing a long, slender thigh.

She wants me, Yashim thought. *And I want her.* Her skin: he longed to reach out and stroke it. He longed to inhale her strange, foreign fragrance, figure her curves with his own hands, touch her dark lips against his own.

Forbidden. This is the path of passion and regret.

This is where you cannot go. Not if you value your sanity.

'You don't understand,' said Yashim desperately. 'I'm a . . . a . . .' What was that word the English boy had used? It came back: 'I'm a freelance.'

Eugenia looked puzzled.

'You want me to pay?' She laughed incredulously and shook her curls. Not only her curls. 'What if I don't?'

Yashim was confused. She saw the confusion on his face, and held up her hands.

'Come,' she said.

She put her hands flat on the bed, behind her back. Yashim groaned softly and closed his eyes.

Five minutes later, Eugenia had discovered what Yashim meant by freelance.

'Better and better,' she said, and threw herself back against the pillows. She raised a slender knee.

'So take me, Turk!' she gasped.

81

Far away, in the first great court of the sultan's palace at Topkapi, the carriages rolled away across the cobbles and through the high gate, to disappear towards the Hippodrome and the darkness of the city. Only one fine carriage still remained, its driver motionless on the box, whip in hand, two footmen standing behind like men of stone, impervious to the light drizzle. As the wind whipped the torches hung up along the inner wall the flare caught the glossy black shellac of the carriage door and lit up the royal arms of the Romanovs with its double-headed eagle: the symbol that so many centuries before had originated in this very city.

If all was ghostly still in the Russian ambassador's carriage, in the boudoir of the Russian ambassador's wife matters had reached a distinctly lively crisis.

With a heave of her shoulders, Eugenia let out a long, satisfied sigh.

Moments later, she was smiling lazily into Yashim's ear.

'I may be vain, but I don't suppose,' she whispered, 'that this is why you came?'

Yashim propped himself up. His eyes were squeezed shut, as though he were in pain. Eugenia put out a hand and stroked his damp forehead. 'I'm sorry,' she said, simply.

Yashim blew out, and opened his eyes. Taking a deep breath, he said: 'The – map – in – the – vestibule. Where's it got to?'

Eugenia laughed, but when she caught the look in his eye she whipped aside and knelt on the bed.

'Are you serious?'

'I need to look at that map,' he said. 'Before your husband gets home.'

'Him?' A look of scorn crossed her face. 'He won't come in here.' She bounced off the bed and retrieved her peignoir, tying the sash with an angry tug.

'He has never forgiven me for marrying him. And you have no idea how *bored* I am.'

Yashim frowned. It was hard to believe that the prince could keep his hands off his wife for a moment. But there it was. Perhaps he, Yashim, was no better than those westerners who imagined the sultan in a scented paradise of houris.

'I've been here six months. I never go out. I change my dress three or four times a day – for what? For who? The sentries? Once a week my husband hosts a very dull dinner.'

She gathered her black curls in one hand and raised them to the back of her head. Then she let the curls fall.

'At home there's a ball every night. I see my friends. I ride out in the snow. I – oh, I don't know, I laugh, flirt, talk about literature and the arts, everything. I suppose that's why I seized on you. You were the first Turk I ever had a chance to speak to. My first Turkish lover.'

Yashim lowered his eyes. Eugenia laughed again.

'I'll show you the map. It's just there.'

She pointed over his shoulder. He looked round and there it was, leaning against the wall, the familiar shape of the city like an animal's snout, rootling the shores of Asia.

'I need to compare,' he explained, reaching for his cloak. He took out Palewski's map, unfolded it, and crouched down by the Hontius map, smoothing Palewski's against the glass.

'I just can't imagine what you're up to, but can I help?'

She laid a hand on his shoulder.

Yashim explained.

'On this map, we have all the religious buildings in Istanbul as they stood about thirty years ago. The ones I'm interested in are the Karagozi tekkes – the symbol seems to be an Arabic letter B, like this.'

'They're awfully difficult to make out,' Eugenia said, pouting. 'It's a complete forest of Arabic squiggles.'

Yashim's eye swept the map. 'Originally I was looking for a fire-tower, but I've had to change my mind. The old map, this one of yours, shows us all the buildings which were standing in 1599. By comparing the two, we should be able to work out where the oldest Karagozi tekkes were.'

'You mean if something shows up on both maps, it was built before 1599.' Eugenia bit her lip. 'You'd do best to split the city

213

into several strips, north-south, say, so that you know where you are and don't miss anything out.'

'That,' Yashim said, 'is a very clever idea. Let's do it.'

Eugenia took Palewski's map and folded it into four pleats. Then she turned the first pleat over, and they began to plot the tekkes.

After twenty minutes they had covered the first quarter of the city and dismissed about a dozen tekkes as being too modern. Yashim struck them off. They were left with two possibilities.

'Next strip,' Eugenia said.

They worked on.

'Some people might think this was an odd way to spend time with a half-naked Russian girl in the middle of the night.'

'Yes. I am sorry.'

'I like it.' Eugenia's eyes crackled. She hugged her knees. 'All the same, you might take me back to bed quite soon.'

They completed the second leaf. A possible candidate had popped up by the city walls, but this time it was the newer map which sowed the confusion, making it hard to say exactly which building had been the tekke.

'Halfway now,' Yashim reminded her.

'More than,' she said. 'The city gets progressively thinner from here on, until it reaches Seraglio Point.'

'Quite true. Go on.'

About ten minutes later they identified the Stamboul Tower as a tekke.

'That's good,' Yashim said. 'It proves the system is working.'

'Pouf! I'm glad you told me now.'

The last fold of the map brought out the Galata Tower and also the old tekke in the Janissary headquarters, now buried beneath the Imperial Stables. As Eugenia had predicted they completed their comparison quicker, for not only did the city dwindle but much of it was covered with the palace and grounds above Seraglio Point. They found nothing there to surprise them.

'It's late,' Yashim said. 'I should go.'

Eugenia stood up and stretched, first on one foot, then the other.

'How? Perhaps it hasn't occurred to you, but the embassy is locked at night. High walls. Vigilant guards. A mouse couldn't get in – or out. Fortunately for me, you are not a mouse.'

With a flourish she slipped the sash from her waist. Her peignoir swung open and she gave a shrug of her shoulders and stepped from it.

'The pleasure is all mine,' Yashim said, with a smile.

'We'll see about that,' she said, and held out a hand.

≪ 82 ≫

The master of the soup-makers' guild took the ends of his moustache in either hand and tugged on them thoughtfully.

Then he picked up the ancient key which the guard had just returned and slipped it back onto the big ring.

He knew that the investigator from the palace had to be right: only the night watchmen could have organised the theft. But why? It had to be some foolish prank, he supposed. Maybe some sentimental ritual of their own. When he explained that one of the cauldrons had gone missing he had expected them to look shifty and ashamed. He had expected them to confess. Confide. He had hoped they would have confidence in him.

Only they stared at him blankly, instead. Denied it all. The soup master had been disappointed.

The soup master began again. 'I am not looking for punishment. Perhaps the cauldron will be returned, and perhaps we need say no more about it. But –' he raised a heavy finger, 'I am troubled. The guild is one family. We have difficulties, and we

215

sort them out. I sort them out. It is what I do, I am the head of this family. So when some outsider comes to tell me about problems I know nothing about, I am worried. And also ashamed.'

He paused.

'A snooping fellow, from the palace, comes to tell me something that has happened in my own house. Ah – I'm getting through now, am I?'

He had detected a flicker of interest – but it hadn't developed.

The soup master pulled at his moustaches again. The meeting disturbed him. The men weren't exactly insolent, but they were cold. The soup master felt that he had run a risk for their sakes, giving them work when they were desperate; but there had been no answering gratitude on this occasion.

He stopped short of dismissing them, with an uneasy feeling that a wordless threat had been issued. That he should mind his own business – as if the theft of a pot, and the subsequent denials, weren't his business entirely! But he could not simply dismiss them now. If they suffered, he might suffer. He could be accused of aiding and abetting the enemies of the Porte.

He crammed his massive hands together, kneading his fingers.

Was there no way of paying them back for their disloyalty? He thought of the eunuch.

The eunuch had some status in the palace.

The soup master wondered how he could become better acquainted with that man.

 83

Yashim spent the morning visiting the three sites he had identified from the old map the night before. He hoped that something would strike him if he searched with an open mind.

A tekke did not have to be large, but a big space might provide a clue. A tekke did not, of itself, have to conform to any particular shape, yet a small dome might suggest a place of worship. So would, perhaps, a stoup for holy water, or a redundant niche, or a forgotten inscription over a doorway, in a corridor – little signs which might seem insignificant in themselves, but taken together would help to point him in the right direction.

Failing that, he could always ask.

The first street he visited was only gradually recovering from the effects of a fire which had burned so fiercely that the few stone buildings had finally exploded. Large, broken blocks still lay embedded in the ash that drifted listlessly up and down the charred-out street. Some men were poking in the ash with sticks; Yashim supposed they were householders, searching for their savings. They answered him slowly, as if their thoughts were still far away. None of them knew about a tekke.

The second place turned out to be a small, irregularly shaped square just within the city walls. It was a working-class district, with a fair number of Armenians and Greeks among the Turkish shopkeepers whose little booths were gathered along its eastern edge. The buildings were in poor repair. It was almost impossible to guess their age. In a poor district buildings tended to be repaired and recycled beyond their normal life-expectancy. Come a fire, and people built afresh in the same style as their fathers and grandfathers.

Across from the shops stood a small but sedate and clean mosque, and behind it a little whitewashed house where the imam lived. He came to the door himself, leaning on a stick, an old, very bent man with a straggling white beard and thick spectacles. He was rather deaf, and seemed confused and even irritated when Yashim asked him about the Karagozi.

'We are all orthodox Muslims here,' he kept saying in a reedy voice. 'Eh? I can't understand you. Aren't you a Muslim? Well, then. I don't see what – We are all good Muslims here.'

He banged his stick once or twice, and when Yashim got away he continued to stand there on his threshold, leaning on his stick and following him with his thick spectacles until he had rounded the corner.

From the shopkeepers he learned that a market took place in the square every other day. But as for any Sufi tekke, abandoned or otherwise, they only shrugged. A group of old men, sitting out under a tall cypress growing close to the base of the old wall, discussed the matter between themselves, but their conversation soon moved on to memories of other places, and one of them began a long story about a Mevlevi dervish he'd once met in Ruse, where he had been born almost a century ago. Yashim slipped away while the men were still talking.

By late morning he had reached the third, and last, of the possibilities suggested by Eugenia's map, a tight knot of small alleys in the west of the city where it had been impossible to pinpoint, with any degree of accuracy, either the street or building the tekke had appeared to occupy.

Yashim wandered around, defining a kind of circuit which he spent more than an hour exploring. But these narrow streets, as always, yielded little: it was impossible to guess what was going on behind the high blind facades, let alone imagine what might have taken place there fifteen or a hundred years before. It was only at the last minute, when Yashim was ready to give up, that he accosted a ferrety man with a waxed moustache who was stepping out of a porte cochère, carrying a string bag.

The man jumped when Yashim spoke.

'Who do you want?' he snapped.

'It's a tekke,' Yashim began – and as he said it he was struck by an idea. 'I'm looking for a Sufi tekke, I'm not sure whose.'

The man looked him up and down.

'Doesn't it make a difference?' He seemed genuinely surprised. 'They aren't all the same, you know.'

'Of course, I understand,' Yashim said peaceably. 'In this case, I'm looking for a particular old tekke . . . I'm an architect,' he added wildly.

He had spent the morning asking people if they remembered a Karagozi tekke. He had supposed that a redundant tekke could become anything from a shop to a tea-room. It hadn't occurred to him until now that the most likely fate for an abandoned tekke was to be adopted by another sect. A Karagozi tekke would become someone else's.

'An old tekke.' The man swung his nose left and right. 'There's a Nasrani tekke in the next street. They've only been there ten years or so, but the building's very old, if that's what you mean.'

The Karagozi were banned ten years ago.

'That,' said Yashim, smiling, 'is exactly what I mean.'

The man offered to show him to the place. As they walked along, he said: 'What do you make of all these murders, then?'

It was Yashim's turn to jump. A street dog got up from a doorway and barked at them.

'Murders?'

'The cadets, you must have heard. Everyone's talking about them.'

'Oh, yes. What do you think?'

'I only think . . . what everyone says. It's something big, isn't it? Something about to happen.' He put his hand into the air as if feeling it with his pursed fingers. 'I keep rats.'

'Rats.'

'Do you like animals? I used to keep birds. I loved it when the light fell on their cages in the winter. I kept them hanging, outside the window. The birds would always sing in the sunlight. In the end I let them go. But rats, they're clever, and they don't

219

mind a cage. Plus I let them out, to run. You can see them stop and think about things.

'I've got three. They've been acting strangely these last few days. Don't want to come out of their cages. I take them out, of course, but they only want to hide somewhere. If it was just one, I could understand. I get times when I don't want to see people, too, just want to stay at home and play with my pets. But all three, just the same. I think they feel it, too.'

Yashim, who had never liked rats, asked: 'What is it? What do they feel?'

The man shook his head.

'I don't know what. People muttering, all closed up. Like I said, something's happening and we don't know what. Here you are, the tekke.'

Yashim looked round in surprise. He had passed the low, windowless box earlier. It looked like a warehouse or a store-room.

'Are you sure?'

The man nodded briskly. 'There might be no one there, but they seem to be around in the evenings. Good luck.' He waved the string bag. 'Got to pick up some food for the rats,' he explained.

Yashim gave him a weak smile.

Then he knocked hard on the double doors.

84

'Yes, Karagozi.' The man continued to smile gently.

So this is it, Yashim thought. At the same time he looked about him with sudden curiosity. Was it here, then, that the Janissaries had indulged in their bacchanalian rites? Bibbing, and women, and mystic poetry! Or something more prosaic, like a chamber of commerce, where business deals were fixed up and the soldiers who had become traders and artisans talked about the state of the market, and what they could squeeze from it.

There was nothing superficially sacred about the place. As it stood, it could easily have been the warehouse that Yashim had originally mistaken it for, a plain, whitewashed chamber lit by high windows, with an oak table running down the middle and benches on either side. A banqueting hall, say. The walls were freshly whitened, but they seemed to have been painted once, to judge by the cloudy images he could still make out behind the lime.

'The walls were decorated?'

The tekkemaster inclined his head.

'Very beautifully done.'

'But – what, sacrilegious?'

'To our minds, yes. The Karagozi were not afraid to make representations of what God has created. Perhaps they were able to do this with a pure heart. Yet those who believe as I do would have found them a distraction. I cannot say that this is why we had them painted over, though. It was more driven by a concern to return to the old purity of the tekke.'

'I see. So wall painting was introduced into Karagozi tekkes more recently? It wasn't the original idea?'

The tekkemaster looked thoughtful.

'I do not know. For us, the Karagozi occupation was an interlude we preferred not to commemorate.'

Yashim looked up at the coffered ceiling.

'Interlude? I don't quite understand.'

'Forgive me,' the tekkemaster said humbly. 'I have not made myself clear, so perhaps you are unaware that this was a Nasrani tekke until the time of the Patrona Rebellion. The Karagozi grew very strong at that period, and they needed more space: so we gave it over to them. Recent events,' he added, with the usual circumspection, 'allowed us to reacquire the building, and the pictures were covered, as you see.'

Yashim turned to him with a defeated look. The Patrona Rebellion had been in 1730.

'You mean, this tekke was built by your order? It wasn't originally a Karagozi foundation at all?'

The man smiled and shook his head.

'No. And so you see, we move in circles. What is open will be closed.'

Five minutes later, Yashim was back in the street.

Palewski's map, drawn up by the Scotsman Ingiliz Mustafa, identified the old tekke correctly – *for the time it was drawn up*. The Karagozi hadn't built it, though: it wasn't one of the original four tekkes.

But the principle had to be right.

Yashim thought again of the little square under the old Byzantine walls of the city.

He pictured it in his mind's eye. The mosque. The row of shops. An old cypress against the weathered stonework of the walls.

The tekke was there. It *had* to be there.

❧ 85 ❧

Half an hour later Yashim approached the square up a long, straight alley from the south.

Straight ahead, beyond the mouth of the alley, he had a clear view of the splendid cypress where earlier he'd stood talking with the old men.

From where he stood, five hundred yards back, he could see what he couldn't see before. He could see over the top of the tree.

222

Just behind its slender tip, in solitary semi-ruined splendour, a Byzantine tower rose from the massive city walls.

The Kerkoporta. The little gate.

Not many Stambouliots learned the story of the Conquest of 1453 in any detail. It was ancient history, almost four hundred years old. It had been the fulfilment of destiny, and the how, or why, of its successful capture from the defending Greeks was a matter of little interest or relevance to people living in Turkish Istanbul in the nineteenth century.

Only two sorts of people had maintained their interest, and told the story to whoever wanted to listen.

The Janissaries, with pride.

The Phanariots, with regret – though whether that regret was perfectly genuine, Yashim had never quite been able to decide. For the Greek merchant princes of the Phanar, when all was said and done, had made their fortunes under Ottoman rule.

Yashim could remember exactly where he'd been when he first heard, in detail, the story of the Turkish Conquest. The Mavrocordato mansion, in the upper Phanar district, was the grandest, gloomiest palace on its street. Locked away behind high walls, and built in a style of high rococo, it was the headquarters of a sprawling family operation which extended to the principalities of the Danube and the godowns of Trabzon, taking in titles civil and ecclesiastical on the way. The Mavrocordatos had produced over the centuries scholars and emperors, boyar overlords and admirals of the fleet, rogues, saints and beautiful daughters. They were fantastically rich, dazzlingly well connected, and dangerously well informed.

There had been seven of them around a table, and Yashim. Their faces expressed many different things – humour and bitterness, dread or jealousy, complacency and contempt: but there had been one lovely face, too, he still saw sometimes in his dreams, whose glance said more. Only the eyes were the same, blue and brooding; Yashim had understood then why the Turks feared the blue eye.

The table had been covered in an Anatolian carpet that must have taken years to make, so tightly was it knotted. Coffee had been served, and when the heavy curtains were closed and the servants had withdrawn George Mavrocordato, the heavy-jowled patriarch of the clan, had invited Yashim to make his report.

Afterwards, George had slowly crossed to the fireplace, and the rest of them drifted over to sit with him in total silence that was like a form of speech. Eventually, George's ancient mother had smoothed the belly of her black silk dress, and beckoned him across.

And she had told him the story of the Conquest.

86

Now, stock-still in the alley, he remembered it all.

Above all he remembered her bitterness when she told him about the Kerkoporta. The little gate.

The siege had already lasted ninety days, when young Sultan Mehmed ordered a final assault on the walls. Exhausted and weak, the few thousand Byzantines who remained to defend their city heard the roll of the kettle drums, and saw the hills beyond the walls move as tens of thousands of Mehmed's troops descended to the attack. Wave after wave broke on the thinly defended walls, raised a thousand years before: the Anatolian levies, the Bashi-Bazouks from the hills of Serbia and Bulgaria, renegades and adventurers from the whole Mediterranean world. With every assault that they repulsed, the defenders weakened, and still the attack came on, with Mehmed's police standing at the rear with thongs and maces to discourage their retreat, the ladders crashing on the walls, the wild skirling of the Anatolian pipes, the fitful light of flares, and the sudden thundering crash of the Hungarian's gigantic cannon.

All the bells of the city were tolling. As the smoke cleared from the breach in the walls where the invading troops lay dying; as the defenders rushed to reconstitute the rubble; as the moon struggled clear of a ribbon of black and flying cloud, Mehmed himself advanced at the head of his crack infantry, the Janissaries. He led them to the moat, and from there they advanced, not in a wild battering frenzy like the irregulars and Turks who had been flung against the walls all through the night but, in the hour before dawn, in steady and unwavering file.

'They fought on the walls, hand to hand, for an hour or more,' the old lady said. 'Believing the Turks were failing. Even those Janissaries losing their momentum. It . . . it wasn't so.'

Yashim had watched her lips working against her toothless gums. Dry eyed, she said:

'There was a little gate, you see, at the angle where the great old walls of Theodosius met the lesser walls behind the Palace of the Caesars. It had been blocked up, goodness knows how many years before. So little, that gate. I don't think two men could pass through it abreast, but there – God's will is infinite in its mystery. It was opened at the start of the siege, for sallies. A party had just returned from a sortie, and – would you believe it – the last man back forgot to bar the gate behind him.'

It was the discovery of the little gate rocking on its hinges – a tiny gap in the whole eight miles of massive wall and inner wall, a momentary lapse of attention in a story that had run for a thousand years – that turned the course of the siege. Some fifty Janissaries shoved through and found themselves between the double walls. But their position was desperately exposed, and they might still have been driven back or killed by the defenders

225

had one of the heroes of the defence, a Genoese sea-captain, not been seriously wounded by a close shot at that very moment. His crewmen bore him from the walls; the Byzantines sensed that he had abandoned them, and gave a shout of despair. The Ottomans made a rush for the inner walls and a giant called Hasan surged over the stockade at the head of his Janissary company.

In ten minutes the Turkish flags were flying from the tower that stood above the Kerkoporta.

All this was four hundred years ago.

But now, rising behind the great cypress in the square, the tower of the Kerkoporta still stood, red and white and empty against the wintry blue sky.

The exact spot where fifteen hundred years of Roman history reached its bloody climax, as the last emperor of Byzantium tore off his imperial insignia and, sword in hand, vanished into the melee, never to be seen again.

The exact place where Constantinople, the Red Apple, the navel of the world, was won by the Janissaries for Islam and the sultan.

Old Palmuk had been right after all.

There *was* a fourth tower.

The fourth tekke.

Shaking his head at the memories he had summoned, Yashim walked forward into the winter sunlight.

87

The stone flight of steps which led up to the inner parapet of the first wall was invisible from the alley. To reach it, Yashim groped his way down an unmarked passage between two wooden houses built against the base of the wall. Reaching the top, he turned back and followed the parapet walk to the Kerkoporta Tower.

At parapet level there was a wooden door set in the masonry. It stood ajar, its hinges rusted, fastened to the jamb with a length of flaking iron chain which almost crumbled at Yashim's touch. He pushed. The door trembled slightly. He put his shoulder to the planks and heaved, until the hinges screamed and the door swung inwards into the dark.

The floor was littered with dust, fallen mortar, and dried droppings. Lifting his sandalled feet with care, Yashim advanced by the slanting sunlight into the centre of the chamber, and looked around. The ceiling was lost in the shadows. The walls showed signs of having been plastered once, but now revealed layers of Roman brickwork interspersed with courses of stone, while in the farthest corner of the chamber a stone staircase spiralled up from the floor below and disappeared upwards.

He crossed to the staircase and peered down. A slight breeze seemed to be coming up towards him, suggesting that the room below had air and maybe light; it carried odours of damp masonry and straw. He felt for the step and began to descend into darkness, his left hand trailing cobwebs from the rough outer wall of the spiral.

For several steps he was in total darkness, and when he thought of the sun on the square, and the tradesmen sitting outside their shops only a few yards away, he knew that this was as lonely and silent a spot as anywhere in the whole of Istanbul.

Another winding turn of the spiral brought a slight change in the quality of the darkness, and as Yashim went on down, and down, it bled to a grey twilight, until he stepped off the lowest tread into a vaulted room, supplied by a shuttered window on either side; only the shutters were cracked, and set with glowing chips of sunlight.

The walls were dark with greenish damp, but they were still plastered, and peering close Yashim could make out shapes like the cloudy shapes he had seen under the whitewash in the Nasrin tekke that morning. He recognised trees, pavilions, and a river. A long oak table ran down the room, and there were benches pushed up against the walls.

He took a step forwards and ran a fingertip along the table top. It was clean.

Yet the chamber overhead was a mess of dust and rubbish.

He faced the window. The chinks of light made it too bright to see, so he raised a hand to block them out, and saw a door. It was locked from the outside.

He stood with his back to the door and surveyed the room. From here he could see beyond the table.

At the far end stood what looked like a wooden chest, with a flat lid.

Yashim crossed the room and stood beside it. The lid was at waist-height. He eased his fingers under the rim, and tried it gently.

The lid lifted smoothly, and he looked inside.

⋘ 88 ⋙

Stanislaw Palewski opened his mouth to groan, as he did every morning when he woke up. But the groan did not come.

'Ha!'

The events of the night before had returned to him with unexpected clarity.

He wriggled his toes and they appeared obediently at the foot of the bed, poking out from beneath the duvet he had long ago adopted, in the Turkish fashion. His toes looked very dirty, until he remembered how he had blacked them with a brush.

He recalled the execrable champagne that he had been about to punish the previous evening. Doubtless some sharp French house had unloaded a bushel of the bad vintage on the unsuspecting Porte, charging top whack and confident that they would not be exposed. After all, who could complain? Not the Turks, who weren't supposed to drink the stuff. And the guests were hardly likely to make a fuss.

All the same, Palewski thought, he didn't get champagne every day, and he could have drunk rather more if that stiff-necked Russian hadn't been so clumsy.

He grinned.

Tossing his drink over Prince Derentsov had been, he thought, a gifted manoeuvre. But swabbing it down afterwards, to ensure the maximum discomfort, was little short of inspiration.

What did it matter if afterwards he got a dressing-down from the sultan himself? The Russian had almost certainly fared worse – it was he who laid down the challenge, after all, and broke the sultan's injunction. Palewski had merely responded as a man of honour must.

He and the sultan had had an interesting discussion, too. Surprisingly frank and friendly, and all because he had spilt his drink and wore a dastardly but inordinately well-contrived apology for the Sarmatian finery of his distant predecessors.

The sultan liked the coat. He had recalled, with Palewski, the old days which neither of them had ever known, but which both of them imagined tinged with a glamour and success that neither Poland nor the empire had ever rediscovered. And the sultan had said, in a voice that sounded suddenly weary and unsure, that all the world was changing very fast.

'Even this one.'

'Your Edict?'

The sultan had nodded. He described some of the pressures that now forced him to make changes in the running of his empire.

Military weakness. The growing spirit of rebellion, openly fostered by the Russians. The bad example of the Greeks, whose independence had been bought for them by European Powers.

'I believe we are taking the right steps,' he said. 'I am very positive about the Edict. But I understand, also, that there will be enormous difficulties in persuading many people of the need for these changes. Sometimes, to tell you the truth, I see opposition everywhere – even in my own home.'

Palewski was rather touched. The sultan's home, as they both knew, contained about 20,000 other people.

'Some will think that I am going too fast. Just a few may think that I have gone too slowly. And sometimes even I am afraid that what I am trying to do will be so misunderstood, so mangled and abused, that in the long run it will be the end of . . . all this.' And he gestured sadly at the decorations. 'But you see, Excellency, there is no other way. There is nothing else we can do.'

They had sat in silence together for some moments.

'I believe,' Palewski said slowly, 'that we must not fear change. The weight of the battle shifts here and there, but the hearts of the men who fight in it are not, I suppose, any weaker for that. I also believe, and hope, that you have acted in time.'

'Inshallah. Let us hope together that the next round of changes will be the better for us – and for you.'

And he had thanked the ambassador again for listening to him, and they shook hands.

As the sultan left to visit the Russian prince, he had turned at the door.

'Forget the incident this evening. I have forgotten it already. But not our talk.'

Unbelievable. Even Stratford Canning, the Great Elchi as the Turks liked to call him, who helped prop up the Porte against the pretensions of the Russians, would have swooned with pleasure if the sultan had spoken to him so sweetly.

Palewski – who normally took mornings one thing at a time – clasped his hands behind his head on the pillow, grinned, wriggled his toes, pulled the bell rope for tea, and decided that the first thing he would do today was pay a visit to the baths.

And later, it being a Thursday, he would dine with Yashim.

89

As the lid swung up on well-oiled hinges Yashim took a cautious peek inside.

The light was dim, and the interior of the chest in shadow, but even so Yashim could recognise something that was as prosaic as it was unexpected.

Instead of the dead cadet he dreaded, a stack of plates.

Beside the plates lay a tray of rather finicky little glasses, turned on their rims to keep out dust. Next to them, a metal goblet covered with what proved to be a folded strip of embroidered cloth. And a book.

Yashim picked it up. It was the Koran.

Otherwise the chest was empty, and smelled of polish.

Yashim smiled, a little grimly.

They're getting the caterers in, he said to himself. For a feast.

A Karagozi bacchanal.

He closed the lid quickly and made for the stairs. Halfway up he found himself swallowed in darkness and began taking the stairs two at a time, surging out of the spiral and across the chamber he had come in by, not caring that his flying feet raised a cloud of dust as he slewed over the floor. Out on the parapet he yanked the door closed, hooked the chain, and leaned back against the wall, breathing heavily. From where he stood he could look down into the branches of the elegant cypress tree.

How is it, he asked himself, that I can be frightened by a set of crockery?

Because, he thought, this time I've got it right. Three bodies turn up, close by three tekke. This would be the fourth. Established on the site of the Janissaries' greatest triumph – the Conquest of Constantinople.

And the body was yet to come.

90

The first person Murad Eslek saw when he strolled into the café for his breakfast was Yashim effendi, the gentleman he had rescued from the tanners.

Yashim saw him grin and wave. He murmured something to a passing waiter, then he was sitting down beside Yashim and shaking hands.

'You're well, inshallah? How's the foot?'

Yashim assured him that his foot was getting better. Eslek looked at him curiously.

'And I believe you, effendi. Forgive me, but you seem like a watered rose.'

Yashim bowed his head, remembering the hours he and Eugenia had spent sheathing the sword last night. He thought of her gasping, flinging back her beautiful head and baring her teeth with frantic lust, almost overcome – as she had whispered to him – by the discovery of a man who could do more than feed her appetite: who could, in the hours they played together, awaken a hunger she had never known before. He hadn't slept a wink.

He hadn't slept too much the night before, either, the night that he'd dropped Preen's assailant into the bubbling vat at the tannery. Since then he'd been constantly on the move – that second time to the Russian embassy, sending Palewski to the party to buy him time, pounding the streets in search of a tekke which meant nothing to anyone but him and – who? All the time his mind had been turning over the possibilities, tracking back over his encounters of the past week, looking for something he could take a grip on.

All the time trying not to think about what had happened last night. The pain, and the desire. The torment he had been powerless to resist.

He'd see what his friend Eslek could do to help him, and then he'd go to the hammam to revive. To wash away the dust of the Kerkoporta Tower. To ease his aching limbs, to dissolve his thoughts, and contemplate the presence of the demon he had fought so long and so hard to control.

Murad Eslek looked up from his coffee to see the expression on Yashim's face.

'You all right?'

Yashim smoothed it away.

'I need your help. Again,' he said.

91

An hour before dusk, Stanislaw Palewski joined a group of men spluttering with indignation at the doors of the Hammam Celebi, one of the better baths of the city on the Stamboul side.

It stood at the bottom of a hill, below a network of crowded alleyways whose relatively generous width suggested that this was, all the same, a prosperous district, neither so crammed that its houses almost jettied into their neighbours across the street, nor so grand that they were hidden behind walls, but a district of

233

well-to-do merchants and administrators who liked to saunter down the streets in the evening, and sit discussing the day's news in the numerous cafés and eating houses. It was not far, in fact, from the Kara Davut, and it was with the idea of stopping for a bathe en route to Yashim's Thursday dinner that Palewski had crossed the Galata bridge on foot, at peace with the world, with two bottles of the bison grass tucked very chill, and snug in their wrappings, into the bottom of his portmanteau.

The Hammam Celebi was unexpectedly closed for cleaning. Disappointed bathers clutched bags of clean linen and fulminated gloomily against the management.

'They are saying to come back in one hour, or even two!' A man with an Arab headcloth complained. 'As if I should spend my evening running up and down hills carrying clothes like a pedlar!'

Another man added: 'And as if this wasn't Thursday!'

Palewski pondered this oracular argument. But of course: tomorrow was a holy day for rest and prayer, to be tackled unspotted, at least on the outer side. Thursday night was always busy at the baths.

'Forgive me interrupting,' he said politely. 'I don't quite understand what the matter is.'

The men turned to look him up and down. If they were surprised or displeased to find a foreigner – and a ferenghi, to boot – with a plain intention of entering their bath, they were certainly too well mannered to let it show. And when it came to bathing, the procedure was, by long tradition, a democratic one. The hours for men to use the hammam were hours when they could be used by all men, infidel or believer, foreigner or Stambouliot.

A third frustrated bather, a man with a small paunch and a few grey curls peeping from his turban, politely offered Palewski an explanation.

'For some reason none of us can fathom, the bath people have taken it into their heads to clean out the hammam in the middle of a busy evening, instead of at night.'

A fourth man spoke up, quietly.

'It may be some sickness. It has never happened before. Perhaps we should be praising the bath manager, instead of being so angry. We should take their advice and return in a short while. As for carrying our linen about, there are many decent cafés in the district, where one could easily while away the time. Is it not so?'

The group slowly dispersed. Palewski couldn't tell if they still meant to return, after the last man had raised the possibility of disease. He thought, probably, yes. The Turks, after all, are fatalists. Like me.

That the baths could be closed down because of sickness surprised him more than the probability that everyone would come back in spite of it.

He wondered what to do. On the one hand, he had been looking forward to rubbing the blacking off his feet. On the other, though the delay might not make him late for Yashim, he was not yet quite as fatalistic as the Turks in the matter of disease.

He decided to sit and have a coffee somewhere, keeping an eye on the hammam. If it re-opened, and the signs were good, he could choose whether to go in. If not, he would simply go on to see his friend at the appointed time, and save his feet for the pump later. Or tomorrow morning, more likely, he remembered, thinking of all the vodka in his bag.

He turned, walked a short way up the hill, and chose a coffee shop from where he could watch the door of the hammam without moving his head. He could even look across the dome of the baths, and over the roofs behind, to watch the sun set into the Sea of Marmara, gilding the rooftops and the minarets, the domes and the cypress trees.

92

Eslek had picked up fast, Yashim thought. He had not refused payment, to his relief: the task was crucial, too important to be carried out purely as a favour. He'd had his favour already, anyway. It was time to make returns.

He slipped off his clothes and handed them to the attendant, shuffling into a pair of wooden clogs to protect the soles of his feet from the hot stone. Inside the hot rooms of the hammam the floors were always dangerously slippery. Naked except for a clout around his hips he clip-clopped through the door into a large domed chamber filled with steam. The dome was supported on squinches which created semi-circular niches around the walls, where one could sit by a flowing spout of hot water that ebbed away downhill to the drain in the centre, scooping up the water to clean one's body to the very depths of one's pores.

Yashim stepped gratefully into the steamy room. He set his feet apart, arched his back, and stretched until the joints in his shoulders cracked. Then he ran his fingers through his black curls and looked around for somewhere to sit. He took possession of a niche, and sat on a small low bench with his back against the wall and his long legs stretched out in front of him. For several minutes he did not move, allowing himself to absorb the heat, feeling his sweat begin to run. At last he bent forward and picked up a tin scoop at his feet.

He stretched out an arm to fill the scoop, and very slowly tipped the water over his head. His eyes were closed. He loved the way the water sought out runnels through his hair and trickled, like soothing fingers, down his neck. He did it again. He heard a man laugh. He smelt the animal scent of clean skin. After a few more minutes he picked up a bar of soap and began to lather himself completely, beginning with his feet, working his way up his body to his face and hair.

He continued to pour the water over his head and shoulders. Eventually he began to wash the soap away, from top to toe, working at his skin with his fingers, watching the way the hairs on his legs followed the course of the water. It always reminded him of Osman's dream, the dream in which the founder of the Ottoman dynasty had seen a great tree, whose leaves suddenly trembled and then aligned, as if in a wind, pointing a myriad sharp points towards the Red City of Byzantium. Finally he gave his feet a thorough kneading with his thumbs, and stood up and crossed to find room on the raised platform in the centre of the room.

He climbed up languidly onto the hot platform, the so-called belly of the hammam, spread out his towel, and lay on it, face down, his head turned to the left and his eyes closed. The huge masseur, bald as an egg, every ripple of his flesh hairless and shining, closed in, and began to work Yashim's feet with great force and dexterity, rhythmically smoothing and digging at Yashim's flesh until Yashim felt his whole body rocking up and down. Up and down. Head to toe on the burning marble.

Invisible shivers ran up his legs. He thought of the pile of plates. He saw Eugenia's white breasts, a tangle of sheets, her lips swollen with the heat. This was another kind of heat, a heat which sucked at his will, sapped him of all his strength. Once or twice he kicked out, involuntarily, as he rose from the sleep he so desperately craved. 'Salright,' he murmured to himself. A few minutes, then the masseur will tap him off the bench and wake him up. Sleep.

Slowly the room began to empty out.

The masseur kept on working on Yashim's body.

Slowly, and more slowly.

There was only one man left in the hammam, asleep on a

bench. The masseur raised his fingers from Yashim's neck. Yashim didn't move.

The masseur went over to the sleeping bather and scooped him up in his powerful banded arms like a little baby. The man started, and opened his eyes, but when the masseur set him down again he was in the tepidarium, facing a cold plunge. The masseur gave him a friendly little shove and he leaped into the cold tub, gasping and laughing. He'd been asleep!

The masseur shot the bolt of the hammam door and folded his huge arms over his chest.

Inside the hot room Yashim slept on, dreaming of melting snow.

93

'How do I look now, old man?'

Fizerly looked his friend up and down with a critical eye.

'Capital, Compston. Or should I say, Mehmed? If we're going out to explore the old city, just remember that you're Mehmed from here on.'

Compston chuckled and looked at himself in the embassy mirror. Fizerly had been awfully clever with the turban – in the end, they'd arranged it so that not a hair of his blond head straggled out, and even if the balance of the turban had suffered slightly in consequence it wouldn't show. 'Just keep moving your head about like a good chap,' Fizerly had suggested, helpfully. Not Fizerly, that is. Ali. Ali Baba, at your service.

Compston-Mehmed giggled and rubbed a little more soot into his eyebrows.

'Let's hope it doesn't rain,' he said.

94

Palewski drank his coffee slowly, watching the sunset. Outside, the hubbub of traffic was subsiding, the porters going empty-handed uphill, a few small donkey carts returning to stables, while the numbers of people taking the evening air increased. Sometimes Palewski recognised them – a palace official he couldn't name, a Greek dragoman linked to one of the Phanariot merchant houses, an imam looking exactly as he had looked fifteen years before, when Palewski had had a discussion with him on the history of the idea of the transmigration of souls. Later he saw a couple of juniors from the British embassy – Fizerly, he recalled, with the straggling whiskers, now smoking a Turkish cheroot, sauntering along with a boy in a curious sort of hat, apparently made out of various pieces of his underwear, nodding and laughing at his side. Palewski wondered vaguely what they were doing, dressed like children out of a nativity play. Nobody seemed to pay them much attention, and they strolled down the hill and disappeared round the corner of the baths.

How much Istanbul had changed in the thirty years he had known it! What was it that he had said to Yashim? He had said he mourned the passing of the Janissaries. Well, the past ten years had been particularly lively. Since the suppression of the Janissaries there had been nothing to restrain the sultan except the fear of foreign intervention, and the sultan was a born moderniser. He'd taken to the European saddle faster than anyone. The change that had come over the city went beyond the gradual but continuous disappearance of turbans and slippers, and their replacement by the fez, and leather shoes. That was a change which Palewski was romantic enough to regret, though he did not expect it to be complete in his lifetime – if only because the great city still drew people from every corner of the empire towards it, people who had never heard of sumptuary laws, or shoe-laces. But more people from outside the empire were coming in, too, and in the gradual rebuilding of Galata after the great fire there were oddities like the French glovemaker, and the Belgian who sold bad champagne, ensconced in their little shops, with tinkling bells, just as if they were in Cracow.

The door opened and a gust of cold air entered the fug of the café. Palewski recognised the man who came in, too, though for a while he couldn't place him: a tall, bullish man in late middle age, distinguished by a white cloak. He was followed in by two European merchants Palewski had seen around, but not spoken to. He thought they might be French.

The three men took a table slightly behind Palewski's line of sight, so it was a while before he glanced back and recognised the seraskier, who had shrugged back his cloak and now sat with booted legs tightly crossed, his blue-grey uniform jacket buttoned to the neck. He was toying with a coffee cup, listening with a slight smile to one of his companions who was leaning forward and making a point, quietly, with the help of his hands. French, then. Or Italian?

Palewski wondered if he might order another coffee himself. He looked down the hill: the doors of the baths were still shut, but another knot of men with bags of linen had gathered outside, presumably rehearsing the complaints he had listened to half an hour before. Cleaning the baths! On a Thursday night, too. Sacrilege! Scandal! Palewski grinned, and waved at the waiter.

Well, he could see that they were cleaning the baths – and thoroughly, too. The little air vent at the top of the dome was releasing a corona of white steam which rose, eddied and then trailed away in the dusk. Caught by the dying rays of the sun, the steam sometimes refracted a rainbow of colour. Very pretty, Palewski thought. Next came a stick, bound with a trailing white cloth, to riddle out the vent. Very thorough, Palewski thought. If they finish in time, I will certainly try my luck.

The waiter brought him a fresh coffee. Palewski leaned back to overhear the conversation going on behind him, but it was being muttered at a distance, over the bubble of pipes, the hiss of boiling water, and the murmur of low conversation around the room. Disappointed, he looked out of the window again.

How odd, he thought. The stick was still going up and down in the hole, and the scrap of cloth was fluttering with it, like a tiny flag.

There's cleaning, Palewski thought curiously, and obsession.

And as he watched, the stick suddenly wavered and keeled over to one side. Stuck at an angle, the little white cloth waved and flapped in the evening breeze like a signal of surrender.

95

Yashim had been dreaming. He dreamed that he and Eugenia were standing naked, side by side in the snow, watching a forest fire crackle in the treetops. It wasn't cold. As the fire advanced, the warmth increased, and the snow began to melt. He shouted 'Jump!' and they both leaped over the edge of the melted snow. He had no recollection of hitting the ground below, but he had started to run across the square towards the huge cypress. Eugenia was nowhere but the soup master reached out with his enormous hands and lit the cypress with a match. It burned like a rocket as Yashim held on to it, pressing his face against the smooth bark; but when he tried to pull away he couldn't, because his skin had melted and stuck to the tree.

He coughed and tried to raise his head. His eyes opened. They seemed to be filmed over: his vision was foggy. He made another effort to raise his head and this time his cheek sucked against the hard top of the massage bench, where he lay in a pool of his own sweat. He rolled over, his whole body slithering on the bench, and swung his legs to the floor.

A dull pain throbbed through his feet, and it took him some moments to realise that the soles of his feet were burning against the stone floor. He sat back on the bench, legs raised, and looked round. There was nobody else there.

The steam was peeling away from the floor in angry ribbons, which blended into a fog that thickened as it approached the dome. Yashim found that he was breathing hard: the air was so hot and humid that every breath stuffed his throat like a rag, and brought him no relief. With a heavy hand he dashed the sweat from his eyes.

The fog felt curiously intimate, as if it were really a problem with his eyes, and this seemed to disorient him: he jerked his head about, searching for the doors. He saw his wooden clogs beside the massage bench. With his feet in the clogs he stood swaying for a moment, holding onto the bench; and then, like a man struggling through the snow, he staggered forwards towards the door. He fell against it, groping for a handle: but the door was as smooth as the walls.

No handle.

Yashim drummed with his fists, unable to shout, his breath sobbing through his teeth. No one came. Again and again he crashed against the door, throwing his whole weight behind his shoulder; but it didn't budge, and the sound itself was flattened against the iron-bound oak. He sank into a squat, one hand against the door for support.

The heat rolling off the floor made it impossible to hold that position for very long. He stood up slowly; bent double, he pushed himself along the wall. The spigot in the first niche had stopped flowing. There was a scoop on the floor, but it contained only an inch of water and the metal was hot.

He could not guess how long he crouched there, gazing down between his arms at the water in the scoop. But when the water started to steam he thought: I'm being braised.

But I am thinking.

I must get out.

Gingerly he raised his head, for it felt as though it must burst at any minute: he needed to keep the water out of his eyes.

A faint pattern of light penetrated the fog above. It came from the pattern of holes let into the roof of the dome, and for a second Yashim wondered if he could somehow climb up and reach it, thrust his hands, maybe, and his lips against the holes.

You can't climb the inside of a dome, he said to himself.

His eye followed the base of the walls, searching for anything that he could use.

He almost missed it: the long bamboo cane attached to the head of a mop, tucked up into the angle between the floor and the wall.

He could hardly pick it up: his fingers were puffy and hard to bend.

Yashim raised the flimsy cane with an effort. Too short.

Once more he started round the room. Twice he almost blacked out, and fell to his hands and knees: but the burning stone tortured him back to life, and he tottered on until he found the second cane.

Now he needed a strip of cloth to bind them together. He tore at a towel with his fingers and his teeth, whimpering now.

At last he managed to create a nick in the hem. Even tearing the cloth he was like a puny child, nearly too weak to raise his arms, but at last he had a bandage of cotton which he secured around the two bamboos. The remaining scrap he tied to the top of the pole, and then he began to raise it up. The bare end struck on the side of the dome. He scraped it upwards.

It was too short.

Through the vapour, against the dome, Yashim could hardly tell how short. His face was set in a rictus now, his teeth bared. He staggered across to the massage bench and clambered onto it. Every movement was an agony. As he raised his arms he noticed that they were almost purple, as if blood was starting to ooze from his pores.

He started to pump the stick up and down, up and down. At every stroke he felt that he was pumping the blood, too, through the pores in his skin. He faintly remembered that he needed to make the stick move, but he could no longer remember why this had seemed important, only that it was all the instruction he possessed. It was all he had left.

≪ 96 ≫

'*Avec permission*, seraskier.' Palewski stuck out his hand as he bowed. 'Palewski, ambassadeur de Pologne.'

The seraskier glanced upwards with a look of surprise. Then he smiled politely.

'Enchanté, Excellence.'

'I'm so sorry to interrupt,' Palewski continued, 'but I have just seen something rather strange and I wanted your opinion.'

'Mais bien sûr.' The seraskier did not sound impressed. What he and the Polish ambassador found strange could be entirely different things. 'What have you seen, Your Excellency?'

It occurred to Palewski that any explanation he could give would sound thin, even laughable. He turned to the seraskier's companions.

'Would you excuse me? I'd like to borrow the seraskier for just one minute. Indulge me, effendi.'

The men made noncommittal gestures, but said nothing. The

seraskier looked from them to Palewski with an impatient half-smile.

'Very well, Excellency.' He was on his feet. 'My apologies, gentlemen.'

Palewski took him by the arm and steered him into the street.

'Something funny just happened at the baths,' he began. 'First they closed them, quite suddenly, on a Thursday night.' He had seized on this detail, which had so baffled him at first, as being the oddest from a Turkish point of view. 'They are supposed to be cleaning them out, but a minute ago I watched someone waving a flag out through a hole in the roof. I say a flag, because there is simply no other explanation I can think of. It looked like, well, a signal. And now it has stopped. D'you see, effendi? It may sound odd to you, but it really did look like that – as if someone had been signalling, and then was stopped for some reason. I wanted to go down there myself, but seeing you – well, I thought you could make an enquiry with greater weight.'

The seraskier frowned. It sounded like rubbish, of course, and whatever went on in a hammam was really no concern of his . . . and yet, the Pole was clearly agitated.

'For your sake, Excellency, we will go and ask,' he said, with as much gallantry as he could muster.

⊰ 97 ⊱

Yashim could hear voices. A tiny sliver of light cut into the darkness as he raised his eyelids a fraction of an inch. Something that soothed him pressed for a moment against his body, and was gone.

Dim shapes moved in the light. *Dreadful accident . . . stroke of luck* . . . Then someone was wiping his face with a cool wet cloth and Palewski's own face swam into view.

'Yash? Yashim? Can you hear me?'

He tried to nod.

Palewski put a hand under his head and tilted him forwards.

'Drink this,' he said. Yashim felt the rim of a glass against his lips, but his lips felt huge. His fingers seemed to be in gloves, they were so hard to bend.

'Can he speak?'

It was the seraskier's voice.

I am dreaming, Yashim thought.

Hands picked him up and moved him through the air. Then he was lying back again, covered with a blanket.

Palewski saw his friend settled on the litter and motioned to the bearers. To the seraskier he said: 'I'll take him to the embassy. He'll be safe there.'

The seraskier nodded. 'Please let me know how he is doing later.'

The litter-bearers shouldered their poles and followed the ambassador out into the night.

Yashim was aware of the jouncing of the litter as they threaded through the dark streets. He heard the slap-slap of the bearers' feet and the jingle of little bells, and wondered how badly he was hurt. Sometimes the fabric of the litter rasped against his skin and he almost shouted out.

A runner had gone on ahead to give Palewski's maid time to make up a bed and lay a fire; when they arrived she was already on the stairs with a wedge of fresh linen. Palewski took candles off a table in the hall to light the bearers' way, and so expertly did they carry him that Yashim only knew they were going upstairs by the slope of the ceiling.

They transferred him to the bed. Palewski settled a fire in the stove that stood in one corner of the room, tiled with a design of twining blue flowers, while Marta appeared with a basin of cold water and a sponge, turning down the sheet so that she could dab delicately at Yashim's inflamed skin.

Yashim felt nothing, only a wave of nausea that now and then clutched at his belly and made him retch. When he did, Marta cleaned him up without a word. He slept for a while, and when he woke she was there again, with a spoonful of liquid so bitter it made his mouth ache; but he swallowed and the nausea slowly dissolved.

Marta brought up a basin of warm water that smelled of lavender and honey. Yashim was breathing steadily now. By the light of the candles he watched the silent Greek girl with her straight brow and olive skin, standing over the basin, absorbed in her task. She took a pile of big linen napkins and one by one she soaked them in the basin, wrung them out, and spread them on a clothes rack to cool. Her straight black hair was gathered in two plaits, pinned to the side of her head; when she bent forwards he could see the little hairs on the nape of her neck as they caught the light.

When she was ready she took the first honey-scented napkin and folded it.

'Please close your eyes,' she said, in a voice as soft as a dove's. She laid the napkin firmly over his forehead, and he felt her fingers smooth the damp cloth over his eyelids, and mould it across his nose and cheekbones.

'Can you roll onto your side? Here, let me help you.'

A moment later he felt another cool cloth pressed around his chin and neck and shoulder. His left arm was lifted, and Marta's fingers smoothed another napkin over the side of his chest and his back.

'Try not to move,' she said. As she worked her way down his body Yashim began to find his sensations returning. He felt her palms on his buttocks and thighs, through the cool cloth. At length she reached his feet, and helped him roll onto his back to finish wrapping his right side.

'I feel like an Egyptian mummy,' Yashim croaked. She put a finger to his lips. His voice had sounded weak and strained: he even wondered if she had heard what he said.

He must have dozed, because suddenly he was afraid he was being smothered, unable to open his eyes, crushed by a fearful pressure on his chest and limbs. He gave a cry, and tried to struggle free, but two small hands pressed him back by the shoulders and a voice whispered softly: 'I am here, don't worry. It's all right. It's better now.'

For a moment he felt her breath on his lips, and then she had removed the bandage over his eyes and he opened them to see her standing over him with the napkin in one hand and a shy smile on her face.

He smiled back. For the first time since she had touched him, he was conscious of his nakedness; conscious that he was, once again, alone with a woman. He raised himself gingerly on one elbow, and she seemed to feel it, too, because she turned to the candle and said: 'If you feel better, you should wash. The honey will be sticky. I will fetch what you need.'

She was gone for a minute. When she returned she carried a basin of warm water and a robe draped over her arm. She set the basin down by the bed and laid the robe near his feet.

'There is a sponge in the basin,' she explained.

As she turned to go, Yashim said: 'My arm is still very stiff.'

She shot him a smile and for the first time he saw her serious dark eyes twinkle.

'Then you will have to wash slowly,' she said, sweetly. And was gone.

Yashim sighed, and heaved his legs off the bed in a rustling cascade of napkins.

He washed himself, as the girl had said, slowly.

Aware that there was little time.

Wondering what had become of Murad Eslek.

Wondering what Marta meant to his friend Palewski – and he to her.

98

'What is the time?'

Yashim had opened his eyes to find Palewski perched at the foot of his bed, his elbows resting on his knees, looking patiently into his face.

'After midnight. Marta has gone to bed.'

Yashim gave him a weak smile as a stray thought entered his mind. To Palewski I am only half a man – but the half he likes. The half he can trust. And he decided never to tell his friend about what happened between him and Eugenia at the Russian embassy.

'I have to thank you, Palewski, for saving my life.'

'And I you, my old friend, for allowing me to hobnob for an hour or so with the sultan.' He clapped his hands together. 'It was a capital party!'

Yashim looked blank. Palewski told him about Derentsov's challenge and the intimate conversation he had held with Sultan Mahmut IV.

'I get the impression, Yash, that the sultan has sleepless nights over this Edict of his. It will make him a very lonely man. He makes a lot of enemies.'

Yashim nodded. 'I'm beginning to think that murder is the least of it. And tonight, but for you, they would have killed me too.'

'You were in a public place.'

But Yashim said: 'I forgot something I'd learned. Working in the stoke-holes of the baths was one of the jobs that Janissaries took up, if they survived the purge. Tell me, you saw my signal?'

Palewski recounted the series of events which had brought him and the seraskier to the doors of the baths.

'The seraskier?' Yashim put in. 'If I hadn't been half-dead – he's the man I need to speak to. I ought to go and find him.'

Palewski put out a restraining hand. 'Marta left me particular instructions, Yashim. She expects to find you here in the morning. You are her patient. Perhaps you would like to drink some tea? Or something stronger?'

Yashim closed his eyes. 'I've found out where the fourth man is going to appear.'

Palewski looked anxious. 'Good, good,' he murmured. He straightened his back. 'I'm sorry, Yashim, but do you know what I think? None of us are players in this scheme. We're witnesses, at best: even you. It's too –' He searched his mind. 'You told me you had the impression that it was like a feast prepared, meze and a main dish, remember. Well, I believe you were right. We're guests. And it's a dangerous party.'

He stood up carefully and approached Yashim, crouching beside his pillow.

'You aren't going to find anyone alive. None of the other cadets were killed where you found them. You won't find this one being cooked in front of your eyes, either. Take this rest. You can go off, if you feel fit, very early in the morning after Marta has seen to you again.'

Yashim stared at the ceiling. It was sensible advice. He'd lost the time he needed, and nothing would bring it back. He wanted so much to do as his friend suggested, sleep – and trust to Eslek. He could be at the Kerkoporta by first light.

It was sensible advice. But in one particular, at least, the Polish ambassador could not have been more wrong.

99

The provisioning of a great city, the kadi liked to remark, is the mark of a successful civilisation. In Istanbul it was a business that had been honed close to perfection by almost two thousand years' experience, and it could truly be said of the markets of Istanbul that there was not a flower, a fruit, a type of meat or fish that did not make its appearance there in season.

An imperial city has an imperial appetite, and for centuries the city had commanded daily tribute from an enormous hinterland. Where the Byzantines had managed their market gardens on the approaches from Thrace and Asia Minor, the Turks, too, raised vegetables. From two seas – the warm Mediterranean and the dark, gelid waters of the Black Sea – it was supplied abundantly with fish, while the sweetest trout from the lakes of Macedonia were carried to the city in tanks. From the mountains of Bulgaria came many kinds of honey to be turned into sweets by the master sweet-makers of Istanbul.

It was a finely regulated business, all in all, from the Balkan grazing grounds to the market stall, in a constant slither of orders, inspections, purchases and requisitions. Like any activity that needs unremitting oversight, it was open to abuse.

The kadi of the Kerkoporta market had taken up his job twenty years before, and earned himself a reputation for severity. A butcher who used false weights was hanged at the doorway of his own shop. A greengrocer who lied about the provenance of his fruit had his hands struck off. Others, who had jibbed a customer, perhaps, or slipped out of the official channels to procure bargain stock, found themselves forced to wear a wide wooden collar for a few weeks, or to pay a stiff fine, or to be nailed by the ear to the door of their own shop. The Kerkoporta market had become a byword for honest dealing, and the kadi supposed that he was doing everything for the best.

The merchants found him officious, but they were divided as to the best way to deal with him. A minority were for clubbing together to manufacture some complaint against him from which he would be unlikely to recover; but the majority shrugged their shoulders and counselled patience. The kadi, some suggested, was merely establishing his price. Will not an ambitious carpet dealer wax lyrical over the colours and qualities and rarity of his carpet, as a prelude to negotiation? Will not a young wrestler hurl all his strength into the contest, while the older man uses no more than he actually needs to use? The time would come, they argued, when the kadi would start to crack.

The action brigade claimed that this man was different. The realists said he was human. And the subtlest minds of all quietly observed that the kadi had two daughters. The eldest, approaching the marrying age, was reputed to be very beautiful.

The kadi's fall, when it finally came, was silent and absolute. The rumour of his daughter's beauty was perfectly true; she was also meek, pious, obedient and skilful. It was these very qualities that caused the kadi such agony of mind, as he tried to choose a husband for her. He loved his daughter, and wanted the best for her; and it was because she was so good that he became so picky. It was because he was so picky that he eventually settled on a renowned teacher at the central medrese, a bachelor from an excellent wealthy family.

The kadi's fortune was by no means equal to providing his daughter with the handsome dowry and memorable wedding festivities that the groom's family customarily provided for their own daughters. They didn't mind, of course; but it tormented the kadi. The cause of the torment was divined by the match-maker, a shrewd old lady who chewed betel and wore a gold bangle for every union she had successfully negotiated: she tinkled like a fountain when she moved. And she moved a lot: that is to say, she visited almost every house in the district on a fairly regular basis, and through one of these visits the Kerkoporta merchants learned of the kadi's dilemma.

The affair was handled with delicacy and tact.

For fixing up a splendid wedding, and clubbing together to provide the girl with a stylish dowry, the merchants asked the kadi for nothing in return. Few markets were as well served as the Kerkoporta by its kadi, who had brought such order and regularity and honesty into the business that even a foreigner, as was widely known, could make purchases there in perfect confidence. Hardly anyone need even know that the dowry and the feast came as a private act of tribute from the market to the judge.

Nothing was said. No deals were struck, perish the thought. The kadi continued to do his job with rigour, as before. He wasn't even particularly grateful.

He was simply weary. Being honest was tiring, but it wasn't as exhausting as carrying on with what he knew: that he had connived with the merchants he was deputed to regulate.

He continued to sit in the market house, hearing cases, investigating abuses, frowning at supplicants and keeping his own counsel. But he no longer punished transgressions with such severity. He no longer really cared whether the merchants cheated their customers or not. If he found gold in his purse, or a freshly slaughtered sheep delivered to his door, it roused neither gratitude nor indignation.

He had another daughter, after all.

100

The donkeys drummed on the cobbles with their little hooves. The two-wheeled carts jounced and swayed behind them, with a noise like sliding pebbles. The thin beams of lamplight careered around the blank walls.

Fourteen. Fifteen. Sixteen.

Murad Eslek raised a hand. The night porter gave a nod and let the barrier swing gently back into the wooden block on the other side of the gate, closing the road.

Eslek called out a brief thanks, and followed his carts into the square.

Sixty or seventy donkey carts jostled through the narrow openings, arguing their passage with a dozen or so much bigger mule carts, a flock of bleating sheep, and vendors still arriving. Space was constricted by the empty stalls Eslek and his men had been putting up over the last couple of hours, each one topped by a lantern. Wagon eight, Eslek noticed, had overshot its stall: no use trying to back up, it would have to be led round again for a second try, when the others were out of the way. One of the stallholders, wrapped in a horse blanket tied on with string, was demanding to know where his delivery was: cart five had got swept away by an eruption of mule carts coming up from the city. Eslek could just about make it out, with its high stack of poultry cages swaying dangerously in the distance. But for the most part everything was in place.

He began to help unload the leading cart. Baskets of aubergines, jute bags of potatoes, bushels of spinach thumped onto the stall. When it was almost done, Eslek wheeled back and began the same routine with the cart behind. The trick was to finish unloading simultaneously, keep the train together, and move out in order. Otherwise it was all back and forth, and no rest till sun-up.

He darted across the square to the poultry cart. Just as he feared, it had got wedged in behind a mule cart loaded with sacks of rice and no one was paying any attention to the driver's shouts. Eslek grabbed the mule's halter and waved his arm at the driver standing in the cart, swinging the heavy sacks into the arms of a man on the ground.

'Hey! Hey! Hold it!'

The driver shot him a glance and turned to pick up another sack. Eslek drove the mule's halter back: the mule tried to lift its head but decided to take a step backwards instead. The cart jolted and the driver, caught off balance, staggered back with a sack in his arms and sat down heavily.

The stallholder grinned and scratched his head. The driver leaped from his cart in a fury.

'What in the name of God – oh, it's you, is it?'

'Come on, Genghis, get this rattletrap backed off half a mo, we're stuck. Here, pull her up.' He gestured to the donkey cart driver, who was sitting on the cart board with his long driving stick poised and ready. The rice carter backed his mule cart, the donkey driver whacked the dust from the donkey's flanks, and the little beast trotted forward.

'Cheers!' Eslek waved, then jogged alongside his cart with a hand on the board. 'Second time this week, Abdul. You're holding us all up.'

He brought the cart to the back of his own train, told the driver to grab a crate and with the stallholder's help they unloaded, dodging up and down the line. Most of the stallholders were already arranging their stock; the scent of charcoal hung in the air as the street-food vendors lit their fires. Eslek felt hungry, but he still had to clear the carts out; it was another hour before he saw them all safely through the gate, where he paid off the drivers.

'Abdul,' he said. 'Just keep your eyes open, understand? Those mule men look tough, but they can't touch you. Not if you don't give them a chance. Just stick to the tail of the man in front, keep your eyes straight. They're all bluster.'

He walked back to the market. Now and then he had to flatten himself against the wall to allow other donkey carts to clatter by, but by the time he reached the square the first hubbub of the night had subsided. The vendors were busy with their arrangements of fruit and vegetables, vying against each other by building pyramids, amphitheatres and acropolises of okra, aubergines and waxy yellow potatoes, or of dates and apricots, in blocks and bands and fancy patterns of colour. Others, who had lit their braziers, were waiting for the coals to develop their white skin of ash, and using the time to nick chestnuts with a knife, or to load a thick skewer with slices of mutton. Soon, Eslek thought with a pang of hunger and anticipation, the meatballs would be simmering, the fish frying, the game and poultry roasting on the spits.

He, too, had another job to do before he could eat. Once he had checked with his vendors, and reckoned their bills, he took a tour of the perimeter of the market. He paid particular attention to dark corners, shadowed doorways, and the space beneath the stalls whose owners he did not serve. He looked men in the face, and recognised them quickly; and now and then he lifted his head to scan the market as a whole, to see who was coming in, and to watch for the arrival of any carts he didn't know.

From time to time he wondered what was keeping Yashim.

A troupe of jugglers and acrobats, six men and two women, took up a position near the cypress tree, squatting on their haunches, waiting for light and crowds. Between them they had set a big basket with a lid, and Murad Eslek spent a while watching them from the corner of the alley beneath the city walls until he had seen that the basket really did contain bats, balls and other paraphernalia of their trade. Then he moved on, eyeing up the other quacks and entertainers who had crowded in for the Friday market: the Kurdish story teller in a patchwork coat; the Bulgarian fire-eater, bald as an egg; a number of bands – Balkan pipers, Anatolian string players; a pair of sinuous and silent Africans, carefully dotting a blanket spread on the ground with charms and remedies; a row of gypsy silversmiths with tiny anvils and a supply of coins wrapped in pieces of soft leather, who were already at work, snipping the coins and beating out tiny rings and bracelets.

He took another look across the market and thought of food, though he knew it would be a few minutes yet before he could eat. The air was already spiced with the fragrance of roasting herbs; he could hear the sizzle of hot fat dripping on the coals. He lifted a cube of salty white bread from a stall as he passed by, and popped it in his mouth; and then, since no one had rebuked him, he stopped a moment to admire the arrangement of the spit, worked by a little dog scampering gamely round inside a wooden wheel. Nearby he saw out of the corner of his eye a man flipping meatballs with a flat knife. He drew a few meatballs to the side of the pan, and Eslek stepped forwards.

'Ready, then?'

The man cracked a smile and nodded.

'First customer Friday is always free.'

Murad grinned. He watched the man scatter a few pitta breads on the hot surface of the pan, press them down with the blade of his knife and flip them over. He pulled one towards him and opened it up with a quick arc of the point and a sliding motion with the flat side.

'Chilli sauce?'

Murad Eslek's mouth watered. He nodded.

The man took a dab of sauce on the end of his knife, spread it inside the bread, scooped up two meatballs and stuffed them home with a generous handful of lettuce and a squeeze of lemon.

With the kebab in two hands, Eslek sauntered happily through the stalls, munching greedily.

He saw nothing to surprise him. Eventually he went down the alley by the walls and found the dark passageway Yashim had mentioned. He mounted the steps carefully, and made his way back to the tower. The door was still on its chain as Yashim had left it. He sat down on the parapet, swinging his legs, licking his fingers, and looked down through the cypress at the market below.

The sky had lightened, and it would soon be dawn.

101

When Yashim opened his eyes again it was still dark. The fire in the grate had died out. Wincing slightly, he eased himself upright and slipped his legs over the edge of the bed. His feet felt bruised and swollen, but he forced himself to stand upright. After he had hobbled up and down the room for a few minutes, he found the pain was bearable. He found his clothes by accident, putting out a hand in the darkness to steady himself. They were neatly piled on a table where Marta must have placed them.

He took his cloak from the hall and stepped out into the early morning air. His skin was tender, but his head was clear.

He walked swiftly down towards the Golden Horn. The lines of the Karagozi poem circled in his head to the rhythm of his footsteps.

> Unknowing
> And knowing nothing of unknowing,
> They sleep.
> *Wake them.*

He quickened his pace to reach the wharves. On the quayside he found a ferryman awake, huddled into his burnous against the dawn chill, and once across he took a sedan chair and ordered the bearers to the Kerkoporta market.

❦ 102 ❦

'I saw you arrive,' Murad Eslek explained. He'd recognised Yashim immediately, and rushed to greet him before he disappeared into the crowd. Now that the day had broken there were plenty of people milling past the stalls, filling their baskets with fresh produce. 'I've been looking about, like you said. Nothing unusual. A few performers I don't know, that's about it. Quiet, everything normal.'

'The tower?'

'Yep, I checked it out. The door you told me about, it's still on the chain. I've been up there for an hour.'

'Hmmm. There's another door, though, from the other side. On a lower floor. I'd better take a look. You stay here and keep your eyes open, but if I'm not back in half an hour, bring some of your lads and come after me.'

'Like that, is it? Half a minute, I'll get someone to go with you now.'

'Yes,' Yashim said. 'Why not?'

It took them only a few minutes to reach the parapet. The porter Eslek had found stamped along incuriously behind Yashim, but he was glad of his presence: the memory of the dark stairs leading down to that clean chamber still made him shiver. He unlooped the chain and once more set his shoulder to the door.

The porter protested.

'I think we didn't ought to go in there. It's not allowed.'

'I'm allowed,' Yashim said shortly. 'And you're with me. Come on.'

It was darker this time, but Yashim knew where to go. At the head of the steps he put his finger to his lips and led the way down. The tekke was just as he'd left it the day before. He tried the door: it was still locked. The porter stood nervously at the foot of the stairs, looking round in surprise. Yashim went over to the chest and raised the lid. Same collection of plates and glasses. Still no cadet.

Yashim straightened up.

'Come on, we'll go back now,' he said.

The porter needed no second bidding.

103

The effendi had told him to keep his eyes open, and Eslek had been doing just that for several hours. He wasn't sure what he was looking out for, exactly, or how he would recognise it when he found it. Something out of the ordinary, perhaps, Yashim had suggested. Or something so very ordinary that no one would give it a second glance – except, he had explained, perhaps Eslek himself. Eslek knew what went where, and who might be expected at a Friday market.

He scratched his head. It was all very ordinary. The stalls, the crowds, the jugglers, the musicians: it was like this every time. The market was busier, it being a Friday. What had happened that didn't happen every day of the week? The meatball man had given him a free breakfast, that didn't happen to you every day!

Thinking about the meatballs had reminded him of something.

He tried to remember. He'd been hungry, yes. And he'd seen that the meatballs were done, hadn't he, before anyone else? Seen that much out of the corner of his eye while he poached a cube of bread –

Eslek jerked his chin. The little cube of bread. Nobody had noticed. There'd been no one manning the stall, and the little dog running round to turn the spit. Something he'd never actually seen before today, not in the market, at least. But so what?

He decided to take another look. As he threaded his way through the crowd, he caught sight of the meatball vendor with the flat knife in one hand and a pitta bread in the other, serving a customer. But he was looking the other way. When Eslek reached him he was still standing, as though transfixed, and the customer was beginning to grumble: 'I said yes to sauce.'

The vendor turned back with a puzzled look on his face. Then he looked down at his knife, and the bread in his hands, as if he wasn't sure why they were there. His customer turned away with a snort.

'Forget it. Life's too short.'

The meatball man seemed not to have heard. He turned his head and looked over his shoulder again.

Eslek followed his gaze. The little dog was still trotting in the wheel, with his tongue hanging out. But it wasn't the abandoned dog which attracted Eslek's attention so much as the meat hanging on the spit. It had been tightly bound to set it once the heat caught it; but with no one about to baste the meat, it was beginning to shrink. The pack of meat was gradually unravelling, stiffening, revealing to Eslek the shape of the beast it had once been. Two of its legs, paring away from the surprisingly slender body, were thick; the other two were smaller, wizened, in an attitude of prayer. It could have been a hare, except that that it was ten times bigger than any hare Eslek had ever seen.

The meatball vendor must have noticed him, because he suddenly said: 'I don't get what's going on. There's been no one at that stall all morning, not since I come. The dog must be fair knackered.' He swallowed, and Eslek could see his Adam's apple bobbing up and down. 'And what the fuck's on the spit?'

Eslek felt the hairs prickling on the back of his neck.

'I'll tell you one thing, mate,' he growled. 'It sure as shit ain't halal.'

He put a hand up to his amulet and gripped it hard. The meatball vendor began to mumble something: he was praying, Eslek realised, running through the ninety-nine names of God while he stared in horror at the trunk and limbs of a human being, popping and blackening over the smouldering coals.

104

Yashim didn't hear the shouts until he was almost out of the tower. He and the porter stood on the parapet, trying to see round the aged cypress tree. In a moment the space below them was thronged with people trying to get away, cramming into the alley, voices raised. He heard several people shout: 'The kadi! Fetch the kadi!' and a woman screamed. One of the juggler's wooden batons sailed up into the cypress and clattered down again, striking against the branches, as the crowd jostled against him.

Yashim looked out over the square. There was no point trying to get down there, he realised, while crowds were still pouring down the alley. Someone beneath him stumbled, and a basket of vegetables went flying. 'Go! Go!' The porter was hopping from foot to foot.

He could see the kadi now, stepping out of his booth into a knot of men all gesticulating and pointing. Further to the left he saw that a ring had formed among the stalls, leaving one of them isolated in the middle. He glanced below. The crowd had stopped running. People were standing in little groups, while those closest to the mouth of the alley had turned around, and were craning their necks nervously to watch the square.

Yashim broke into a trot along the parapet, leaped down the steps and darted up through the passageway. Somebody clutched at his arm, but he shrugged them off, dodging his way back into the square between the knots of bystanders. As he ran towards the ring of men he saw Murad Eslek leading the kadi forwards. The men shuffled aside to let them through, and Yashim dashed through on their heels.

One glance showed him all he needed to see.

The kadi was speechless. The spit was still turning; at every turn one of the wizened arms flopped towards the ground. Yashim stepped forwards and put his hand on the wheel, and the little dog simply sank down inside it, panting.

'We need to rake out the fire,' Yashim said, turning to Eslek. 'Get the porters, and a barrow. A donkey cart will do. We've got to get this . . . this thing out of here.'

Eslek closed his eyes a moment and nodded. 'I . . . I never thought –' He didn't finish his sentence but turned away to organise the porters.

The kadi, meanwhile, had started ranting at the crowd, waving his fists.

'Get away! Go back to work! You think I'm finished, do you? I'll show you! Some kind of joke, is it?' He clapped his fists to his temples and stared at them all, rocking on his heels. In his market! Disgrace. Disgrace and shame. Who had done this to him?

He stalked forwards, and the men stumbled back to get out of his way. He strode to his booth and went in, slamming the door.

In the stunned silence which followed a few men, like Yashim, seemed to notice the smell for the first time. Pleasant, rich without being heavy, like veal. They, too, turned away.

The meatball vendor was loudly and violently sick.

Yashim saw Eslek returning with the porters, carrying brooms and rakes.

He spoke to him for a few minutes. He interviewed the meatball vendor, who was unable to stop himself shuddering.

No one had seen anything. As far as the meatball vendor was concerned, the spit was already running before he started setting up. He'd thought it strange, yes, but he had work to do and hadn't given it another thought until after daybreak. He'd been concerned for the dog, really.

It was the dog that had caught his attention, at the first.

105

The validé's jewels sparkled in the yellow light. In that greasy chamber they were the only objects that could catch the eye.

There was magic in them. The magic that conferred power. No one could look away from these jewels, any more than a rabbit could take its eyes off a snake.

The smooth fingers stole forward and stroked them.

Ferenghi magic, maybe. What difference could that make? The fingers stiffened. There might be words that needed to be said. Invocations. Incantations. That was an unforeseen possibility. This zigzagged figure that appeared on each of the jewels could be a word, perhaps, or a sound.

No. Possession was what mattered most. Whoever held the jewels enjoyed the power they conferred. Napoleon, to scatter even the armies of the faithful – everyone knew that he had luck beyond the ordinary share. Fool! He had parted with the jewels and his luck had changed. And the validé, too: she'd done well for herself ever since the jewels arrived. Clawed her way to the top, across a battleground far more dangerous than any the French emperor had ever faced, where whispers were lances, and knowledge battalions, and beauty marched in the ranks.

We knew all about that, didn't we? Knew how hard it was to emerge standing from that melee, not to be kicked back, pulled down, to wither in obscurity. And then to reach one's goal, to stand at the apex, to have complete power over creatures who grovelled and cringed at a single word!

Nothing could destroy that. No one could take that away.

Not with these in one's possession.

And a pair of lips puckered and came forward to kiss the jewels.

106

Yashim curled his fingers around the little cup and stared down gratefully at the black liquid settled heavily inside. No spice and a hint of sweet. As he brought it to his nose, a shadow fell across the table and he looked up in surprise.

'Please,' he said, motioning to a stool.

The soup master placed his enormous hands on the table and sank his weight onto the stool. His eyes swung around the café, taking in the other customers, the two stoves, the glittering wall of coffee pots. He gave a sniff.

'The coffee smells good.'

'It's fresh Arabica,' Yashim replied. 'They roast the beans here every morning. Too many people buy the Peruvian kind, don't you think? It is cheap, but it always tastes stale to me.'

The soup master nodded. Without moving his hand from the table he raised his fingers and nodded solemnly at the proprietor, who came forward bowing.

'Coffee, very sweet, with cardamom. No cinnamon.' The café

owner walked over to his stove. 'I don't like cinnamon,' the soup master added.

They discussed the question politely until the coffee arrived. Yashim was inclined to agree with the soup master that cinnamon in bread was an abomination.

'Where do we get these ideas?' The soup master's eyebrows shot up in perplexity. 'For what?'

Yashim shrugged and said nothing.

The soup master put down his cup and leaned forwards.

'You wonder why I am here. Last night the guards did not show up for work. It is the first time. I thought you might be interested.'

Yashim cocked his head. He was wondering why the big man had come. He said: 'I'd rather talk about the past. Twenty, twenty-five years ago. The Janissaries kicked up trouble, didn't they? What did they do, exactly?'

The soup master ran his fingers over his moustache.

'Fires, my friend. We had men in the corps who could lead a fire easy as a gypsy with a bear. I said we – I meant they. I was not involved. But this was how they made their feelings known.'

'Where were the fires, mostly?'

The soup master shrugged. 'In the port, in Galata, over here by the Golden Horn. Sometimes it was as if the whole city was smouldering, like underground. They had only to lift a cover somewhere and – whoosh! Everyone felt it. Danger all around.'

Like now, Yashim thought. The whole city knew about the murders. They understood what was happening. The place was tense with expectation. There were three days to go before the sultan proclaimed his Edict.

'Thank you, soup master. Did you notice the direction of the wind today?'

The soup master's eyes suddenly narrowed.

'Off Marmara. The wind has been set from the west all week.'

107

The seraskier pursed his lips.

'I doubt it can be done. Oh, operationally, yes, perhaps. We could flood the city with the New Guard, a man at every corner, artillery – if we could get it through – in the open spaces. Such as they are.'

He scrambled to his feet and went to stand by the window.

'Look, Yashim effendi. Look at these roofs! What a mess, eh? Hills, valleys, houses, shops, all straggling around little lanes and alleys. How many corners do you think I could find out there? Ten thousand? Fifty thousand? And how many open spaces? Five? Ten? This is not Vienna.'

'No,' Yashim agreed quietly. 'But nevertheless –'

The seraskier raised a hand to stop him.

'Don't think I misunderstand you. And yes, I think something could be done. But the decision would not lie with me. Only the sultan can order troops into the city. Troops under arms, I mean. You think he can take this decision so fast?'

'He did thirteen years ago.'

The seraskier grunted. 'Ten years,' he echoed. 'Ten years ago the people were united with the sultan's will. Nobody could deny that the Janissary menace had overwhelmed us all. But today – what do we know? You think Stambouliots will welcome my men with open arms?

'There is another thing I hesitate to point out. What happened ten years ago was not the work of a day. It took months, you could say years, to prepare for victory over the Janissary rabble. We have twenty-four hours. And the sultan is – older. His health is not so good.'

He drinks, you mean, Yashim thought. It was common knowledge. Everyone knew that M. Lebrun, the Belgian wine merchant in Pera, handled far more stock than the foreign community could account for. And what about the discovery only last year of a veritable mountain of long-necked bottles, in the woods close to where the sultan liked to take his family for picnics?

'There will be a Janissary insurrection,' said Yashim flatly. 'I think it will take the form of a fire, or many fires, I don't know. Either sooner or later the sultan will have to order in the Guards, to keep order and deal with the conflagration, and I for one would prefer it was sooner.' He stepped away from the window and turned to face the seraskier.

'If you won't, I will try to talk to the sultan,' he said.

'You.' It wasn't a question. Yashim could see the seraskier weighing him up. He stood with his back to the light, his hands clasped behind his back. The silence deepened.

'We will go together, you and I,' the seraskier announced at last. 'But you, Yashim effendi, will make it clear to the sultan that this was your suggestion, not mine.'

Yashim stared at him coldly. One day, he thought, he would come across a man in the sultan's service who was not a trimmer, who would stand up and stand out for his beliefs. But not today.

'I will take responsibility,' he said quietly.

I'm only a eunuch, after all.

⋙ 108 ⋘

Their footsteps echoed off the high walls of the seraglio as they walked across the first court. Usually on a Friday the place would have been busy, but a combination of grey skies and the suppressed tension hanging in the air had left the great court all but deserted. Ceremonial guardsmen stood to attention around the perimeter walls, as silent and immobile as the Janissary guards whose stillness had once struck chill into the hearts of foreign envoys. Yashim wondered if the New Guards were not, in their own way, more sinister: like German clockwork dolls rather than real men. At least the Janissaries had possessed their own swaggering panache, as his friend Palewski had pointed out.

His fingers closed on a scrap of paper tucked beneath his belt. Coming across the Hippodrome, he had swerved on an impulse from the bronze serpent and cut across the dirt to the Janissary Tree, knowing what he would find: the same mystic verses that had been puzzling him all week.

They had been pinned to the peeling bark. This was how the Greeks advertised their dead, Yashim thought, with a piece of paper nailed to a post or tree. He had pulled down the paper and studied it again.

Unknowing
And knowing nothing of unknowing,
They sleep.
Wake them.

A fire in the night, Yashim thought. A call to arms. But what did this mean?

Knowing,
And knowing unknowing,
The silent few become one with the Core.
Approach.

He folded the paper and tucked it into his belt.

The sultan kept them waiting for an hour, and when he met them it was not in the private apartments, as Yashim had expected, but in the throne room , a room that Yashim had seen only once fifteen years before.

He had not seen the sultan, either, for several years. Mahmut's beard, which had been jet black, was red with henna, and the keen dark eyes had turned watery, sunk beneath folds of fat. His mouth seemed to have drooped into a pout of permanent disappointment as if, having tasted everything that money could buy in the world, he had found it all to be sour. He waved them in with a chubby hand, larded with rings, but made no effort to rise from the throne.

The room itself was as Yashim remembered it, a jewel box of the coolest blues, tiled from the floor to the apex of the dome in exquisite Iznikware, a frozen dream of a garden that twined and dripped and hung festooned around the walls.

Yashim and the seraskier entered stooping at the waist, and after they had advanced five paces they prostrated themselves on the ground.

'Get up, get up,' snapped the sultan testily. 'About time,' he added, pointing at Yashim.

The seraskier frowned. 'Your Imperial Majesty,' he began. 'A situation has arisen in the city which we believe – Yashim effendi, and myself – to be of the gravest potential consequence to the well-being and security of the people.'

'What are you talking about? Yashim?'

Yashim bowed, and started to explain. He spoke of the Edict, and the murder of the cadets. He described a prophecy uttered centuries ago by the founder of the Karagozi order of dervishes – and caught the sultan's warning frown.

'Be careful, lala. Be very careful of the words you choose. There are some things one cannot speak about.'

Yashim eyed him levelly. 'Then I don't think it will be necessary, sultan.'

There was a silence.

'No,' Mahmut replied. 'I have understood. Both of you, approach the throne. We don't want to shout.'

Yashim hesitated. The sultan's words had reminded him of the last lines in the verse: *The silent few become one with the Core. Approach.* What could it mean? He took a step closer to the sultan. The seraskier stood stiffly beside him.

'What do you say, seraskier?'

'There may be upwards of fifty thousand men preparing to take to the streets.'

'And Istanbul could be burned to the ground, is that it? I see. Well, we must do something about that. What do you have in mind?'

'I believe, sire, you must let the New Guards occupy the city temporarily,' Yashim explained. 'The seraskier is reluctant, but I can't see a better way of guaranteeing public safety.'

The sultan frowned and tugged his beard. 'Seraskier, you know the temper of your men. Are they ready to take such a step?'

'Their discipline is good, sultan. And they have several commanders who are level-headed and decisive. With your permission, they could take up positions overnight. Their presence alone might overawe the conspirators.'

Yashim noticed that the seraskier sounded less hesitant now.

'All the same,' the sultan observed, 'it could become a battle, in the streets.'

'There is that risk. In those circumstances we would simply have to do our best. Identify the ringleaders, limit the damage. Above all, sultan, protect the palace.'

'Hmm. As it happens, seraskier, I hadn't been planning to remain in the city.'

'With respect, sultan. Your safety can be guaranteed, and I think that your presence will help to reassure the people.'

The sultan answered with a sigh.

'I am not afraid, seraskier.' He rubbed his hands across his face. 'Get the men ready. I will consult with my viziers. You can expect an order within the next few hours.'

He turned to Yashim.

'As for you, it is high time you made progress in our enquiry. Be so good as to report to my apartments.'

He dismissed them with a gesture. Both men bowed deeply and walked backward to the door. As they closed on the audience room, Yashim saw that the sultan was sitting on his throne, his fist bunched against his cheek, watching them.

⊰ 110 ⊱

Outside the door the seraskier stopped to mop his forehead with a handkerchief.

'*Our* enquiry? You should have told me that you were working on a case in here,' he muttered reproachfully.

'You didn't ask. Anyway, as you heard, I gave yours priority.'

The seraskier grunted. 'May I ask what the enquiry concerns?'

The seraskier was too brusque. On the parade ground it would do, perhaps: soldiers promised their unwavering obedience. But Yashim wasn't a soldier.

'It wouldn't interest you,' Yashim said.

The seraskier's lips drew tight.

'Perhaps not.' He stared Yashim in the face. 'I suggest, then, you do as the sultan said. As I will.'

Yashim watched the seraskier stepping briskly towards the Ortakapi, the central gate leading to the first court. It wasn't a position he'd enjoy to be in himself. On the other hand, if the seraskier handled it well, both he and the Guard would emerge with honour. It was an opportunity to restore the reputation of the Guards, somewhat tarnished by their failures on the battle-field.

And a duty, too. Not just to the sultan, but to the people of Istanbul. Without the Guards, the whole city was in danger from the Janissary rebels.

There was no doubt in Yashim's mind that the fourth murder had completed a stage, established the preliminaries. The old altars had been re-consecrated, in blood. The second stage was underway, Yashim felt sure of that.

Wake them. Approach.

What did it mean?

Within the next seventy-two hours, he sensed, they would all find out.

He saw the seraskier disappear into the shadow of the Ortakapi. Then he turned and headed for the harem apartments.

❧ III ❧

'Hello, stranger!'

It was almost a whisper. Ibou the librarian doubled up his long arm and waggled the fingers in greeting.

Yashim grinned and raised a hand.

'Off to work?' he asked in a low tone. By long-established cus-tom, no one ever raised their voice in the second court of the palace.

Ibou cocked his head.

'I've just finished, actually. I was going to get something to eat.'

Yashim thought he sensed an invitation.

'Well, I wish I could come with you,' he said. And then: 'You've come out of the wrong door.'

Ibou gave him a solemn look, then turned his head.

'It looks all right to me.'

'No, I mean from the Archives. I . . . I didn't know you could get through on this side.' Yashim felt himself blushing. 'It doesn't matter. Thanks for your help the other night.'

'I only wish I could have done more, effendi,' Ibou replied. 'You can come and see me again, if you like. I'm on nights for the rest of this week.'

He salaamed, and Yashim salaamed back.

Yashim went into the harem by the Gate of the Aviary. He could never pass this gate without thinking of the validé, Kosem, who two centuries before was dragged here from the apartments naked by the heels, and strangled in the corridor. That had been the finale to fifty terrifying years, in which the empire was ruled by a succession of madmen, drunkards and debauchees – including Kosem's own son Ibrahim, who had his rooms papered and carpeted in Russian furs, and rode his girls like mares . . . until the executioner came for him with the bowstring.

Dangerous territory, the harem.

He stepped into the guard room. Six halberdiers were on duty, standing in pairs beside the doors which led to the Court of the Validé Sultan and the Golden Road, a tiny, open alleyway which linked the harem to the selamlik. The halberdiers were unarmed, except for the short daggers they wore stuffed into the sash of their baggy trousers; they only carried halberds on protective duty, as when on rare occasions they escorted the sultan's women out of the palace. In the meantime they had a single distinguishing characteristic: the long black tresses which hung from the crown of their high hats as a token that they had been passed for entry into the harem. Yashim remembered a Frenchman laughing when the function of the hair was explained to him.

'You think a mane of hair will stop a man from seeing the sultan's women? In France,' he had said, 'it is the women who have long hair. Is it so, that they cannot steal glances at a handsome man?'

And Yashim had replied, rather stiffly, that the halberdiers of the tresses only went into the more public areas of the harem, to bring in the wood.

He laid his fist against his chest and bowed slightly.

'By the sultan's order,' he murmured.

The halberdiers recognised him, and stood to let him pass.

He found himself beneath the colonnade which ran along the western edge of the validé's court. It had been raining, and the flagstones of the court were gleaming and puddled, the walls greenish with damp. The door to the Validé Sultan's suite was open, but Yashim stood where he was, turning the situation over in his mind.

What was it, he asked himself, that created danger in the harem?

He thought of the halberdiers he had just met, wearing their long hair like blinkers.

He thought of the chambers and apartments that lay beyond, as old and narrow as Istanbul itself, with their crooked turns, and sudden doorways, and tiny jewel-like chambers crafted out of odd corners and partitioned spaces. Like the city they had grown up over the centuries, rooms polished into place by the grit of expediency, rooms hollowed out of the main complex on a whim, even doorways opened up by what must have felt like the pressure of a thousand glances and a million sighs. None of it planned. And in this space, scarcely two hundred feet square, baths and bedrooms, sitting rooms and corridors, lavatories and dormitories, crooked staircases, forgotten balconies: even Yashim, who knew them, could get lost in there, or find himself looking unexpectedly from one window into a court he had thought far away. There were rooms in there no better than cells, Yashim knew.

How many people trod the labyrinth every day, unravelling the hours of their existence within the walls, treading a few well-worn paths which led from one task to the next: sleeping, eating, bathing, serving? Hundreds, certainly; perhaps thousands, mingling with the ghosts of the thousands who had gone before: the women who had lied, and died, and the eunuchs who pitter-pattered around them, and the gossip that rose like steam in the women's baths, and the looks of jealousy and love and desperation he had seen himself.

His eye travelled around the courtyard. It was only about fifty-foot square, but it was the biggest open place in the harem: the only place where a woman could raise her face to the sky, feel the rain on her cheeks, see the clouds scudding across the sun. And there were – he counted them – seven doors opening into this court; seven doors; fifteen windows.

Twenty-two ways to not be alone.

Twenty-two ways in which you could be watched.

As he stood below the colonnade, staring at the rain, he heard women laugh. And immediately he said to himself: the danger is that nothing you ever do is a secret in this place.

Everything can be watched, or overheard.

A theft can be observed.

A ring can be found.

Unless –

He glanced at the open door to the validé's suite.

But the validé wouldn't steal her own jewels.

He heard the door behind him open, and turned round. There,

puffing with the exertion and filling the doorway with his enormous bulk, stood the Kislar Agha.

He looked at Yashim with his yellow eyes.

'You're back,' he piped, in his curiously tiny voice.

Yashim bowed.

'The sultan thinks I haven't been working hard enough.'

'The sultan,' the black man echoed. His face was expressionless.

He waddled slowly forwards, and the door to the guard room closed behind him. He stood by a pillar and stuck out a hand, to feel the rain.

'The sultan,' he repeated softly. 'I knew him when he was just a little boy. Imagine!'

He suddenly bared his teeth, and Yashim – who had never seen the kislar smile – wondered if it was a grin, or a grimace.

'I saw Selim die. It was here, in this courtyard. Did you know that?'

As the rain continued to patter onto the courtyard, seeping through the flagstones, staining the walls, Yashim thought: he, too, feels the weight of history here.

He shook his head.

The Kislar Agha put up two fingers and pulled at his pendulous earlobe. Then he turned to look at the rain.

'Many people wanted him to die. He wanted everything to change. It's the same now, isn't it?'

The Kislar Agha continued to stare out at the rain, tugging on his earlobe. Like a child, Yashim thought vaguely.

'They want us,' he said in a voice of contempt, 'to be modern. How can I be modern? I'm a fucking eunuch.'

Yashim inclined his head. 'Even eunuchs can learn how to sit in a chair. Eat with a knife and fork.'

The black eunuch flashed him a haughty look.

'I can't. Anyway, modern people are supposed to know stuff.

They all read, don't they? Eating up the little ants on the paper with their eyes and later on spraying the whole mess back in people's faces when they don't expect it. What do they call it? *Tanzimat* – the reform era. Well, you're all right. You know a lot.'

The Kislar Agha raised his head and looked hard at Yashim.

'It may not be now, maybe not this year or the next,' he said slowly, in his mincing little falsetto voice, 'but the time will come when they'll just turn us out into the street to die.'

He made a flapping gesture with his fingers, as if he were batting Yashim away. Then he stepped out ponderously into the courtyard, and walked slowly across to a door on the other side, in the rain.

Yashim stared after him for a few moments, then he went to the door of the validé's suite, and knocked gently on the wood.

One of the validé's slave-girls, who had been sitting on an embroidered cushion in the tiny hall, snipping at her toenails with a pair of scissors, looked up and smiled brightly.

'I'd like to see the validé, if I may,' said Yashim.

112

By the time Yashim left the palace that Friday afternoon it was almost dark, and at the market by the Kara Davut the stallholders were beginning to pack up by torch light.

For a moment Yashim wondered if he should have gone to eat lunch with Ibou, the willowy archivist, for he had had nothing to eat all day and felt almost light-headed with hunger. Almost automatically he brushed the idea aside. Regrets and second thoughts seldom occupied him for long: they were futile emotions he had trained himself to resist, for fear of opening the floodgates. He had known too many men in his condition eaten up by bitterness; too many men – and women, too – paralysed by their second thoughts, brooding over changes they were powerless to reverse.

George the Greek came swarming out from behind his stall as Yashim stood picking over the remains of a basket of salad leaves. The sight seemed to drive him into a frenzy.

'What for yous comes so late in the day, eh? Buying this old shit! Yous an old lady? Yous keeping rabbits now? I puts everything away.'

He set his hands on his hips.

'What you wants, anyways?'

Yashim tried to think. If Palewski came to dinner, as promised, he'd want something reasonably substantial. Soup, then, and manti – the manti woman would have some left, he was sure. He could make a sauce with olives and peppers from the jar. Garlic he had.

'I'll take that,' he said, pointing out an orange pumpkin. 'Some leeks, if you have them. Small is better.'

'Some very small leeks, good. Yous making balkabagi? Yous needs a couple of onions, then. Good. For stock: one carrot, onion, parsley, bay. Is twenty-five piastres.'

'Plus what I owe you from the other day.'

'I forgets the other days. This is today.'

He found Yashim a string bag for his vegetables.

The manti woman was still at work, as Yashim had hoped. He bought a pound of meat and pumpkin manti, half a pint of sour cream in the dairy next door and two rounds of borek, still warm from the oven. And then, for what felt like the first time in days, he went home.

In his room he lit the lamps, kicked off his street shoes and hung his cloak on a peg. He trimmed the wicks and opened the window a fraction of an inch to clear the accumulated air. With an oil-soaked scrap of rag and a handful of dry twigs he started a fire in the grate and scattered a few lumps of charcoal on top. Then he started to cook.

He dropped the stock vegetables into a pot, added water from the jug, and settled it on the back of the stove to reach a simmer. He slid a ripple of olive oil over the base of a heavy pan and chopped onions, most of the leeks, and some garlic cloves, putting them on to sweat. Meanwhile with a sharp knife he scalped the pumpkin, scooped out the seeds and put them aside. Careful not to break the shell he scraped out the orange flesh with a spoon and turned it with the onions. He threw in a generous pinch of allspice and cinnamon, and a spoonful of clear honey. After a few minutes he set the pan aside and dragged the stockpot over the coals.

He put a towel and a bar of soap in the empty water basin and went downstairs to the stand-pipe in the tiny back yard, where he unwound his turban and stripped to the waist, shivering in the cold drizzle. With a gasp he ducked his head beneath the spout. When he had washed he towelled himself vigorously, ignoring his smarting skin, and filled the water jug. Upstairs he dried himself more carefully and put on a clean shirt.

Only then did he curl up on the divan and open the valide's copy of *Les Liaisons Dangereuses*. He could hear the stock bubbling gently on the stove; once the lid jumped and a jet of fragrant steam scented the room with a short hiss. He read the same sentence over a dozen times, and closed his eyes.

When he opened them again he was not sure if he had been asleep; there was someone knocking on the door. With a guilty start he scrambled to his feet and flung back the door.

'Stanislaw!'

But it wasn't Stanislaw.

The man was younger. He was kicking off his shoes, and in his hand he carried a silken bow string, looped around his fist.

113

The seraskier walked briskly across the first court of the palace, and stepped out through the Imperial Gate, the Bab-i-Humayun, into the open space which separated the palace from the great church, now a mosque, of Aya Sofia. After the unnatural stillness of the palace he was struck by the returning noises of a great city: the rumble of iron-hooped cart-wheels on the cobbles, dogs worrying and growling at scraps, the crack of a whip and the shouts of mule-drivers and costermongers.

Two mounted dragoons spurred their horses forwards and brought up his own grey. The seraskier swung up gracefully into the saddle, settled his cloak, and turned the horse's head in the direction of the barracks. The dragoons fell in behind him.

As they passed beneath the portico of the mosque, the serask-ier glanced upwards. The pinnacle of Justinian's great dome, second in size only to the basilica of St Peter's in Rome, stood high overhead: the highest spot in all Istanbul, as the seraskier well knew. As they jogged along, he scanned the lie of the land for the hundredth time, mentally setting up his artillery batteries, disposing his troops.

By the time they reached the barracks, he had made decisions. To scatter his forces through the city would be futile, he reck-oned; it might even increase the danger to his men. Better to choose two or three positions, hold them securely, and make whatever forays were necessary to achieve their ends. Aya Sofia was one assembly point; the Sultan Ahmet Mosque to the south-west would be another. He would have liked to put men into the stables of the old palace of the Grand Vizier, just outside the seraglio walls, but he doubted that the permission would be forthcoming. There was a hill further west which provided a clear trajectory towards the palace.

It was the palace, essentially, he had to think about.

Having regained his apartments, he summoned a dozen senior officers to a briefing.

He followed the briefing with a short pep talk. Everything, he said, depended on how they and their men conducted themselves over the next forty-eight hours. Obedience was the watchword. He had every confidence that together they could meet the challenge that had presented itself.

That was all.

❮❮ 114 ❯❯

Yashim made a grab for the door. The man on the threshold sprang forwards and for several seconds they fought for purchase, separated only by the thin door which lay between them. But Yashim had been caught off balance, and it was he who yielded first: he leaped away from the door and his assailant came barrelling into the room, almost stumbled, but whipped round fast to face Yashim at a sagging crouch.

A wrestler, Yashim thought. The man was completely shaved. His neck sloped into his big shoulders, which bulged from the arm-holes of a sleeveless leather jerkin. The leather was black and glistened as though it had been oiled. He was short-legged, Yashim noticed, his bare feet planted a yard apart on the rug, knees bent, slim-waisted. There was no sign of a weapon beyond the string in his right fist.

A man who could crack me apart without even trying, Yashim thought. He took a backward step, sliding his bare feet on the polished boards.

The man gave a grunt and lunged forwards, lowering his head like a ram, coming at Yashim with surprising speed. Yashim flung back his arm as he leaped backwards, and swept his hand across the kitchen block. His fingers felt the knife, but they only knocked it: it must have spun, for when he tried to close on the hilt his fingers met in the air, and as the wrestler's huge shoulder crashed against his midriff he was rammed back hard against the block with a force that made his head whiplash. He gasped for breath and felt the wrestler's arms fly upwards to pinion his own.

Yashim knew that if the wrestler got him in his grip he was finished. He lunged to the right, throwing all the weight of his upper body against the wrestler's rising arm, flinging his own arms out at the same time to grab at the handle of the stock pot. With a wrench he snatched it up and swung it round over the man's shoulder, but the lid was stuck and he had no room to do more than swing the pot and clamp it against the wrestler's back before his arm was caught in his grip.

A band of leather was sewn round the collar of the man's jerkin, and as the pot slid up the lid must have snagged against it. The man flipped back as the boiling stock sloshed over his neck, and let Yashim go.

The surprise on the assassin's face when he slammed his taloned hand into Yashim's groin and squeezed down hard was palpable. Certainly more palpable than Yashim's groin.

The assassin jerked back his arm as if he'd been stung. Yashim slid his right hand up the assassin's left arm as hard as he could and then brought his left down hard, gripping his wrist as he pivoted the man's arm against his own hand. There was a crack and the arm went limp. The assassin clutched at it with his right, and in a moment Yashim had taken his right wrist out away from his body and with a heave sent the assassin curving in an arc which brought him round, doubled up, and his right arm in a tight half-nelson. The assassin had neither screamed, nor spoken a word.

Five minutes later, and the man had still not spoken. He had barely grunted. Yashim was at a loss.

And then Yashim saw why the man had failed to speak. He had no tongue.

Yashim wondered if the mute could write. 'Can you write?' he hissed in the man's ear. The look was blank. A deaf-mute? Long ago, in the days of Suleyman the Magnificent, it had been decreed that only deaf-mutes should attend the person of the sultan. It was a way of ensuring that nothing was overheard; that nothing they saw could be communicated to the outside world. They signed at one another instead: ixarette, the secret language of the Ottoman court, was a complex sign language which anyone, hearing or deaf, speaking or dumb, was expected to master in the palace service.

The palace service.

A deaf-mute.

Frantically, Yashim began to sign.

At the other end of the city, Preen the köçek dancer lay back on the divan, staring at the dark window.

A jet black wig of real hair, bolstered with horse-hair plucked from the tail, was draped over a stand. Her pots of make-up, her brushes and tweezers, stood unused on the dressing table.

Preen tried to wriggle her frozen shoulder. The bandages the horse-doctor had applied creaked. When it came to treating breaks and bruises, the girls always turned to the horse doctor: he had more practice and experience in a month than ordinary sawbones saw in a lifetime, as Mina said, because the Turks looked after their horses even better than themselves. He had probed Preen's twisted shoulder, and diagnosed a sprain.

'Nothing broken, God be praised,' he said. 'When my patients break something, we shoot them.'

Preen had laughed for the first time since her attack. Laughter wasn't the only medicine the horse doctor used, either: he had salved her shoulder and neck with a preparation of horse chestnut. He had then applied the bandages and painted the result with hot gum.

'Tastes dreadful,' he observed. 'And stops the loops from sagging and coming apart. Whether or not it is medically necessary, who knows? But I'm too old to change my prescriptions.'

The gum had set and dried, and now it creaked whenever Preen moved her shoulder. At least she could work her fingers: two days ago they had been swollen and immovable. Mina had come to help her eat, bringing the tripe soup she loved in an earthenware bowl. Apart from the horse doctor, and her friend Mina, Preen had no visitors: she had resolved to turn even Yashim away, should he come. Without her war-paint she felt sure that she looked a fright.

She looked different, certainly. Her own hair was cropped close to a downy fluff, and her skin was very pale; yet Mina could see in the shape of her head and the high-boned face more than a trace of the boy she had once been, eager and fragile at the same time. With her big brown eyes she had pleaded with Mina to stay the night, and Mina had curled up beside her friend and watched her sleep.

On the third morning Preen had had to tell her landlady that she had no intention of paying extra for her so-called guest. The conversation had been conducted through the door, because Preen refused to let the old woman come in.

'Perhaps I should deduct rent when I am not home for the night?' she called out. 'It is your fault, anyway, that I have to have a nurse. I trusted you to keep an eye on people coming and going! And you let in a murderer!'

There was an outraged silence, and Preen grinned. Nothing could be more mortifying to the landlady than to be accused of slackness when it came to peering through her lattice. It was like doubting her faith.

That was earlier. Now Mina was coming in with bread and soup for their supper.

She helped prop Preen upright on the divan, and handed her a bowl.

'You're missing a lot of excitement, darling,' she said, sitting on the edge of the divan. 'A positive invasion of handsome young men.'

She arched her eyebrows. 'Men in tight trousers! The New Guard.'

Preen rolled her eyes.

'Doing what, exactly?'

'That's what I asked them. Taking up *positions*, they said. Well, I couldn't resist it, could I? I said I could show them a few they hadn't thought of.'

They giggled.

'But what does it mean?' Preen demanded.

'It's for protection, apparently. All that plotting and killing, it's coming to a head. Oh, Preen, I'm sorry – you look white as a sheet. I didn't mean . . . I mean, I'm sure it's got nothing to do with what happened the other day. Look, why don't you ask your gentleman friend?'

'Which one? Yashim?'

'That's right, dear. Yashim. Come on, eat your soup and put on your face. I'll help you. You can walk, can't you? We'll get a chair and go and find him right now.'

The truth, of course, was that Mina was getting just a tiny bit bored of her nursing duties. She fancied an outing, especially when there was something exciting going on outside. So she was her most persuasive, and overruled Preen's doubts.

'It's just that . . . I don't feel safe,' Preen admitted.

'Nonsense, darling. I'll be with you, and we'll find your friend.

It'll be fun, who knows? You'll be perfectly safe going out. Just as safe as staying here. Safer.'

Later, Preen was to remember that remark.

⋙ 116 ⋘

Yashim, as it happened, was already dealing with his second visitor of the evening.

Palewski had come up the stairs to sniff the aroma on Yashim's landing, but for once he was disappointed. There was a faint smell of onions, he imagined, and perhaps boiled carrot, but the insubstantial clues failed to gel: it could be any number of recipes. Then he noticed the shoes, a pair of sturdy leather sandals.

Company, he supposed. He knocked on the door.

There was a slight delay, and the door opened an inch.

'Thank God it's you,' Yashim said, pulling the door open and scooping Palewski through into the room.

Palewski almost dropped his valise in surprise. Yashim was holding a large kitchen knife, not that it mattered. What struck his notice instead was the body of a huge man, face down on the carpet, largely enveloped in a knotted sheet.

'I've got to do something about this maniac,' Yashim said shortly. 'I've tied his wrists with the corner of a sheet but now I'm out of ideas.'

Palewski blinked. He looked at Yashim, and back at the body on the floor. He realised that the man was breathing hard.

'Perhaps what you need,' he said quietly, fumbling at his waist, 'is this.'

He held out a long cord, made of twisted silk and gold thread.

'It went with my dressing gown. My Sarmatian finery, I should say.'

Together they bound the man's wrists tightly behind his back. Yashim undid the sheet and wrapped it round his legs: the man was so docile that Palewski found it hard to credit what Yashim was saying.

'A wrestler?' Then he silently mouthed the word: 'Janissary?'

'Don't worry, he can't hear, poor bastard. No, not a Janissary. It's odder than that. Worse than I thought. Look, I have to reach the palace immediately. I don't know what I could have done with this fellow if you hadn't come. Will you stay? Keep an eye on him? Prick him if he tries to move.'

Palewski was staring at him in horror.

'For God's sake, Yash. Can't we get him to the night watch?'

'There isn't time. Give me an hour. There's bread and olives. You can leave him here after that. If he gets free, so be it – though you could try knocking him on the head with a saucepan before you go. For my sake.'

'All right, all right, I'll stay,' Palewski grumbled. 'But it's not what I joined for, you know. One night, intimate conversation with the sultan. Next night, quiet evening with friends. Third night, silent vigil over murderous twenty-stone wrestling deaf mute. I think I'll have a drink,' he added, sliding his valise closer.

But Yashim was hardly listening.

'It's two I owe you,' he said over his shoulder, as he cleared the top flight of stairs in a single jump.

❧ 117 ❧

The Kara Davut was always busy on a Friday night. The shop-keepers and café owners set out lanterns above their doorways and after mosque families paraded up and down the street, stopping for a sherbet or an ice, queuing for hot street food and thronging the coffee shops. Children chased each other in and out of the crowds, shouting and laughing, only occasionally called to order by their indulgent parents. Young men gathered round café tables, those who could afford it sitting with a coffee, the others at their elbows chatting and trying to catch a glimpse of the local girls, decorously swathed in chador and yashmak, who walked accompanied by their parents, but all the time signalling with their gait and the movement of their heads and hands.

Yashim didn't think he was imagining that the atmosphere tonight was different. The street was as full as ever, even more crowded than usual; but the children seemed quieter, as if they were playing on a shorter rein, and the knots of youths in the cafés seemed larger and more subdued than usual.

This impression of subdued expectation didn't evaporate as Yashim hurried towards the palace. He had failed to find a chair, and guessed that the chair-men would contribute to the confusion approaching the city: if not ex-Janissaries, they were still a rough crew, the sort of men who went to swell a mob or serve the rabble if they scented an opportunity.

As he half-walked, half-jogged through the streets and alleys, he was surprised to meet no soldiers on the way, none of the little platoons the seraskier had forecast at every street corner. How soon would they secure the city?

He had an answer of a kind as he swept out of the maze of streets behind Aya Sofia and onto the open ground that lay between the mosque and the walls of the seraglio. A pair of uniformed guardsmen ran towards him, shouting: behind them he could see that the whole space was occupied by soldiers, some on horseback, several platoons in what looked like a drill formation, and others simply sitting quietly on the ground with their legs crossed, waiting for instructions. Beyond them he thought he could make out the silhouettes of mounted cannon and mortars.

This has the makings of a complete disaster, he thought fiercely – an opinion confirmed on the spot, as the two soldiers ran up to block his way.

'The way is closed! You must go back!'

They were holding their guns across their chests.

'I have urgent business at the palace,' Yashim snapped. 'Let me through.'

'Sorry, mate. These are our orders. No one is to come through here.'

'The seraskier. Where is he?'

The nearest soldier looked uneasy.

'Couldn't say. He'll be busy anyways.'

The second soldier frowned.

'Who are you?'

Yashim saw his chance. He jabbed a finger.

'No. Who are *you*? I want your rank, and your number.' He didn't know much about military organisation, but he hoped he sounded better than he felt. 'The seraskier is going to be very unhappy if he gets to hear about this.'

The soldiers glanced at one another.

'Well, I don't know,' one of them muttered.

'You know who I am,' Yashim asserted. He doubted that, very much, but there was an angry edge to his voice which wasn't faked. 'Yashim Togalu. The seraskier's senior intelligence officer. My mission is urgent.'

The men shuffled their feet.

'Either you take me to the Imperial Gate right now, or I will speak to your commanding officer.'

One of the soldiers glanced round. The Imperial Gate loomed black and solid in the darkness only a hundred yards away. The corps commander – he might be anywhere.

'Go on, then,' said the soldier quickly, with a jerk of his head. Yashim walked past them.

After he'd gone, one of the men let out a sigh of relief.
'At least we didn't give our names,' he remarked.

※ 118 ※

Yashim felt the hairs prickling on the back of his neck as he picked his way among the soldiers waiting patiently on the ground. At any minute he expected to be challenged again, delayed again. A shout was all it would take.

There it came. One shout, and another. He saw the men around him turn their heads.

But they weren't looking at him. Another shout: 'Fire!'

Yashim swivelled, following the men's gaze. Over their heads, beyond the silhouette of the great mosque, the sky had lightened like an early dawn. A dawn rising in the west. A dawn rising upwind of the city of Istanbul. As he watched, he saw the light go yellow and flicker.

For a few seconds he stood transfixed.

Around him the men strained uneasily, taking up their rifles, awaiting the order to rise.

Yashim broke into a run.

※ 119 ※

The flap in the lattice dropped open with a click as Preen and Mina reached the corridor at the foot of the stairs, but they sailed past it without a word, noses in the air. On the street they nudged each other and giggled.

For ten minutes they walked eastwards, looking for a chair to carry Preen, at least. Preen seemed to have recovered her poise on leaving the house, leaning only slightly on Mina's arm, looking hungrily around as if she had been in bed for a month instead of a couple of days. A few men threw them curious glances, but finally she could bear it no longer.

'Where are the handsome soldiers, then?' she demanded.

Mina snorted.

'And I thought you wanted to come out to get reassurance from your friend! Really, Preen!' Then she looked round and shrugged. 'There were dozens of 'em earlier, honest. I can't say I'm not a bit disappointed myself. Oh, where are all the chairmen?'

'That's all right,' said Preen, smiling and patting her friend's arm. 'I'm getting on all right now.'

There was a buzz of excitement in the street behind them, like a sudden cooing of pigeons, Preen thought. She turned her head to see a man running up the alley, pumping his arms and flinging out his chest: he wore a beard and a high red cap with a white pennant flying from its crown. In each fist he carried a flaming torch.

'Fire! Fire!' He bellowed suddenly. He swerved to the wall: there was a sound of breaking glass and the man lunged, reappeared and sped across the alley.

'Fire!'

He was only holding one brand now, but there was a bottle in his other hand and he was sloshing gobbets of liquid from it over a doorway. 'Fire!'

'What are you doing?' Preen screamed, breaking away from Mina who had clapped a hand to her mouth.

She put out her hands without thinking and felt the bruise ripen in her shoulder.

The man touched the brand to the door: as Preen reached him it sprouted a lovely mass of blueish flames and the man wheeled round, grinning wildly.

'Fire!' he roared.

Preen slapped him hard across the face with her good hand. The man jerked his head back. For a moment he narrowed his eyes and then he dodged down and sped past her, up the street, before she could think what to do next.

Preen threw an alarmed look at the doorway: the blue flames suddenly started to spit. Some were turning yellow as they licked upwards, snapping at the old wood.

'Mina!'

Mina hadn't moved, but she was looking from Preen to the other side of the street where a shattered window was leaping in and out of view as the flames guttered and shrank inside.

'Let's go back!' Mina wailed.

Preen acted on impulse. People were already running in the street, in both directions. A few had stopped and were making an effort to smother the flames creeping round the doorway. But even as they beat the fire with their cloaks flames had started to shoot from the window opposite.

'No! Go on, to Yashim's!' she shouted. She glanced back: a light seemed to hover at the corner of the alley, and then a wall of turbanned men with flickering torches surged around the corner, blocking the alley. 'Run!'

The pain in her shoulder seemed to fade away as she began to run uphill. After a moment she put out a hand and rested it on Mina's shoulder. Both dancers stopped and kicked off their shoes, those two-inch pattens on which they liked to totter into male company; and both, as women will, snatched them up and carried them as they ran barefoot through the alleyways towards the Kara Davut.

They didn't get so far. As they turned into the alley which led to the open space beneath the Imperial Gate, they flung themselves into a packed crowd of men, jostling and elbowing against each other. Almost immediately they were hemmed in by other

293

people running up behind them: Preen grabbed Mina by the arm and spun her round. Together they fought their way back to the street corner, and took the turn to the right.

'We'll go round behind the mosque,' Preen whispered in Mina's ear.

They slackened their pace, partly to avoid the people running up the alleyway towards them, partly because among so many people Preen felt unwilling to surrender herself to the panic that was already developing around them.

But at the next crossroads they had to push and shove their way through the crowd, and turning her head left, back west, Preen saw the flicker of fires smoking on the hill above.

Beyond the crowd the side-street was also heaving with men, and women, too, some of them leading children, trying to protect them from the constant buffeting of people running back and forth. Everyone seemed to be shouting, screaming to make way, bellowing about fire.

Two men, running into each other from opposite directions, suddenly stopped shouting and fell to exchanging blows.

A man called Ertogrul Aslan, who had just poked his head out from his doorway, got a smack on his ear from a wooden box carried by a man dodging down the alley close to the wall.

A printer who ran into the street was carried away by a tide of people racing for the next corner.

A little boy in a nightshirt, who would one day sit as a deputy in the Kemalist National Assembly and spend an evening drinking raki with an air ace called Baron von Richthofen, had his little hand popped out of his mother's grip and was scooped up and passed overhead by total strangers for several minutes before he found himself being pressed to her bosom again, an experience he could later recall perfectly from other people's memories.

Alexandra Stanopolis, a Greek girl of marriageable age, had

her bottom pinched sixteen times and hoarded the secret to her death in Trabzon fifty-three years later, when she finally revealed it to her daughter-in-law, who herself died in New York City.

A notorious miser known as Yilderim, the Thunderbolt, lost a wooden chest he was carrying to a cheerful thief who later found it contained nothing but a silk scarf with a very tight knot in it; the miser died later in an asylum and the thief in Sevastopol, of dysentery, still wearing the knotted scarf.

Several hundred worshippers at the great mosque, formerly the church of Hagia Sophia, found themselves trapped inside the building and had to be escorted in batches by armed troops who led them to an alleyway beneath the seraglio and told them to find their own way home. Two of the worshippers, swathed in their ostlers' cloaks and hiding their frightened faces underneath their hoods, quailed at the soldiers' appearance and in the melee around the great door followed instead a notorious army deserter into a former side-chapel of the cathedral, where they sank down behind a column and communicated in nervous glances. Their names, unusual for Muslims, were Ben Fizerly and Frank Compston.

And all the while, west of the city, the fires raged and raced towards each other like members of a scattered regiment, plunging and burning through the obstacles which lay between them. So that Stanislaw Palewski, Polish ambassador to the Sublime Porte, with a kitchen knife in one hand and an eye on the window, retrieved the golden threaded cord to his dressing gown and without a word to the man stirring on the carpet beat a hasty retreat to Pera, across the Golden Horn.

In times of crisis, he told himself, foreign representatives needed to make themselves available at their embassies.

As Yashim ran across the first court of the seraglio he noticed that it was almost completely deserted: with the New Guard installed in the square and preventing anyone from crossing it was something he might have expected. The few men who remained seemed to have gathered beneath the great plane tree. The Janissary Tree. Yashim shot them a nervous glance as he scuttled over the cobbled walk, his brown cloak billowing behind him.

At the Ortokapi Gate five halberdiers of the selamlik, not wearing curls, stood forward in a body to challenge him. Two of them held pikes in their hands; the others were armed only with the dagger, but their cloaks were pinned back and they stood legs akimbo with their right hands cradling the hilts stuffed into their pantaloons.

'Bear up, men!' Yashim cried as he stepped into the light. 'Yashim Togalu, on the sultan's service!'

They stepped warily aside to let him pass.

The wind which had been whipping his cloak against his legs was still: for a moment he marvelled at the great space that opened up in front of him before he plunged down an alley of cypress, struck by the still blackness of the trees, by the darkness that enveloped him almost at the centre of Ottoman power. Only the thin spark of a lamp at the far end of the tunnel prevented him from succumbing to the frightening atmosphere of a wood at night.

He burst out of the alley and crossed swiftly to the portico of the last, most numinous gate of all the gates that defined the power of the Sublime Porte: the Porte del' Felicita, the Gateway of Happiness, which led from the workaday second court where viziers, scribes, archivists, ambassadors kicked their heels or rapped out the orders which controlled the lives of men from the Red Sea to the Danube. Beyond it lay the sacred precincts of the third court, where one enormous family led an existence made precious by the presence of the sultan, the Shah-in-Shah, God's very representative on earth.

The representative's doors, however, were firmly closed.

His fist made no echo on the iron-studded gates: he might have been beating stone. Exasperated, he took a few steps back and looked upwards. The huge eaves jutted forwards ten feet or more, in classical Ottoman style. He ran his eyes along the walls. The outer walls were built up with the imperial kitchens, a long series of domes, like bowls stacked on a shelf: there was no way through there. He turned to the left and began to walk quickly towards the Archives.

No one challenged him as he placed his hand on the inlaid doors and pushed. The door creaked back, and he stepped into the vestibule. The door ahead stood slightly ajar, and in a minute Yashim was back in the familiar dark archive room.

He called softly.

'Ibou?'

No answer. He called again, a little louder.

'Ibou? Are you there? It's me, Yashim.'

The tiny candle at the far end of the room was snuffed out for a moment; then it reappeared. Someone had moved in the darkness.

'Don't be afraid. I need your help.'

He heard the slap of sandals on the stone floor and Ibou stepped forwards into the light. His eyes were very round.

'What can you do?' he almost whispered.

'I need to use the back door, Ibou. Can you let me through?'

'I have a key. But – I don't want to go.'

'No, you stay. Do you know what's happening?'

'I am new. I wasn't asked – but it is some kind of meeting. Dangerous, too.'

'Come on.'

The little doorway gave onto the corridor in which the Val…dé Kosem had been dragged to her death. Yashim clasped Ibou's hand.

'Good luck,' the young man whispered.

The door to the guard room was closed. Yashim opened it with a quick flick of the handle and stepped inside.

'I am summoned,' he announced.

Approach.

The halberdiers stood frozen.

They made no effort to stop Yashim opening the door, as though they were clockwork soldiers that someone had forgotten to wind.

For a moment he, too, stood transfixed, looking into the Courtyard of the Validé Sultan.

Then he took a step back and very softly closed the door.

✦ 121 ✦

The sleeping quarters of the harem slaves lay above the colonnade which spanned one side of the validé's court: quietly trying the door, Yashim found himself in a small, bare chamber strewn with rugs and mattresses and dimly lit by a few short candles set on plates on the floor. The beds were empty: dark shadows at the latticed window showed him that the harem slaves were crowding there for a better view.

One of the slave-girls gave a gasp as Yashim stepped up behind her. He put a finger to his lips, and looked down.

Never in all his life would Yashim forget that sight. To the left, the Validé Sultan stood at the doorway to her apartments, at the head of a crowd of harem women that spilled from the doorway and lined the walls three deep: a hundred women, maybe more, Yashim guessed, in every state of dress and undress. Some, roused from their beds, were still in their pyjamas.

Across the courtyard, massed in their finery, stood the palace eunuchs, black and white. Their turbans sparkled with precious jewels, nodding egrets. There must have been three hundred men, Yashim guessed, rustling and whispering like pigeons roosting in a tree.

A silence fell on the eunuchs: they turned their faces to the doorway below Yashim's window, and slowly they began to move aside, creating a corridor. Yashim could see them better now, even recognise a few faces: he saw sables, and kaftans of cashmere, and an imperial ransom of brooches and precious stones. They were more like magpies than pigeons, Yashim thought, drawn to everything that glittered, amassing their nests of gold and diamonds.

He reached up on tiptoe to see who was coming through the crowd, though he already knew. The Kislar Agha looked magnif-icent in an enormous dark pelisse so spangled with the moisture in the air that it sparkled. He walked slowly, but his tread was surprisingly light. His hand, clutching at the baton, was thick with rings. His face was lost beneath a great turban of whitest muslin, wrapped around the conical red hat of his office; so Yashim was unable to gauge his expression. But he saw how the other eunuchs lowered their eyes to the ground, as if they didn't quite dare to look him fully in the face. Yashim knew that face, wrinkled like an ape: the bloodshot eyes, the fat, blubbery cheeks, it was a face that carried the stamp of vice, and wore its vice with an air of blank unconcern.

The eunuchs had now formed two wedges, leaving the Kislar Agha standing alone between them, facing the validé across the court. He didn't raise his hands: he didn't need to. Nobody stirred.

'The Hour has come.'

He spoke slowly in his high, cracking voice.

'We, who are the sultan's slaves, proclaim the hour.

'We, who are the sultan's slaves, assemble for his protection.

'We, who kneel beside the throne, uphold the sacrament of power.

'We will speak with your son, our lord and master, the Shah-in-Shah!'

The chief eunuch's voice rose as he cried out: 'The hour has come!'

And a wavering cry rose from the ranks of the eunuchs: 'The Hour! The Hour!'

The Validé Sultan never moved, except to tap one dainty foot on the stone step.

The chief eunuch raised his arms, his fingers curled like talons.

'The banner must be unfurled. The wrath of God and the people has to be appeased. He shall draw back from the abyss of unbelief, and wield the Sword of Osman in defence of the faith! It is the Path.

'It is written that the knowing shall approach, and become one with the Core. Caliph and sultan, Lord of the Horizons, this is his destiny. The people have risen, the altars are prepared. It is God who has awoken us, at the eleventh hour, the Hour of Restoration!

'Produce him!' He bellowed, in a terrible voice. He curled his fingers into loose fists and let them sink to his sides. His voice sank to a hoarse whisper. 'Reveal the Core.'

Like Yashim, the Validé Sultan seemed to find the chief's performance somewhat hammy. She turned her head to murmur something to an attendant, and Yashim saw her perfect profile, still clear and beautiful, and recognised the lazy look in her eyes as she turned back and focused on the chief eunuch. Lazy meant danger. He wondered if the Kislar Agha knew.

'Kislar,' she said, in a voice that rang with amused contempt. 'Some of our ladies present are not at all well dressed. The night, I may point out, is chill. As for you, you are not suitably attired.'

She raised her chin slightly, as if inspecting him. The eunuch's eyes narrowed in fury.

'No, kislar, your turban seems to be in order. But you do seem to be wearing *my* jewels.'

Good work, Yashim thought, bunching his fist. The validé certainly knew how to use information.

The chief eunuch's nostrils flared, but he looked down quickly. Whether that movement – made, as it were, under the influence of a woman more powerful than him – put him off his stroke, or whether it was the sheer unexpectedness of the validé's remarks, Yashim could not guess. But he opened his mouth and shut it again, as if he had a speech he couldn't make.

The validé's voice was like drawn silk.

'And you murdered for them, too, didn't you, kislar?'

The eunuch raised a forefinger and pointed it at the validé. Yashim saw that he was trembling.

'They are – for my power!' he screeched. He was improvising now, drawn into an argument he didn't mean to have, and couldn't win. His power was lessening with every word he spoke.

Out of the corner of his eye, Yashim saw a white shape stirring close to the wall. A girlish figure sprang forwards, like a cat, and began to run towards the eunuch.

The eunuch didn't see her immediately: she was blocked by his outstretched arm.

'Produce the sultan, or suffer the consequences!' The Kislar Agha screamed. Then his head turned a fraction, and at the same moment Yashim recognised the girl.

The girl who had stolen the gözde's ring.

Yashim closed his eyes. And in that second he saw her beautiful, unyielding face again, when she had closed her mind to him.

Only now he recognised that look. A mask of grief.

A slave-girl gasped at his side, and Yashim opened his eyes. The girl had hurled herself upon the enormous eunuch: he swatted her aside like a fly. But she was on her feet in a moment, and for the first time Yashim saw that she carried a dagger in her fist, a long, curved steel like a scorpion's sting. She sprang again, and this time it was as if the two embraced, like lovers: the slim white girl and the huge black man, staggering as she clung to him.

But she was no match for the kislar. His hands closed around her neck and with a tremendous thrust of his arms he pushed her off. His long fingers spread around her neck like a stain. Her feet kicked wildly but skidded on the wet stone. Her hands came up to his, clawing at them: but the Kislar Agha's strength was far greater. With a grunt he flung her aside. She crumpled back against the floor, and lay still.

Nobody moved. Even the validé's foot had stopped tapping.

Suddenly one of the women screamed and clapped her hand to her mouth. The Kislar Agha swung round, his head moving from side to side as if expecting another assault. Yashim saw the women shrink back.

The Kislar Agha opened his mouth to speak.

He coughed.

His hands went to his stomach.

Behind him the eunuchs stirred. Their chief started to turn towards them, and as he moved Yashim saw very clearly what had made the women scream.

The jewelled hilt of a Circassian blade.

The kislar spluttered as he turned, and then he began to twist towards the ground, his enormous torso slowly sinking as he wheeled. His legs gave way and he sank to his knees, still holding the hilt of the dagger in his abdomen, wearing the look of horrified surprise that he would take to the grave.

Yashim heard the thump as the Kislar Agha's body pitched headfirst to the ground.

There was a momentary silence before the court erupted in pandemonium. The eunuchs swarmed towards the doors in a frenzy to escape, anything to put some distance between them and their fallen chief. Men were slithering and scrambling over each other to reach the doors, some running into the Golden Road, others pouring below the colonnade where Yashim could no longer see them. Doubtless those clockwork halberdiers would stand immobile as dozens of men fled to the sanctuary of their own quarters. Tomorrow you would not find one, Yashim reflected, who would admit to having been there that night.

They'd accuse each other, though.

There was one, at least, he could vouch for personally. He was glad that Ibou had chosen the right course, sticking to his world of musty texts and tattered documents.

The eunuchs had all but cleared from the court, leaving jewels, slippers and even their batons strewn across the flagstones. A few men had attempted to stem the rout at the first panic, dragging at the crowd, shouting encouragement. 'It is still the Hour!' But the eunuchs had run like chickens in a yard, and the words of encouragement had died away. Everyone had gone.

Still the women had not moved, waiting for their mistress's signal. The chief eunuch and the dead girl still lay on the gleaming flagstones like pieces seized from a giant game of chess – white pawn sacrificed for the black castle. It was a self-sacrifice, though. It had been her ring, all along. A token she had asked her lover to wear, Yashim supposed. There were other forms of love inside these walls than the love of a woman for a man – if the performance of the act could be considered love. What had the dresser told them? That this ring turned up here and there, with its esoteric symbol, its concealed meaning. It was clear enough, now. An endless circuit, snake swallowing snake. Frustration and excitement and pleasure in equal measure – and without issue.

The validé had stepped down into the courtyard, and the women were crowding round the body of the girl, lifting her up, moving her beneath the colonnades.

Even now, Yashim felt a pang of pity for the man who had killed her, and her lover, too. Only a few hours earlier they had spoken together, just where he lay now, and he had reminded Yashim of the murder of the sultan's father, Selim, as he played music on the *ney* for the entertainment of the palace girls. It was his own predecessor who carried out the killing. Was this one of the traditions he was seeking to uphold: the murder of sultans by their Kislar Aghas?

But why did he take the validé's jewels? Perhaps, in some crazy way, he had explained it himself: in his narrow, cunning, super-stitious old mind he had come to associate the jewels with power, and stole them as a talisman, a juju that would see him through the greatest crisis of his career.

The slave-girls had crept out already. Yashim followed them, making his way down the steps and through the guard room to the corridor.

He paused with his hand on the handle of the archive door. What should he tell the young man?

He pressed the door and it opened. Ibou was standing just inside, holding a lamp.

'What happened? I heard shouts.'

He held up the lamp higher, to cast a light behind Yashim, into the corridor.

'What's the matter?' Yashim asked.

Ibou peered over his shoulder. He seemed to hesitate.

'Are you alone? Oh. I . . . I thought I heard someone.' He put up his arm and fanned his face with his hand. 'Whooh, hot.'

Yashim smiled.

'It will be soon,' he said, 'if we don't get the fires put out.'

'That's true,' Ibou said, with a weak smile.

Yashim put a hand against the door jamb and rested his weight against it, staring at the floor. He thought of Ibou working on all alone while the eunuchs bayed for their sultan in the validé's court. He thought of the little back door he'd just come through so conveniently, and of the knot of men he'd seen beneath the Janissary Tree outside. The timing was tight, wasn't it? The uprising in the city, and the persuasion of the sultan. The conspirators would need some way to communicate – to carry news of the sultan's mystical apotheosis to the rebels outside.

A go-between. Someone who could bring word from the closed world of the harem to the men on the outside who threatened the city.

He felt a great weight in his throat.

'What fires, Ibou?' he asked quietly.

Yashim didn't want to see Ibou's face. He didn't want to learn that he was right, that Ibou was the hinge on which the whole plot turned. But he knew from Ibou's stuttering effort to reply. From the simple fact that no archivist, corralled within the high walls of his archives room, could have seen or heard the fires that Yashim had seen lighted only moments before he entered the half-deserted palace.

Ibou had already known what would happen.

Reluctantly his eyes travelled upwards to the young man's face.

'It didn't work, Ibou. The chief eunuch is dead. You needn't expect anyone else.'

305

He looked past the archivist down the darkened stacks towards the door. The lamp ahead twinkled and glistened. Yashim squeezed his eyes shut and opened them again. The light burned clear.

Ibou turned and carefully set the lamp down on the table. He kept his fingers on the base, as though it were an offering, as though he were praying, Yashim thought. Ibou stared into the little ring of flame, and something in the sadness of his expression reminded Yashim of the man whose corpse lay neglected in the rain-swept courtyard outside. Years ago, the Kislar Agha must have been a man like Ibou. Soft and slender. Charming. Time and experience had made him gross: but once he had been lovely too.

'It isn't over, Ibou,' he said slowly. 'You have to tell them. Stop what's happening. The Hour isn't come.'

Ibou was breathing rapidly. His nostrils flared.

Very gently he took his fingers from the lamp. Then he put up a hand and pulled at his earlobe.

Yashim's eyes widened.

'Darfur?' He said.

The young man glanced at him, and shook his head.

'There is nothing there. Huts. Crocodiles in the river. Little bushpig in the road, dogs. He told me I should come. I wanted to.'

Yashim bit his lip.

'I've got four brothers, and six sisters,' Ibou continued. 'What else could I do? He sent us a little money now and then. When he became chief, he sent for me.'

'I see.'

'He is my mother's uncle,' Ibou said. Yashim nodded. 'My grandfather's brother. And I wanted to come. Even at the knife, I was glad. I was not afraid.'

No, thought Yashim: you survived. Whether it was anger or desperation, one or the other would help you survive. In his own case, anger. For Ibou? A village of mud and crocodiles, the knife wielded in the desert, the promise of escape.

'Listen to me, Ibou. What's happened has happened. You have no protector any more, but I will vouch for you. You must come with me now, and tell the men outside that the game is finished. The Hour has passed. Do this, Ibou, before many people die.'

Ibou shivered and passed his hand across his face.

'You . . . you will protect me?'

'If you come with me now. It has to come from you. Where are they waiting – beneath the Tree?'

'By the Janissary Tree, yes,' Ibou almost whispered.

We must go now, Yashim thought, before he has time to grow afraid. Before we are too late.

He took Ibou's arm. 'Come,' he said.

❦ 123 ❧

When they reached the Ortakapi Gate, Yashim checked his stride.

'Ibou,' he said in a low voice. 'This is as far as I can go. My presence won't do any good. You must say that the Kislar Agha is dead, and the palace is quiet. Just that. Understand?'

Ibou clutched his arm.

'Will you be here?'

Yashim hesitated.

'I have to find the seraskier,' he said. 'There's no danger for you: they expect the messenger. Now go!'

He patted Ibou on the shoulder, and watched as the young man sauntered through the gateway and headed for the group of men in the darker shadows of the planes. He saw the men stir and turn and, certain that Ibou had their attention, he slipped through the gate and made his way around the opposite wall of the first court, sticking to the shadows.

⚜ 124 ⚜

Bombardier Genghis Yalmuk slipped a finger beneath his chin strap and ran it round from ear to ear, to soothe the pressure. He had served in the New Guard for fifteen years, graduating from common soldiering to the artillery corps five years ago, and his only complaint in those fifteen years had been the headgear that soldiers were expected to wear: ferenghi shakos, with tough leather straps. Now he commanded a battalion of ten guns and their crews: forty men, in all.

He glanced over the Hippodrome and grunted. He'd slogged through the sand and heat of Syria. He'd been in Armenia, when the Cossacks broke through the infantry lines and charged his redoubt, with their sabres flashing in the sunlight and their horses foaming at the nostrils, and his commanding officer offering to shoot down any man who deserted his post. Battle, he'd learned, was days and hours of waiting, putting off thought, punctuated by short, savage engagements in which there was no time to think at all. Leave all that, he'd been told again and again, to the commanding officers.

Well, he was one of them now himself, and the injunction against thinking still held, as far as he could discover. His orders had come direct from the seraskier himself, who had been moving through the lines like a man demented, setting the position of the guns, instructing the troops, fixing elevations and exhorting them all to obedience. Genghis had no quarrel with that, of course, but he was a Stamboul man himself, not one of your Anatolian recruits, and he found it strange to be in his own city, under arms and idle while the place was bursting into flames.

He wished he'd been detailed to the Sultan Ahmet, perhaps, or the other, unidentified location deeper in the city, where the men would no doubt be tackling the fires head-on, instead of being told to train their guns every which way and stop the crowds from approaching the palace. But the seraskier had been very exact in his instructions. They had synchronised their time-pieces, too, ready for the barrage that was to open in almost exactly one hour. The barrage whose purpose Genghis Yalmuk neither questioned, nor understood, but which the seraskier had personally prepared, working from gun to gun with a sheaf of co-ordinates as if his bombardier could not be trusted to fix the co-ordinates himself.

And meanwhile, he thought wretchedly, they were waiting again. Waiting while the city burned.

He caught sight of a man in a plain brown cloak speaking to two sentries outside the seraglio gate, and frowned. His orders were very clear, to keep civilians out of the operational area: this man must have slipped through the gate, from the palace. Genghis Yalmuk threw back his shoulders and started to march towards them. This fellow had better just slip back the way he'd come, and at the double, too, palace or no palace, or he'd know the reason why.

But before he had walked five yards the man in the brown cloak had turned and was scanning the ground; one of the sentries pointed, and the man began to walk towards him, holding up a hand.

'Look here,' Genghis began to say, but the civilian cut him short.

'Yashim Togalu, imperial service,' he said. 'I need the seraskier, and fast. Operational need,' he added. 'Vital new intelligence.'

Genghis Yalmuk blinked. The habit of obedience was very

deeply ingrained, after all, and he had an ear that was tuned to the commanding style.

As for Yashim, he crossed his fingers.

For a moment the two men looked at one another.

Then Genghis Yalmuk raised his hand and pointed.

'Up there,' he said, crisply.

Yashim followed the direction of his finger. Over the walls and trees surrounding the great mosque. Beyond the minarets. Higher, and further away.

He was pointing at the dome of Hagya Sophia.

'Then I'm too late,' said Yashim, crisply. 'I'm afraid I have to ask to see your orders.'

❦ 125 ❧

The seraskier leaned back against the lead casing of the buttress, and put his cheek to the smooth metal. He had not realised how excited he was. His face seemed to be burning like the city which lay about him, at his feet.

Out here, on the leads, he had the perfect view. From down below, Hagia Sophia seemed to rise in a single burst, the massive central dome supported on a buttressed ring that floated in the air over two half-domes on either side. This was how artists since time immemorial had pictured it, round-shouldered like so many mosques; but in this they erred. Built in the sixth century, the Byzantine Emperor Justinian's great church was a reconciliation of two opposed forms. The great circle of the dome, rising on a round gallery of arches, thrust itself skywards through a lead-covered square. There was space at the four corners, where the pitch of the roof was slight, at most; and so it was from here, two hundred feet above the ground, that the seraskier saw across the Seven Hills, over the seraglio to the dark waters beyond, touched here and there by a bobbing lantern. Further west he imagined the water reflecting the flames that even now were shooting skywards, sending out brilliant showers of sparks, springing their way from rooftop to rooftop, consuming the wooden walls of the old portside houses, bursting through doorways, roaring down alleys. An unstoppable, purifying furnace fuelled by two thousand years of trickery and deceit.

The flames belonged to the city. All those long centuries they had smouldered, now and then breaking loose, feeding on the packed-up tinder that had been sifting into the shadows and the corners of Istanbul, its crooked angles dredged with dust and detritus and the filth of a million benighted souls. A city of fire and water. Dirt and disease. A city that stank on the water's edge like a decaying corpse, too rotten to be moved, shining by the oily bloom of putrefaction.

He turned to the south. How dark the seraglio looked! Shuttered behind its ancient walls, how it brooded on its own eminence! But the seraskier knew better: it was a vulture's nest, scattered with the filth and droppings of the generations, piled on the bones of the dead, filled with the insistent gaping cry of fledgelings warmed by their own excrement and fed with filth plucked from the surrounding midden of the city in which it had been built.

The seraskier stepped forwards to the gutter, and looked down into the square where his men were standing by their guns. Order and discipline, he thought: good men, moulded these last twenty years in proper habits of deference and obedience. They knew the penalty for stepping out of line. Order and obedience made an army, and an army was a tool in the hands of a man who knew how to use it. Without order you had only a rabble, that snarled and bit like a mad dog, ignorant of its purpose, open to every suggestion and prey to every whim.

Well, this night he would show the people who was stronger: the blind rabble and the vulture's nest, or lead and shot and the power of discipline.

And when the smoke cleared, a new beginning. A brave new start.

He smiled, and his eyes glittered in the firelight.

Then he stiffened. He eased away from the wall and slid the pistol from his belt.

He cocked the firing pin and laid the barrel in a straight line, pointing back towards the arch.

Someone was coming up the stairs.

The shadow lengthened, and the seraskier saw the eunuch blinking as he turned his head from side to side.

'Well done, Yashim,' said the seraskier, smiling. 'I wondered if you would come.'

❈ 126 ❈

The seraskier tapped his foot on the sloping roof.

'Do you know what this is? Do you see where we are?'

Yashim gazed at him.

'Of course you do. The roof of the Great Mosque. You see the dome, above your head? The Greeks called it Hagia Sophia, the Church of the Holy Wisdom. One hundred and eighty-two feet high. Enclosed volume, nine million cubic feet. Do you know how old it is?'

'It was built before the days of the Prophet,' Yashim said cautiously.

'Incredible, isn't it?' The seraskier chuckled. He seemed to be in the best of spirits. 'And it took just five years to build. Can you imagine what an effort that must have required? Or what we could do with such energy today, applied to something actually worthwhile?'

He laughed again, and stamped his foot.

'How does something so old get to last so long? Well, I'll tell you. It's because no one, not even the Conqueror Mehmed himself, had the wit or courage to knock it down. Do I surprise you?'

Yashim frowned.

'Not entirely,' he replied quietly.

The seraskier looked up.

'Thousands of sheets of beaten lead,' he said. 'Acres of it. And the pillars. And the dome. Just imagine, Yashim! It's been weighing on us all for fourteen hundred years. We can't even see beyond it, or around it. We can't imagine a world without it. Can we? Do you know, it's like a stench, nobody notices it after a while. Not even when it's poisoning them.' He leaned forward. The gun, Yashim noticed, was still steady in his hand. 'And it's poisoning us. All this.' He waved a hand. 'Year after year, habit piled on prejudice, ignorance on greed. Come on, Yashim, you know it as well as I do. We're smothered by it, aren't we? Tradition! It's just grime that accumulates. Why, it even took your balls!'

Yashim could no longer see the seraskier's face against the light of the fires at his back, but he heard him snicker at his own thrust.

'I've just come from the palace,' Yashim said. 'The sultan is safe. There was a coup of sorts –'

'A coup?' The seraskier ran his tongue across his lips.

'Yes. The palace eunuchs, led by the Kislar Agha. They were set to turn back the clock. Re-instate the Janissaries. It was all in that Karagozi verse – remember?'

The seraskier blew out his cheeks. 'Come, Yashim. This isn't important. You know that, don't you? Eunuchs. Sultans. The

313

sultan's finished. The Edict? Did you really think the Edict was going to make a difference? You saw him today, didn't you, the old boozer? What makes you think any of them can do a thing? They are half the problem. The Edict is just another worthless piece of paper. Equality, blah blah. There's only one equality under these skies, and that's when you're in the line, shoulder to shoulder with the men beside you, taking orders. We could have figured that out years ago, but we grew crooked.'

'The Janissaries?'

The seraskier gave an amused grunt.

'The Janissaries – and their Russian friends. Some of them, I gather, were living in Russian territory. And the rebels wanted Russian help.'

'Who warned you?' Yashim asked. 'Not Derentsov?'

The seraskier chuckled. 'Derentsov doesn't need money. It was your friend in the cab. The scarface.'

Yashim frowned. 'Potemkin . . . kept you informed?'

'Potemkin informed me, initially. But he was too expensive. And too dangerous.'

Yashim regarded the seraskier in silence. 'So you found some-one else to keep you up to date with the Janissary plot. Somebody safe, who wouldn't be much noticed.'

'That's right. Somebody cheap and inconsequential.' The seraskier grinned, and his eyes widened with delight. 'I found you.'

'I gave you the timing of the rebellion.'

'Oh more, much more. You kept the plot alive, didn't you? You helped to create the atmosphere I needed. Down there, a city in panic. They're defeated already. The Janissaries. The peo-ple. And now the palace, too.'

He ran his hand around his chest: a gesture of relish.

'For you, I'm afraid, I have a choice prepared between life and death. Or should I say, between devotion to the state and . . .

what, a romantic attachment to an outdated set of traditions.' He paused. 'For the empire? Well, the choice is made. Or will have been made in' – he drew a glinting orb from his pocket – 'approximately eighteen minutes. The choice between all this, this weight and history and tradition, this great weight squatting over us all like the dome of Justinian's cathedral – and starting fresh.'

'But the people –' Yashim began to interrupt.

'Oh, the people.' The seraskier half-turned his head, as if he wanted to spit. 'The world is full of people.

'We're well placed, up here, aren't we?' the seraskier went on. 'To watch the palace burn. And with the dawn, a new era. Efficient. Clean. The House of Osman served us well in its time, yes. Reform? An Edict? Written in water. The system is too crazy and tottering to reform itself. We need to start fresh. Sweep away all this junk, these pantaloons, sultans, eunuchs, whispers in the dark. We have suffered under an autocracy that doesn't even have the power to do what it wants. This empire needs firm government. It needs to be run by people who know how to command. Think of Russia.'

'Russia?'

'Russia is unassailable. Without the czar it could beat the world. Without all its princes and aristocrats and courts. Imagine: run by experts, engineers, soldiers. It's about to happen – but not in Russia. Here. We need the Russian system – the control of labour. The control of information. That's an area for you, if you like. I've said you're good. The modern state needs ears and eyes. We'll need them tomorrow, when the first day dawns on the Ottoman republic.'

Yashim stared. He had a sudden vision of the seraskier the first time they'd met, reclining so awkwardly on his divan in trousers and a jacket, reluctant to sit at the table with his back to the room. A fine western gentleman *he* made. Was that what all this was about?

'Republic?' He echoed the seraskier's unfamiliar word. He thought of the sultan and the validé, and all those women in the court: and he remembered the glittering fanatical light in the eyes of the leading eunuchs, and the unexpected death of the chief.

The seraskier had known that they would gather together. And he, Yashim himself, had persuaded the sultan to let the artillery into the city.

'That's right,' said the seraskier curtly. 'We've seen those weak old fools for the last time. Blathering about tradition! Padding round in their own nest, like silly chickens. Defying history.'

He drew himself up.

'Think of it as . . . surgery. It hurts, of course. The surgeon's knife is ruthless, but it cuts out the disease.'

Yashim felt his heart grow still. With it, his mind cleared.

The seraskier was still talking. 'For the patient the agony brings relief,' he was saying. 'We can be modern, Yashim: we must be modern. But do you really think modernity is something you can buy? Modernity isn't a commodity. It's a condition of the mind.'

Something stirred in Yashim's memory. He clutched at it, an elusive shape, a form of words he'd heard before. The man was still talking; he felt the memory slipping away.

'It's an arrangement of power. The old one is over. We have to think about the new.'

'We?'

'The governing classes. The educated people. People like you and me.'

No one, Yashim thought, is like me.

'People need to be directed. That hasn't changed. What changes is the way they are to be led.'

None of us are alike. I am like no one.

I will stay free.

'I'm going down, now,' the seraskier said quietly. 'And you – you'll stay up here, I'm afraid. I thought you might come with me, but it doesn't matter.'

He gestured with his gun, and Yashim stepped out of the archway onto the sloping roof.

'Shall we just change places, slowly?' The seraskier suggested. They circled each other for a few seconds, and then the seraskier was in the arch.

'You see, I'm not going to shoot you. I still think you might want to change your mind. When the troops fall back. When this place starts to burn.'

But Yashim wasn't really listening. The seraskier had seen his eyes stray from his face, and then widen, almost involuntarily. But he mastered an impulse to turn around. Deflection tactics were no more than he expected.

Yashim's surprise was not at all affected. Behind the seraskier, up the stairs, two extraordinary figures had made a silent appearance. One was dark, the other fair, and they were dressed like believers, but Yashim could have sworn that the last time he had clapped eyes on these two they had been wearing frock coats and cravats in the British embassy.

'*Excusez-moi*,' the fair one said. '*Mais – parlayvoo français?*'

The seraskier spun round as though he had been shot.

'What's this?' he hissed, turning a wary look on Yashim.

Yashim smiled. The fair young man was glancing round the seraskier, putting up a hand to wave.

'*Je vous connais, m'sieur* – I know you, don't I? I'm Compston, this is Fizerly. You're the historian, aren't you?'

There was a tinge of desperation in his voice which, Yashim thought, was not misplaced.

'They are officials at the British embassy,' he told the seraskier. 'Much more modern than they look, I imagine. And efficient, as you say.'

'I'll kill them,' the seraskier snarled. He jabbed his gun at them, and they shrank back.

'I wouldn't if I were you,' Yashim said. 'Your republican dawn could quickly turn into dusk if you bring British gunboats to our doorstep.'

'It's of no consequence,' the seraskier said. He had regained his composure. 'Tell them to get out.'

Yashim opened his mouth to speak but his first words were drowned by a muffled crump that sounded like a clap of thunder. The ground trembled beneath their feet.

As the sound of the explosion died away the seraskier jerked the watch from his pocket and bit his lip.

Too early, he thought. And then: it doesn't matter. Let them begin the barrage.

He waited, staring at his watch.

Fifteen seconds. Twenty seconds. Let the guns fire.

The sweat had broken out on his forehead.

There was another bang, slightly fainter than the first.

The seraskier looked up and flashed a look of triumph at Yashim.

But Yashim had turned away. He was standing on the roof, hands held aloft, staring out over the city as the wind caught at his cloak.

Beyond him, the seraskier saw the burst of light. It glanced off the pillars of the dome, flinging Yashim into brilliant relief where he stood against the skyline. The seraskier heard the rumble of the guns which followed. There was another burst of light, as of an exploding shell, and another deep rumble, and the seraskier frowned. He knew what was puzzling him. The sound and light were the wrong way round.

He should have heard the guns roar, and then seen the light flash as the shell reached its target.

The seraskier leaped from the archway and began to run, his feet making no sound on the thick lead sheets.

Yashim made a lunge for him, but the seraskier was too quick. In an instant he had seen what he had not expected to see, and with brilliant military intuition he had grasped precisely what it all meant to him. The guns were working the wrong end of the city, the shells exploding far away. He did not break stride. He shrank slightly as Yashim reached out, but a moment later he was over the gutters and half-running, half-sliding down the leaden roof of the supporting half dome.

He moved with a speed that was terrible to see. Yashim darted to the edge and began to lower himself down onto the conical roof, but the seraskier had already dropped from sight. Then he suddenly re-appeared, lower down, loping south across a cat-slide roof.

For a moment the whole city lay spread out beneath the seraskier's feet. He saw again the dark mass of the seraglio. He saw the lights twinkling on the Bosphorus. He saw men and women streaming through the square beneath him, and in the distance the chutes of flame that peeled away from the sudden yawning gaps that the artillery was making in their path.

As for him, there was only one direction he could take.

For many years after that, an Armenian army contractor who married a rich widow who bore him six sons would tell the story of how he was almost crushed by an officer who fell on him from the sky.

'Not a common soldier, mind you,' he would end his story, with a smile. 'God, in his Grace, sent me a general: and I've been dealing with them ever since.'

319

'I need an escort, Palewski,' Yashim was explaining. 'You know, somebody with an 'in' with the sultan. He'd expect that. And you two are very pally, aren't you?'

It was Saturday morning. The rain which lashed against Yashim's windows had been falling steadily since before dawn, much to the advantage of the New Guards struggling to extinguish the city fires. With the breaks their cannon had opened in the night, the fire had been contained to the area of the port, and although the damage was said to be serious, it did not approach the scale of 1817, or 1807, or of almost a dozen major fires which had broken out in that district in the previous century. And the port, when all was said and done, was not the most prized Istanbul quartier.

Palewski put up two fingers and touched his moustache, to hide a smile.

'Pally's the word for it, Yash. I've a mind to present the sultan with a little something which arrived for me this morning, saved by providence from the fire in the port.'

'Ah, providence,' echoed Yashim.

'Yes. I happened to notice that stocks were getting rather low last Thursday, so I ordered another couple of cases out of bond immediately. What do you think?'

'Yes, I think that the sultan would appreciate the gesture. Not that he'd drink it, of course.'

'Of course not. No bubbles in it, for one thing.'

They smiled at each other.

'I'm sorry about the thug last night,' Palewski said.

Yashim yawned, shaking his head.

'I don't know what you hit him with. He was gentle as a lamb when I got back. Preen and her friend were chatting away with him, you can't believe. Not that he said much, naturally, but he seemed to be enjoying their company. Preen said she could take him to a doctor. I think she said a horse doctor, but there you are. He seemed very grateful when I explained it to him.'

'In mime?'

'In sign. It's a language I learned when I was at court.'

'I see.' Palewski frowned. 'I didn't hit him, you know.'

'I know. I'm glad. Will you call for me at six?'

129

Yashim slept deeply until one o'clock, then dozed for another hour, sliding in and out of dreams where he heard only voices speaking to him in tones he knew and languages he didn't understand. Once he saw the seraskier, talking perfect French with a light Creole accent, and lashed himself awake. Was it a dream that the seraskier had spoken to him in the language of his dreams? *A condition of the mind.* The phrase rolled around his head, and he sat up, feeling lightheaded.

He got up, leaving his cloak on the divan. The room felt warm, the stove was lit: his landlady must have crept up to light it while he was asleep. He picked up the kettle and settled it onto the coals. He took three pinches of black tea and dropped them into the pot. He found a pan by the stove with a few manti inside: Preen seemed to have cooked his supper and eaten it with her friend; and the mute, too, maybe. They'd saved something for him.

He set it on the stove and watched the butter melt, then stirred the manti with a wooden spoon. He thought of making a tomato sauce with the jar of puree, then decided that the manti were ready and he was too hungry, so he simply tipped them onto a plate and ground a few rounds of black pepper over them.

They were not excellent, he had to admit; slightly hard around the edges, in fact, but wonderfully good. He poured the tea, and drank it with sugar and a cigarette leaning back on the divan and watching the raindrops sparkling on the lattice: the rain had stopped and a weak wintry sunlight was making a last appearance before it faded for the night.

Palewski had been almost right, he thought. A dangerous party: always a guest, never a player. Only obliged to stand by, confused and helpless, as the old, grand battle raged, a battle that would never be won between the old and the new, reaction and renovation, memory and hope. Coming in too late, when last night's manti were already curling at the edges. Until he spoke to the bombardier, who swung the guns in time.

After a time he began to look around the room, not stirring but glancing from one object to the next before he saw what he wanted. He reached out and took it in his hand, half-smiling: a little cloisonné dagger with no pommel, only its beautifully enamelled hilt and scabbard making a single crescent, tapering to a fine point. He slid the dagger halfway out, and admired the gleam of its perfect steel, then pushed it back, hearing the tiny click as it settled into the scabbard again.

Damascus steel, cold drawn, the product of a thousand years' experience – and the finer it was worked, the less it showed the labour. It was not as they crafted such things now. He wondered if she'd know the difference, not that it mattered. It was a beautiful and satisfying thing. Dangerous, but protective too. Perhaps she'd look at it now and then, and in her white northern world of ice it would bring back some memory to make her smile.

For several minutes he weighed the dagger in his palm, thinking of it; and then he frowned and set it gently aside, and got up and washed in the basin as best he could.

130

'We have orders to admit no one until the disturbance has sub-sided,' the butler intoned, placing his large body in the doorway of the embassy.

'There is no disturbance,' Yashim said. The butler merely pursed his lips.

Yashim sighed, and held out a small package. 'Would you see to it that this reaches Her Excellency the Princess?'

The butler glanced down and sniffed. 'And from whom shall I say it comes?'

'Oh – just say a Turk.'

'Yashim!'

Eugenia was coming slowly down the stairs, one hand floating by the rail and the other at her cheek.

'Come in!'

The butler stepped back and Eugenia took Yashim's hands in hers and led him to the sofa. The butler hovered over her.

'That's all right,' she said. 'We're friends.'

'From the gentleman, Your Highness.'

The butler handed her Yashim's packet, and stood back.

'Tea for our visitor, please,' Eugenia said. When the butler had gone she dropped the packet on her lap, took hold of Yashim's hands again and looked him steadily in the eye.

'I think . . . we are going home.' She flashed a sudden smile, and squeezed his hands. 'Derentsov – my husband – is furious. And frightened. He thinks he's been betrayed.'

Yashim nodded slowly.

'You know who it was, don't you?' Eugenia tilted her head back and appraised him with a slow smile. 'They all think that you don't matter. But you are clever.'

She saw Yashim glance away. 'Do you want to know?' he

323

asked her, quietly.

She shook her head. 'It would spoil everything. I have a duty to my husband, and there are some secrets I can't keep. He was raving this morning, saying he'd been compromised. No choice but to resign. Determined to return us to St Petersburg, and face the czar.'

'And the balls, and the dinners, and the ladies with their fans. I know.'

'It will be hard.'

'But you have a duty to your husband.'

They laughed softly together.

'What is this?' She said, hefting the packet in her hand.

'Open it, and see.'

She did, and watched him showing her the tiny catch which slipped the dagger from its scabbard.

'It reminds me of something,' she said mischievously. 'And someone.'

Their eyes met, and the mischievous look disappeared.

'I don't think –'

'That we'll meet again? No. But . . . I will always dream. Of you.'

'If I told the ladies of St Petersburg –'

'Don't say a word.'

Eugenia shook her lovely head. 'I won't,' she said. 'I never would.'

She leaned forwards, tilting her head slightly to one side so that a lock of her black hair swung free.

'Kiss me,' she said.

They kissed.

Russian or otherwise, a butler is a butler. He is unflappable. He is discreet.

Yashim had gone before he served the tea.

131

'So it seems that the seraskier was right,' said Mahmut IV. 'It's good that we had him in the city. But what a terrible accident, just when everything was going so well.'

'Yes, sultan.'

'They say he fell. I suppose he'd climbed up somewhere for a better view. Fires to fight, and all that, eh?'

'Yes, sultan.'

'We'll give him a splendid funeral, don't worry about that. You two got along pretty well, didn't you?'

Yashim inclined his head.

'Something new, he'd have liked that. Gun carriages, maybe, and a few platoons of Guards firing volleys over his grave. Show that the sultan doesn't forget his friends. We might even name the fire-tower at Beyazit after him. Ugly object. Seraskier's Tower. Hmm. The empire honours its heroes, you know.'

The sultan picked at his nose.

'I never liked him much. That's the worst I can say of him. At least he knew his duty.'

Yashim kept his eyes fixed on the ground.

The sultan looked at him with narrowed eyes.

'My mother says that you did a great deal to prepare her for the ordeal she passed through last night. It seems to me you did very little.'

He snuffed. Yashim looked up and caught his eye.

The sultan blinked and looked away.

'Hrrmph. I suppose it was enough in the end. And frankly, the eunuchs are perfectly quiet now. Takes one to catch one, I imagine.'

He picked up a little whisk and began to twirl it between his fingers.

'The point is, I need someone in here, since the kislar's gone. Someone who knows the ropes, but a bit younger.'

Yashim froze. It was the second job he'd been offered in the last twenty-four hours. The eyes and ears of the new republic? Now it was power and the promise of riches. The second job he didn't want.

He began to say that he wasn't young. He was white. Whiteish, anyway – but the sultan wasn't listening.

'There's an archivist,' he said. 'New man. Keen, good looking, it'd frighten some of the old men, wouldn't it? I can't replace them all. And I could keep an eye on him, too. Reminds me of the kislar when he was young, before he started spooning up this tradition stuff and murdering the girls. He wasn't in on the whole charade, either. That's what I like. Give him a frock coat and a baton. That's it. My man.'

Yashim felt a flood of relief. He had no doubt that Ibou would prove to be a perfect Kislar Agha; a little young perhaps, but time would offer its inevitable solution. At least he would vault straight over all the terrible compromises and feuds that had driven the former incumbent to the verge of madness as he clambered his way to the top. And he would be quick to learn his duty. Maybe even genuinely grateful.

'The sultan is most wise,' he said. It was better not to say more.

'Well, well.' The sultan rose from his chair. 'This has been a most interesting discussion. To be honest, Yashim, I sometimes think you know more than you say. Which may be wise in its way, too. It is for God to know everything, and for us to learn only what we need.'

He scrabbled short-sightedly at the little table, and picked up a leather purse.

'Take this. The seraskier would no doubt have rewarded you, and in the circumstances the task is left to me.'

Yashim caught the purse in mid-air.

He bowed. The sultan nodded shortly.

'The validé wants a gossip, I understand. There was an Edict,' he added, 'but it will have to wait after all. We'll see the household settled before that. And the city, too.'

He waved a hand, and Yashim bowed as he withdrew.

❦ 132 ❧

'Was there a twist?' The validé smiled. 'I like a twist.'

'Yes,' Yashim said. He thought of telling the unvarnished truth, but knew that it would never make a proper story. 'The seraskier was rotten to the core. He planned the whole thing.'

The validé clapped her hands.

'I knew it!' she cried. 'How did you guess?'

'It was a number of little things,' Yashim told her. He told her about the seraskier's awkwardness in western dress, and the way he had claimed to speak French, and then denied it. He told her how eager the seraskier had been to spread panic at the murders, at which the validé had nodded vigorously and said that he was obviously being used. How, exactly, had the men been murdered, she wanted to know?

And Yashim told her.

He explained that his friend Palewski had overheard him speaking French – he thought it was French – at a café one evening.

'When he denied all knowledge of it! Ha ha!' The validé wagged a finger.

He told her then about the Russian, Potemkin.

'What a villain!' the validé snorted. 'Ruined by his scar, no doubt. He must have been charming, in his way, to lure the fellows into his carriage. But all the same,' she added, putting the image of the wounded charmer to one side, and considering the practicalities, 'what did the Russians have to gain by getting involved?'

And Yashim told her.

'They're poised for a takeover of Istanbul,' he said. 'Ever since the days of the Byzantines they've dreamed of the city. It was the second Rome – and Moscow is the third. They wanted anarchy in Istanbul. They didn't care how it happened – a Janissary coup, the seraskier going mad and proclaiming himself ruler, anything. If the House of Osman was extinguished, imagine the consequences! They're camped a week or so away. They'd claim to be restoring order, or to be protecting the Orthodox, or to be being sucked into the vortex one way or another, it wouldn't matter how. Just so long as they could occupy the city and provide themselves with a reasonable excuse afterwards, when the European Powers started kicking up a fuss. The French, the English, they're terrified of letting the Russians in – but once they're in, they'd be here to stay. Look at the Crimea.'

'What brutes!' the validé breathed. The Crimea had been taken by the Russians, by a combination of threats and stealth and bloody war. 'They backed the Greeks, as well!'

'Everyone backed the Greeks,' Yashim reminded her soberly. 'But certainly the Russians lit the spark there, too.'

The validé was silent.

'To think that all this was hovering over our heads while I dealt with the kislar in the palace,' she said after a pause. 'I thought that was a drama, but it was a sideshow.'

'Not really,' Yashim suggested. 'If the seraskier's plans hadn't come off – and they didn't, did they? – there would still have been a revolution, but for you. A counter-revolution, as they call it, going back to the old ways.'

'It was the girl,' the validé pointed out. 'I've seen plays, you know. When I was young, I saw them in Dominique. If I set the scene, she performed the final act. Thanks to you, Yashim.'

Yashim bowed his head.

The validé reached for a bag by her divan, and pulled the string at its mouth.

'I've got just the thing for you,' she said.

She fished inside the bag and brought out a book with paper covers.

She held it up between her two hands and let Yashim read the title, emblazoned in red.

'*Père Goriot*,' he read. 'By Honoré de Balzac.'

'There.' She held it out. 'Quite disgusting, I'm afraid.'

'What makes you give it to me?'

'They say it's all the rage in Paris. I've read it now, and it's all about corruption, deceit, greed, lies.'

She patted the cover of the book and held it out to Yashim.

'Sometimes, you know, I am so glad I never got to see France.'

Acknowledgements

I owe a debt to all the historians who have broadened our appreciation of the Ottoman Empire; I've also drawn constantly on the observations of contemporary travellers. The errors and manipulations are entirely mine.

Daisy Goodwin encouraged me to take a detective-story approach to the Ottoman Empire. Yashim waited to live on the page until I hit on a period, Istanbul in the 1830s. Christine Edzard, who adapted *Little Dorrit* to film, has shared her passion for nineteenth-century costume – and mores. Richard Goodwin read the book in Dickensian instalments, as it flowed forth; having filmed various Agatha Christie novels, he was well-positioned to advise on everything from plot tweaks to dialogue. Jocasta Innes, an inveterate thriller reader, steered me away from potential failures of continuity. I'm grateful to them all, and to Sarah Wain and Clare Michell and Mary Miers for their readings and comments.

Sarah Chalfant, my agent at the Wylie Agency, brought me together with Sarah Crichton in New York, and then with editors around the world. Sarah Crichton has been matchless in her encouragement – and who says editors these days don't edit? Julian Loose, at Faber, unlocked the whole thing for me: all thanks to him.

In Istanbul, I'd particularly like to thank Professor Norman Stone of Koc University, and John Scott, the editor of *Cornucopia*, the beautiful and intelligent magazine devoted to all things Turkish.

My oldest boys fought me for control of the computer with remorseless cunning; they proved themselves to be Turing-level code-breakers but they never, ever wiped the hard drive and I'm grateful to them for that. The younger two took a more remote interest in the coalface, but cheered me along by wandering in for more paper and chats. All my books have been for them.

This book wouldn't have been written, though, without Kate's encouragement and enthusiasm. It's a few years since we tramped down together from Poland to Turkey, saw the storks flying north across the Sea of Marmara, and took our final steps towards the domes of Istanbul, and the great Bosphorus below, into the city that had fed our imaginations for six months. We were not disappointed.

The book is dedicated to her.